Any Dream Will Do

ANY DREAM WILL DO

MARIA DUFFY

HACHETTE
BOOKS
IRELAND

To my husband Paddy, and our children
Eoin, Roisin, Enya and Conor,
with all my love.

CALM BEFORE THE STORM

CHAPTER 1

Bloody hell! They're coming in less than *two* weeks! What on earth possessed me to throw a scantily thought-out invitation to the world and its mother on Twitter? I should have known better. And the fact that they're coming during the run up to Christmas is only adding to my stress. Why, oh why, couldn't I have thought before I tweeted? Oh, no – that wouldn't do for me. In school, I was *always* the one to stick my hand up to volunteer for something before I even knew what it was; and it was rarely something exciting.

'So who's going to do a job for me?' My hand would be waving in the air before Miss Pitcher could finish and, inevitably, it would be something disgusting like emptying the bins or checking to see if the loos were clean. I just couldn't help myself. And I'm still doing it now, as a thirty year old.

Anyway, back to the dreaded invitation and the drunken tweeting that brought it on. I love Twitter. I discovered it about a year ago on a Saturday night when nobody was available to go out and I was spending yet another night home alone. My *real* friends were ... well, let's just say they were busy with their own lives and loves. While most of them are changing nappies and basking in domestic bliss, I'm still avoiding the whole relationship thing and pretending that I'm far younger than my thirty years.

So I decided to check out this thing that everybody seemed to be talking about and, within minutes, I'd created an account. I couldn't make up my mind whether to call myself by my mundanely ordinary name, Jenny Breslin, or to go for something progressive like Lipstickchick or Jennycool – in the end, I played it safe and just went for JennyB. It wasn't long before I'd made loads of friends. Most of us hooked up through our mutual love of anything that smelled of reality TV – *Big Brother*, *X Factor*, *I'm a Celebrity* – we followed and tweeted through them all. I became close to a few, well as close as is possible via a social network! Hardly a night went by without me meeting up on Twitter with Fiona, Kerry and Zahra. There were others, of course, but it's funny how you get drawn to a certain few. It was one of those nights, almost exactly a year after I had first started tweeting (I think Lord Sugar had fired the sexy, posh bloke from *The Apprentice* and I was drowning my sorrows), that I felt an overwhelming love for these virtual friends and sent out a tweet:

@JennyB So who's on for a few days in Dublin, then? Would love to meet you all in person – I have spare room in my house.

I should have known. Mention a free bed and there'll always be takers!

@zahraglam Count me in for sure. I'm due some time off and would love to meet.
@fionalee Ooh, yes. A trip to Dublin would be fab. I'm in!
@kerrydhunt Yahooo! A Twitmas Party! Haha!

Eeeek! It seemed like a good idea after I'd downed four glasses of red in quick succession, but that was six weeks ago. Now as the time is drawing closer, I feel like running away. I mean, these people – they all sound so interesting. Zahra is a celebrity make-up artist in London, for God's sake. She brushes shoulders with the rich and famous every day and now she's coming to see what Dublin has to offer! Fiona seems lovely too. She's a happily married mum of a little boy and seems to eat, drink and sleep domesticity. And then there's Kerry. She's a bit of an enigma. She's the only one who doesn't have her picture up on Twitter – she says she's not showing her face until she loses at least a stone. Still, she seems lovely. She's a nurse so she must be. If I'm honest, I feel closest to her. She's single too and I feel I can be more myself with her than anybody else on Twitter. And then there's me, an insecure, commitment-phobic party girl whose biggest achievement in life is managing to get two piercings squeezed into my belly button! Oh bloody, bloody, bloody hell!

My insecurities started while I was still at school. I wasn't a looker, like Ellen O'Brien with her long blonde curls and perfect skin. Nor did I have an hourglass figure, like Sinead Byrne. I hated how I looked. I hated my boyish figure, my mousy, thin hair and insipid greenish-brown eyes. 'They're hazel,' my mum used to say. 'You have beautiful hazel eyes, Jenny.' But in my mind, 'hazel' was just a word people used when your eyes were neither one colour nor another.

At twelve, I had entered the wonderful world of puberty and had grown buds of breasts. Oh, how exciting that had been – just to have a little something to protrude through my T-shirt. I felt that with a pair of boobs I would start to look like a woman. But sadly that's where my development began and ended. Those buds never flowered, I never grew hips and, as a result, my last few years in secondary school were hell.

Jerry, they called me. They thought I couldn't hear the whispers – or maybe they just didn't care. 'Is she a lesbian, do you think?' Cruel, heartless bitches.

Now don't get me wrong, I didn't cower into a corner and cry into my soggy cheese and cucumber sandwiches. I'm not, and never was, that sort of a girl. I took comfort in the company of Louise and Sally, my two very best friends. We'd chat for hours about how I was going to get a boob job for my eighteenth birthday and how those stuck-up bullies would envy my fabulous body. It kept me sane.

At seventeen, I had my first sexual experience. Ronan Byrne was the heartthrob of Leixlip, where I lived with my mam and dad. We slipped out of the local disco and he pulled me down on the soft grass behind the building. It felt good – dangerous and thrilling as his hand fumbled around to find its target. I remember marvelling at how he was able to slip a condom on with one hand while expertly pleasing me with the other. For the first time in my teenage life, I felt really happy. I felt as though I was the most special girl in the world – not only because this gorgeous boy had chosen me, but because I finally felt like a woman.

The lovely Ronan didn't want to be my boyfriend. Bastard. He'd gotten what he wanted and moved on – wait for it... to Louise bloody Molloy! She was supposed to be my friend. I was gutted. During those precious moments of loving, I imagined myself basking in newfound respect from the other girls. They'd envy the fact that I managed to snare such a fabulous specimen and I'd generously forgive their past taunts.

I don't know if it was the fact that I was at such a vulnerable age or just the build-up of years of bullying, but, that night, I vowed I'd never let my guard down again. If anything, I'd turn the tables and *I* would be the one in control from now on.

I decided I'd do something about my lacklustre appearance. That's when I began to dye my limp mousy hair various shades of red and to layer on the make-up so thick that my face was barely recognisable. Over the years, I've added a few piercings too – nothing major but just enough to draw attention away from my plainness and give me a bit of confidence. I started with my belly button and a couple of extra ones in my ears and then bravely acquired a little black diamond in my eyebrow. I've toyed with the idea of other places but, to be honest, I'm a bit of a coward. As there was nothing I could do about my five foot nothingness and my boyish figure, I developed a quirky style of dress – sort of punkish, but without the hob-nailed boots. I love my shoes too much for that!

Most people see me as a good-time girl, someone who parties a lot and revels in the single lifestyle that allows nights of wild abandon and days conked out under the duvet. And mostly that's what I am – I enjoy having a good time and really love my nights out, but lately when I'm sticking yet another Marks & Spencer ready meal for one in the microwave, sometimes … only sometimes … I wonder what it would be like to be in a relationship, to have somebody who's always there to talk to, to laugh with, to love me. For feck sake, cue the violins!

On Twitter, I can be myself. I don't have to hide behind my mask of heavy-duty Mac foundation or make sure I plaster a smile on my face. I can have a good old moan with the rest of them. That's not to say I'm always completely honest. I may have invented a few extra friends and fabricated the odd date with a handsome man – well, I couldn't have my virtual friends thinking I'm a complete loser, could I? Oh and I've used a picture of myself that was taken one or two, or maybe eight, years ago. Come on, let's face it – who wants to admit they're getting old?

Now I have two weeks to plan a fun-packed few days for these girls. God knows I've tweeted enough about wonderful Dublin and how I have such a brilliant life here. I hope they're not looking to do the museums and historical tours of the city, though, that's not really my thing. It's not that I'm not cultured

– I do read the newspapers on Sundays very thoroughly – but I always hated history in school and, to be honest, I couldn't tell you the first thing about Ireland's past. I'm hoping more for shopping and lunch during the day and pubs and clubs at night.

Right, enough procrastinating – I need to start planning. In just twelve days, I'll have the three of them here, so I may as well get used to the idea. Let's see if anyone is online and maybe I'll have a chat with them about planning some stuff.

> *@fionalee* Was thinking about our trip to Dublin. Would love to do a historical tour of the city.
> *@zahraglam* Oooh, yes, and maybe take in some museums and art galleries. That would be fab. What you think, Jen?

Shit! I snap my laptop shut and head to bed.

CHAPTER 2

Friday – Twelve Days to D-Day

I'm running for shelter from the ferocious rain that's just begun out of the blue. Big, icy cold drops are pelting at my face, and slowing me down. It's dark, and the streets are deserted. I just need to get home – but, suddenly, I'm lost. I stop to get my bearings when a scarecrow jumps from an alleyway and grabs my hand.

'Come on, Dorothy. We'll get you home,' he says.

'But ... but ... I'm not Dorothy,' I say.

But my protests are ignored as the scarecrow, now joined by a tin man, takes my hand.

'Just click your ruby slippers and chant "there's no place like home",' says the tin man.

'Oh, but it's all a terrible mistake,' I cry. 'I don't even have a pair of ...'

I glance at my feet and it seems my Faith boots have turned into a sparkling pair of ruby slippers. For God's sake, they don't even have a heel!

Whoa! What a trippy dream. I'm trying very hard to open my eyes but they're firmly stuck together. God, what's wrong with me? Maybe I'm coming down with some terrible disease. What if I die here alone? What a thought.

I try again valiantly to prize my eyes open and just about

manage a slit. As things begin to come into focus, I spot an empty wine glass on my pine locker. So *that's* the culprit. Bloody hell, was I really drinking in bed last night? Jesus, I need to cop on to myself. That's a terrible carry on altogether. I should be going to bed with a nice camomile tea and waking up fresh as a meadow of sunflowers. It's all coming back to me now, but things are looking up already – eyes are open and in proper working order and seems I'm not dying after all.

The clock beside the bed says it's 8.50 a.m., but I know different. In a moment of genius, I set it twenty minutes fast to fool myself into actually getting up in time for work. WORK! OMG it's Friday and I'm dead late again. Why did I think it was Saturday? I untangle myself from my olive green duvet and leap out of bed like a first-class gymnast, forgetting my previous near-death state. Clothes, clothes, clothes! I spy my knee-length black skirt and grey sweater on the floor and a quick sniff tells me they'll do for another day. Within minutes, I'm out the door and heading down the Old Lucan Road to the bus stop. Isn't life strange at times? There I was only twenty minutes ago on my death bed, and now here I am dressed and waiting for the 25A that'll take me to the job I hate.

I manage to shove my way onto the packed bus and even nab a seat beside an old woman. She must be over seventy and she's wearing a skirt that's far too short, exposing extremely knobbly knees and a ridiculously low cut T-shirt. The T-shirt, by rights, should have exposed some cleavage, but I suspect her boobs are so far down to her waist at this stage, all I can see is a mass of saggy, draggy skin. Her face is overloaded with make-up that only serves to accentuate the myriad of wrinkles.

I know I should think 'fair play to her for trying to stall the tides of time' but, to be honest, I favour the little old lady type of pensioner, with no make-up, a hunched back and permed, bluish-grey hair. I never knew either of my grandmothers and I like to think of them as the little old lady variety.

It's 9.25 as the bus pulls up just past the Ha'penny Bridge and I know I haven't a hope of making it on time for my 9.30 start. Shit! I hate giving that bitch Brenda 'Bootface' Delaney another excuse to haul me into her office.

Bootface has made my life a living hell since I moved to the O'Connell Street branch of the bank a little over eighteen months ago. Having worked in head office since I'd left school at eighteen, I'd felt it was time for a change and had applied for a transfer to a branch where I'd anticipated more action. Well, they say to be careful what you wish for, don't they!

It had only been twenty minutes into my first day and I'd been hoping to get a bit of inside gossip from the girls in the canteen who all seemed very nice, when I'd heard, 'Jenny Breslin, I think we need to have a little chat.'

Naively, I'd felt quite cheery as I'd followed her into her tiny office, expecting a nice, warm welcome and a low down on what I was expected to do. So imagine the shock fest when she shook her head and fixed a look of pure disgust on her face.

'Jenny,' she'd said, still shaking her head. I did wonder for a moment if she had some sort of tick – you know when people twitch or make involuntary movements.

'Now you may have got away with that sort of dress code in the *department* you worked in up until now, but be under no illusion, it's completely unacceptable here. We are a public office and it's imperative we look respectable at all times.'

As soon as she'd spat out the word 'department' I'd known I was in trouble. There's an unspoken rivalry between those who work in the branches, dealing with the public face to face, and those who work in the background in the departments. Some branch staff seem to think that those who work in departments have it easy – that they can breeze in at whatever time they like and sit back in their chairs dunking their Mars bars into their coffee. It's not true of course – well the Mars bar bit anyway – but Brenda was obviously one of the begrudgers and would be making sure I was on my toes at all times.

Since that first day, she hasn't let me get away with anything. She regularly hauls me into her office for a telling off and it's always for teeny weeny things that shouldn't matter. Like the time I dared to paint my nails at my desk while she was out at a meeting. It was half four on a Friday and everyone was winding down for the weekend. I was just applying the last coat of the black varnish to my right hand when her voice boomed, almost making me spill the whole bottle all over my desk.

'Jenny Breslin! What in the name of God are you doing? A word in my office please! NOW!'

I'd been tempted to ask if she could wait until the nails were dry as it had taken me ages to get them just right, but I thought that might be pushing things a little too far. Her eyes were glistening with what I thought at the time was rage but, on reflection, I think it was more delight at having witnessed a true crime against banking!

Bloody hell. It's 9.40 and I'm surely going to get a bollocking. Letting myself in through the staff door, I slip quietly to my desk, one of six just inside the public counter. The branch doesn't open its doors to the public until ten, so all is quiet at the moment. I'm bracing myself for the royal summons into her office, which is no more than ten steps away from my desk, but all is quiet. Could it be that I've got away with being late this time? It's not like Bootface to let a punishable crime slip through the net.

Would it be too much to push my luck and take a quick look at my Twitter and see what's happening? I had intended to check in on the bus but was distracted by the colourful old lady. Ah, what the hell? I whip my iPhone out of my bag and quickly log in, keeping one eye on Bootface's office door.

@JennyB Hellooo. Anyone here. I'm just having a sneaky peek. In work. Shouldn't be on here at all.
@fionalee Hi Jenny. I'm here. Just having a bit of quiet time. Hubbie gone go work and Ryan at playschool.
@JennyB Lucky you. I hate being here. I wish I was—

'You jammy cow,' comes a voice from behind, scaring the life out of me and forcing me to throw my phone into my bag. 'She's been on the phone in her office for the past ten minutes, so it looks like you got away with it.'

Paula Farrell is my best friend in work and, without her, my days would be an unbearable blur of meaningless numbers. She too works at the public counter and her desk is just a few away from mine. Mad as a hatter and only twenty-five years old, we hit it off from the first day I came here and we've remained friends ever since.

'Jesus, you scared the shit out of me,' I say, my heart beating like a dentist's drill. Thought I was a gonner there.'

'Sorry, I couldn't resist,' laughs Paula, twisting her long strands of sleek black hair around with her fingers. 'You must be feeling lucky today; being late *and* daring to look at your phone.' I'm momentarily distracted by the number of hairs that are falling to the floor. I really should lecture her on overuse of straighteners.

'I'll probably be for it when she's off the phone,' I say, removing a few of the piercings from my ears. 'Well, before she comes out, are we still planning to go out tonight? I'm dying for a good old bop.'

Paula winces as I stretch the skin at my eyebrow to get a hold of the miniature stud. 'Yes, I'm looking forward to it. Now quick, here she comes. Look busy.' Paula shuffles some papers she's holding in an effort to look busy and scurries back to her desk.

The old boot stares straight at me from her office door. God, she's scary. Without opening her mouth I can tell her mind is saying, 'Damn you Jenny Breslin, for managing to slip in unnoticed and escape a royal bollocking from me.'

I can't seem to get this stupid tweet-up or tweet-meet or whatever it's called out of my mind. Maybe I'll pop over to Sally in the morning and have a chat with her about it. With the new electronic toll on the motorway, the traffic flows brilliantly now, and I can be at her place in Santry in fifteen minutes. I love the fact that we've remained such good friends even though our school days are far behind us. I was telling her the other day about my guests arriving and she thought I was completely off my head.

'Why would you invite people you don't know to stay in your house?' she'd asked. 'Sure they could be axe murderers for all you know.' A little dramatic, I thought, but she probably had a point.

Still, these twitter girls seem nice enough. I've known them for a year now and they seem to be open and honest about their lives. And it's only for four days. How hard can that be?

*

'Wow, this place is buzzing, isn't it?' says Paula, elbowing a couple of girls out of the way so she can squeeze in beside me. Having spent the hours from eight until eleven having a relatively quiet chat in O'Neill's pub on Suffolk Street, we've now come down to a club in Leeson Street for a bit of a bop. I love it here, and hardly a weekend goes by without me taking a trip to the famous dancing strip. For a moment, the girls look as if they're going to tear her hair out but then get distracted by a group of tattooed men who've just appeared at their sides.

'Jesus, Paula,' I whisper, keeping one eye on the girls. 'How long have you and I been coming to these clubs? You can't just push people around unless you have a death wish.' Even without the pushing and shoving, Paula often earns us death stares from other women. In her heels, she towers six foot tall and her size ten waist and ample bust are the cause of much envy. Even with barely any make-up, her skin is pale and smooth and beautifully contrasted by her sleek black hair. Paula isn't aware of any of this nor is she fazed by the girls as she passes me my vodka and Coke.

'You worry too much, Jen,' she says, sipping on her own gin and tonic. 'People don't come here and expect they'll have their own space. It's always bumper to bumper.'

I'm not really listening to what she's saying because I've been distracted by a man wearing the sexiest aftershave I've ever smelled. He's just passed by and is standing a few feet away with two other guys. His rugged face and tight cut hair wouldn't usually attract me – I prefer the more baby-faced guys – and I can't quite put my finger on it, but there's just something about him. His ruggedness mixed with the heady scent has my sexual antenna going wild!

'Should we move over nearer the dance floor,' I say, noticing an unclaimed space just behind the scented man. 'Sure we might even have a dance when we get this drink down us.'

'Good idea,' Paula says, downing most of her gin and tonic in one.

'*Paula!* I didn't mean we have to dance this minute. Take it easy, or I'll be carrying you home!'

'He's been eyeing you up too, you know,' she says, once we've moved over to our new spot beside the dance floor.

'What? Who has?'

'The fella in the purple top. I can see you looking at him. I just wish ... I wish ... ' She takes the last gulp of her drink as though she needs some Dutch courage. 'I know you like to have a bit of fun with these guys, but I really wish you'd consider actually going out with one. I'd love to see you in a *proper* relationship, like me and my Ian.'

'Eh ... I hate to be the one to point this out to you, but didn't you and Ian split up again a few weeks ago?'

'Ah, Jenny, sure you know us? Ian is all over the place at the moment, what with losing his job and everything. He'll be back again in no time.'

'I'm sure he will,' I say, patting her hand reassuringly. I do love Paula but I just can't stand the loser she's been with on and off for the past year. Ian is her first proper relationship and she's hell bent on getting him up the aisle. As far as I can see, he has no intentions of any such thing and I just wish Paula would realise it.

I get really fed up with people telling me that I should find myself a nice man to have a relationship with. As far as I can see, relationships aren't all they're cracked up to be. I see so many girls wasting their lives, checking their mobiles every few minutes to see if their latest squeeze has texted. Then there are tears and cries of, 'I'll never find anyone like him again.' What's the point in that? There was one time when I was twenty-five that I fell completely head over heels for baby-faced Shane Lonergan. I don't know what it was about him but I completely forgot my rules about men and was only too willing to make a date. We were together for a whole year. I'd never felt so happy or fulfilled. I thought that was it. I'd married myself off in my head – white picket fence, 2.5 kids and the big Old English sheepdog from the Dulux ad. He loved me – he said so every single day – and I adored him.

Until one day, out of the blue, almost a year from the day we first got together, he announced we were over. Finished. He'd fallen in love with somebody he worked with. I was devastated. I imagined he'd left me for a goddess – a six-foot, blonde-haired, blue-eyed, big-boobed woman. Somebody who was everything I wasn't. I thought that would be the worst scenario. Until I found out his new love was a six-foot, blond-haired, blue-eyed, big-muscled man. It just proves that when you think things can't get any worse, they can.

Since then I just don't do dates.

'Well, maybe one of these days you'll kick that Ian into touch and you can join me in a bit of harmless flirting,' I say, noticing my scented man is looking in our direction.

'Ah, Jen, sure God love him,' she says, shaking her head. 'He's having a hard time at the moment so I really want to be there for him.'

There you go! Paula is a typical example of the girl consumed by waiting for phone calls and texts from the man who'll never be as interested in her as she is in him. And a 'hard time' my arse! Yes, Ian lost his job as a builder a few months ago, but has he tried to get anything else to replace it? Not a chance. He uses Paula as his meal ticket and the poor girl is so besotted by him, she just can't see it.

The dance floor is getting packed and we're being pushed over to the side by the overflow. Suddenly, there's a big shove and I somehow end up with a pint of Guinness down my front.

'Jesus, sorry about that – hold on, I'll get some tissues.'

It's the scented man. I'm torn between disgust at my sodden top and excitement that it's *his* drink and he seems keen to make amends.

'Aw, your lovely top,' says Paula, swaying from side to side.

'Not to worry, I've got it,' says the scented one, arriving back with a clump of tissues. 'I'm Matt, by the way.' He proceeds to rub the tissues on the wet stain on my top. Jesus! I'm frozen to the spot.

'Em ... thanks for that but I can take it from here,' I say, suddenly aware that I'm standing there allowing this man to practically massage my breasts!

'No problem,' he says, flashing a mouthful of bleached-white teeth as he hands over the tissues. 'And sorry about your top.

Can I buy you a drink to make up for it?'

Ooh, the night is looking up. But where on earth has Paula gone? Jesus, she was standing right here just a minute ago.

'Sorry, I just need to go check on my friend,' I say, fully aware that I sound like a kid in the playground. 'I'll be back in a minute.'

I find her wandering towards the exit. Ah, feck it. She's a lot more drunk than I thought. 'Paula, where are you going? I turned around and you were gone.'

'Ah howareya, Jenny?' she slurs. 'I seem to be a tinsy winsy bit tipsy, so I'm going home.'

Fuck! Just when I've clicked too. Maybe I could just stick her in a taxi and go back to the lovely Matt. But I'm not the sort of girl who'd abandon her friends, and after briefly toying with the idea of letting her go home alone, I know what I need to do.

'Right, just hold on there for a second. I'll be back,' I say, propping her up against the wall beside the exit. She's too far gone to protest.

I hurry back over to explain to Matt that I can't stay for that drink after all. He doesn't notice me as I gather our two jackets from the floor beside where he's standing and I'm about to tap him on the shoulder when I hear him talking to his friends. 'She's well up for it. Did you see her face when I was rubbing her tits? It works every time! And she looks like a bit of a goer too. Looks like I'm in for a night of it!' They all guffaw and I can't get away quickly enough.

Thankfully, Paula is still leaning against the wall where I left her, smiling to herself in a drunken haze. I can't help wishing for that blissful haze myself! 'Come on,' I say, linking my arm through hers. 'Let's get you home.' There are plenty of taxis outside, so I bundle us both into one, giving the driver Paula's city-centre address. Thankfully, she immediately falls asleep and the driver is listening to the radio so there's no need for chatter. When Paula is safely in her flat and we're en route to Lucan, I finally let myself think about what happened in the club and how I feel about it. All I know is I'm disgusted – disgusted that a man could talk about me like that but even more disgusted that I allowed myself to get into that situation at all. I'm an eejit – a bloody, bloody eejit!

The taxi pulls up at my door just as I can feel tears forming in the corner of my eyes. I quickly throw thirty euro to the taxi man and wave away the change. Somehow, money doesn't seem to matter much tonight. Inside, in the safety of my lonely house, I sit down on the beige carpeted stairs and let the tears fall. I can't ever remember crying this much – I can't ever remember feeling this bad. God, what the hell is wrong with me? I usually wouldn't let a comment like that from a drunken idiot in a nightclub affect me. But for some reason, it has.

They say thirty can mark a change in your life. I've always thought that was a load of rubbish, but maybe there's something to it.

I have a pretty good life really. I don't have anyone else to worry about except myself. But maybe that's part of the problem. Oh, God, my head is spinning. I've got to stop analysing it all. I'll have a good old moan to Sally tomorrow – she'll be able to sort me out. But, for now, sleep is what I need. I drag myself up the stairs and strip off quickly before curling into my bed. I begin to drift off immediately with my heavy-duty mask of make-up still on my face.

CHAPTER 3

Saturday – 11 Days to D-Day

I'm sitting on an inflatable ring, bobbing up and down with the waves. I can see Sally on the beach making sandcastles with her girls. They're having a ball. The sun is beaming, the sky is blue and life is good. I close my eyes and breathe in the fresh, salty air. When I open them, the beach is no longer in sight. I'm out in the middle of the sea, completely removed from any bit of land. Think! Think! What should I do? Then I spy them. There must be five of them at least. They've sensed the fear and they've come to get me. I know what I have to do. Without further thought, I open the little rubber fixing on the ring and the air begins to slowly blow out. I'm sinking now; lower and lower and lower. I close my eyes and succumb to the hungry sharks.

'Thanks, Sal,' I say, mopping up the last of my runny eggs with a piece of fried bread. 'That was delicious.'

It's eleven o'clock on Saturday and I'm sitting in Sally's house after a very welcome greasy fry-up. There's something very comforting about being here in the bosom of domestic bliss, especially after last night. Besides Paula, Sally is my only other friend in the world. We used to go out together all the time until she settled down and had her two girls.

Sally is great in a crisis and always knows what to do. She's a head of sense. Well except for the few months after her youngest daughter Abbey was born when all sense seemed to desert her. She was a complete mess. One day she almost drove off with Abbey sitting comfortably in her car seat on the roof of her BMW! Honestly, only for a neighbour tapping on her window before she reversed the car out of the driveway, the poor child would have been catapulted through the air. I wonder if the car seat would have been at all useful in that situation, being as she was firmly strapped into it. But that was three years ago and she's well back to sensible Sal now.

'Ah it's no problem, Jen,' says Sally, lifting Abbey out of her chair. 'Sure we're delighted to see you, aren't we, John?'

'Course we are,' Sally's husband agrees, his oversized belly peeping out from beneath his T-shirt as he stretches. 'Now, why don't I take these two little missies into the playroom and leave you two to have a good old gossip?'

'Yay, Daddy's gonna play dollies with us,' says Sinead, grabbing Abbey's little hand and dragging her into the playroom. At six, Sinead is clearly the boss of her three year old sister.

'Can't wait,' he says, rolling his grey eyes. 'But I bagsy to be Ken.'

'Thanks, John,' I say, laughing. 'You're a pet.'

I like John. He wouldn't exactly be my type and I don't find him at all attractive. Well except for when he does that thing with his tongue. Now, there's no way John is actually *trying* to be seductive – he's not that sort – but he has a habit of opening his mouth slightly and running the tip of his tongue over his bottom lip. I try not to notice but it's hard not to.

'Now,' says Sally, loading the last of the dishes into the dishwasher and filling the kettle. 'I'll make us a cuppa and you can tell me all the gossip.'

'Eh ... maybe we should go straight to the whiskey,' I say, trying to gauge whether I want Sally to be the 'best friend' Sally or the 'Mammy' Sally. You see, Sally covers both those roles very well. As a friend, she's fiercely loyal and supportive. I can tell her about anything and she'll listen and won't judge. The Mammy Sally is comforting. She'll put her arms around me and make me feel as though I'm five years old. But she'll also take a dimmer view of my shenanigans. She'll repeatedly tell me off for behaving like a teenager and tell me she just wants to see me settle down with a nice man.

I decide that today, I need *all* the above.

'Sal, it's about last night. I ... there was this man ... I ... ' I sort of don't know how to tell her about this Matt bloke without seeming like a total loser. But I have her attention now and she plonks back down in a chair beside me.

'Jesus, you're scaring me, Jen. What happened?'

I begin, tentatively at first, to fill her in on last night's happenings. But then it all starts to flow out. I tell her about the spilled drink, the breast rubbing and the fact that I was enjoying it. I tell her about my initial annoyance at Paula for putting a stop to my fun, but also how I copped on to myself and knew I had to leave with my friend. I blush at the memory as I tell her about what I overheard. I finish with the grand finale of me crying myself to sleep on a sodden, mascara-covered pillow. Well maybe I exaggerated that last bit, but I really feel I need a bit of Sally loving today!

I wait for her reaction, but there's none. Jesus, she looks positively bored! I expected cries of 'oh God' and 'poor you' at the very least, but instead she looks as though she's thinking through the shopping list for her trip to Tesco later.

'Well say something,' I whisper, slightly irritated that it hasn't made a bigger impact!

'Fuckin' ... fuckin' ... fuckin' bastard,' is her response.

Okay, so maybe I did her an injustice.

'Jenny, that's awful. Did you let him know you'd heard? What a horrible, horrible thing to happen.'

'I know,' I sigh. 'But the thing is, I've come across idiots like that so often in clubs. They're out with the lads for a night and get themselves sozzled and don't really care who they hurt along the way. I can usually laugh it off or even find a smart answer, but I don't know why last night was different. It really got to me, Sal.'

'Of course it did. Sure you wouldn't be human if it didn't. Those types of guys aren't worth a second thought. What you need is somebody who'll treat you well, show you a good time and prove to you that relationships can actually be nice.'

Sally has often given me the 'you need to find yourself a decent man' lecture and usually it's like a red rag to a bull, so why are there tears rolling down my face? Jesus, not again. I'm becoming a snivelling wreck!

'Ah, Jen,' says Sally, getting up off the chair to come over to me. 'It's terrible that you had to go through that. And don't mind me trying to bulldoze you into a relationship. It'll happen when the time is right. I'm just a silly old romantic who believes in happy ever after.'

Yay! It's Mammy Sally. She's hugging me now and I feel everything is going to be all right. In a way, it's sad how my friend is more of a mother to me than my own mother. My mam is a bit of a looper. At fifty-six years old, she's lived on her own since my dad left twelve years ago. It was a shock when he went. I blamed her, I suppose, because in my eyes my lovely dad could do no wrong. I used to live in hope that he'd change his mind and come back, but my hopes were firmly dashed by his untimely death two years later. I was never all that close to my mother in the first place, but the events surrounding my dad's departure and death firmly sealed the distance between us. Now don't get me wrong, I do love her and I wish we had a better relationship. She only lives five minutes away in Leixlip and I drop into her a couple of times a month. I even play the dutiful daughter and accompany her to bingo every now and again. But we never do – and never have done – the usual mother and daughter things like going shopping or having girlie chats.

Last week, I spotted her in Liffey Valley, wearing a pair of skin-tight black leather trousers and an equally tight Lycra top. It was clear to everyone that she wasn't wearing a bra and, at that moment, I wished I was an orphan. She was walking towards Marks & Spencer as I was coming out but I ducked into Next just in the nick of time. Within seconds, the 'wish I was a teenager' person I call my mother was gone and I was relieved.

'Jenny ... Jenny ... JEN, are you okay?'

I realise I'd been lost in thought and hadn't noticed Sally breaking away from our embrace. I'm still sitting in a sort of foetal position on the chair as though her arms were still around me. What am I like?

'Em ... sorry Sal. I was just thinking about Mam and wishing she was more of a mumsy type. I wish I could share stuff with her. Can you imagine her sitting beside me on the sofa, arms around me and advising me on how to live my life?'

We both laugh at the unlikely picture, lightening the moment.

'Mummy, what are you and Aunty Jenny laughing at?' asks Sinead, wandering into the kitchen.

Sally sighs and looks hassled. 'Nothing, darling. Go on back in to Daddy, will you?'

'But Mummmmy! I need something to eat. It's been ages since my breakfast.'

'Sinead Kinsella!' Sally says, ushering the child back into the playroom. 'It's about twenty minutes since your breakfast and you had heaps of food!'

'But I want—'

'SINEAD!'

That seems to do the trick because there isn't another word

from the child. It's not like Sally to be so short with the children. She usually comes across as the all-singing, all-dancing mother who can make dinner with her right hand while playing the Wii with her left.

'What's up with you, Sal?' I ask, fully realising I've monopolised the conversation up until now. I suddenly notice she looks tired. She has black shadows under her eyes and her skin looks dehydrated and dull. Sally was always a bit of a looker, but the past few years haven't been kind to her. When she's made up and hair done, she has a look of Holly Willoughby about her, but she never lost the baby weight after Abbey was born and doesn't bother much now with trying to look good.

'Oh nothing much that a good night out wouldn't fix,' she says, sitting back down heavily on the wooden chair.

'Well why don't you and me go out then?' I ask, suddenly cheered at the prospect of a night with my very best friend. 'It's ages since we both went out. It would be fun.' Oh this day is really looking up. I know I don't have a shortage of nights out, and Paula is fabulous and everything, but I really miss the old days when it was just me and Sally. We used to have great nights out until she stepped onto the treadmill of domestic bliss.

Sally sighs heavily. 'Jenny, don't take this the wrong way, but if you really want to help, maybe you *could* see your way to minding the girls for us some night. I really think me and John need a night out. It's been hard these past couple of years with the girls taking up so much of our time. Abbey usually ends up in our bed most nights, so we get very little time to ourselves. We've barely left the house together in three years.'

I'm completely deflated.

She quickly adds, 'We could go out some night as well, but if you could just give me and John a night out for now, it would be brilliant.'

Sally is always there for me so how can I say no to her when she's obviously desperate enough for a night out to have asked *me* to babysit? And, besides, listening to her talk about the past few years being difficult for her makes me realise I must be a crap friend.

'No problem at all, Sal. How about next weekend? I could come over on Friday or Saturday night if you like.' Her eyes light up at this.

'Ah, Jen, you're the best.' She's back over hugging me again. I don't enjoy this one quite as much. Why the bloody hell did I offer to mind those two whiny kids? But maybe if I paid more attention to Sally instead of always keeping her at arm's length, I'd have a better relationship with her kids. Besides, they're not babies any more, so there'll be no bottles and nappies and all that stuff. I can bring a DVD and stick them in front of that until they go to bed. No problem at all. And I suppose it'll be good practice in case I ever decide to settle down and have kids.

I realise John has come back into the kitchen with the girls and Sally is just telling him they have a babysitter for next Saturday.

'Thanks, Jenny,' he says, tousling the top of my hair. 'You're a life-saver. We've been dying for a night out together for ages but Sally won't trust anyone to mind these two.'

'Don't *want* Aunty Jenny to mind us,' spits a vicious-looking Abbey, appearing at the kitchen door.

'Abbey! That's enough,' shouts Sally. 'You apologise to Aunty Jenny straight away!'

'Will not,' says the stubborn three year old. 'She doesn't bring sweeties and she *never* talks to us.'

I suppose the child has a point. I never think of bringing presents for them and, to be honest, I can't think of anything more boring than trying to make small talk with a three or six year old. I mean, what would I say? How could anything I say possibly interest them, and vice versa? But maybe it's just that I'm not used to kids. I should probably try to engage more with them – for Sal's sake.

'Abbey Kinsella! If you don't apologise to Aunty Jenny right now, you're going to your room for a whole hour.'

You see, I really don't understand this kiddie thing. I assume that sending her to her room is some sort of punishment, but I would have put it in the treat category myself. I mean, being asked to go into a room where there's books and a bed and you can have a snooze with nobody disturbing you or not having to be up for work is a good thing as far as I'm concerned!

'Sally, it's okay,' I say, looking at the child's pouting face. Maybe this is my 'get out of jail free' card! 'I wouldn't want them to be upset. Maybe me babysitting isn't such a good idea after all.'

'Oh there's no way a three year old is going to dictate what goes on in this house,' declares Sally, fixing the child with a death stare. 'Whether or not they both hate you, you're coming on Saturday!'

Eeeek! That was a bit of a blow. I'm not fond of the kids, but they *hate* me? Gosh, am I that horrible a person? Oh I can see I'm in for a great night on Saturday. Well, if they decide to take on their Aunty Jenny, they'd better be ready for war. Bring it on. It's Jenny versus the brats!

★

Although it's just two in the afternoon when I arrive back home, I'm exhausted. I'm not used to analysing my thoughts so much, and Sally really has a way of making me question things. Flopping down on the sofa in the living room, I open my laptop which I've left on the coffee table and log on to Twitter. I see Kerry is online and chatting about her night out last night. I think I'll send her a private message rather than tweeting her for everyone to see.

Private messages, or DMs as they're called, are great – it's like having a chat to someone where nobody else can hear.

> *@JennyB* Hi, Kerry. I see from your tweets you had a good night last night.
> *@kerrydhunt* Hi, Jenny. Yes, it was a laugh. How did your night go?
> *@JennyB* Well between you and me, it was a bit of a disaster.
> *@kerrydhunt* Oh, why? What happened?
> *@JennyB* Sigh! It seems silly even as I say it but a guy I thought might be interested in me turned out to be a right idiot. I don't know how I get myself into those situations!
> *@kerrydhunt* Oh, are you all right? Did he do something to you?
> *@JennyB* Ah, no, nothing like that, but he just made me feel like a real loser. Why do things like this always happen to me?
> *@kerrydhunt* Well, you're lovely so he's the loser, if you ask me! Don't give him another thought. You deserve way better than that.
> *@JennyB* Thanks, Kerry. I love how you always cheer me up. I'd better go though – I've a million and one things to do.
> *@kerrydhunt* No problem. Chat to you later.

Kerry is just such a nice person. The more I chat to her, the more I'm beginning to actually look forward to the girls' arrival. It might be just the distraction I need. Right, well an afternoon of telly awaits, but I might just have a tweet or two first.

> *@JennyB* Just back from a lovely breakfast with my very best friend and her family. Love being with them.
> *@fionalee* Oh, lucky you. Me, hub and Ryan only had boring cereal. Did you go somewhere nice?

@JennyB Just over to their house. Only ten minutes away. Her hub cooked the works – the full Irish!

@fionalee Sounds fab. I wish me and hub could have a bit of time on our own. Love Ryan but hard work.

@JennyB Oh, it wasn't adults only. They have two girls, 3 and 6. They're gorgeous and they even call me aunty!

@fionalee 3 and 6 is a handful – one 4 year old is hard enough work. Do you spend much time with them?

@JennyB Oh, yes. The girls adore me and since I have none of my own, I'm always taking them out and buying them things. Love them to bits.

@fionalee Lucky them. You sound like you'd make a lovely mammy yourself.

@JennyB Hmm! Maybe some day. Are you looking forward to your Dublin trip?

@fionalee Can't wait. Hub is taking time off work to mind Ryan. Can't believe I'll be free for a few days.

@JennyB Well, bring it on. I'm off to buy toys for the girls. I love to spoil them. Babysitting for them next week. Can't wait.

@fionalee Lucky girls to have somebody like you in their lives. Enjoy shopping. Catch up with you later. x

For feck's sake! Why am I such an idiot, pretending the girls love me and that I adore them back? It's just that Fiona seems like such a great mammy. She's always tweeting about Ryan. And her husband sounds lovely. She seems to have a life of domestic bliss in Galway. But everyone to their own, I suppose, and maybe my life looks just as appealing to others.

Right, enough of the deep thoughts. Pyjamas, telly and a cool glass of white wine – that's what's on the menu for me for the rest of the day! Tomorrow I might even take a trip over to Mam. With Dad gone and having no brothers or sisters, she's the only family I've got. Thinking about her today made me realise that I should really make more of an effort.

With only a few weeks left to Christmas, I need to shake off this dark cloud and look at things in a more positive light. There'll be no crying into my trifle this year. Actually, I might even ditch the trifle for a strawberry cheesecake! Oooh, things are looking up!

CHAPTER 4

Sunday – 10 Days to D-Day

Why is my mam walking on her hands? It doesn't make sense. I hide myself inside the door of River Island as she passes by. Liffey Valley is buzzing with people doing their last-minute Christmas shopping. Why is it that nobody else seems to notice her? I walk a safe distance behind. Her skirt is around her waist, exposing bright-pink knickers. I've got to do something about it. I run up to her.

'Mam … Mammy … What are you doing? Stand up, will you, for God's sake?'

'Ah howarya, Jenny love. Come on – try it. It's great fun.'

I don't remember thinking about it or I don't remember getting into position, but it seems I too am walking on my hands beside her. It's strangely liberating. I'm aware that my knickers are exposed too and don't really care. We're having fun.

I'm on my way to see my mam. I haven't been able to get her out of my mind since yesterday. With Christmas almost upon us, I'm determined that this year will be different. Although we always spend Christmas day together, it's usually a bit of a non-event as we both count down the hours until we don't have to play happy families anymore. I want us to start actually enjoying each other's company.

Mam was never like the other mothers who stood at the school gates in their mummy clothes. She'd always be there, wearing a flamboyant top with more than a little cleavage showing and tight leggings sculpting the shape of her enormous bum. Unlike the other mothers who'd always complain about putting on weight, mam embraced her curves and used every opportunity to show them off. Dad was a quiet man, but never blinked an eye at my mother's wacky ways.

I loved my dad. I was always a bit of a daddy's girl growing up, and I think sometimes that Mam sensed that. He told the best stories and never had to read them from a book. He had them all in his head, and I loved all the whacky characters he created. Even into my teenage years he used to tell his stories, and even though I used to roll my eyes and tut-tut the way only teenagers can, I secretly enjoyed his tales.

Anyway, I was just twenty-two when I got that dreaded call in work. It was Aunty Polly, Dad's sister. The words were all a blur to me ... heart attack ... sudden ... no pain ... gone ... GONE! My lovely, fabulous dad was dead. Those next few days went by in a haze. Fifty years old and seemingly healthy. Nobody could believe it.

I kept imagining the 'what ifs'. What if they hadn't split up and he'd still been living at home? Would we have noticed something amiss with him and insisted that he saw a doctor? What if the heart attack was brought on by the stress of having his family torn apart? I suppose I was looking for somebody to blame and, unfortunately for my mother, she seemed like the easiest target.

Losing my dad has had a profound effect on my life. Being left in the lurch by a passing fling or being dumped by a boyfriend is one thing, but having the man who's always been there whipped away so suddenly was almost too much to bear. I relied heavily on my dad. He was the one I confided in when I got my first period as Mum was off with her friends for the weekend. He was the one who noticed when I became withdrawn as a result of bullying at school.

Dad was a gardener – not just a 'pull up a few weeds and plant a bunch of roses' gardener but a proper landscape gardener. He was very fortunate to have benefited from the property boom and right up until the day he died, there was always plenty of well-paid work for him. Don't get me wrong, we weren't rich or anything, but it did mean that Dad could pick and choose his hours and, luckily for me, he chose to spend a lot of time with his family.

I've never told anybody just how much I miss him. Often on Sunday afternoons while my friends are busy with their families, I'll take a plant or a few flowers up to his grave in Glasnevin cemetery. I sometimes even talk to him and convince myself that a gust of wind or a sudden rain shower is him saying that he hears me and that he's looking down on me.

I pull Betsy up on the kerb outside Mam's driveway. Betsy, my beloved lime green Volkswagen Beetle, is my pride and joy. I used to sneer at those who treated their cars like some sort of family member. I'd tut-tut when I'd see a man out washing his car for hours while his wife multitasked and managed a career, the house and ten kids. But now I can understand it. I've cherished Betsy since that first day I brought her home from the garage, all shiny and new. I fell in love with her well before that day, but it was only when I got her home that we started to bond. I wash her lovingly every weekend and make sure she gets a quick lick and spit daily.

I didn't bother telling Mam I was coming today as I'm quite sure she would have put me off.

Walking up the driveway, I notice the curtains are still closed. It's twelve o'clock and she's usually an early riser, so it's a little strange. Maybe she's watching telly. The frosty sun is gleaming this morning so there would have been a shine on the screen, hence the closed curtains. I'm about to ring the bell when a movement inside prompts me to press my nose up against the stained glass of the front door instead.

What the fuck? What's my mother doing on the kitchen counter? Has she completely lost her marbles? She's just lying there completely still, wearing some sort of silk get up and staring up at the ceiling. Oh, I suppose it'll be one of her new-fangled ideas – she'll be listening to some native Indian meditation tape that promises to change your life.

Balancing the box of cakes I picked up from Avoca in my left hand, I ring the doorbell with my right. I won't let on I've seen her lying there. She'll only be all defensive if I do and it'll get us off on the wrong footing.

Suddenly, the door is swung open and I'm frozen to the spot. My mouth has gone dry and I can't get any words out.

'Thanks, love,' says a hairy-faced man in boxer shorts and T-shirt, grabbing the Avoca box from me and shoving a twenty-euro note into my hand.

'And keep the change,' he says generously, closing the door again.

Did that just happen? I feel like I'm in one of my dreams and need to wake up. That's it. Yes, it'll be one of my loopy dreams. I'll wake up in my bed and have a good laugh at it. I'm waiting ... and waiting ... nope ... still here!

Just as I'm trying to make sense of what happened, the door opens again and Mr Hairy is back. He looks angry this time and shoves the Avoca box back into my hands.

'Where's the chicken with cashew nuts?' he says, puffing out his chest, causing his tight T-shirt to rise over the top of his boxer shorts, exposing an expanse of white flesh. That's what I ordered, with two portions of egg fried rice.'

'I ... eh ... I think ... maybe ...' I'm at a loss.

'*Jenny!* What on earth are you doing here?' Mam has come out to join Mr Hairy at the door and I look from one to the other in complete confusion. Then it hits me. Jesus, the kitchen counter ... the man ... the half nakedness . . .

'Eh ... I just wanted to drop in for a chat.' The words come out strangled. 'I brought these.' I thrust the box into her hand. What the hell do I do now? Do I leave or do I invite myself in? Mr Hairy has retreated into the kitchen, realising I didn't come bearing chicken with cashew nuts.

'I suppose you'd better come in,' she sighs, reluctantly opening the door.

I hesitate for a moment and then it hits me. Why the hell should *I* be made to feel like an intruder? This is *my* house – the house where I grew up. I have more right to be here than Mr Hairy. I puff out my own chest and follow Mam into the kitchen.

'Jenny, I've been meaning to ring you, but I'm glad you're here now. This is my boyfriend, Harry.'

Jesus! Her *boyfriend*! She can't call him that at her age. And she didn't even flinch when she said it.

'And Harry, this is my ... my daughter, Jenny.'

Hairy Harry seems to be completely okay with the fact he's standing in my mother's kitchen in his boxers and extends his hand to shake mine.

'Nice to meet you, Jenny,' he says, gripping my hand tightly. Am I imagining it or is he looking at me strangely? He looks vaguely familiar too but he probably just has one of those faces.

'Eh ... you too,' I say. 'Mam didn't tell me she had a ... she had a ...' Oh, God, I can't say the word. It sounds so juvenile! 'Mam didn't say she was seeing someone.' Much better.

'Darling,' she says, fixing me with one of her glares. 'You know how I hate it when you call me Mam. Just call me Eileen.'

Jesus! First I heard of that!

'And Harry,' she continues. 'Go on up and get yourself dressed, will you? The food should be here in a few minutes and I want to have a little word with Jenny here before she goes.'

Harry does as he's bid and I watch in amazement as his back disappears out the kitchen door.

'MAM! What the hell is going on?' I'm still standing in the middle of the kitchen, feet glued to the floor.

'What do you mean "going on"?' she asks innocently, flicking in the switch of the kettle. 'I'm a grown woman, Jen. I have needs just like everyone else, you know. And for your information ... '

But she's lost me at 'needs'. I know she's only fifty-six and I know she's a good-looking woman, but when your mother starts talking about her 'needs', it's time to go.

'Look, Mam ... Eileen ... don't get me wrong. Fair play to you and all that but it's just a shock. I mean, I was coming over for Sunday afternoon tea and cakes and instead I've been met with ... with *that*!' I gesture in the direction of her sexy lingerie and blush at the thought of what was happening before I arrived.

She seems completely unperturbed by it all and busies herself pouring two cups of tea. She plonks them down on the counter.

'Come on, Jen. Harry's a keeper. He's been really good to me these past few months. We've been . . .'

'*Few months*?' I practically spit out. 'You've been seeing him for a few months and you didn't think it worth your while to tell me about him?' I feel hurt. I know ours isn't a traditional type of family, but it would have been nice to have been told.

'Come and get your tea, love. He'll be down in a minute.' She gestures to the steaming hot tea on the counter and I realise I'm still rooted to the spot.

'Well maybe just a few sips,' I say, plonking down on a bar stool beside her. 'So where did you two meet?' There's no point in fighting it.

'I met Eileen at a party in a mutual friend's house,' says Harry, appearing at the kitchen door. He's looking a lot better in a pair of chinos and an open-neck polo shirt.

'Harry came to chat to me when he heard that I work in the

Department of Health,' my mother adds, beaming at the object of her affection. 'It turns out he's not long retired from there himself. He took one of those early retirement packages – lucky sod.'

'It was love at first sight – well on my part anyway,' he continues. 'Your mam took a bit of persuading, but she eventually agreed to go out with me.'

'Nice,' I say, completely lost for words. I feel uncomfortable. I know Mam has seen men in the past, but I've never actually met any of them. Well except for Billy. And he doesn't count – he only had one leg. Now I don't mean I'm discounting him as a boyfriend because of his disability but I know that Mam really only went out with him because he was a neighbour and he'd been asking her for ages and, as I said, he only had one leg. It lasted for two dates – once to the cinema and once for a walk in the park. The walk wasn't one of Mam's better ideas.

I'm saved from further conversation by a ring at the door.

'That must be the food now,' says Mam, heading out to the door. 'You'll stay for a bit, won't you, Jen?'

'I ... um ... I'll leave the two of you in peace and head off I think.'

'Ah don't go, Jenny,' says Harry. 'I'm sure Eileen will be delighted for us to get to know each other a little better.'

What can I say to that? 'Okay, then, maybe just for a while. I'll just have one of my cakes while you're having your dinner.'

Mam comes back into the room with the hot food and we all gather around the counter.

'Let's not bother with plates,' she says, ripping open the bag and letting a delicious aroma escape. She grabs a couple of forks and they both proceed to eat from the foil containers. My mam was never the domestic goddess type.

There's silence for a few minutes as they eat and I take one of the enormous chocolate éclairs out of the Avoca box. I leave it down on the counter as I take a sip of my now cold tea. Taking a huge bite of the cake it suddenly dawns on me. Fuck! The counter! What was going on before I arrived? Why was my mother lying on the counter? With no serviettes or tissues in sight, I just spit my mouthful out on the counter.

'Jenny Breslin!' shouts my mother, in a tone she used to use when I was five. 'That's disgusting. What did you do that for?'

'Jesus, sorry about that, Mam … Eileen,' I say, mortified. It was just going down the wrong way.' I could hardly say that I couldn't swallow a cake that had touched a counter that had been possibly used for sexual intercourse not twenty minutes before!

'Anyway,' I continue, getting up from the stool. 'I'm going to head off and leave you two to it.' Oh God! 'I mean, I'll leave you to … em … I … I need to be somewhere.'

I can't get away quick enough and nobody is protesting.

'All right, love,' says Mam. 'You'll let yourself out, won't you? Don't want this food getting cold.'

I feel overwhelmed by motherly love – not!

'Bye now, Jenny,' says Harry. 'Lovely to meet you.'

'And you too Hairy … uh I mean Harry.' Jesus!

★

Bloody hell! It's only two in the afternoon and I'm already home. All of a sudden, I feel very lonely. Sunday is normally my day for burrowing under the duvet after a long night out on the town, revelling in the fact that I'd nobody else to worry about and could spend the day in my pyjamas, eating microwave food.

Right, enough of the moping! I'll really have to get my act together and start planning some things to do when the girls come over. I wonder is there anyone online now or are they all having a busy Sunday. Sighing, I open my laptop.

@JennyB Just popping in for a mo. I've a very busy day planned. Anyone here?

@zahraglam Yes, I'm here, but like you, just on for a moment. What are you up to?

@JennyB Just been to my mam's for dinner. I've had a lovely day.

@zahraglam But it's only after 2 – you must have had an early one?

I've really got to watch what I say. I'd hate to be caught out telling lies.

@JennyB Yes, unfortunately, I had to leave straight after. She wanted me to stay but I have plans.

@zahraglam Anything interesting?

@JennyB I'm meeting a few friends in town for a drink. Looking forward to it.

@zahraglam Lovely. I'm working myself. I have to be at the studios in an hour. But I really don't mind – it's a brilliant place to work. Everyone is so nice.

@JennyB Oh, it sounds so exciting. I've never been in a television studio before. You're so lucky to love your job so much.

@zahraglam I know. It's good to get into work and away from the boredom at home. And lovely to get a glimpse at the dressing rooms of the rich and famous!

@JennyB But you must get more than a glimpse if you're there to do their make-up. And don't you have parties with them at least a few times a week?

@zahraglam Yes, yes, always parties. But I have to fly now. I'll catch up with you tomorrow.

I'm just about to snap the laptop shut when another tweet beeps at me. This time it's a DM. It's Kerry. Oh, I love when her messages appear in my inbox.

@kerrydhunt Hi, Jenny. Are you ok?

@JennyB I'm fine. Why do you ask?

@kerrydhunt Was just watching you tweet to Zahra and got the impression all wasn't well and what with your disastrous night on Saturday, I just wanted to check in on you.

Gosh, she's very perceptive! I'm quickly checking back on my tweets but I don't seem to have given any indication something is wrong. But isn't she lovely to be extra sensitive because of what I told her yesterday?

@JennyB I wouldn't say there's anything specifically wrong, Kerry, just a combination of things.

@kerrydhunt Well is there anything I can do? Do you want to chat about it?

@JennyB I just can't quite put my finger on it but it's like there's a bit of a cloud over me these past few weeks. I'm not enjoying stuff like I used to.

@kerrydhunt I think we all get a bit like that at times, Jenny. To be honest, I've been feeling a bit like that myself.

@JennyB Really? You always seem so happy with your lot. So what's up with you then?

@kerrydhunt The single life of hell! That's what's up! I'm fed up being on my own – I want someone special in my life. So there! I've said it now.

@JennyB Hmmm! The single life's not so bad. But I know what you mean about wanting someone special. I never really thought about it much but these past few days has me rethinking stuff.

@kerrydhunt Looks like the other night has really affected you. I'm sure there's someone out there for you.

@JennyB Hmmm! I wouldn't be so sure. I'm not the nicest person in the world sometimes. I honestly don't know why

anyone would want to be with me.

@kerrydhunt Jenny Breslin! Stop that now. You're lovely, as I've told you again and again. Stop putting yourself down.

@JennyB I don't mean to be so self-indulgent but sometimes I just hate who I am. I wish I loved my job like you or Zahra does or that I was happy in domesticity like Fiona.

@kerrydhunt Sorry to cut you short but I have to go – only half an hour to get ready for my shift. Let's chat about this more tomorrow. Looks like we could both do with a bit of a change!

@JennyB And you'll be here very soon and we can have a nice girlie face to face chat. Imagine being able to talk in more than 140 characters! Talk tomorrow. x

Oh, God, cue the tissues again! I'm in danger of becoming a right softie. What a lovely girl Kerry is. Imagine she picked up on the tone of my tweets to Zahra and knew something was up. She seems like the sort of girl I could be very good friends with. It's a pity she doesn't live closer. But I'm feeling a lot more positive about our Twitter weekend now. It'll be good to be able to chat to her face to face. I think Sally was wrong about the axe murderer thing – well at least where Kerry is concerned!

Right, I need to get my act together and stop wallowing. I had planned to strip off and hop into bed for a few hours but not now. I'm going to slip down to Marks & Spencer and buy a few of those lovely red, Christmassy plants they have on display and bring them down to Dad's grave. Dad always liked those flowers and we used to have the house full of them at Christmas. Yes, he'd love that and I might just have a quiet word with him while I'm there!

CHAPTER 5

Monday – 9 Days to D-Day

The music starts and I take a deep breath. I never thought I'd see this day. It's exciting but terrifying at the same time. I only wish my dad was here to walk me up the aisle. I slip my veil over my face and step onto the red carpet that will lead me to my destiny.

'Go on, Jen,' comes a shout from the congregation.

'Stick it to him,' shouts another.

'Show us what you're made of.'

Uh … this feels all wrong. Why are they shouting things like that? I'm getting nervous now as I reach the altar and can feel the tension in the church. But what's this? There's no altar – only a boxing ring! Jesus, is that Hairy Harry waiting for me in the ring? He's wearing the shorts he had on at Mam's house and a pair of boxing gloves. Before I know what's happening, somebody whips off my fabulous white dress and hands me a pair of boxing gloves. I suppose I may as well go with the flow.

'Right then, Harry! Give me what you've got!'

I hide a smile as I sit on the 25A on my way to work. That was a strange dream all right; me and Harry in a battle. But a battle for what? For my mam? Ha! Maybe I *am* feeling a teeny weeny bit jealous. It's a bit of a double whammy, isn't it? Not only am

I trailing leagues behind my own mother in the relationship stakes, but it also means there's now even more distance between us. Does that sound childish?

I suppose what I'm trying to say is that I won't feel comfortable just popping over to my childhood home any more. I certainly wouldn't want to be interrupting their counter-top shenanigans again! I shudder at the thought.

It's only 8.30 a.m. as the bus pulls up on the quays. I pull my jacket tighter around my neck to fend off the cutting wind and I consider going for a walk up Grafton Street to take in the atmosphere. I love it there in the early mornings. The flower sellers are usually setting up their brightly coloured stalls as the aroma of coffee from Bewley's hangs in the air. And December time is the best. I don't think I'll ever be too old to enjoy the magical Christmas displays in the windows of Brown Thomas, nor will I tire of looking at the enormous Christmas tree that crowns the street at Stephen's Green.

But it's the first day of the week and I decide I'm going to get to the office early for once. Bootface won't be able to believe her eyes when she sees my diligence. Maybe I'll even get a glimmer of a smile from her. On second thoughts, I don't think she knows how to smile. Her facial muscles would need retraining for that! I think she'd be scarier if she smiled anyway. There's something comforting about her permanent scowl.

I slip in through the staff door, my takeaway coffee in hand, and head straight for the ladies. It's actually quite nice to be in early for a change. I usually spend my first hour in work bursting for the loo as I've only just made it to my desk on time. A quick top-up of lip gloss and an extra layer of black eyeliner and I'm done.

I flick the switch on my computer and sit back, enjoying sipping my delicious choca mocha in peace.

'But I *can't* just up and leave like that – I've told you already. Why can't you just *understand*?'

Fuckity, fuckity fuck! I jump up from my chair as half my chocolaty coffee spills right down my top. I thought I was the only one in. But seems Bootface is here and by the sounds of it, she's having a good old barney with somebody on the phone.

'No, no, *no*! I'll be there as soon as I can, so just hang on for today, will you?'

I'm in a dilemma. Do I go to the loos to sort out my coffee-sodden top and scalded chest or hang around to listen to the old bag's conversation? It's not often I get the opportunity to hear something like this, so I opt for sprinkling cold water from the water cooler on my top while shuffling a little nearer to her office. It's gone quiet again, so I tiptoe right up to the door.

Suddenly the door is swung open and Bootface storms out. She stops dead when she sees me crouched down on my hunkers outside her office but instead of shouting at me, she lets out a little high-pitched noise and runs off to the loos.

Well that was all very strange. And I'm sure she was crying. God, maybe something terrible has happened. I feel weird. I sort of pity her, but I don't want to feel like that. The only thing that gets me through the day is my dislike of Bootface. It would completely upset the dynamics of the place if I was to feel sorry for her.

Should I go in after her and see if she's okay? I realise I'm still crouching down on my hunkers so I hop up and follow her. But she's already coming out, head up and mouth fixed into the stern look we all know and love. But her eyes reveal more. They're red and bloodshot and it's obvious she's been crying.

'Brenda, are … are you okay?' I ask, tentatively. 'It's just that I heard … I saw …'

'Jenny Breslin, you're not paid to play hide and seek around the office, you know,' she sneered.

'But I … I was just …'

'And look at the state of you.' She's looking at the coffee stain right down my front. 'What have I told you about the dress code here? Tsk!'

She click clacks back to her office and slams the door hard. Hooray! I can go back to disliking her. Although I can't help wondering what all that was about. I like to think of Bootface as this lone, hard-nosed creature who doesn't have a life outside of this place. She's like the banking ogre who sleeps in her office and never enters the outside world. I smile to myself with this picture in my head as I head back to my desk, ready to begin the day's work.

'What's with you being here this early?' asks Paula, rambling into the office and throwing her bag on the floor beside her desk. 'And what the hell happened to your top?'

'Long story,' I say, beginning to realise just how bad I look and smell. 'Come on into the loos and I'll tell you.'

I whip off my grey cotton top and quickly run it under the cold tap. Thank God I have another vest top underneath. That's stained too but it'll have to wait until I get home.

'So what's up?' asks Paula, sitting up on the ledge beside the sinks.

I quickly fill her in about Bootface and the coffee spill while holding my top under the hand dryer.

'I'm glad I didn't see that,' says Paula. 'I certainly wouldn't want to be feeling sorry for her or anything.'

'That's exactly what I thought,' I laugh. 'But, thankfully, she was back to her crabby old self within minutes, so no sympathy needed.'

'And what's the story with you being in so early?' she asks, rolling her eyes at my attempts to dry the top under the pathetic blow of the dryer.

'I'm just sick of always rushing at the last minute and ...'

'And what, Jenny? What is it?'

'It's the whole bloody Friday night saga. It's just made me rethink a few things, that's all.'

I'd had a good chat to Paula on the phone on Saturday night and filled her in on all she missed while she was blotto. 'Ah, Jenny, don't let one eejit in a nightclub put a stop to your fun. There are plenty of men like him about but there also plenty of decent ones.'

'That's just it, Paula. It's not really fun anymore.' I hoosh myself up on the counter beside her, abandoning my efforts to save the stained top. 'Honestly, I'm sick of messing around. And I'm certainly not giving up on men because of that pig! I might even dip my toe into this whole dating scene – that is, if anyone decent comes along!'

'Oh that's great, Jenny! It will be brilliant to see you in a proper relationship at last – just like me and my Ian! How lovely.'

Not like her and Ian!

'And won't it be great if we can double date at last? It'll be fun. Oooh that's the best news I've heard in ages.'

Now I'd rather flush my own head down a toilet than endure a double date with Paula and that prat, but I smile sweetly and nod.

The sudden rush of women into the toilets, flinging handbags and coats on the counter, alerts us to the fact it's half nine so we head back out to our desks. Jesus, is it really only half nine? How am I going to survive until lunch-time? I feel as though I've put in hours already. Maybe I need to rethink this whole 'early to work' malarkey!

★

'Gosh, it's mental in here today, isn't it?' says Paula, grabbing two chairs at the end of an already packed table. Lunch-time in the staff canteen doesn't usually attract so many but the freezing cold weather has made staying in so much more enticing.

'Well there's no way I was going out in that,' I say, gesturing to a window that had suddenly turned white from a heavy fall of icy hailstones. 'I wish to God this bloody weather would get its act together and actually snow – proper fluffy snow! I hate how we're teased with a sprinkling of it and then it turns to hail and all we get is icy pavements where we're likely to break our necks!'

'Ha, I know what you mean,' says Paula. I love a bit of snow at Christmastime. It makes it all so magical.'

'Well, we've a few weeks to go, so fingers crossed for a white Christmas.'

'Oooh don't look now but here comes Tom Delaney,' says Paula.

Why do people say that? There's nothing more likely to make somebody look than being told not to!

'He's a bit of all right, isn't he?' she continues.

'*Paula Farrell*! I know what you're doing and you can stop it, *right now*!'

'What?' she asks, innocently. 'I'm not doing anything! Howareya, Tom. Are you going to join us?'

Bloody hell. I'll feckin' kill her. I can tell now she's got a bee in her bonnet about me finding a *nice* man and she won't stop until she's found one. Had I known she was going to entice that Tom Delaney over, I would never have purposefully swung my elbows about until the girl beside me had no choice but to leave. I can't stand being squashed at a table and in fairness, she was almost finished. Now it looks like Tom is going to take her place! Shit!

'Eh ... hi girls ... eh ... well, if you don't mind, I'll grab that chair so. I'll be gone again in a few minutes.'

'No problem at all,' says Paula, suddenly jollying her voice up a notch. 'So how are things with you?'

Jesus, you'd swear Tom was one of her long-lost friends. I think we've probably only ever said two words to him in the whole time we've been working here. He works upstairs in accounts and, being such a large branch, it's impossible to get to know everyone properly.

'Good, good, thanks,' he says, breaking up pieces of his bread roll and floating them on top of his soup. 'So what are you girls talking about?'

'Oh just the weather and the general state of the country,' I say, watching in amazement as he continues breaking the bread into the bowl until the soup disappears.

'And we're discussing which places are best for drinks around here,' adds Paula, kicking me under the table. I'm giving her the evil eye, but she's ignoring me.

'So where do you usually go?' asks Tom. 'The pubs around here are great – always buzzing come five o'clock.'

'Oh, we vary it,' says Paula, before I can get a chance to speak. 'Actually, Jenny was dying to go out tomorrow night and I can't make it. Maybe *you* could keep her company instead!'

'*Paula!*' Oh fuck! I'm mortified. I can't believe she just said that. I want to roll up in a ball under the table!'

'What?' asks Paula, innocently. 'I'm only suggesting a drink – what's wrong with that? But I have to fly off and make a call before lunch-time is over so I'll leave you two to make arrangements.' She's gone before I can fix her with my death stare. And to make it worse, Tom is watching her run out, a smile on his face. I bet he's enjoying my mortification!

'Jesus, Tom. I'm sorry about that. I'll kill her when I get my hands on her!'

'She's a right firecracker, that's for sure,' he says, still smiling. 'But how about it, then?'

'Em ... about ... em ... Do you mean ... ?' Oh shit! Now I look like an eejit. Is he asking me out? God, I'm so relaxed in a nightclub environment and well used to chatting to men but put me in a similar situation in my workplace and I become unable to put a sentence together!

'Well since Paula made such an effort to get us out together, it would be a shame to disappoint her, wouldn't it?'

'Oh ... em ... yes, it would.' He has a nice, warm smile and his grey eyes twinkle when he laughs. He's actually quite attractive – how did I never notice that before? He's one of those ordinary-looking guys that just blend into the crowd and it's only up close I can see his handsome features. Maybe a date with him wouldn't be such a bad thing after all.

'Great, so tomorrow evening it is then,' he says, standing up. 'Have a think about where you want to go and I'll pop down to your desk later to make arrangements.'

'Okay, see you later so.' I watch his retreating back and I'm not sure how I feel. In shock? Yes. Ready to kill Paula? Yes. A little excited? Yes! Well, I did say I was willing to give this whole dating thing a go – I just didn't expect it to happen so soon. And I wouldn't say I fancy Tom or anything, but who knows? That might change once we've been out.

I can't believe lunch-time is almost over! I feel as though I've just sat down, and with all the comings and goings, I've only managed a few bites of my salad baguette. But somehow, my appetite has deserted me. Maybe I'll check and see who's online and report about my date for tomorrow night.

> @*JennyB* What a day it's been so far today! Guess who's got a date?
>
> @*kerrydhunt* Oooh, is it you? Tell us more.
>
> @*JennyB* Well he's pretty damn gorgeous for starters!
>
> @*kerrydhunt* Lucky you. So where did you meet him then?
>
> @*JennyB* He's the heartthrob of the office. He's asked me out before but I didn't want to get involved with someone in work.
>
> @*kerrydhunt* So what's changed then?

Fair play to Kerry. She's tweeting as though I haven't been telling her anything in secret. At least she has the cop on not to tell the world my problems!

@JennyB I just decided to see what happens. He's really nice so it seems silly to refuse him just because we work together.

@kerrydhunt Well I hope it works out well for you. I take it you're feeling a bit better today?

@JennyB Yes, much better thanks. Sorry for moaning yesterday. It was just one of those days.

@kerrydhunt No problem, Jenny. You can moan to me anytime. I'm a good listener.

@JennyB Yes, you certainly are. I'm really looking forward to having a face to face chat when you're here.

@kerrydhunt Oh, me too. But got to go – ward sister is on my back this morning. Talk later. x

I feel bad about lying to Kerry but when I'm chatting to her by DM, I can be more honest with her. She's turning out to be a really good friend, which seems funny since we've never even met. At least I haven't lied about anything big and when the girls are over we'll probably all have a laugh about the little porkies we've told. After all, I'm sure nobody is one hundred per cent honest on a social networking site.

But, for now, I have other things to think of, such as how to act on a date! Honestly, I haven't been on a proper date in years but how hard can it be? I'm actually feeling okay about it. Right, I'd better go and find Paula and tell her she's off the hook and that I won't be killing her today after all!

CHAPTER 6

Tuesday — 8 Days to D-Day

I'm standing in the front garden of what I can only describe as a fairytale house. It's a small cottage painted white with roses growing up either side of the hall door. There's a white picket fence around the garden and little birds seem to be whistling all around my head. I shoo them away but they seem determined to make their presence felt. I begin to walk towards the door but trip up on my skirt.

'Oh bothersome,' I say, picking myself up off the ground.

Bothersome? Since when do I speak like that? This is all very weird. I glance down at the layers of skirt that caused me to catch my heel and I can't believe what I see. It seems I'm dressed in some sort of Snow White get up! Jesus! That's so not me — what's going on? Two little birds suddenly appear in front of my eyes, carrying a little mirror. They hold it up to my face and I realise what's happening. I am Snow White — black hair, blue hairband, red lips! Ah well, I'd better get cooking — those dwarves will be home for dinner soon!

I'm standing in the shower, allowing the lovely hot water to sluice over my body. I can hardly believe I'm getting ready for a date. And what's more, I'm actually looking forward to it. I'm meeting Tom in a local pub at eight. The original plan was to just go out somewhere in the city centre after work, but it turns out he lives in Celbridge, a mere ten-minute drive from my house.

'So where do you want to go?' he asked, arriving at my desk just before home time yesterday.

'I dunno really,' I said. 'Maybe somewhere close to my bus stop so I can hop on a bus afterwards.'

'So where do you live then ... or should I not ask ... you don't have to tell me if ...'

'Jesus, shut up, will you,' I said, laughing. 'I'm in Lucan so I can get a bus from the quays.'

'Lucan? That's gas. Sure I'm only down the road in Celbridge. If you like we can just go local and then you won't have to worry about getting home.'

Sure we're practically neighbours! Who would have thought? I clocked that one up as a good sign of things to come. I'm a firm believer in signs. For instance, I'd often say to myself that if the next three sets of traffic lights are green, then I'm going to have a good day. Or if one of my favourite songs comes on the radio within five minutes, something good is going to happen. I'm not completely mad and I do know this isn't an exact science, but it keeps me going because I usually cheat so that the signs work to my advantage!

So eight o'clock in Courtneys in Lucan village. I love Courtneys, but don't get much of a chance to go down there as I usually just go into the city centre when I'm going out.

I squeeze some Body Shop White Musk shower gel on a sponge and lather it over my body. I sigh, as I always do, at the tiny buds of breasts that belong to a teenage girl and not a fully grown woman. I never did get that boob job at eighteen but if everything goes to plan, it may very well happen soon!

I feel sort of grown-up going out on a date like this, and I have to admit it feels exciting. I'm not suddenly going to go all gooey-eyed and put my dancing days behind me for a hand-in-hand walk in the park. Nor am I going to sit at home waiting for the phone to ring. But maybe it will be nice to have somebody special to go to a club with or even to help fill the void of those lonely Sundays.

Maybe Tom is going to be *the one*! He seems really nice and how handy would it be to have a boyfriend just down the road? I'm going to make sure he knows where he stands though. There'll be no funny business (well not on the first night anyway!). If there's a next time, we'll see about it, but tonight will just be a few drinks, a chat and maybe a little goodnight kiss.

Get a grip, Jenny! What am I like? Sure the poor man was practically forced into going out with me. Maybe he doesn't even fancy me at all! Although, thinking about it, he has given me the eye more than once. I saw him staring at me and Paula from the photocopier the other day and last week I caught him peering over his newspaper at us when we were in the canteen.

But I really need to get a move on now if I'm to be on time. I've been in the shower for ages and I really don't want to keep Tom waiting. I don't want to be one of those girls who tries to be clever and play hard to get by being late. I never really understood that.

Ten minutes later, I'm standing in my underwear with half the contents of my wardrobe on the bed. What on earth do I wear? To be honest, there isn't much of a choice. I've never been a girlie girl with masses of coloured dresses and pretty accessories in my collection. I do like fashion, but tend to stick to what I know best – short skirts with thick tights or leggings with a long top. Maybe it's a reaction to my mother's vibrant wardrobe that I tend to stick to greys and blacks but whatever the reason, the choice is looking pretty grim at the moment.

A glance at the clock tells me it's already after half seven and I still have a fifteen-minute walk to the village. I quickly make my choice and slap on my usual face of make-up. At least that's something that never changes, a thick layer of pale Mac foundation with layers of silver eye-shadow and thick black-black eyeliner. I don't bother much with lipstick, preferring a brown-tinged lip gloss instead.

I grab my jacket from the banisters and head out the door. Although my shoes are four inches high, they're one of my comfiest pairs, so walking isn't an issue. But I am conscious of my dark purple mini-skirt as it rides up dangerously close to my bum. Still, I reckon I look pretty much okay, at least I've made an effort.

It's five past eight when I nod at the doorman at Courtneys and head in to meet my date. My heart is beating madly, and I feel like I'm twelve years old and going to meet Johnny O'Byrne. Despite living only doors away from each other and being in the same class, Johnny and I never spoke. At twelve years old, it was way too embarrassing to engage with boys, but one day we ended up sort of walking home from school together. When I say 'sort of' I mean he walked three paces ahead while passing a few words back to me.

'Howareya?' he said, while keeping his head down.

'All right,' I said, blushing from my head to my toes!

'Do ya want to walk to school together tomorrow?' he whispered.

'Em ... well ... okay then,' I said.

I remember thinking I must have been in love.

We'd arranged to meet at the end of the road at 8.15 a.m., and I'd been up since 7.00, washing my hair and making sure I looked and smelled nice. I couldn't even eat breakfast as my stomach was churning at the thought of walking side by side with this gorgeous boy. But there was still no sign of him at 8.20. And still no sign at 8.30. Eventually, I gave up and began to walk myself. On the way, I spotted him with two of his friends. They were all laughing. He looked over and gave me a wink and I knew I'd been set up.

The pub is quiet enough as I head into the lounge. I spot him straight away, nervously fiddling with a beer mat with one hand and checking his phone with the other. He doesn't look much different to what he did in work today, except for the top button of his shirt being open and no tie to be seen. I feel inexplicably annoyed by his failure to dress to impress. I know we didn't make the date in a traditional sort of way, but am I not worth making an effort for?

'Hiya Tom, hope you weren't waiting long.'

'No, no, not at all,' he says, jumping up to pull out my chair.

Jesus, I thought they only did that in the movies. Or have I just been so out of touch with the dating scene that it's come full circle and it's considered hip and current to act like Cary Grant? It's kind of nice though, so I gratefully take the weight off my feet.

'And what can I get you?' he gushes. 'I would have had it ready but didn't know what you wanted. The barman is quick though, so won't be a minute.'

'Vodka and Coke please,' I say.

God, he's keen, isn't he? I'll have to be careful with this one. I don't want him to get the wrong idea about me. There'll be nothing of a sexual nature happening, no matter how much he kisses my ass (so to speak!). I notice with a flicker of delight that he's drinking Guinness. There's just something about a Guinness drinker. I love to see a man take a big gulp of the stuff, leaving a froth moustache on his upper lip.

'There you go,' he says, placing my drink in front of me and lining a second pint up for himself. 'So … how have you been?'

Crikey. This is going to be a long night. He only saw me a few hours ago and the best he can come up with is, 'How have you been?'

'Ah grand,' I say, taking the beer mat from under my drink.
'It's a nice place, this, isn't it?'

'Em ... yes,' he says, staring at the beer mat which I've
proceeded to tear into shreds.

His eyes are darting all over the place and he looks panicked.
What on earth's wrong with him?

'Here, have this one,' he says, taking another mat from the
empty table beside us and placing it neatly under my drink.

He spends maybe a little too long fixing the edges so they fall
in line with the edge of the table.

'I wouldn't want your drink dripping on your lovely clothes
now, would I?'

I give him the benefit of the doubt. He's just being gentle-
manly.

'So, Tom,' I say, trying to get something resembling conversation started. 'Do you like working in the bank?'

'I do, yes, it's a great job,' he says, his eyes lighting up. 'I've
always loved numbers so it seemed like a perfect job for me.'

'But what about Bootface ... I mean Brenda? Doesn't she
drive you mad? Sure we can't so much as blink without her
coming down hard on us.'

'Ah Brenda's okay, really,' he says. 'She's never really had an
issue with me so I can't complain. But I suppose being upstairs
makes it easier to escape her. She seems to be on your case a
lot though.'

'Tell me about it,' I sigh. 'Honestly, that woman must spend
her life planning ways of tricking me into doing or saying the
wrong thing. I can't stand her.'

He laughs at that, thank God. I'm beginning to think this was
a mistake. Now I know why dates have never been my cup of
tea. It's so hard to make small talk with somebody you don't
know and to pretend that you're interested in what they have to
say. I'll give it another half hour and if things don't improve, I'll

go to the loos and ring Paula. I'll tell her to ring my mobile and pretend there's some sort of emergency so I have to leave.

'So it's all thanks to your friend that we're here,' he says, relaxing back into his seat. 'What made her try to push us together?'

Oh this is embarrassing! 'Well, I've never really been one for dates in the past. I'm more of a … a party girl … I mean … I … I just haven't been ready to settle down.' Oh fuck! Now I sound like a prostitute who's looking to snare him into marriage! But thankfully he doesn't seem to pick up on any of that.

'Why's that?' he asks, sounding genuinely interested. 'I'm sure a gorgeous girl like you has had plenty of offers.'

'I suppose just the whole idea of settling down scares me. I don't want to give everything I have to one man and risk being let down.' Gosh, listen to me, opening up like a real adult. He's actually really easy to talk to.

'I'm sort of the opposite,' he says. 'I love to have a woman in my life. It feels good to have somebody who'll love you no matter what and to know they'll always be there for you.'

'And do you not have anyone like that in your life at the moment?' I ask, sipping my drink. I'm curious now. The conversation is a little easier and I'm beginning to relax. This mightn't be as bad as I'd initially thought.

'Nobody at the moment – except my mam,' he laughs. 'But I did have a girlfriend for two years. We split up last year and there hasn't been anyone since.'

'Ah, sorry about that,' I say, noting the change in his face when he mentioned her. 'You must have really loved her then?'

'I did, yes,' he says, bowing his head.

Oh, Jesus, please don't cry. I'm suddenly conscious of being in the middle of my local pub with a man who could be about to start blubbing. I frantically search my brain for something funny and appropriate to avert disaster.

'Look, we're getting through these quickly,' I say, indicating the barely touched drinks on the table. 'I'll just go and get us another couple.'

I hop up from my seat before he can protest and hotfoot it to the bar. I like him – I really do, but, honestly, if he starts crying, I'm out of here. I give the barman my order and steal a quick look over at Tom. Thankfully, he's not crying but what the hell *is* he doing? Seems he's messing with the beer mats again and fixing the ones on the table beside us too. He's turning them all the same way around and looks as though he's measuring the distance between them. I'm reminded of the soup yesterday and how he managed to cover the whole surface of it with pieces of bread. Jesus! Last thing I need is taking on somebody with an obsessive compulsive disorder while I'm trying to tackle my own problems.

'Here we go,' I say, arriving back to the table with the new drinks. 'You've done a … em … fine job with those mats there.'

'Sorry,' he says, at least having the cop on to look embarrassed. 'It's a bit of a nervous habit of mine. Some people shred mats, I arrange them!'

Okay, so he has a point. Maybe I'm doing him an injustice. It's just that I remember Paula telling me about a friend of Ian's. Apparently, he was completely obsessive about stuff. He'd wash his hands a million times a day and couldn't leave the house without checking the door about twenty times. His girl-friend put up with it for a while because she loved him. But things got really out of hand when he had to count how many times he'd rise and fall during love-making. If he didn't make it to thirty each time before ejaculating, he'd have to get up and do fifty press-ups to make up for it. Not surprisingly, she left him soon after that. Last Ian heard of him, he was spending some time in a hospital in London where they specialised in that sort of thing.

'So I was just thinking,' says Tom, 'after we have a few, do you fancy getting a taxi back to my place so you can ... '

'Tom, I may as well tell you here and now, I'm not interested. You're very nice and all that but I'm not sleeping with you tonight. I thought we were having a nice date – a proper chat like normal people do. Now I don't know what you've heard but ... '

'Jenny, if you had let me finish, I was just about to say, "So you can meet my mam"'!'

Oh, God, I'm absolutely mortified. It just shows how much I know about dates. The mere mention of going to his house and I thought he was looking for one thing!

'Jesus, you must think I'm a total gobshite,' I say, barely daring to look at him. 'It's just that ... it's just that I really would prefer for us to get to know each other first ... I mean before we ... em ... oh God, feel free to stop me whenever you like!'

Thankfully he laughs at that.

'Don't worry, Jenny. I suppose it did sound a bit suspect. But how about it? I know it might seem strange to ask you, but it's just me and Mammy at home and when I told her I was going out on a date, she suggested I bring you back. She loves to meet people I'm seeing.'

I'm not sure how to take this. It's nice he wants me to meet his mother, but surely not on a first date? It's a little weird really. But, again, I'm not exactly expert on the ins and outs of dating, so who am I to say?

'I won't tonight, Tom,' I say. 'It's only Tuesday and I'm knack- ered. Maybe another time?' Good thinking, gently refusing the invitation while still letting him know I'm interested in another date. I'm getting good at this relationship thing!

'Well maybe you could come over for tea on Friday night then – just to keep her happy? Mammy has her bridge tomorrow night and I have chess club on Thursday.'

I'm not listening to what he's saying. He has that froth moustache which he's licking off with his tongue. Doesn't he know how seductive that is? Gosh, I almost wish he *had* been suggesting what I thought he was suggesting in the first place! Would it be so wrong to do it on a first date? I wish there was a rulebook I could refer to! And really, he's more or less my boyfriend now anyway, so it wouldn't be like sleeping with just anybody!

'Jenny ... Jenny ... are you okay? Did you hear me?'

'Oh ... um ... sorry,' I say, conscious I'd been staring at his mouth. 'I was miles away. You were saying about your mother.'

'Yes, I was asking you if you'd like to come to tea on Friday,' he says, taking a tissue out of his pocket to wipe the froth from his mouth, putting a firm end to the scene of seduction.

'Oh yes ... of course ... that would be lovely.' I'm not sure if it would be lovely, but I'm so addled from my runaway thoughts that I can't think straight. I think I'd have agreed to anything he asked. But at least I've snapped out of it now and using the tissue to wipe his mouth sort of broke the spell anyway.

'Fantastic,' he says, draining the last drop from his glass. 'I'll just go get us another couple of drinks. Same again?'

'Lovely, thanks.' I relax back into my seat and watch as Tom banters with the barman. This whole dating thing isn't so bad after all. I'm surviving date number one and have already made another for later in the week. Easy peasy. I'm on a roll!

@JennyB Just back from my fabulous date. Had a brilliant night. How's everyone here?

@zahraglam Ooh, get you and your date. Glad you had a good night. So are we going to get to meet him when we're in Dublin?

@JennyB Ah, it's early days yet to say that, but you never know.

@zahraglam It's getting closer now. I can't wait. You'll have to tell us what you've lined up for our visit.
@JennyB I've a few exciting things planned. I might just keep them to myself for now – would be nice to surprise you.
@zahraglam Fab. I'm sure it will be brilliant no matter what we do. Looking forward to it.

I close my laptop and sigh heavily. I guess I'm going to have to start educating myself on what our city has to offer. God, I can't think of anything worse. Maybe I'll ask Tom about it. He strikes me as a cultured sort of guy. I'm cheered up by that thought. Yes, I'll ask my fella about it. He'll know what I should do!

CHAPTER 7

Wednesday – 7 Days to D-Day

The girls have arrived at last and I've brought them to a fabulous new amphitheatre in the middle of O'Connell Street. Tom knows somebody who knows somebody who managed to erect it overnight in honour of my guests. I'm proud of the fact I've gone all cultured and the girls are impressed.

The music begins and two dancers twirl out onto the stage. OMG, it's Tom! He's a ballet dancer? How did I not know that? But what's he doing? He and his female dancer seem to be … em … getting intimate on the stage! He's on top of her and they're moving to the rhythm of the music. This is worrying. Now Tom is getting off her. He lies down on the floor and begins doing push-ups. The girl stares for a moment, then rushes off the stage in tears.

I'm exhausted but can't get back to sleep. My trusted alarm clock tells me it's only 6.20 a.m. but I think I'll get up anyway. Imagine dreaming about Tom after our first date. I wonder if that means something. I must google dreams later on and see what all mine mean. I've certainly had some strange ones of late.

I shiver as I pull myself out of my tangle of olive green duvet and quickly wrap myself in my worn grey robe. I think it's definitely time to set the timer to have the heat on in the mornings.

I've gotten away without it until now because it's been mild enough but the weather fairies seem to have copped on to the fact that it's December and the temperature has all of a sudden dropped dramatically.

A thought suddenly occurs to me. Maybe it's snowing! Maybe the reason it's so cold this morning is that we're under a blanket of snow. Oooh, how exciting. I rush to the window in anticipation but am disappointed to see nothing but a covering of glistening frost on the ground. Damn!

Downstairs in my small beech-wood kitchen, I fill the kettle and stick a tea bag in a cup. I wonder if there is anyone on Twitter this early. Probably only Americans or Australians. I follow people from lots of different countries, but don't tend to get into many conversations with them. Now don't get me wrong, I'm not in any way prejudiced. In fact, I once slept with a man from Texas with a Stetson and pointy boots, but I have to admit being a bit put off when he took out a huge cigar the moment we'd done the deed and proceeded to puff it in my face.

Overall, I'm following about three hundred people but a lot of those are celebrities like Jonathan Ross and Alan Carr. If Jonathan Ross tweets that he's wearing odd socks, Twitter goes wild and within minutes he's trending. Trending is where a word is the most mentioned one on Twitter at any given time. I make a note to tweet about my socks later and see if that'll get *me* trending!

I open my laptop on my coffee table and wait for it to warm up. Out of the girls who are coming for our twitter meet-up, Zahra is the one I'm most nervous about. She's following about the same number of people as me, but there are more than 1,000 people following *her*. I was checking out her profile the other day and it seems Jonathan Ross himself is following her. That's mad. He has hundreds of thousands of followers and yet he's following her! What can I possibly offer her here in Dublin that'll compare with the celebrity lifestyle she lives over there?

I'll have to have a think about what might impress her. I do know somebody who's an author. Well, when I say I know them, it's my mother's next-door neighbour's uncle. But, still, it might be enough to make her think she's not the only one who mixes with the rich and famous.

I scroll down through the Twitter feed and none of my buddies are online. Damn! I'd have loved a bit of a chat. But I have a sudden brainwave. Instead of stressing about what I'm going to do with the girls, I should start googling things to do in Dublin. Great idea. If I can find something cultured to do for one of the nights, surely they'll be happy with the pub for the other two? After all, nights at the theatre are expensive (so I'm told) so one night should be enough.

I look through the theatre listings but nothing is appealing at first. *Romeo and Juliet* just isn't my thing, nor is *Swan Lake*, An Evening of Classical Music, *Oliver* or *Riverdance*! Now if there were tickets available to see *The Script* in the O$_2$, that would be right up my street but apparently their concert sold out in the first couple of hours.

But hang on, now there's something interesting. Keith Barry is doing his show, The Asylum, in the Olympia Theatre next week. That's definitely something I could watch. I haven't been but I've heard it's a brilliant show. Paula's cousin went last year and she ended up on the stage being hypnotised. Apparently, she was stripping half-naked because he had her convinced it was roasting and then she was cuddling up to the person beside her because she thought it was freezing. Ha! That'd be a right laugh. There's no way I'd volunteer to get up on the stage, but it would be brilliant to watch. Tickets are cheap enough so, feck it, I think I'll just go ahead and book them. The girls can fix up with me when they arrive.

Ten minutes later, four tickets are booked for the Thursday night and I'm feeling less stressed about their visit. It's a start anyway. And that Keith Barry is a fine thing. When he does that *Deal or No Deal* show on TV3, he seems like the boy next door, all clean cut and polite, but I've watched him on other shows where he drives celebrities around while blindfolded and catches a bullet between his teeth and his nice-boy image is replaced by a dangerous, sexy beast one.

I wonder if he's on Twitter. Now there's an idea. Maybe if I could make contact with him on there, I could claim I know him. Wouldn't the girls be impressed with that? I quickly type his name in the Twitter name search. There's loads of Keith Barrys but I reckon I've found him – *@keithpbarry*. I tick the box to follow him and send him a message:

@JennyB Hi, Keith. I've just found you on Twitter. I'm coming to The Asylum soon. Heard it's fab.

I wait for a few minutes but he doesn't seem to be online. I suppose it was a bit of a long shot. I'll type a few more messages anyway and leave it at that. Maybe if he's online later, he'll see them.

@JennyB I've heard you meet the audience after your shows. Would love to meet you.
@JennyB I'll be bringing some friends who'll be visiting Dublin for weekend so would be nice if we could say hello.

I'll just leave it at that. I don't know where the last hour and a half went. I'd better go and get showered and ready for work. This tweet-up as we've christened it is shaping up quite nicely. I feel so much more relaxed about it now – maybe that's down to a few things in my personal life looking up. I'm really looking forward to meeting them all face to face – especially Kerry. I just know we're going to be very good friends.

★

'So, tell me,' said Paula, pulling a chair up to my desk. 'I'm dying to know how it went.' We're both in early this morning. Bootface is in her office on the phone again but she can hardly take issue with us for talking since we're not due to start work for another half hour.

'It was actually quite okay,' I say, doodling on a Post-it. 'Better than I thought it was going to be.'

'Oh, brilliant,' she says, grinning. 'I just knew you two were going to get on. Trust your Aunty Paula to know what's best for you!'

'Well, I wouldn't be marrying us off just yet,' I say, laughing at her enthusiasm. 'But he's a nice guy – I could certainly do worse.'

'Yes, he *is* lovely, isn't he? If I didn't have my Ian, I'd be going after him myself! So did anything ... em ...' She lowers her voice conspiratorially, '... you know ... *happen*?'

'Of course nothing happened, Paula. Jesus, didn't I tell you we were just having a drink and a chat – nothing more!'

'Oh, so-rry,' she says, looking hurt. 'Forgive me for thinking that maybe if you both got on so well, there might have been a little something afterwards.'

'Sorry, I didn't mean to snap,' I say, thinking of Tom's froth moustache and realising I'm probably more than a little put out that he didn't make a move. For God's sake, he didn't even kiss me at the end of the night!

When we got over the misunderstanding about him asking me back to his, I felt more relaxed. He wasn't just out for one thing and he seemed interested in actually finding out more about *me*. He walked me outside to the taxi rank afterwards and I decided I'd let him kiss me. I was feeling quite turned on at that stage and thought that a nice, lingering kiss would be perfect. We hung back from where the taxis were parked and chatted for a little longer. At that stage, we'd had five drinks at least and the conversation had become fluid and easy.

'So Friday then,' he said, making sure I remembered our date for tea at his house.

'Yep,' I said, shivering in the cool night air. 'I'm looking forward to it.' I moved in a little closer to him. He should have taken his cue from the shivering. He had the perfect opportunity then to put his arms around me and move in for the kiss. I licked my lips in anticipation and even closed my eyes.

'You're shivering,' he said. Well spotted – cue the arms, the hug, the kiss.

'Come on. Let's get you into a taxi before you freeze to death. Sure that jacket is paper thin.'

He ushered me quickly over to a waiting taxi, patted me on the back and opened the door for me. I've never wanted anybody to kiss me more than I wanted him to at that moment. I paused before getting in, giving him further opportunity to move in for the kill, but nothing. I hopped in before I could embarrass myself any further and gave him a little wave as we sped away.

'So are you seeing him again then?' asks Paula, dragging me back to our conversation.

'Em ... yes, Friday evening after work. I hope you don't mind, Paula. I know we usually go out but a date's a date.'

'Of course I don't,' she says, generously. 'Actually, Ian rang me last night and he's coming over on Friday night. So looks like we might both get lucky. So where are you off to?'

'I ... em ... we're going to ... to his place for tea.'

'You're *what?*' she giggles. 'That's hilarious. He's already asking you over for tea? And I suppose you'll tell me next that he wants you to meet his mammy!'

I'm a bit put out by Paula's hysterical laughter. Does she not think I'm capable of the normal stuff that most couples do? Or maybe having tea isn't normal any more. Oh I don't know! I make a mental note to have a look in Eason's for a book on the ins and outs of dating.

'Well, actually …' I begin. 'He … em … *is* bringing me to meet his mother.'

That stops Paula's hysterics dead – for two seconds!

'Hahaha! Oh you're meeting the in-laws already. This is brilliant. Wait until I tell Ian, he'll get a right laugh out of it. Jesus, he must be mad about you if he's bringing you home to Mammy already!'

'Will you shut up, for God's sake,' I say. 'Bootface will be out of that office in a minute with the noise.'

'Ah sorry, Jen,' she says, calming herself down. 'I'm laughing at the idea but, to be honest, I envy you.'

Now she has me confused. 'What are you talking about – one minute you think it's the funniest thing ever and next thing you envy me? Make up your mind, will you?'

'I just think it's funny that it's all happened so quickly and it's as a result of me pushing the two of you together. But I'd love a fella who'd want to show me off like that. I've never even met Ian's mother and look how long I've been going out with him. No, I shouldn't have laughed. I think he's lovely to treat you like that. I really hope it all works out for you.'

I'm about to reply when I notice Tom striding towards us. God, is it my imagination or is he looking sort of sexy? Did he just develop that overnight? I mean, I still don't think he's up there with Brad Pitt or George Clooney, but there's just something about him.

'Hiya, girls,' he says, all six feet of him standing over us. 'Great night last night, Jen, really enjoyed it.'

'I … em … yes, it was a good one all right,' I say, aware that Paula is sitting with her mouth gaping open. What the hell is wrong with her?

'And how are you, Paula?' he says, turning his eyes to her.

'I ... I ... I'm fine,' she says.

'Good, good,' he says. 'I must say thanks for the little push the other day. It's thanks to you that Jenny and I got together.'

Paula doesn't respond. She just stares.

'Well I'd better get to work,' he continues, realising he's not going to get much of a conversation. 'I'll catch up with you ladies later.' He winks, sticks his hands back in his trouser pockets and heads off to his own desk.

'Jesus,' says Paula.

'What's wrong with you?' I ask, following her stare as she watches Tom head up the stairs.

'Jesus,' she says again.

'Paula! Snap out of it. What the hell is wrong with you?'

'Jesus, that man really has something about him, doesn't he?' she says, managing at last to tear her eyes away from him. 'He's no hunk or anything but he's just so ... you know ... so ...' She bends over to whisper, 'Yummy!' How did I not notice that before? I mean ... Jesus!'

You see, she's noticed it too. Isn't it funny how when somebody makes a comment like that, it makes you want the man even more? Like when I was sixteen and didn't fancy Cormac McCormack one bit. He was always asking me out, but I wasn't interested. Too geeky for me. But one day, I overheard Ellen O'Brien (with the long blonde curls and perfect skin) say she thought he was hot and was hoping he'd ask her out. All of a sudden, I saw Cormac through different eyes. He was suddenly not geeky at all but intelligent and gorgeous. I went out to the pictures with him just to make Ellen green with envy, and it worked too. One up for the girl they called Jerry!

'He is, isn't he?' I say, smugly. 'He's got a sexy glint in his eye.'

'And did you smell him?' she asks, dreamily. 'He smells good enough to eat.'

'Steady on,' I laugh. 'As I said, nobody will be eating anybody – at least not for a while yet!'

'Lucky bitch,' she mumbles, getting up from her chair. 'Almost half past – I'd better look busy. Catch up with you later.'

A few minutes left and Bootface is still in her office so I whip out my iPhone for a quick look. I log in to Twitter and there are a number of messages waiting for me. Oh, my God! I can't believe it. The first one reads:

> @*keithpbarry* Thanks for that, Jenny. I'll be signing autographs after the show so please come and say hello.

Bloody hell! Keith Barry, world famous illusionist, is sending me a message! That's mad. And another one:

> @*keithpbarry* And if you or any of your friends want to volunteer to come up on stage, I guarantee an amazing experience.

Ooooh! Wait until I tell Zahra about this. This is brilliant news. I don't have to rely on a dodgy author as being my only famous friend. Now I'm best friends with Keith Barry.

Bootface throws her office door open all of a sudden, reminding me it's time I started work. I throw my phone into my bag under my desk. Just in the nick of time as she casts her beady eye around the room. But I'm smiling to myself. I love it when a plan comes together and there are certainly plenty coming together for me at the moment!

*

I opt for a walk at lunch-time because Paula has some phone calls to make and I don't want to look like a Billy-no-mates sitting alone at my desk. Bootface has taken the afternoon off again, so it won't matter much if I'm a few minutes late back.

I pull my cotton jacket tighter around my neck as I cross a

bustling O'Connell Bridge. I really must invest in something warmer – especially if the promised snow ever arrives! I'll keep going until I get to Stephen's Green and maybe pick up a sandwich to eat back at my desk. Just as I reach the top of Grafton Street, I notice Bootface waiting to cross the road. She's pushing an old woman in a wheelchair. I have to do a double take to make sure it's her because she seems so out of place in this scenario.

It's her all right. I duck into a shop door to watch her. The woman in the wheelchair must be at least ninety and seems to be quite disabled. Her arms and hands are all twisted and her face is lobbing to the side. Bootface takes a tissue from her pocket and bends down to wipe the drool from the old lady's mouth. She looks different. Her features are softer and she smiles as she attends to her charge. She kisses her lightly on top of the head and crosses the road with the rest of the pedestrians.

I don't know what to think. I can feel those damn feelings of compassion coming to the surface again. I try very hard to remember that I dislike her because it's a familiar and comforting feeling, but now my thoughts are clouded by frantic phone conversations, tears and wheelchair-bound people!

Who was that woman with her? A sick relative maybe? She's been taking a lot of time off lately, which isn't like her. Maybe there's more to her story than we know. Maybe I'll make a better effort with her and see if I can find out a little more. I'm not going to do a complete turnaround and be best buddies with her or anything, but maybe there's some middle ground. As I pay for my cheese salad sandwich, I'm thinking of some of the awful things I said about her. Now it's true she deserved a lot of them, but I'm sort of feeling bad for the pure venom I've been spitting about her over the last year.

God, what am I like? Paula would faint if she knew I was thinking like that. Our hatred of Bootface is one of the things that gets us through the day. I head back to the office to eat my sandwich and can't seem to get the picture out of my head of a woman who's supposed to be so horrible, wiping the drool off an old lady's face!

CHAPTER 8

Thursday – 6 Days to D-Day

I seem to have no control. My wheelchair has a mind of its own and I'm bombing down the middle of the M50. Cars are beeping from every direction and swerving to the side to avoid a collision. How is it that I can't stop it? I'm pulling the brake but nothing's happening.

'Serves you right,' says a voice from behind.

I look over my shoulder and realise Bootface is pushing me, an evil grin on her face.

'You should never have painted those nails black,' she screams, cackling manically. 'Now you have to pay!'

Isn't it amazing (and a little bit scary) that you can google anything these days? Gone are the times when you'd have to go to your local library to research something or send off a stamped addressed envelope to some company or other for information.

I must be really bored because I'm finding myself sitting on the sofa with my laptop, googling lots of stuff, including my own name (which proved fruitless!), breast surgery and bosses from hell! Now I'm just in the process of googling sex addiction. Paula made some flippant comment the other day when I kept bringing the conversation back to sex and she accused me of being a sex addict! Now she was laughing when she said it and I know she didn't mean it, but it got me thinking. I have been thinking a lot about sex lately and find I'm getting turned on very easily. To be honest, I think it's just the lack of any action in that department that has me in that frame of mind but, still, there's no harm in checking!

My 'sex addiction' search has been very fruitful and, thankfully, it's proved to me (and of course I knew it already) that I am *not* a sex addict!

You see, I don't ever 'get into debt for the purpose of paying prostitutes for sex or paying for online pornography or sex chats'. I did once, however, get charged five euro for clicking a link on my mobile that brought me into a sex site. I just got a message that said: 'Click to see some amazing shoes.' How was I to know they'd be modelled by people wearing nothing else?

Another thing that confirms my non-sex addict status is that I don't 'expose myself in public places with the intention of people witnessing'. I did have a gym membership once and there was a lot of exposing going on there. Honestly, the women walked around the changing rooms completely naked, regardless of how far their boobs fell to their waist or how many cheeks they sported on their bum. I wanted to join in and be cool about it but I just couldn't bring myself to do it. So, you see, I'm actually the complete opposite of wanting to expose myself!

There are a couple of things there which I'd have to hold my hand up to, such as preoccupation with thoughts of sex and finding it difficult to form relationships, but I don't think those alone mean anything.

With the girls descending on me soon and my date with Tom, I have lots of other stuff to occupy my mind.

I need to get myself organised for 'the big tea' tomorrow night. My legs are badly in need of a shave. Paula is always trying to convince me to get them waxed but I really have no tolerance for pain. I can't even take a plaster off without spending an hour picking at it and bracing myself for the big pull. Honestly, why would I just lie there and let somebody slather boiling hot wax on my legs and then, bit by bit, pain by pain, rip the hairs right out? I can have it done in a jiffy with a razor.

I'll just have time for a quick shower when I get home from work tomorrow, so any major preening has to be done tonight. My eyebrows could do with a bit of a pluck and I should really sort out the two big spots that have appeared on my chin. I know it's just tea and I know his mother will be there, but you'd never know what might happen afterwards. I could drive over, but I was thinking that if I got a taxi, maybe he'd drop me home and I could invite him in. It is our second date, after all, and I'm planning on seeing him again too.

Maybe I'll just have a peep and see who's on Twitter before I head to the shower.

@JennyB Helloooo! Anyone here tonight?

Gosh, Twitter is a bit quiet tonight. There seems to be plenty online but nobody answering me. I'll try again.

@JennyB I'm just popping in for a few minutes. Have to get organised for my date tomorrow night. Who's here?

The thing about Twitter is that sometimes you can feel like the most important person in the world. Sometimes there can be lots of people chatting to you at once and including you in conversations and you can feel really popular and in demand. Then other times, like tonight, it can make you paranoid. Even though I have over four hundred followers, not one of them has answered my tweet. A couple of weeks ago, the same thing happened three nights in a row. I got really paranoid and ended up checking back through all my tweets for the previous week to see if I'd said something offensive. But often a tweet can just get lost in the stream of tweets, especially when there are a lot of people chatting at once.

@kerrydhunt Hey, Jenny, I'm here. How's it going?

@JennyB Ah hiya, Kerry. I'm good. How about you?

@kerrydhunt Exhausted. Just home from a twelve-hour shift. Can barely keep my eyes open, so it'll be shower and bed.

@JennyB Poor you. Nursing must be such a demanding job. At least you have a few days off to look forward to.

@kerrydhunt Can't wait. Have you managed to organise anything or are you going to wait till we arrive?

@JennyB Well, I wasn't going to say but I've actually booked a fab show for the four of us.

@kerrydhunt Oooh, really? What is it? Come on, tell me!

@JennyB Going to see Keith Barry in his Asylum show on Thurs. Heard it's fab. And he's a friend of mine, so we'll prob meet him after the show.

@kerrydhunt Fab. Dying to see that. And I didn't know he's a friend of yours. He's from just down the road here.

Shit, shit, shit. There I go again. Getting myself caught up in lies. Why couldn't I have just said I'd spoken to him on Twitter? Bloody eejit, I am!

@JennyB Oh, I didn't realise. Well, he's more a virtual friend really. I chat to him a lot on Twitter.

@kerrydhunt Well that's brill, Jenny. Can't wait for the show and can't wait for weekend.

@JennyB Me neither. Won't be long now.

@kerrydhunt So, I take it your date went well the other night?

Saw your tweets to Zahra.

@JennyB Oh, yes, it was great. He's really lovely. I'm actually going to meet his mother tomorrow night.

@kerrydhunt Oh wow! You must really be getting along so. I'm really happy for you.

@JennyB Thanks, Kerry. But these legs won't shave themselves so I'll have to say goodnight. Talk tomorrow. x

It's almost nine o'clock, so I'll have a shower and be back down before ten. I might just catch up on some Corrie and go for an early night.

I strip off the clothes I've worn all day and throw them in the overflowing laundry basket. One of these days, I'm going to get organised and catch up on all the things I need to do in this house.

I turn on the electric shower in my little en-suite and am just about to dip my toe in to test the temperature when my mobile rings. Sticking a towel around me, I rush out of the en-suite to grab the phone from the bed. It's Tom. He must be looking to confirm our plans for tomorrow night. The poor guy – I don't know how many times he tried to catch me today. I noticed him on a few occasions trying to catch my attention but there was an endless queue at the counter and I was dealing with customers all day. That's the trouble with Thursdays. It's late opening and one of our busiest days. I won't answer it now though. I'll just have my shower and I'll give him a buzz back when I'm relaxing later.

Back to the shower and I'm just about to hop in when the doorbell rings. Shit! Who could that be at this time? Well I'm not expecting anyone, so I'll just ignore it. Honestly, sometimes I could go for weeks without anyone phoning or calling at the door. It's all go tonight! I turn the heat down as the water is too hot and the bell goes again. This time, a voice comes booming up the stairs.

'Coo-eeeee! Jenny, it's only me. Hurry up and let me in – I'm bursting.'

Jesus, my mother! What on earth is she doing calling at this time of night? And she never just drops in on me like this.

'Coming, Mam,' I shout, throwing my robe on and bounding down the stairs. I swing the door open and there she is, hopping from foot to foot with Harry at her side.

'Hiya, love,' she says, pushing past me. 'I couldn't have waited another second.'

'Eh ... howareya, Harry,' I say, holding open the door for him and indicating into my sitting room.

'Thanks, Jenny,' he says, stepping in and giving me a little nod. 'We were just on our way home from late shopping in town when your mam needed the loo. She just couldn't wait to get home so we thought we'd stop off here instead of a pub.'

Mam is coming out of the little downstairs toilet just as I'm showing Harry into the sitting room at the back of the house.

'Thanks love. Jesus, I was bursting. The ol' pelvic floor isn't what it used to be, you know.

'Mam! Is nothing sacred with you? We don't want to know about your pelvic floor, or lack of it, thanks very much!'

'Ah don't be so prudish, love,' she says, plonking down on my brown leather sofa. 'And it's Eileen, remember? I'd murder a cuppa though.'

Shit! This is all I need. I'll never get my shower if I don't go now. And why on earth is Harry staring at me like that again? I'm definitely not imagining it. It's the same look he gave me the other day in Mam's house. But I need to get on with things.

'Listen, Mam ... Eileen. Go on in and stick the kettle on, will you? I've left the shower on. I was just about to hop in when you called. Just give me ten minutes and I'll be back down. Make yourselves a cuppa while you're waiting for me.'

'Right, love,' she says, picking up the remote control for the telly. 'Go and take your time. We're not in a hurry, are we, Harry?'

'Nope,' agrees Harry. 'Sure it's early yet.'

Bloody hell! I was sure they'd just leave when I said I was busy. Ah, well, I suppose it's sort of nice that Mam dropped in and Harry doesn't seem so bad really.

I step into the shower and let the delicious warm water relax me. I lather my hair in a gorgeous cucumber-scented shampoo and leave it in so I can breathe in the heady scent. I squeeze out some rose shaving gel into my hands and cover my left leg with it. Just as I'm running the razor up my leg, I hear a very loud guffaw from Harry. I can't help smiling. Maybe it's because of my own new-found love of this whole relationship malarkey, but it's good to see Mam with somebody. I know it was a shock at first but, to be fair, they were in the privacy of the house and didn't expect to see me on their doorstep.

It's sort of weird though to think of my mother having sex. I can't seem to ... HOLY FUCK! The computer ... the sites ... the sex addiction ... Jesus, I've left the computer open on the coffee table. Oh fuckity, fuckity, fuck! Maybe that's what they're laughing at. I have to get down there.

In my haste, I cut a slice out of my leg and squeal with the pain. The suds from my hair are mixing with the blood in the shower tray and not making a very pretty picture. I rinse off everything as quickly as I can and hop out. Towelling myself down quickly, I wrap the towel around my wet hair and curse the two-week-old razor that's made a shambles of my leg. I know from experience I'll have to just ride out the bleeding. Nothing is going to stop it and I can't afford to sit here and wait. I throw on my robe and tear down the stairs. I burst in the door of my living room, ready to explain that I'm helping a friend do some research for a book she's writing.

'Jenny, love,' laughs Mam, pointing at the telly. 'I stuck on one of your *Desperate Housewives* DVDs. It's hilarious. I must start watching it.'

I eye my computer nervously but there's no sign anybody has been near it. They're both curled up on the sofa together, enjoying a laugh at the telly. I quickly grab the laptop from the coffee table and close it over. Sticking it into one of my dresser drawers just in case, I breathe a sigh of relief. Jesus, imagine if they'd seen that I'd been googling sex addiction sites. I'd have been mortified.

'You can take the whole set home with you if you like,' I say, generously, plonking down on the armchair. 'I've seen them all a hundred times.'

'Thanks, love,' says mam. 'Jesus, what's happened to your leg? You're gushing!'

Ah Jesus, I'd forgotten about that. The blood has now rolled down into my slipper and it looks as though my leg has been hacked with an axe!

'Have you a first aid kit?' asks Harry, jumping up from the sofa. 'That looks nasty.'

'No, no, don't worry,' I say, fearing Harry might go all doctorly on me and try to perform repair work on my leg. 'It's just a nick, honestly. It looks a lot worse than it is.'

'Ah were you shaving your legs?' Mam asks, nodding knowingly. 'That'll be our fault for rushing you. We should go really and let you get on with it. Come on, Harry.'

'Right so,' says Harry, rooting in his jacket pocket. 'Thanks for the tea, Jenny. We'll leave you to it.'

'You don't have to go on my account,' I say. *Please go, please go, please go!*

'Sure it's getting late anyway,' says Mam. 'And we want an early night ourselves.'

Eeeek! Too much information. But thank God they're going. Harry pulls out car keys from his pocket and is putting on a pair of glasses. He must need them for driving because I haven't seen him wear them yet. I'm walking towards the front door with them when Harry turns to me.

'It's really lovely to meet you again, Jenny,' he says. 'You must come over and have dinner with us at your mam's soon.'

Oh … my … God! I can't speak. Suddenly my tongue is glued to the roof of my mouth and no words will come out. It's the glasses. He looks completely different with them on. Oh holy fuck! What am I going to do now?

'Night, Jenny, love,' says Mam, bending to give me a kiss on the cheek. 'Now sort that leg out, won't you? I'll give you a ring over the weekend.'

'N … n … night. Talk soon,' I say, forcing the words from my lips.

I don't even wait until the car pulls off, but close the door as soon as they turn their backs. I'm in a daze as I walk into my little front kitchen. Flicking on the switch of the kettle to make a cuppa, I curse the thumping that's started in my head. I let myself flop down onto one of the chairs and put my head in my hands.

What are the chances? And what the hell am I going to do? As if I haven't already got a million things going on in my head – and now this! How on earth am I ever going to tell my mother that I've snogged her boyfriend?

CHAPTER 9

Friday – 5 Days to D-Day

I'm running through a forest. It's dark and very scary. I'm going as fast as I can, but I'm in my bare feet, and the twigs snapping underfoot are slowing me down. I can feel my pursuer closing in. It's no good. I'm going to have to just give in and accept my fate. My blood-soaked feet can't take it any more. I stop and lean against a big oak tree, gulping mouthfuls of air. I turn to face my pursuer and can't believe what I see. It's me. My pursuer is me! How can that be? She ... I ... she's stopped and looking at me strangely. Are we enemies? I don't know what to think!

Why am I so nervous about this stupid tea tonight? You'd think I was going to meet the Queen! I've taken most of my piercings out and put them back in about five times already. I'm just not used to this. Should I just be myself and let the woman see who I am? I'm not a bad person. Or would the piercings be all too much for an old lady to handle? When I eventually rang Tom back last night, he told me his mother is seventy-five and has a weak heart, so I don't want to be the cause of her having a massive coronary!

Right, enough flapping around or I'm going to be late. I've called a taxi for 7.30 and it's already 7.15. Thankfully, Bootface didn't turn up for work today and I was able to slip out a little early again. Otherwise I wouldn't have had a hope of being ready on time. Though I do wonder why she's missed so much time lately. Maybe it's something to do with the woman in the wheelchair. She does seem to be really preoccupied too. I know we don't get on, but I feel bad for the fact that she doesn't seem to have any friends to talk to in work. I make a mental note to see if I can engage her in a chat sometime soon.

In the end, I leave a few piercings in each ear because I really don't want to pretend I'm something I'm not, but I take the one out of my eyebrow. I'm not sure she'll be able to handle too much of me in the one night. I'm happy with the puffball long cotton top I'm wearing over my leggings. It sort of gives the impression I have hips and a bum – not that Mrs Delaney will be impressed by that, but it makes me feel good.

I'm trying to push all thoughts of my own mother and Harry out of my head. I hardly got a wink of sleep last night for thinking about the whole damn situation. I can feel my heart plummeting all over again when I think about the moment I saw Harry with the glasses on. It's amazing how one little thing can change a person's look. But I have no doubt that it's him. And by the way he's been looking at me, I suspect he recognises me too. God, what are the chances? Bloody hell!

It was quite a while ago when it happened – definitely more than a year because Paula hadn't met Ian at that stage and she was going through her big knicker phase. The big knickers were of the 'suck it all in variety' and made her look super skinny. She ditched them when she met Ian because, number one, they weren't the sexiest of things for Ian to meet when heading that direction and, number two, she felt she didn't need them since she'd snared her man.

Anyway, we'd been out for hours, having gone straight from work for a few drinks and eventually ended up in a club. I remember noticing Harry because he seemed to be on his own and he stood out from the crowd in his unusual, and very expensive-looking, suit. I'm not well up on fashion but when his jacket was on the seat beside me, I noticed it was Issey Miyake. I was wearing Issey Miyake perfume at the time and I remember thinking it was some sort of sign; sign I should have run a mile probably.

We'd had quite a lot to drink and Paula wanted to dance. Now I love dancing too, but even in my inebriated state, I was a little embarrassed by her head-banging display and her numerous failed attempts at the splits. I decided to watch from the sidelines for a while and that's when I got talking to Harry.

His hair wasn't quite as black then as it is now because I remember thinking how the splattering of grey gave him such a distinguished look. He had the start of a beard, but nothing like the forest that's now growing from his chin. I liked his glasses too – they suited him and he seemed comfortable in his own skin. He was nice. It was as though he didn't quite belong in the wild surroundings of clubland.

I'm not usually drawn to older men but there was just something about him. We chatted for a while, nothing personal, just superficial stuff, and soon found ourselves sitting at the back of the club having a good old snog. But that's all it was – an innocent snog. There was no groping, no fumbles in the dark, nothing at all of a sexual nature.

But a snog is a snog, and my mother deserves to know the truth. Nice and all as he seemed, he was still hanging around nightclubs on his own, willing to pick up a younger woman. Poor Mam, but tonight I have a different mother to worry about and I'm hoping she'll be easier to deal with than my own.

The taxi ride takes less than ten minutes and all too soon, I'm standing at the Delaneys' front door. As a result of a last-minute thought, I had the taxi man stop at the Eurospar down the road and am now holding a selection of Mr Kipling cakes — apple slices, almond fingers, French fancies and even Christmas slices. It occurs to me that this is turning out to be an expensive night.

I can't help feeling slightly irritated that I have to ring the doorbell. I expected Tom to have his nose pressed up against the window, waiting with excitement for me to arrive. I suddenly have visions of myself as an excitable child. Dad used to bring home a bag of assorted chocolate bars on Friday and I'd wait for hours at the window until he came home. I suppose Tom is a bit past the nose against the window stage.

At last the door is opened and Tom is standing there looking dead sexy in a pair of beige chinos and an open-necked, sky-blue Tommy Hilfiger shirt. So he doesn't live in suits after all. This triumph of fashion sends a tingle of excitement through my body and makes me want to kiss him. But my sensible side takes over and, instead, I push the cakes into his hands.

'Hiya, Jenny,' he says, balancing the cakes with one hand and closing the door with the other. 'Was that a taxi I saw you arrive in?' Aha! So, he was looking out the window. Then why the hell didn't he rush to the door to welcome me?

'Yeah, blooming car wouldn't start for me,' I say. *Liar, liar, pants on fire!*

'Oh that's bad luck,' he says, leading the way through to the back of the house. 'Sure I can drop you home later if you like?'

Result! 'That would be great, thanks, if you're sure.

'No problem at all. Now give me your jacket and I'll bring you in. She's dying to meet you.'

Mrs Delaney is pottering around the friendly kitchen, filling the table with all sorts of goodies. I can't help feeling like I'm coming to a six-year-old's birthday party. There are sausage rolls, little sandwiches with the crusts cut off and a whole variety of what look like home-made cakes. I suddenly want to hide my shop-bought offerings, but it's too late as Tom has already put them on the counter top.

'Well you must be Jenny,' she says, wiping her hands in her apron and holding one out to shake mine. 'Tom has told me so much about you.'

He has? That's kind of weird since we've only had one date and never really knew much about each other before then. But, still, she seems nice, which is helping my nerves to dissolve. I feel a little thrill too that she's of the little old lady variety that I love. With her grey-blue permed hair and her back stooping her into four foot nothingness, I feel I want to claim her as my own.

'Nice to meet you too,' I say, genuinely. 'And what a lovely spread. You must have been baking all day.'

'Mammy likes to busy herself in the kitchen. Don't you, Mammy?' Tom says, pulling out a chair for me to sit down.

'Oh, yes,' says Mammy, beaming. 'My Tom loves a bit of home baking, so I like to spoil him.'

'Ah she's very good to me,' says Tom, smiling sweetly at the object of his affection. 'Since there's only the two of us here, we have to look after each other.'

Now, it's nice to see a man being good to his mother and it's touching to see a mother and son who are close, but this 'Mammy' thing is grossing me out. I did worry a little when I heard that he was still living at home at his age, but I never for a minute expected him to be such a mammy's boy! He's thirty-five years old, for God's sake, not five! And surely he should be looking at *me* with those adoring eyes, not his mother!

'So tell me, Jenny,' says Mrs Delaney, delicately choosing a sandwich from the pile and placing it on her plate. 'What are your intentions regarding my son?'

I'm just about to swallow a mouthful of salad sandwich but, on hearing her question, I gag and a piece of cucumber hops right out of my mouth and onto the table in front of me. I'm mortified.

'Jesus, sorry about that,' I say. 'It just went down the wrong way.'

'Eh ... not to worry, Jenny,' says Tom. 'I'm sure Mammy doesn't mind.'

Mammy doesn't mind? I've just almost choked to death on a piece of cucumber and he's worried about his mammy minding? I glance at Mrs Delaney, a smile still fixed on her face. I'm not buying the eyes though. My initial impression of a little vulnerable old dear is slipping.

'So back to what we were saying,' she says, as if I hadn't just had a near-death experience. 'Is this just a fling you're having with my Tom or are you looking on it as something more serious?' My eyes dart in Tom's direction in the hope that he'll rescue me, but he doesn't seem even the slightest bit embarrassed by Mammy's question. In fact, he actually looks like he's waiting to hear the answer! Bloody hell!

'I ... em ... I hadn't really thought too far ahead, Mrs Delaney,' I say, thankful for the thick coverage of make-up that's hopefully disguising my blushing. 'We've only just started to see each other, so we'll see how it goes.'

'Hmmm,' she says, stirring her tea in a little china cup.

'Jenny is going to see Keith Barry in the Olympia in a couple of weeks, Mammy,' says Tom. 'He's the nice boy from *Deal or No Deal* you like.' At least he's diverting attention from the probing questions. Mrs Delaney, however, still has a smile on her face but the corners of her lips are twitching. I'm guessing she's not impressed.

'Are you *really?*' she asks, eyes boring into mine. 'From what they've been saying at the bridge club, I don't think he's such a nice boy when he's on stage – quite rude, I've heard. But maybe you're into that sort of thing.'

'Ah, Mammy, that's a bit unfair,' says Tom.

Yay! He's taking his mother on. Things are looking up.

'I'm sure if Jenny thought he was rude or crude,' he continues, 'she wouldn't be going.' My heart sinks. Is he for real? I'm ready to spit fire but manage to stick a lump of cake in my mouth and chew on that instead of Tom's ear!

'This Christmas pudding is gorgeous, Mrs Delaney,' I say, attempting to lighten the mood. 'I think I'll have another slice.'

'Thank you, dear,' she says, clearly pleased at the compliment. 'Tom loves it, don't you, love? I always make a few coming up to Christmas and we can never resist cutting one to test it.'

'Ah you do make the best cakes, Mammy,' he says, placing a slice on his own plate.

'Jenny, you've hardly touched your tea,' says Mrs Delaney. 'Maybe a mug would be more your style, dear?'

I glance at her to see if that was meant as a slur – I'm sure it was, but her face isn't giving anything away. 'Ah no it's fine, Mrs Delaney – or can I call you Lily? Tom told me that's your name. I had an aunt called Lily too. It's a lovely name.' Maybe if we're on first name terms, things might feel a little more relaxed. She's smiling sweetly and all seems well, but I can feel the tension in the room.

'I prefer Mrs Delaney, if you don't mind, dear,' she says, placing her cup down a little too hard on her saucer. 'I like to think there's still a little respect in the world for the elderly.'

'Oh ... I ... of course ... I didn't mean ... I only thought ... '

'Mammy, Jenny's only trying to be nice. She didn't mean anything by it,' says Tom, who actually sounds cross. At last! Although I'm half waiting for a 'but'!

'I know, I know,' she says, in a much softer tone. 'You know how I get with the youth of today though, Tom. There just seems to be such little respect.'

Her stony eyes seem to have warmed and the smile seems a little more genuine. Maybe I've got her wrong. Maybe she's just an old lady who thinks the world doesn't have much tolerance for the elderly. She's obviously very close to Tom, so maybe she's just looking out for him as well. I really want her to like me – I feel it's all part of cracking the whole relationship thing.

'That's a nice necklace, Mrs Delaney,' I say, gazing at the gold twisted chain around her neck. 'Is it antique gold?'

'Yes, yes it is,' she says, fingering the chain. 'I like understated jewellery. There's nothing worse than gaudy, cheap-looking pieces.' She's looking at my earrings! Honest to God, she's staring right at them. Her whole face is lit up in pleasant chit-chat mode, but she's making sure I know what she's thinking.

'My father always bought Mammy an antique piece for her birthday before he died,' says Tom, gazing lovingly at his mother. 'He always had such good taste, just like Mammy.'

'He certainly did, love,' she says, her eyes glazing over. 'And he had such good fashion sense. He loved it when I made an effort to dress up, and I always do, you know.' The glaze is gone from her eyes and she's looking at me pointedly now. Her mouth is saying all the right things, she's coming across as friendly and welcoming, but every look she's giving me tells me she dislikes me immensely. I can't take much more of this. It's torture.

'Mammy was a bit of a looker in her day,' says Tom, obviously completely oblivious to his mother's jibes. 'She even won a few beauty pageants back in the fifties.'

'Oh, that's amazing,' I say, trying to imagine this old woman as 'a looker'. 'And have you any photographs?' Good thinking! Old people always love to show photos.

'Oh, I have somewhere, dear, but I couldn't put my hand on them right now. It was different in those days. We were judged for our natural beauty. We maybe put a smattering of rouge on our cheeks and coloured our lips and that was it. Not like the young ones today who completely hide their faces under a covering of vulgar make-up.'

That's it. If I stay any longer, I swear, I'll say something I'll regret.

'Thanks again for all this,' I say, smiling sweetly at Mammy Delaney. 'But I probably should head home. I'm on babysitting duty for my friend's two kids tomorrow night, and I'll need plenty of energy.'

'What, already?' Tom asks, looking shocked that I suggested breaking up the fun party. 'But it's only just gone nine.'

'I know, Tom, but I'm exhausted and I'm sure your mam is tired too after all her work preparing this lot.'

'I am a little tired, dear,' she says, faking a yawn. Thankfully, she seems to feel the same as me!

'Come on then,' says Tom, getting up from his chair. 'I'll drive you home.'

'Ah Tom, love,' says the mammy from hell. 'Why don't you just call a taxi for Jenny? I'm sure she wouldn't want you to have to go out to bring her home this hour of the night.'

Stupid old bag! He at least owes me a lift home after me putting up with that abuse all evening. And I'm still hoping to entice him in for a bit of something else. That would certainly make up for the sham of a tea.

'No, Mammy, I don't want her to have to get a taxi. I promised I'd bring her home and it's only down the road. I won't be long.'

'Thanks,' I say, giving him a grateful look. 'And thanks again, Mrs Delaney, for such a lovely tea.'

'No problem, dear,' she says, lips clenched. 'And, Tom, I'll stick on the kettle and make a fresh pot of tea for when you get back. Sure you hardly touched yours earlier.'

'Great, Mammy,' he says, kissing her on the cheek. 'I'll be back in a jiffy.'

I welcome the cool night air after the stilted stuffiness of the kitchen. Thank God that's over. I like Tom – really I do – but if getting close to him means getting close to that old bat, then I'm honestly not sure it's worth it. He carefully reverses his Ford Focus out of the driveway and at last we're heading for my place.

'That was a nice evening, wasn't it?' he says. 'I think Mammy likes you.'

'You've got to be kidding, Tom,' I can't help saying. 'Didn't you see the way she was looking at me? She hates me!'

'Don't be ridiculous, Jenny. Sure she spent all day baking for you. And, anyway, Mammy isn't capable of hate – she's such a gentle soul.'

I have to bite my tongue. It's no use. Tom and his mother adore each other and there's no way I could come between them. I wouldn't want to really, but it would be nice if he could at least acknowledge that she'd been goading me all night. Anyway, we're almost home and hopefully we can put all thoughts of Mammy aside for a while and get to know each other a little better. I'm not talking about luring him into bed or anything – to be honest, I'm still not sure if I fancy him – but I'm beginning to hate the loneliness of being on my own in the house night after night, and a bit of company would be a welcome change.

'Just turn left down here,' I say, 'and straight to the end of the road. I'm number sixty-nine.'

'There we are,' he says, pulling right up behind Betsy in the driveway. 'Service to your door!'

'Thanks, Tom. So are you going to come in for a while? As you said, it's still early.'

'But I thought you wanted an early night,' he says, not taking the bait.

'Well …' I say, not sure how to play it. 'I just thought maybe we could get to know each other a little better, without your mother breathing down our necks.'

'Ah, Jenny, I'd love to, but Mammy will be expecting me home. I should really get back.'

For fuck's sake! I can't believe I'm being shoved aside for a seventy-five-year-old woman. What's the story with that? Is he really so attached to her, or is it that he just doesn't fancy me? Despite being unsure of my feelings towards him, I feel a bit miffed that he may not fancy me either! I'll give it one more shot.

'Would you not just like to pop in for ten minutes or so? You could even ring your mam if you like?'

'Honestly, I'd better not,' he says. 'Maybe another time.'

'Right so,' I say, opening the car door slowly, hoping he'll do as they do in the movies and grab me back for a long, lingering kiss.

'Night, Jenny,' he says, bending over to kiss me on the cheek. 'I'll give you a ring over the weekend.'

Shocked and disappointed, I step out of the car and slam the door. He waits until I turn the key in my hall door and then speeds off down the road, breaking speed limits in an effort to get back to Mammy!

What a bloody night. I flick on some lights and head straight into the little kitchen. I grab a half full bottle of white wine from the fridge and pour myself a large glass. This relationship thing is harder than I thought. I can't believe how difficult it's proving to get physically close to him. It's not even about the sex; it would have been nice if he'd have come in and at least had a kiss and cuddle with me. I wonder what it is. Maybe he's gay. Jesus, maybe that's it – it's not as though it hasn't happened to me before. Thoughts of Shane Lonergan flood my mind and I wonder if he's living a happy gay life without a thought for the hearts he broke when he pretended to be straight.

Taking my wine into the living room, I take a few big gulps and place it on the coffee table. Maybe I'll have a chat with the girls on Twitter. They always cheer me up. And it will give me a break from the million things swirling around my brain. I take my laptop out of the dresser drawer where I left it last night when Mam was here. I open it and wait for it to warm up.

It won't be long now before the girls are here. I'm really getting excited. It's funny to think I hated the idea of them coming, but between our lovely Twitter chats this week and my private chats with Kerry I'm starting to actually look forward to the visit. Thursday night at Keith Barry should be a good night – even if Mammy Delaney doesn't approve!

I click on the Twitter icon and the live chats appear immediately on the screen. It seems Zahra is chatting about another secret celebrity makeover she's been doing today. I wish she'd tell us who these celebrities are. I'm still a little bit in awe of Zahra. I know she's not a celebrity herself, but she's rubbed shoulders with so many of them, it feels as though she is.

Fiona's little boy seems to be running a temperature and Kerry is giving her tips on what to do. Fiona is such a good mam to that little boy. She seems so happy with her little family – so sure of herself and happy with her life. And I envy how much Kerry loves her job. Nursing seems to be her life and she's always in good form.

My fingers hover over the buttons to join in the conversations. But what have I to offer? More lies? I certainly don't feel like announcing to the world that I'm a failure in the romance department. I could DM Kerry, but I don't want her to get sick of my moaning. Well! So much for Twitter cheering me up! I close the computer. Grabbing my wine, I flick off the lights and head up to bed. Maybe things will look more positive in the morning.

CHAPTER 10

Saturday – 4 Days to D-Day

'Congratulations,' says the midwife. 'You have yourself a beautiful baby daughter.'

I can't believe it. Tom squeezes my shoulder as the nurse places the baby in my arms.

'Let's call her Lily,' says Tom. 'Mammy would be so proud.'

'But ... but I thought we'd picked Katie. We said if it was a girl, we'd call her Katie.'

I'm panicking now. There's no way I want my baby to be a constant reminder of that old bag. I can't believe he wants to call her Lily. He knows how I feel about his mother.

'But, darling,' says Tom, smiling. 'It has to be Lily – have you seen her face?'

I glance down for the first time at my baby daughter. But ... oh no ... it can't be ... how can this happen? My precious little girl has been born with the face of Lily Delaney!

I'm in the pink aisle of Smyths toy store. God, I never realised there was such a variety of dolls out there. When I was little, I had one precious Barbie doll that I kept for years. Every Christmas, Santa would bring me something for the doll – a little pony, a wardrobe, a car – and I looked after everything so well.

Kids these days seem to treat toys as though they're disposable. Take Sally's girls, for example. The dining room in the house looks as though it's been invaded by aliens from Planet Pink as every corner of the room is heaving with girlie toys. Yet I hear them constantly complaining to their mother that they have nothing to play with. It's unbelievable. Okay, now I'm sounding like my mother and that's a very scary thought!

So, anyway, I may as well be looking into a pit of snakes as I don't have a clue what I should buy. I have to admit to being a bit hurt when Sally said that they hated me. I'm not overly fond of them either but, to be honest, I've never really tried to engage with them. Not having brothers or sisters growing up meant that I was never really exposed to babies or younger kids. I was never one to babysit like a lot of girls did when I was a teenager, so really my experience of children is zero.

Well, let's see. I'm going to have at least two hours with them before they go to bed. I don't think Barbies will buy me much time because, as far as I can remember, they account for about half the pinkness in their playroom. What I need is something to keep them occupied – something creative that will keep their attention and take the heat off me. I abandon the doll aisle for the arts and crafts one.

Right, I'm not wasting any more time here. I pick up the first box I see that looks vaguely interesting and check the blurb on the side. Hmmm! A vase-painting set – that should hold their attention for a while. I grab an extra set of paints and some paper for good measure and head to the checkout. As the usual Christmas panic has started, there are about ten people ahead of me in the queue. I decide that, as I'm going to be standing here for a while, I may as well see what's happening on Twitter. A touch of a button and I'm in – honestly, I could do it with my eyes closed at this stage.

Ah, Kerry has sent me a DM to see how my tea went last night. Fair play to her for remembering. I'll just let her know because I can't see myself doing much tweeting tonight. I'll just stick with DM though – especially if I'm going to be honest about things!

@JennyB Thanks Kerry. It wasn't great to be honest. Tom is really quite nice but his mother was awful.

@kerrydhunt Ha! It's a bit early for mother-in-law syndrome, isn't it? You've been going out with him for, what? All of four days?

@JennyB Haha! She probably does fit the stereotypical wicked mother-in-law. But let's not get carried away just yet!

@kerrydhunt So are you feeling better about things in general? You sounded so down the other day.

@JennyB I'm not too bad, actually. I'm excited about you guys visiting and, in the meantime, I have something even more exciting to do on Monday.

@kerrydhunt Oooh, tell me, tell me!

@JennyB Well let's just say that I've been unhappy about a part of my body for a long time and I'm finally plucking up the courage to go for a consultation about having it fixed! That's all you're getting!

@kerrydhunt Very intriguing! Well the best of luck with it. Let me know how you get on and whenever you can tell me more, I'd love to hear about it.

@JennyB Thanks, Kerry. But I'd better go. There's just one person in the queue here before me now. Talk later.

I'm feeling quite pleased with myself. I'll show Sally that I'm a good aunty and the girls will see that I'm not as terrible as they thought I was. I'm actually quite looking forward to it now. How hard can it be? It's not as though they're babies. Now *that*

I wouldn't be able to handle – changing nappies and making bottles just wouldn't be my thing. But at 3 and 6, at least I can reason with them and they can look after themselves in the toilet department! I'll have them worn out so they'll be conked out by nine and I can catch up on *X Factor*. Bring it on!

★

'But, Mummmyyyy! You *can't* go out. You *never* go out and leave us all on our own like this.'

I've just arrived for babysitting duty and Sinead is having a fit. I get the impression this has been going on for a while because Sally is looking completely frazzled.

'Don't be silly, Sinead, love,' she says, prizing the six-year-old's fingers from her arm. 'Sure Aunty Jenny will be here with you. You're not going to be on your own.'

I'm still standing just inside the front door, unsure whether to go on in or run for my life! Abbey is sitting on the stairs sucking her thumb. She doesn't look too happy either, but at least she isn't screaming like her sister.

'But *I don't want* Aunty Jenny,' continues the wailing child. 'I just want you, Mummy.'

'Sorry about this, Jenny,' says Sally, looking dangerously near tears herself. 'Go on into the kitchen and I'll sort these two out.'

I'm thinking now might be a good time to produce the presents I bought earlier. On further examination, I realised the vase-painting set was for ages eight and over so I had intended to wait until Sally and John were gone before I produced it. I'm banking on it keeping them entertained for the night and I'd be gutted if Sally confiscated it. But feck it, I'd say she'd agree to a knife-juggling set at the moment if she thought it would keep them happy so I may as well go and get the less dangerous art set from the car!

'I just need to get something from the car first,' I say. 'Won't be a minute.'

'Okay, Jenny. These two are going to say a proper hello to you when you come back in, aren't you girls?'

I'm not holding my breath. That Sinead is a right handful. I'm glad I brought those jelly snakes too. If I play my cards right, I should have enough bribes to last until bedtime.

Back inside with my bags, I follow them into the kitchen. The two girls are sitting quietly at the table and Sally is standing over them, arms folded in a teacherly fashion.

'Now, girls,' she says crossly. 'What have you to say?'

'Hello, Aunty Jenny,' they say in unison.

'Hi, girls,' I say in my best Nanny McPhee voice. 'Look what I've got for you. We're going to have a lovely time tonight.'

I empty the contents of the Smyths bag onto the kitchen table and, thankfully, the girls' eyes light up at the sight of the colourful bits and pieces.

'Ah, Jenny, you shouldn't have,' says Sally. 'You're so good – isn't she girls?'

'Thank you, Aunty Jenny,' says Sinead.

'Thank you,' whispers little Abbey.

'No problem at all,' I say, delighted that everyone seems to be happy now.

'What's all this, then?' says John, arriving into the kitchen and looking very dapper in a grey suit with an open-neck black shirt.

'Daddy, Daddy,' shouts Abbey. 'Aunty Jenny bought us all this stuff and we're going to make things and everything. Can you stay and play with us too?'

'Don't be silly, darling,' says John, kissing his youngest daughter on top of her head. 'You know Mammy and I are going out for a while. I'm sure Aunty Jenny will be brilliant at making stuff.'

'But … but … I want you and Mammy to make it with us too,' says Abbey, lip wobbling.

'Yes, stay and play with us,' chimes in Sinead, pouncing on the opportunity to use her doey eyes on her mother again.

'Girls, your daddy and I *are* going out! We are *not* leaving you alone, we're leaving you with Aunty Jenny, who's brought you lots of nice things to play with. Now that's the end of it, do you hear me? We'll be back in a few hours when I hope you'll be both fast asleep!'

Go Sally! She's not taking any shit from these two. Fair play to her. I can see she's frazzled and it probably wouldn't take much for her to cancel the whole night, but she's determined not to let them win. She really must want this night out badly, though, as she seems to have made a lot of effort to get ready. She's usually quite conservative in her dress, but she's opted for a black knee-length pencil skirt that shapes her beautifully and gives her a J-Lo bum. I haven't seen her wear make-up in a while and together with her blonde curls spilling down to her shoulders, she looks a lot younger than her thirty-two years.

'Go on you two,' I say, ushering Sally and John towards the door. 'We'll be fine here, won't we, girls?'

The two girls are pouting and Abbey has big tears forming in the inside corners of her eyes.

'But I have a sore tummy, Mammy,' says Abbey. 'I think I'm going to spew.'

'Oh for God's sake, Abbey,' says John, glaring at his daughter. 'That's not going to work on us tonight.'

'And I have too,' cries Sinead. 'Right here.'

She points to her chest and I have to stifle a giggle. They must really hate me. Now that in itself isn't funny, but really the whole scenario is hilarious. At just three and six, the girls are well able to fight for what they want. But it's not going to work tonight!

'Bye, girls. Now be good for Aunty Jenny,' says Sally, kissing both girls on the cheeks.

'Go on,' I say. 'They'll be fine.'

'Thanks for this, Jen,' says Sally. 'You've no idea how much we need a night out. You have our mobile numbers if there's a problem. We're only ten minutes away anyway if we need to come back.'

'Go and have a good night,' I say, shoving them both out the front door. 'I'll text you later on to let you know they're both fine.'

I take a deep breath before heading back into the kitchen. It's only just gone seven, so I'll set the girls up with the vase-painting thingy and go see what's on telly. I imagine that'll keep them going for an hour or so, and then maybe I'll give them something to eat and get them to bed.

'So do you want to paint these lovely vases, girls?' I ask, joining them both at the kitchen table.

'S'pose,' says a sulky Sinead. At least that's a start.

'And what about you, Abbey? Are you going to help too?'

'My tummy is sick,' she says, sucking her thumb.

'Well maybe if you help with this, you might forget all about your sick tummy and I might even have some treats for you both later.'

'Okay,' says Abbey reluctantly.

'Well why don't I leave you two to set up everything and see if you can figure it out. I'll come back and check on you in about twenty minutes and see if you need help. How does that sound?'

'Okay, Aunty Jenny,' says Sinead, looking much happier as she spies all the stuff in the box. 'And I can read properly now, too, so I can read the *structions*!'

'Brilliant,' I say, delighted it's all running so smoothly. 'I'm just going to make a cup of tea and go into the sitting room, okay?'

The girls busy themselves setting everything up as I make myself a cuppa. That was a genius idea, making them organise it all themselves. It'll buy me more time before I have to join them. I take my cup into the sitting room and plonk down gratefully on the suede sofa. *X Factor* has started, but as Sally has it on Sky+, so I'll catch up on it when the kids are in bed. I might just have a peep at Twitter while I'm drinking my tea. Ah, I see Zahra is on. I must tell her about next Saturday night. She should be impressed, I'd imagine.

@JennyB Hi, Zahra. What you up to?

@zahraglam Hey there, Jenny. Just relaxing tonight. I've been so busy these past few weeks, it's good to have a quiet one.

@JennyB Well, get all the rest you can before coming to Dublin – I have some exciting things planned!

@zahraglam So I heard. Kerry was telling me about the show on Thursday night. Sounds fab.

@JennyB And did she tell you I've been chatting to Keith and he said we can meet him afterwards?

@zahraglam Yes. She told me that all right. It should be a good night.

@JennyB I know you're used to meeting celebs but I thought it would be nice for the others to meet someone famous.

'Aaaarrrrgh! My hand … my hand!'

Fuck! I fling my phone onto the sofa and run into the kitchen to see what's happened and I almost faint when I see Sinead holding a dripping red hand aloft.

'Jesus, what's happened?' I say, scanning the room quickly, half-expecting to see a carving knife on the counter with a finger. Thankfully, it only takes me a few seconds to realise it's red paint dripping from the child's hand. Abbey is just looking on, crying quietly. So much for a quiet cuppa!

'It's okay, Sinead,' I say, in the most soothing voice I can muster. It's only a bit of paint. We can sort you out in no time. What happened anyway?'

'I ... I ... was reading the *structions*,' she sobs, 'and I ... I ... was opening the pots of p ... p ... paint like it said and ... and ... and I just knocked over one of them.'

'Ah it's easily done. Not to worry, we'll have you cleaned up in a jiffy.' I whisk her over to the sink and proceed to use one of Sally's dishclothes to clean the offending hand. At least her wailing has died down.

'I have a sore tummy,' cries Abbey. 'I want my mammy.'

Oh for feck's sake! 'It's okay, pet,' I say, putting on my best Mammy voice. 'You just got a fright when Sinead screamed. It's all sorted now, isn't it Sinead?'

'Y ... hic ... yes,' she says, still gulping for air after her wailing session.

'Come on, girls,' I say, realising that I need to get things under control. 'Let's clean up this mess and I'll see have I something nice in my handbag for you.'

'Okay,' says Sinead, looking a little brighter at the mention of something nice. 'And can we watch a DVD while we're having our treat? I don't want to paint anymore.'

'Yes, that's a good idea, isn't it, Abbey?' I say, looking at the sulky three year old.

'Can we watch *Little Mermaid*?' she asks, finally taking her thumb out of her mouth.

'Of course you can ... that is if Sinead agrees to it. What do you think, Sinead?'

'Come on, Abbey,' says Sinead, grabbing her little sister's hand and leading her into the playroom. 'Let's get comfy with our blankets and pretend we're in the cinema.'

Thanks be to God! I'll dole out the jellies I brought and hopefully that'll keep them quiet until bedtime. I put the last of the painting things back into the box, thanking my lucky stars I had the presence of mind to put newspapers on the table to protect it. I flick in the switch of the kettle again. That last cup just went cold on me with all the drama. I sit down heavily on one of the wooden chairs. God, Sally and John are saints. How do they manage these kids? I thought it would be a cinch but there's more to this parenting lark than I thought.

Actually, it can work the other way too – looking out for a parent can be quite tricky, as I've learned these past few days. Oh, God, what the hell am I going to say to my mother about Harry? I know I have to say something, but it's definitely not going to be easy. She seems to really like this guy for some reason.

'Aunty Jenny,' comes a voice from the playroom. 'Abbey's stinky.'

What? What exactly does that mean? Abbey has been out of nappies for the last few months. I distinctly remember Sally telling me how much money she's saving with not having to buy them any more. I'd better go and see what's up.

'What do you mean, Sinead?' I ask, noting how Abbey is sitting with her bum pushed up off the sofa.

'I mean you need to change Abbey's pull-up – it's stinky.'

'But ... but she doesn't wear nappies any more,' I say, panicking slightly.

'It's not a nappy, silly,' says Sinead, shaking her head. 'It's a pull-up for night-time. Mammy puts one on her when she gets her jamies on.'

'Oh,' I say, stunned. 'And c ... can't you do it? I mean ... I ... she mightn't want me to change it for her.' Jesus, listen to me – asking a six year old to change a three year old's nappy! The poor kids are just looking at me. What must be going through their heads? In their minds, adults know everything and can do everything. I'm certainly challenging them on their beliefs tonight!

'Come on, Abbey,' I say, resigned to the fact that I'm the only adult and therefore have to do the necessary. I take her upstairs to the bathroom and take off her pyjama bottoms. Thankfully, the pull-up has contained the foul-smelling excretion but how am I going to get it off her without making a total mess? I try to think of the ads where there are loads of happy babies running around but can't remember seeing any of the mothers in this predicament.

'I want clean pull-ups,' says Abbey, getting impatient with my dithering.

'I know, love. I'm doing that for you now. Just step out of these ones carefully and I'll get you another.'

I don't know how I manage to do it, but five minutes later, the dirty pull-up is in a bag in the bin. Abbey is changed and heading back down to the movie. I actually have wet patches under my arms from the stress of the situation. Not long now, though, and they'll be in bed. Back downstairs, I fish out the jellies from my bag and place a few in two bowls.

'Here you go, girls,' I say, handing them a bowl each. 'You can have another half hour and then it's time for bed, okay?' Back in the sitting room, I curl my feet underneath me on the sofa, grateful for the bit of peace.

I have newfound respect for mothers. I've never had any time for Sally's complaints in the past. She'd moan about being exhausted and never having a minute to do anything for herself. I always felt she'd a cheek moaning when she was able to sit at home all day every day when I had to go to a job I hate five days a week. Much as I dislike my job in the bank, I think it's a hell of a lot easier than having to look after two children. No wonder poor Sal's exhausted. I must try to drag her away for a night somewhere soon. John is great with the girls, so I'm sure he'd help out. Oooh, maybe we could nip up to Belfast for a bit of Christmas shopping. I'll talk to her about it tomorrow.

When I check my watch again, it's almost nine, so I head back into the playroom to the girls.

'Come on now, girls, time's up. Go and brush your teeth and

hop into bed and I'll come up and say goodnight to you in a few minutes.'

'Okay, Aunty Jenny,' says Sinead. 'But I think Abbey is already asleep.'

My heart melts a little when I see the poor little thing; head resting on the arm of the sofa and hand clutching her blanket. She hasn't even touched the sweets I brought in for them. Sinead has demolished hers, but at least they seem to have done the trick and she seems much happier with me now. I scoop Abbey's little body up in my arms and head up the stairs to their bedroom. I place her gently into her bed while Sinead goes to brush her teeth. I stand and watch the covers rising and falling as Abbey sleeps. I find it strangely relaxing. Sinead bounds back into the room and hops into the other bed.

'Night, Sinead,' I say, daring to place a little kiss on her forehead.

'Night, Aunty Jenny,' she says. 'And thank you for bringing us things and minding us tonight. You're not as horrible as I thought you were.'

I have to stifle a giggle. Well, at least she's honest, and I'm really thankful I seemed to have turned things around. Sally will be impressed when she comes home. I flick off the light switch and leave the door halfway open, as instructed by Sally. She said the girls like to see the light from the landing when they're in bed.

Peace at last. I finally make that cup of tea I've been gasping for all night and grab a Kit-Kat from the fridge before heading into the sitting room. Bliss! Tea, chocolate and *X Factor* – a perfect Saturday night.

'Aunty Jenny, Aunty Jenny! Come quickly.' Sinead's voice booms down the stairs.

Jesus, what now?

'Abbey has just thrown up all over the place. And it smells sooooo bad!'

Fuck!

CHAPTER 11

Sunday – 3 Days to D-Day

I've just come home and I can't believe what I'm seeing. Somebody has turned my living room into a hospital ward while I've been gone! There are six beds, three on each side. There are children in all the beds with various injuries. What the hell is going on? A very cross-looking man hands me a chart and tells me I'm late. Late for what? And this bloody uniform is making me itch like crazy. Hang on! What uniform? Jesus, how did that happen? I'm in a nurse's uniform!

'Nurse, nurse,' cries a little voice. 'I think I'm going to be …'

Eeeek!

Bloody hell! What a night. Thanks be to God I'm finally out of that house and on my way home. Although, on the plus side, I think I managed to get the girls to like me. And funnily enough, I sort of like them now too! After they'd gone to bed, I stood at their bedroom door, watching them curled up in pinkness and I felt a strange and unfamiliar feeling and maybe it was more of a hot flush from the stress of the evening, but I did feel my heart warm a little.

That was until I was met by a scene from *The Exorcist*! Jesus, I've never seen anything like it. When Sinead called me, I ran up the stairs and before I even got halfway up, I could smell the foulness seeping out of the room. To be honest, I wanted to run in the opposite direction, but I knew I had to check it out. Abbey was sitting up in the bed crying, a pool of puke all around her, dripping onto the floor and soaking her various toys and books beside the bed. Sinead had buried herself under the duvet to escape the scene and I was very tempted to join her.

My first reaction was to ask the crying child why she couldn't have gone to the bathroom. I mean, would it have been too much to ask for her to aim it all into the toilet instead of taking the lazy way out and doing it in the comfort of her bed? But she was far too upset for a telling off, so I did my best at making some comforting 'ahhh' sounds and telling her everything would be all right.

Twenty minutes later, I had a very pale Abbey back on the couch in the playroom watching a DVD, a large bucket at her side just in case. I'd gathered up the bed covers and shoved them all into the washing machine and bundled up the ruined books and toys into a bin liner.

I was never so relieved to see anyone when Sally and John came home soon after and I gladly passed things over to the experienced mammy. I did sort of feel sorry for them though, their one night out in ages and they had to come home to that. But Sally in her mammy mode was like a whirlwind, spraying disinfectant into every single corner of the house while still managing to comfort a distressed Abbey. I just wanted to go home to my own, non-disease-filled house and get into my own comfy bed. But I'd promised Sally I'd sleep over, so I could hardly change my mind. I tried to block out the noise during the night but every hour or so, I could hear Abbey's pitiful retches and the low mumblings of her parents trying to comfort her.

I'm shattered. What I'd really love to do is go home and grab a few hours' sleep, but there are too many things running around in my head – things I need to get sorted. I've been stressing since last week about my mother's relationship with Harry. Although we're not close, she's still my mother and I feel it's my duty to be honest with her. If Harry is the sort that hangs around clubs picking up younger girls, she should know about it. But God, I don't relish the thought of telling her that I've snogged her man!

God, what a mess. And here I am like a bloody fool trying to sort out my mother's love life when my own is heading up the Swanny fast! I honestly don't know what to make of Tom. I have mixed feelings about him. He rang me when I was on my way over to Sal's last night and we talked briefly. I told him I was babysitting and that I'd give him a buzz today. I thought he may have been ringing to apologise, but he sounded chirpy and not like a man who felt guilty about anything. He's a nice enough bloke and we've hit it off pretty well, but I'm not sure he's *the one*. For starters, if I had to spend another evening in the company of that mother of his, I'd lose my reason! And it's not just her, it's how they are together. That 'mummykins' behaviour was a bit off-putting to say the least!

I was so pissed off that he didn't come in with me on Friday night. I was left feeling needy and lonely. I know we only got together because Paula pushed us into it but, to be honest, I've really warmed to the idea of having a man in my life, especially at this time of the year. I love the whole build up to Christmas – I love the decorations, the carol singers, the hustle and bustle in the shops – but I'm really not all that gone on the actual day. Usually it's spent with just me and Mam eating lots and getting bored with each other's company after a few hours. But this year Mam has Harry and I'd love to have someone special too – even if he's not *the one*!

And as if all that isn't enough, the Twitter girls are coming in a couple of days. I need to do a million and one things before they arrive. I'm going to have to go shopping for a load of new bed linen and towels, give the house a major clean and think of some more interesting things to do with them while they're here.

Anyway, first things first – I'm going to head straight to Mam's before going home. I'm hoping Harry won't be there so I can have a good chat with her. It will be better to have it all out in the open. I'm sure he recognises me – bloody fool! Does he actually think I'm not going to say anything?

I rang Mam before I left Sally's – more to make sure I didn't have to endure the embarrassment of what I saw last Sunday. She seemed happy enough for me to call over, though I'm not expecting to have a home-cooked dinner put in front of me. That's not my mam's style! I'll be lucky if I get a cup of tea and a custard cream. Apparently, Harry is there too but he's heading off to meet a friend so I should have an opportunity to have a chat with her in private.

I park Betsy and ring the doorbell. This time, thankfully, the blinds aren't closed. The door is swung open and Harry is standing in front of me, fully dressed and looking quite handsome. He's ditched the glasses again and I can't get over how different he looks without them.

'Hi, Jenny, come on in,' he says, pleasantly, holding open the door.

'Thanks, Harry,' I say, stepping inside and following him into the kitchen.

'Your mam will be down in a few minutes – she's just drying her hair. Cuppa?'

'Eh ... well ... okay then, I'd love one,' I say, beginning to feel uncomfortable being alone with him. I don't mean uncomfortable in a he's-going-to-jump-my-bones sort of way, but uncomfortable in an I-remember-what-we-did-when-we-were-last-alone sort of way.

'Here we go,' he says, placing a pot of steaming tea on the table and taking out three cups. 'I'm sure there's a few chocolate biscuits in here too.'

He has his head in the fridge and is taking far too long to find the aforementioned biscuits. He's playing for time! I knew it. He *does* know who I am and he's afraid to sit down in case I confront him.

'Ah don't worry about biscuits for me,' I say, toying with the idea of challenging him. 'I haven't had dinner yet, so I'll save my appetite for later.'

'Well, if you're sure, then,' he says, hovering over the table and checking his watch. 'Your mam is taking ages. Maybe I'll see if she's nearly done.'

Definitely avoiding me. That's it, I can't help myself. I have a million words bubbling on the surface of my tongue and I need to spit them out.

'Do you think I don't know who you are, Harry?' I sort of shout to his retreating back.

Oh fuck, fuck, fuck! He's stopped dead. He hasn't turned around yet, but he's just standing there. I want to run away. Why, oh why, did I say it like that? Why did I have to have a 'ta da' moment instead of just discussing it with him like an adult? I'm a bloody eejit. He turns around and I can see there's a defeated look on his face. He comes back into the kitchen, closes the door and sits down heavily on a chair beside me. I don't know where to look.

'Jenny,' he says, fidgeting with the placemat. 'I knew this would come up at some stage. I suppose I was avoiding it.'

'Look, Harry,' I say, a lot more confidently than I feel. 'My main priority here is my mam. I know we're not terribly close but I hate to think of her being hurt.'

'Ah, but, Jenny, I'd never hurt your mother. I love her ... I swear to you ... I really do.'

Well that's a bit of a shocker! I didn't expect to hear that. But, still, it just doesn't feel right knowing what I know and keeping my mother in the dark about it.

'I met you at a really bad time in my life, Jenny. My wife of ten years had just walked out on me and I was devastated. That nightclub phase was just that – a phase. It wasn't me and I soon realised that.'

'I'm sorry you've been through all that, Harry, but what about now? I know you say you love my mother but what are your intentions towards her?' Oh bloody hell – did I really say that?

'Well I'm planning to stick around as long as she'll have me,' he says, and I can't help believing him. 'My wife – the one who left me ... '

I'm tempted to ask if there was another one, but I let him continue.

'She went off with a man much younger than me and he had everything I didn't. I suppose I went a bit mental for a while. I got myself a bachelor pad and a whole new wardrobe of young-looking clothes and hit the nightclubs. I wanted to prove that I wasn't ready for the scrapheap just yet.'

'So do you think my mother is a rebound thing?' I ask, not daring to meet his eyes.

'Definitely not, Jenny. To be honest' – he pauses, reluctant to continue – 'you were more my rebound thing.'

Oh, lovely! I don't know whether to be relieved for my mother or insulted for me. But I don't have time to respond as the kitchen door flies open and my mother appears.

'Ah, howareya, Jenny, love,' she says, sitting down beside the two of us. 'I see my Harry has been looking after you.'

'I'm grand, Mam. And, yes, Harry's been keeping me company.'

She looks different. I'm not sure what it is about her. It could be that she's had her hair cut differently but, if I didn't know better, I'd almost swear she's had a face-lift. Or maybe she's had some Botox. Well, whatever it is, she's looking fantastic and a lot younger than her fifty-six years.

'So, tell us,' she says, pouring herself a cup of tea from the pot. 'How did the "meet the mother" date go the other night?'

'Oh, don't ask,' I say, aware of Harry's pained expression. He's probably terrified I'm going to spill about us.

'That bad, was it?' she asks, smugly. 'What did I tell you? Imagine him wanting you to meet his mother at this early stage! Bonkers!'

'It *was* a bit bonkers,' I say, laughing at how different our two mothers are. 'But I'll tell you all about it again. I'm not staying for long. I just wanted to drop in for a quick cuppa.'

'And it's great to see you, love, isn't it, Harry?'

'Y ... yes, of course it is,' says Harry, looking as though he might cry.

My head is in a spin. What should I do? I was determined to tell my mother about me and Harry but after what he has told me – and I honestly believe him – I'm reluctant to say anything. I need to think.

'I'm just running to the loo, Mam, then I'll head off. Maybe we can catch up for longer next week.'

In the safety of the little downstairs toilet, I pull my iPhone out of my bag. I know it seems desperate, but I just need to talk to somebody about this. I hope one of the girls is online. I'll have to chat to them by private message though, because I don't want the whole world to hear my problems.

@JennyB I'm looking for advice – are any of you here *@zahraglam @kerrydhunt @fionalee?*
@kerrydhunt What's up, Jen?
@JennyB Quick, turn to DM.

@kerrydhunt I'm here. Why the secrecy?

@JennyB Oh, God, in a nutshell, I've just discovered I've snogged my mother's boyfriend and don't know whether to tell her.

@kerrydhunt Jesus, Jen. How can you just discover something like that? Does he have both of you on the go together?

@JennyB God, no. It was a once off for me ages ago, and now he's seeing my mother. They seem happy, but I dunno.

@kerrydhunt Ah! That's different. If your mam is happy and he's treating her ok, then why bring it up? But, Jesus, that's gas!

@JennyB Thanks, Kerry. You're right! I'd better get back to them. I'm tweeting from the loo!

@kerrydhunt Don't forget to wash your hands now! Good luck and talk later.

I throw my phone back in my bag and flush the chain as a last-minute thought. As I'm heading back into the kitchen, I can hear my mother guffawing with laughter. It's been a long time since I heard her laugh like that.

'Oh, Jenny,' she says, wiping her eyes. 'Harry here was just telling me about a girl in his office who was bringing a tray of coffee into the manager one time when she tripped and everything on the tray went all over some very important people. I'd have loved to have seen that!'

'That's funny all right,' I say, noticing how Harry has stopped laughing and is looking worried again. 'I'm going to head off now and I'll give you a ring during the week.'

'All right, love. Those girls are coming on Wednesday, aren't they? I hope it all goes well for you.'

'Thanks, Mam. I'll let you know.'

I'm suddenly feeling overwhelmed. My relationship with my mother doesn't feel strained. I still wouldn't call it perfect, but it's definitely improving. To her surprise, I put my arms around her and give her a kiss on the cheek. And while she's recovering, I bend over and place a kiss on Harry's cheek. At the same time I whisper in his ear, 'Everything's forgotten. Don't let me down.'

They both walk me to the door and I'm feeling better than I have in years. I'd swear there's a tear in my mother's eye and Harry is beaming from ear to ear. I've figured out now what's so different about my mother. I've finally put my finger on it. She's happy, happier than I've seen her in ages. And it's all because of Hairy Harry!

CHAPTER 12

Monday – 2 Days to D-Day

O'Neill's pub in Suffolk Street is buzzing and I'm having a ball. I love just sitting back and taking in the atmosphere. I can't wait for my date to arrive. Here he is now. He walks over to the table I've held for the two of us, and everybody in the pub stops and stares. It's not often they see somebody as famous as Hugh Grant just stroll into their local. He takes me by the hand and helps me up onto the table. I start to dance – a slow, seductive dance – and everybody begins a slow clap. I'm loving it now. I get more and more into it and my movements become raunchier with every shimmy.

I was made for this. Hugh is staring up at me with adoring eyes. He loves me. He must do. I place my hand on my neck and begin to run it sugges-tively down the rest of my body. But what's this? Jesus, no! I couldn't have! I wouldn't have! Is that why they're all staring? Bloody hell. I've forgotten to put my top on. There I am in my Lycra leggings and killer heels and my top half completely exposed. All of a sudden, I see my nipples hanging on a paltry bit of flesh and realise I look like a freak. The clap turns to low chants of 'Jerry, Jerry, Jerry, Jerry …' I jump down from the table, covering myself with my arms, grab my bag and run out of the pub. Needless to say, Hugh doesn't follow!

For feck's sake! I'm so pathetic. It's almost twelve and I'm sitting here in a sweat. I need to be out of here in the next hour if I'm to make my appointment on time, but building up to faking an illness is actually making me ... erm ... ill.

Bootface has been unusually quiet this morning, but that doesn't mean she'll be a walkover. I'm trying to decide whether I should go down the vomiting route or the back pain one. I'm thinking that if I put on an I'm-just-about-to-spew face, there might me more of a chance that she'll wave me off.

Paula is the only one who knows where I'm going this morning so I tried to chat to her about it during tea-break. I wanted her advice on how best to fake an illness, but she's in such a deep wallow over that prat Ian that she's completely useless.

She rang me last night in a state to tell me that they were finished – again! How many times have I heard that? But according to her, it's definitely over this time, something about him cadging money off her supposedly to pay his rent but actually using it to feed his gambling habit. Apparently, he's been begging money off her for ages now. Good riddance to him is what I say. But, honestly, she'd want to cop on to herself soon. I appreciate that it's hard when you break up with somebody you love, but she's got a constipated look on her face and I can barely get a squeak out of her.

Right, I'm off to the loo to slap my face a few times to give myself a flushed look. I can see Bootface giving me the evil eye already as I leave my desk, and it's not giving me much confidence about how she'll react when she hears I want to go home. Thankfully, there's no one else in the toilets. Looking at my face in the mirror, I have that sinking feeling in my stomach again. I'd give anything to be pretty. I hate the make-up-caked, dull-eyed face staring back at me. One of these days, I'm going to pluck up the courage to visit a make-up counter in town and see if they can work their magic on me. They'd want to be bloody good magicians though.

I'm beginning to wonder why I didn't just ring in sick this morning. It would have been a whole lot easier to do it over the phone rather than having to face Bootface now. But there's no point in thinking any more about it – I'll just go out there and tell her I'm not feeling well. She can shout and she can lecture me, but she can't stop me from going home if I'm sick – nothing is going to stop me going to that appointment today. They just rang me with a cancellation on Friday. If I don't go today, it'll be months before I get another appointment.

Taking a deep breath, I head out of the loo towards her office. I give a little courtesy knock before pushing open the door.

'What is it, Jenny? What do you want?' she asks, hastily replacing the phone in its cradle.

'I ... erm ... I'm really not feeling well, Brenda, and I was hoping I could head home.' I brace myself for the inevitable onslaught and begin listing a thousand ailments in my head in case she wants to know exactly what's up.

'Fine so,' she says, rubbing her temples with her thumbs. 'You head on home and get yourself to bed.'

Excuse me? Did she just tell me to go home without question? I know it sounds ridiculous, but I sort of feel cheated. I've had myself so psyched up for the nasty Brenda, I'm completely thrown by an unfamiliar nice one!

'Are you sure?' I say, gawping. 'It's just that ... It's just ...' Jesus, Jenny, quit while you're ahead!

'I know – it's just that you were expecting me to shout and complain and refuse to let you go home.' She sighs heavily and I feel more than a little awkward. 'I'm not an ogre, Jenny, I do understand that life doesn't always run smoothly, and sometimes we just need time to sort it out.'

'I ... yes ... that's true.'

'So was there anything else, then?' she asks, looking at me with tired eyes. 'It's just that I've a lot to do here.'

'I ... eh, no, that's all. Eh ... thanks, Brenda. I'll see you bright and early in the morning.' I'm up and out of the office like a hot snot, before she changes her mind. God, that was weird. Whatever's going on for her at the moment is certainly bringing out her softer side. Who would have thought it – she really must have a heart after all!

It's only 12.30, so I have plenty of time. I only have a short bus journey, so I'll head out early and go for a cuppa before my appointment. I quickly shut down my computer and grab my bag from under the desk. I glance across at Paula to give her the thumbs up, but she's in a world of her own so I don't bother.

Not ten minutes later, I'm sitting on an almost empty number 123 bus on my way to my long-awaited appointment. I'm really excited about it. I'd love to tell the Twitter girls, but I'm not sure it's something I want to tweet about. Maybe I'll tell them when they're here. I can't believe they'll be here the day after tomorrow. I noticed they were talking to others on Twitter last night about our tweet-up and they seem really excited. I'll just have a peep and see if there's anyone on now. I take my phone out of my bag and I'm into Twitter in a second.

@JennyB I'm escaping work for the afternoon. I suppose everyone's still working. Anyone here?
@zahraglam Hiya, Jenny. How come you're escaping? Going anywhere nice?

Maybe I'll tell Zahra. With the world she lives in, she's bound to know all about it. It will be good to chat to somebody about it. I daren't tell Sally because she'd only try to talk me out of it. I'll probably tell her eventually but not until I've made up my mind.

@JennyB You'd never guess where I'm going. Very exciting.
@zahraglam Oh where? Tell me, tell me!

It's just suddenly dawning on me that anybody could be watching my tweets. Jesus, imagine if Bootface looked me up on Twitter and saw me tweeting about this. I don't really think she's the tweeting type but you'd never know. It wouldn't do to be found out. I'd better backtrack.

@JennyB Yes, very exciting – going home sick to curl up in bed and sleep it off!
@zahraglam Oh!

Phew! That was close. I throw my phone back in my bag. I'd better stay off Twitter at least until later on tonight. Anyway, I haven't had much of a chance to think about the appointment and I want to jot down a few questions for the doctor. I can't believe, after all these years of thinking about it, that I'm at last going for a consultation for a boob job.

★

I'm sitting twiddling my fingers in the unhospital-like waiting room. I'd been brought in by a very relaxed and friendly nurse who'd told me I wouldn't be waiting long and had even asked if I'd like a cup of tea. My brain hadn't really processed the fact that it was a private clinic I was coming to and not a hospital A&E, so I was pleasantly surprised that it didn't smell of disinfectant and puke, have peeling lino and a frazzled, all-singing, all-dancing nurse. I'm leafing through this month's *Hello!* but, to be honest, I just want to get in there and see what the doctor has to say.

'Jenny Breslin,' the nurse calls, appearing at the door.

'Yes,' I say, abandoning *Hello!* and jumping to my feet nervously.

'Dr Hanley will see you now,' she smiles, extending her arm in the direction of an open door.

Dr Joanna Hanley – I've had a picture of this woman in my head for the past few months, ever since my doctor recommended her. She'll be a walking advertisement for her own work. She'll have long, wavy blonde hair (not sure why) and long svelte legs. There won't be an extra ounce of flesh on her athletic frame, nor a wrinkle on her face.

'Hello, Jenny,' says a small, friendly looking woman, her eyes disappearing in a bed of wrinkles. Definitely not what I was expecting! She grasps my hand with her podgy little one and shows me into the office. Maybe she's an assistant or a student doctor, although surely Dr Hanley would help her with her double chin and crooked nose.

'I'm Dr Hanley,' she says, sitting down behind a cluttered desk. 'So I believe you're here to talk about breast augmentation?'

'Eh ... yes,' I say, shocked that *this* woman is the plastic surgeon.

'Okay, so, tell me a little about why you want to have the surgery and how long you've been thinking about it.'

'Well,' I say, trying to figure out if I should tell her I've wanted it since I was twelve or thirteen. 'I've been really unhappy with my ... em ... breasts since I was a teenager.' Teenager sounds better – covers a wide range!

'I never really developed much,' I continue. 'And, to be honest, it's really embarrassing.'

'When is it embarrassing?' she asks. Jesus, I thought I was coming here to decide what cup size I wanted to be, not for a counselling session.

'Well I'm embarrassed about it pretty much all the time. I can't wear anything low cut because no matter how hard I try, I can't push what I have close enough together to get any sort of cleavage. Even padded bras don't shape me enough, so I end up stuffing the cups so that I look like I have something there!'

'I see,' she nods knowingly. 'I understand how you must feel. And is it only your breasts that you're unhappy with, or are there other things about your body you'd change if you had the chance?'

What is this? Is she looking for more business? How unprofessional! Or maybe she thinks I need a nose job or a facelift. Good God! A girl could get paranoid.

'I'm just asking so I can get a full picture about how bad you feel about your breasts specifically,' she says. 'Are they what bother you most?'

'Well,' I say, concluding she's probably just being thorough. 'There are probably other things I'd change too but, to be honest, getting my breasts sorted would be a huge thing.'

'Right so,' she says, scribbling frantically on her notepad. 'Let's take a look.'

I'm mortified, but I take off my top and bra and stand as requested while she's examining my non-existent boobs!

'Hmmmm!' she says, pursing her lips. That doesn't instil me with a lot of confidence.

'You really don't have any breast tissue there, do you? It's just nipple on skin.'

Ouch! But she's right. 'Now do you see why I'm so keen to have this done?'

'Of course,' she says, indicating to me to dress and sit back down. 'Now I'm going to have a chat with you about types of implants and sizes and I'd like you to go away and think about it. Maybe you'll come back in a few weeks and bring somebody with you.'

'Okay, that sounds fine,' I say. 'I've told one of my friends about it, so she'll probably come with me.' I'm sure Paula won't be so miserable in four weeks' time and, besides, she's the only one I've told about this so she'll have to come.

'Now there are two types of implants – round and teardrop,' says the doc, fishing around in a big box she has behind the desk. 'It's totally up to you which shape you prefer. Here's a sample of each so you can have a look.'

She produces two big blobs from her box of tricks and I can't help noticing how they look like a stress reliever I bought for one of the guys at work for our Kris Kindle last year! They feel strange and yet wonderful and I'm beginning to get excited about the thought of feeling them under my own skin.

'And then, of course, we have to decide on a size for you.'

'Well I was thinking of a D-cup,' I say, confidently. I've thought about it for years and I reckon if they're going in, they may as well be a decent size because I won't be going back for more. But she's shaking her head. I'm sensing she doesn't agree.

'We don't really guarantee a cup size here. We decide on a size of implant, which is worked out in millilitres, and the end result can vary from person to person. For example, if you get the same size implant as somebody who already has quite a bit of breast tissue there, you're both obviously going to end up with different size cups.'

It makes sense, I suppose, but it's mad to think of ordering my boobs in millilitres!

'So what we suggest,' she continues, 'is that you go home and measure out different amounts of rice, place them in freezer bags and put them into a bra. It's not an exact science, but it will give you an idea of what size you feel comfortable with. Looking at you now, I'd say maybe 200 or 220mls.'

'Um … okay, then,' I say, thinking this is getting more and more bizarre!

'You can make an appointment with Sara on your way out. Let's say about four weeks and have a good think about things. I want to be sure it's what you really want.'

'Thanks,' I say, standing up to leave. 'You've given me plenty to think about. I'll see you in a few weeks.'

Outside in the crisp air, I smile to myself. Wait until Paula hears about this. She'll wet herself laughing. Imagine having to measure out rice into bags and stuff it in my bra. It's hilarious. Wouldn't you think in this day and age they'd have a more technical way of doing things? I search in my little denim bag for my phone as I head for the bus stop. Four missed calls. God, I'm popular! Two from Paula, one from my mother and one from Tom. He's being quite attentive really, which is sort of nice. He must have heard that I went home sick and is checking to see if I'm okay. I'll give him a buzz in a while. I wonder what's up with Paula though. She must be still in work. I'll give her a buzz and see.

'Hello,' comes Paula's whispered voice. 'Is that you, Jen?'

'Yes, it's me. Were you looking for me?'

'Yeah, though I can't talk for long. Bootface is hovering. I just wanted to say I was sorry for being such a bitch today. I know you were going for your appointment. I should have shown a bit more interest.'

'Ah, don't worry about it,' I say, generously. 'Sure you're in bits at the moment about Ian. I don't expect you to be worrying about me.'

'But I know how much this means to you. I'm glad you managed to get out all right. Did Bootface make it difficult?'

'Not at all, actually. She was even nice about it. It was all a bit surreal.'

'Are you serious? That's not like her at all. I thought she'd go mad. So how did it go anyway?'

'Great,' I say. 'The doctor is lovely and seems to really know what she's talking about. I have to think about a few things and go back for another chat in a few weeks. I'm supposed to bring somebody with me next time. Will you come?'

'Of course I will,' she says. 'I look forward to having a proper chat about it.'

'Well, when these girls are gone back home at the end of the week, why don't you come over for a night and I'll tell you all about it. You could even help me measure out some rice!'

'That'd be great,' she says. 'But what do you mean "measure out rice"?'

'Well, apparently, in order to decide what size I want, I have to measure out rice and stick it in my bra!'

'What? Oh, that's hilarious! That's brilliant. Isn't science amazing? Hahaha!'

I'm delighted to hear her laughing. She's really taking her split from Ian very badly. Although it's not the first time they've split, she says it feels very final this time.

'Mad, isn't it?' I say, noticing a bus stopped at the lights.

'Hilarious. But I'd better go before I'm caught on the phone again. I'll catch up with you tomorrow.'

'Great,' I say, sprinting to the bus stop. 'I'll be in early to make up for my time off sick today. Talk to you then.'

I get to the stop just in time to hop on the bus. I notice the battery in my phone is running low, so I decide not to return the other calls until I get home. I wonder what my mother wants. That whole situation with her, Harry and me is bizarre. I really hope I'm doing the right thing by not telling her. I like seeing her happy. I don't think about it from her point of view too often but it must have been tough for her when Dad left. I've always felt so sorry for myself that I didn't really stop to think about her.

Gosh, listen to me getting all compassionate! Between feeling sorry for Bootface and worrying about my mother, I'm in danger of actually becoming a nice person. Well my mother always said that life is full of twists and turns and you'd never know where it might take you. Maybe she talks some sense after all!

CHAPTER 13

Tuesday – 1 Day to D-Day

'Ring around the rosie, a pocket full of posies …'

I'm playing one of my favourite games from my childhood. I'm spinning around and around, holding hands with all my friends. There's Paula and Sally and … hold on, I can't quite make out that face. Oh yes, it's Zahra. And that must be Fiona, although she looks younger in her picture. But … oh my God … who's that other person? They haven't got a head. How weird! It must be Kerry. I must tell her to put up her picture on Twitter because it's just not right to not have a head!

Jesus! I can't believe how much dust is living behind my telly. It's disgusting. It's even formed into filthy clumps and has wrapped itself around the wires. Ugh! You'd swear I never cleaned the house before. Sure only about a month ago I gave the whole place a once over – guess I must have forgotten about the back of the telly!

It's 7.30 a.m. and I should be thinking about getting ready for work, but I'm starting to panic now about the girls' imminent arrival and realise I'm really not prepared. If I can just get the house in reasonable order, I'll nip into Penneys after work and get some new bed linen. I'll stick two of them in the spare room, but one will have to take the sofa. One thing I'm *not* prepared to do is to give up my own bed. I couldn't bear the thought of somebody having free reign over my knicker drawer, and perhaps finding some of the ... ahem ... play things I've hidden at the back!

Right! Zahra and Fiona can go in the spare room and I'll keep Kerry downstairs on the sofa. That way, I'll have more of a chance to have a one-to-one chat with her when the others go to bed. Hopefully she won't think I'm weird sticking around until I have her on her own, but I get the impression she feels the connection between us too. It's as though I've known her for years and I feel very comfortable talking to her.

Zahra kind of scares me with all her stories about hob-nobbing it with the rich and famous. I feel as though I should be rolling out the red carpet for her! And Fiona is lovely, but with her life of domestic bliss with her husband and son, I don't feel we have so much in common. Fingers crossed we can have a fantastic few days.

*

I've claimed a corner of the back of the bus for myself and the mountain of bags I've acquired. After a painfully boring day in work, I was more than happy to wave goodbye to the place for the rest of the week. It's all getting a bit weird in there to be honest. Firstly, there's Paula moping around the place because of her and 'her Ian'. Then there's Tom, popping over to my desk whenever he gets a chance and although it's sort of nice, it's just a bit ... well ... weird. And then Bootface is probably the weirdest scenario of all. She seems to have mellowed a lot these past few days and – and I can't believe I'm saying this – I've slightly warmed to her. I'm guessing she has something going on at home and it's making her subdued. Maybe I've misjudged her. Maybe it's her circumstances that have made her hard and I should give her more of a chance.

Anyway, enough of that. I need to think about the evening ahead and all I have to do. When I left work, I launched myself on Penneys and spent a lovely hour picking up all sorts of bits and pieces. I've never been into interior decorating much and, as a result, my house isn't very homey. I sometimes watch those house makeover programmes on the telly and marvel at how they can take a dull, boring room and by the end of the half hour episode it's a burst of colour and style. Now I don't think I could go as far as some of those shows, but I definitely wouldn't say no to an injection of colour.

I feel exhausted when I finally turn the key in my door and throw all the bags into the hall. At least the house smells a bit better than it did before. Thank God I got stuck into the cleaning this morning, otherwise I'd never be organised. Right, first things first. I'm starving, so I'll throw some frozen chips in the oven, open a tin of beans and change into an old tracksuit whilst it all cooks.

God, even though I spent so long with cleaning this morning, there's still so much to be done. It's times like this I wish I had a fairy godmother who'd appear and turn all my pumpkins into carriages, so to speak.

My thoughts are interrupted by a banging at the front door. Shit! I'm not in the mood to humour another sales person. What is it about these people that they always start their pitch with 'Don't worry, I'm not trying to sell you anything.' Do they think we're absolute idiots?

'Coo-eeeeee! Jenny, love. It's your mam.'

Oh, God, that's all I need! I really don't need the distraction of Mam and Harry while I'm trying to get organised. Sure I told her I'll be up to my eyes tonight – why on earth would she choose now to pay me a visit?

'Jenny, are you there, love?' comes a voice through the letter box. I suppose I can hardly pretend I'm not.

'Coming, Mam,' I say, reluctantly opening the front door and looking for Harry to follow her in.

'Howareya, love,' she says, pushing her way in. 'I just thought I'd come over for a while to see if you ...'

'Mam, it's nice to see you and everything, but I'm really up to my eyes tonight. Have you forgotten my visitors are coming tomorrow?'

'Of course not, Jenny, love. Sure that's why I'm here.'

Now I'm confused. Does she intend to muscle in on my few days with the girls? Is she looking to be included in our plans? Jesus, perish the thought! There's still no sign of Harry coming in so I'm guessing she's on her own. I shut the door and follow her into the kitchen.

'Right,' she says. 'Let's make sure you've plenty of room in your fridge and cupboards and then we'll bring the shopping in.'

What's she talking about? She's beginning to scare me. Oh, God, maybe she's taken something. It sort of reminds me of when Paula once took a few puffs of a joint and she went really weird. She seemed normal enough and didn't look as though it had affected her but then she started saying things like, 'Why is the moon looking at us?' and 'Let's go look for werewolves', without even batting an eyelid. I glare at my mother to see if there'll be any mention of howling at the moon.

'Em ... Mam ... why don't you sit down and I'll make you a nice cup of tea. Where's Harry tonight? Maybe I should give him a call.'

'Ah don't worry about him, love,' she says, rummaging around in my fridge. He's busy tonight. Actually, it was him who suggested that I get the shopping and come and help you out.'

Now I'm completely at a loss. 'What shopping, Mam?

'Shopping, Jenny – groceries. I got all your shopping in for the next few days. Harry suggested that you might need a hand to get organised for the girls. I remember you saying you were going to go to Tesco in the morning, but I thought it would help if I did it for you today. I'm off work this week and next so I have plenty of time on my hands. It's in the car. Come on and help me bring it in.'

I'm gobsmacked. My mother has actually done my shopping? Wow! Harry must be having some influence on her. Sure she doesn't even do a proper shop for herself. I follow her out to the car and can't believe my eyes when she opens the boot and half of Tesco falls out.

'Mam ... I ... I don't know what to say. Thanks for this. God, you're a star.'

'Ah it's no problem, Jenny,' she says. 'I've brought over a few bits and pieces to brighten up the house too. Now I know you're not as ... let's say ... colourful as me, but I really do think you need some accessories.'

So this is what it must feel like to have a *real* Mammy. I'm completely overwhelmed as I carry in bag after bag from the car and see the array of both food and knick-knacks she's bought.

Half an hour later, all the food is unpacked and neatly stored away and we're both sitting eating my chips and beans together with a vegetable quiche from the hot food section of the supermarket.

'So I take it things are going well with yourself and Harry,' I say, stuffing a mouthful of the delicious quiche into my mouth.

'Ah he's great, Jenny,' she says, her eyes glazing over in a sort of I'm-in-love expression. 'You know, I haven't been this happy since ... since ... you know . . .'

I know she means since my dad left. We've never really spoken about it, but I think a reconciliation was always on the cards. Dad didn't move too far away – choosing to rent an apartment a few miles down the road in Clondalkin. But then when he died, Mam sort of went off the rails, a bit like a teenager rebelling against the injustice of homework or not being able to stay out beyond ten o'clock. She didn't want to discuss it with anyone and I suppose it sort of made her look cold. I didn't see her cry at all but I did suspect she shed her tears in her bedroom when she was alone.

'I'm glad you're happy, Mam,' I say, tears threatening to spill out of my own eyes. 'And I know ... I know ... ' I'm not sure whether to say it or not. 'I know Dad would want you to be.' And it's true, he would. Dad was a very generous and loving man. He loved his family beyond anything else in the world and I know he never stopped loving my mother.

'Right, now, let's get this house looking like a home,' she says, all emotion firmly swept aside. 'Let's start with the living room.'

I'm dubious at first as she empties out the bags she's brought. There are multicoloured cushions and shiny satin throws, pictures that look as though a child has splattered paint on the canvas and gaudy looking candles. God, I know my living room is dull as it is, but I'm not sure I want it to look like the set from *Charlie and the Chocolate Factory*! But I decide to leave her to it and go and make up the beds with the new linen I've bought. I can always make some adjustments when she's gone.

Within minutes, the boring bedrooms are already looking cheered up with the matching yellow-print duvets in the spare room and the rose-coloured one in my room. It's amazing how a little splash of colour can make a difference. Heading into the en-suite to replace my grotty grey towels for some fluffy pink ones, I have to do a double take at the shower tray. It's *white*! It's actually, gleaming, shiny white! Wow! I always thought it was *supposed* to be grey. Ugh! Just shows the squalor I've been living in.

I head back downstairs to see how my mam is getting on. I don't have much faith in her newfound Laurence Llewelyn Bowen impersonation and I dread to think what I'll find.

'Just a minute, love,' she shouts, as I'm opening the door. 'I'm almost done – I'll tell you when to come in.'

I honestly feel I'm on *30 Minute Makeover*. Now I know how those people feel when they have their eyes covered and they're trying to fix a smile on their faces just in case.

'Right, come on in,' she says, and I nervously push open the door.

Bloody hell! The gaudy cushions, the tasteless throws, the mismatch of bits and bobs – it's fantastic, it's bloody-well fantastic!

'Oh, Mam, I don't know what to say. It looks amazing. How on earth did you manage to turn my living room into this?'

The boring wine-coloured sofa is brightened up with yellow and green cushions, the pictures that looked childish suddenly look like works of art when hung on the walls and the candles scattered here and there add a sense of warmth and homeliness to the dull room. Even the lime green satin throws just seem to blend in – even with the beady bits hanging off the ends!

'Well you know me, love,' she says, clearly delighted to have made such an impact. 'I always did like my flamboyant colours and Harry has been doing a course on interior decorating since he retired last year. He noticed your house needed a bit of a lift when we were here last, so he gave me a few tips.'

Shock is not the word! Hairy Harry – an interior decorator? What next? I'm half-expecting my mother to announce she's giving up her civil service job to retrain as a doctor!

'Well tell him thanks,' I say, still shocked by the whole bizarre situation. 'Thanks to both of you. I'll be proud to have the girls here now.'

'No problem,' she says, sitting down on the newly dressed sofa. 'But there's something else, Jenny. There's something I need to tell you and you should probably sit down for this.'

She's looking very serious now. Oh, God, maybe she's sick or something. Maybe she's going to tell me she's terminally ill and only has months to live. Maybe that's why she's turned all mammyish. She's trying to make up for her lack of maternal guidance over the years. Jesus, for the first time in my life I feel I have a real mother and now she's going to die!

'I know it will come as a shock, love,' she continues. 'But you need to know and I want you to hear it from me.'

'It's okay, Mam,' I say, sitting down beside her and taking her hand. 'I'm here for you. We'll get through this together.'

'Harry is going to move into the house with me.'

'And whatever you need,' I continue, 'you only have to ask.'

'Did you hear me, love,' she says, breaking my train of thought. 'Harry and I are going to live together.'

'Oh,' I say, a little confused. 'And does he know about … about your condition? Is he moving in to help you through it?'

'What condition?' she asks. Now it's her turn to look confused.

'What you were going to tell me – you're sick, aren't you?'

'Of course I'm not sick,' she laughs. 'Just the opposite. I'm fitter than I've ever been … and happier.'

I'm struggling to get my head around it all. One minute I'm going to be nursing her to her deathbed and next she's happier than she's ever been. God, my mother is so complicated. 'So … so … Harry's moving in with you, that's all you were going to tell me? There's nothing else?'

'No, love, there's nothing else. I just wanted to make sure you were okay with it. I know I haven't always been the ideal mother, but I am aware that it must be hard for you to see me with some-body else. And I just thought it might be difficult for you to see me moving him into the home I shared with your dad.'

'Mam, I'm happy for you, I really am,' I say, genuinely. 'I can see that Harry is good for you and once he's treating you well, I'm fine with it.'

'Thanks, Jenny, that means a lot. He really is good to me, you know. I never thought I'd feel this happy again. And he's even made me realise ... ' She trails off and I can see her eyes are welling up.

'Go on, Mam,' I say, wondering where this is going.

'He's made me realise what a precious gift I have in you, Jenny. Harry never had kids with his wife and it's something he really regrets.'

I honestly don't know what to say to that. The emotional show is so unlike my mother that I almost feel uncomfortable. This day is getting weirder and weirder – but in a good way. I just hug her briefly until she speaks again.

'Right, I'd better get going and leave you to it. Let me know how it's going while the girls are here and give me a shout if you need anything.'

The moment has passed, but I won't be forgetting it in a hurry.

'Will do, Mam,' I say, holding her coat while she slips her arms in. A whoosh of bitter cold wind hits my face as I open the front door and I'm sure I can smell snow in the air.

'God, it's freezing, isn't it, love? I hope you have a nice warm scarf to wrap around your neck when you're going out. Sure that wind would cut right through you.'

I can't remember the last time Mam showed an interest in what I was wearing, or whether or not I might catch a cold. It feels strangely comforting. 'Thanks again for everything, Mam.' I hug her tightly before she heads out to the car and I'm sure I see her wiping away a tear as she drives off.

So Harry is moving in! Wow! Just a couple of weeks ago I didn't even know he existed and now he's going to be living with my mother. I can't help wondering if I would have reacted differently if she'd told me that first. It's kind of like the reverse psychology Sally uses on the kids. If she wants them to go to bed by eight o'clock, she knows they won't be happy, so she'll first tell them they have to go at seven. By the time she's negotiated eight, they think they've won!

But, anyway, my analysis of the whole Harry situation will have to wait because I have visitors to prepare for – though, thanks to Mam, I'm pretty well organised. Nobody is arriving until late afternoon, so it'll give me the morning to get myself ready. I wonder how they're all feeling tonight. Are they as nervous about meeting as I am? I'll log on to Twitter for a few minutes and then maybe I'll have an early night.

Opening up my laptop, I feel a real rush of excitement. If they're online now, it's probably the last time I'll tweet to them before seeing them in real life. Imagine! It feels like we're all such good friends and yet we've never even met. How weird is that? I tap the button that brings up my Twitter screen.

@JennyB Well are any of you here *@zahraglam @kerrydhunt @fionalee*? Are you girls looking forward to your trip? Can't believe you'll actually be here tomorrow!

@fionalee Oh, I can't wait, Jenny. Been a bit stressed trying to get Ryan organised but have it sorted now.

@JennyB Why have you to get him organised? Didn't you say your husband will be looking after him?

@fionalee That was the plan, but he's to go off for a couple of days on business. A friend is stepping in.

@JennyB Phew! That's good. Thought you were going to say you couldn't make it.

@fionalee Well, it was looking like that at one point, but all's fine now. Thank God for good friends.

@zahraglam I can't believe it's tomorrow. My cases are packed and ready to go. Can't wait.

@JennyB Brilliant! What time is your flight arriving in at?

@zahraglam Arriving from Gatwick at 3.10.

@fionalee My train is arriving in at 5.30, so I'll get a taxi straight to your house. I know traffic will be murder so no point in you coming.

@JennyB That would be great if you don't mind.

@fionalee Not at all. Is *@kerrydhunt* arriving by train too? If our times are close, maybe we could share a taxi.

@kerrydhunt Sorry, but decided to drive. Was going to get train but changed my mind.

@fionalee Ah, not to worry. What time are you planning to be at Jenny's then?

@kerrydhunt Roughly around six. We'll probably be there around the same time.

@fionalee Brilliant. I'll see you then.

@JennyB Great. Glad all is sorted. I'll see you at airport tomorrow Zahra and I'll see you at the house Kerry & Fiona. Can't wait.

I close my laptop and put it away. Guess I won't be tweeting much over the next few days. I'm exhausted. The past couple of weeks have been a real roller-coaster and I could be in for more of the same over the next few days. Who knows what will happen, but it's definitely exciting. I switch off the lights and set the house alarm. Padding up the stairs I have a strange feeling in my stomach. What am I letting myself in for? Well I'll know soon enough!

THE STORM

CHAPTER 14

Wednesday – D-Day

I emerge from my new crisp, rose-coloured duvet and rub my eyes. What's this? No dreams? God, that's the first time in weeks, I slept really soundly and don't remember any weird or wonderful things filling my head. Uh oh! Maybe it's a sign that I'm about to actually *live* the nightmare!

Half eight. I snuggle back into my duvet for another while, delighting in not having to go to work. When we initially planned this tweet-up, it was supposed to be on a weekend. The girls were going to come on Friday and go back Monday. It seemed like the most sensible arrangement. But then Zahra said she'd prefer to come during the week because she'd a party to go to on the Sunday and Kerry agreed, saying that it's harder for her to get time off work at weekends. Fiona didn't seem to care either way so Wednesday until Saturday was decided.

I love being in bed when the weather is bad outside. Of course the snow didn't come last night and, instead, there's an icy rain pelting the window. I imagine my 25A bus packed to capacity with dripping bodies and poking umbrellas. There's nothing worse than public transport on a rainy day. A normally empty bus suddenly finds itself heaving with people and the warm air blowing from the vents mingling with the damp bodies makes for a very nauseating ride. And don't get me started on umbrellas. I've lost count of the number of times I've been prodded and poked by those menacing objects. You'd think by now somebody would have invented something better. I mean, it's all very well having a micro umbrella that folds up small enough to put in your handbag but when it's dripping wet, who's going to wrap it back up into its micro state and stick the sodden thing in their bag?

I can't believe the girls are actually coming today. It'll be late afternoon by the time they arrive so if they're happy enough, I'm just going to suggest we order in a Chinese. I can say I didn't prepare anything because I didn't know what they liked and it will save me having to admit I'm no Nigella.

There I go again – trying to portray myself as all singing, all dancing. Would the girls really expect me to be a whiz in the kitchen? I feel I need to prove myself, but I don't know why. Maybe it's because I'm good at nothing. I'm not wallowing in a bath of self-pity or anything, but it's true. I can't paint, can't cook, don't play any musical instruments (well, except for 'Silent Night' on the recorder which I learned in primary school), don't do sports, can't sing … Jesus, now I *am* wallowing in self-pity! That's a pretty heavy list of 'can't dos'!

Well, there'll be enough time for panicking later when I'm trying to make my thin hair look full and healthy and trying to get a bit of a glow from my dull skin. For now, I'm going to take full advantage of the quiet house and sleep for another hour or two. Sure I've loads of time.

★

Oh for feck's sake! How could I have slept until 12.30? How could I – on the very day I need a major overhaul to my appearance – have conked out so soundly for so long? I was planning to leave here at two to allow for parking and to appear relaxed and composed when Zahra emerges like a goddess from her flight. And I'm quite sure she will. Judging from what I know of her, she'll be dripping in designer gear, hair bobbed to sleek sophistication and a face of make-up Lady Gaga would be proud of.

Eeeek! An hour and a half to transform myself – I'll need a miracle! Oh how nice it would be to forget about the day ahead and just let myself nod off again. It's still raining outside and this bed is so comfy. But no, I drag myself out of the warm mess of bedclothes and head to the en-suite. Isn't it funny that the more sleep we have, the more we seem to need? I've been known to go to bed at five in the morning only to be up for work two hours later. But when I have twelve hours' sleep, I'm like the living dead!

Twenty minutes later, I'm standing in front of the mirror, blow-drying my hair. Damn this bloody plum colour, but at least it's faded a little over the past week. Thankfully, my hair only takes ten minutes to sort out, leaving plenty of time for me to do something with my face. Sometimes, I forget what I actually look like with no make-up. Honestly, I live my life hiding beneath such a thick covering, sometimes even forgetting to take it off, that I honestly don't see my naked face too often. Surveying it now, I'm actually quite surprised at how smooth it looks. Sally is constantly complaining about wrinkles but I seem to have avoided them so far. Maybe I should think of toning down the make-up to show off my newly found fresh skin. Then again, maybe not. My signature make-up is what gives me my personality – it's who I am. I'd feel naked without it. So despite my brief dalliance into the bare-face zone, I proceed to load it on as I always do.

★

'So are you waiting for somebody special?' asks the very over-weight girl sitting beside me. She's nervously twisting the strap of her handbag and I want to slap her hands to make her stop. After my initial panic and mad rush to get organised, I made it to the airport with loads of time to spare.

'Well, I'm sort of ... she's ... em ... '

'Because I'm waiting for my boyfriend,' she continues. 'He's coming over from Greece to live here with me.'

'Oh, that's nice,' I say, trying not to stare at her double chin.

'It's soooo romantic,' she gushes. 'We met on holiday during the summer and he's already been over to visit. He says we're soul mates and should be together.'

'Um ... nice.' I really don't want to engage in conversation with this girl. She seems nice enough, but her enormous thighs are unnerving me. She has on a tight pair of black leggings but they're pulled so tightly across her expanse of leg that they're practically see-through. The airport is busy and I was lucky to get a seat at all but her right thigh is shoving me dangerously close to the edge.

'You should see him – he's pretty gorgeous,' she says, totally oblivious to the fact I'm trying to read my magazine. Then she comes a little closer and lowers her voice to a whisper. 'And he's great in bed!'

For fuck's sake! I really don't want to hear this. What sort of weirdo meets a total stranger and discusses her bedroom habits? But I suspect this girl is probably only twenty or twenty-one, despite looking twice that. And, God love her, she really doesn't have much going for her. She hasn't done much to cover up the blemishes on her face and her unruly greasy hair could do with a bit of a trim. I can't help but notice that her jowls wobble even when she's not talking. I wonder what her Greek man is like – if he even exists.

'So, you didn't say,' she wobbles. 'Are you waiting for someone special too?'

You didn't give me the chance to answer, I want to say but

instead I decide to be nice. 'I'm just meeting a friend. She's coming over from London.'

'Ahhh, I see,' she says, knowingly. 'And this ... this *friend* – is she the *someone special* in your life?'

'What? No, no, nothing like that,' I say. 'She's just a friend friend – nothing more.'

'Whatever you say,' she says, nodding in an all-knowing, woman of the world sort of way.

Shit! I feel I've got to tell her now. 'Would you believe she's actually somebody I've met on the internet – we haven't met in person before?'

'Oh how exciting,' she says, shifting position and leaving me with about two inches to perch my bum on. 'Well they say that's the way to meet people these days. Good on you for being so open about it.'

Why do I feel it's important to make this girl understand that I am not a lesbian nor do I intend to perform any lesbian acts with the girl I'm meeting here today? 'Listen,' I say, attempting to claim back at least half of the seat but it's not proving easy. 'It's not just her who's coming for the weekend – there's a group of girls meeting in Dublin. We met through Twitter and are meeting in real life for the first time this weekend!' There, that should get it through to her.

'Gosh, really?' she says, staring at me with eyes that say 'I don't know whether to believe you or not'. 'So you've never, ever met these girls before and you're going to spend a whole weekend with them?'

Is it really that big a deal? 'Yes, that's the plan. But we've known each other for the past year so it doesn't feel like meeting strangers.'

'Oooh wait until I tell Demitri – he's mad into Twitter, but I don't think he's ever met anyone he tweets with before.'

I take it Demitri is the Greek boyfriend. I'm getting more and more interested in seeing what this man is like. I'm guessing maybe forties or even fifties, greying hair greased back to cover bald spot and beady eyes that will immediately fix themselves on this girl's enormous breasts. I can't help hoping he comes out before Zahra does so I can have a nosy. By my reckoning, Zahra's flight should be landing in five minutes, so it'll be at least another twenty before she comes through.

'So are you staying in a hotel in the city centre?' she asks, pulling a king-size Mars bar from her bag and proceeding to stuff half of it in her mouth. Jesus! It takes me three or four bites to eat a mini one but she'll have this one demolished in two clamps of her jaw!

'Eh ... no, actually,' I say, eyes focused on the Mars bar. 'They're all coming to stay in my house. Saves on accommodation costs.'

'*What*?' she says, not disappointing me by swallowing the last of her bar on the second bite. 'Are you out of your mind? Sure they could be axe murderers for all you know.'

Hmmm! It's interesting that it's the same choice of words Sally used last weekend. I mean there are lots of different ways to murder people so the fact they both chose the axe is a little daunting. Maybe it's a sign. Maybe they're right and one of the girls is an axe murderer and has been stalking people on Twitter for years in order to find the right person and place to commit the crime. Or maybe I'm getting completely carried away with myself and need to cop on!

'Hopefully not,' I say, trying to sound confident, though she's giving me the willies. 'And I've spent so much time chatting to these girls over the past year that I really think I know them quite well.'

'Well I hope it all goes well,' she says, flashing a sort of pitying smile at me. 'But be careful.'

'Ah it'll be fine,' I say, wondering if there's any way I can cancel this whole thing without causing too much disruption. This girl has me shitting myself. 'And it's only for a few days and then we'll all be back to tweeting each other again.' That is, if we get through the weekend without any murders!'

She's back to twirling the straps of her handbag again and she's looking at her watch nervously. Maybe he's stood her up. Maybe he's not coming at all. Or maybe he's only a figment of her imagination. I remember seeing a movie a few years ago where a young girl who wasn't very blessed in the looks department made up a whole imaginary world for herself because she was so unhappy with her own life. She made up stories with pretend people and it got so intense that the lines of reality and fiction became blurred. She was eventually committed to an asylum where she lived for most of her life. God, I hope this girl isn't the same. She's looking pretty worried now as she's checking her phone so maybe she's at the blurry stage where the lines of fiction and reality have crossed.

'Demitri, Demitri,' she shouts suddenly, jumping up from the seat with the agility of a sprightly six year old. 'Over here.'

Alarmed by this sudden development and the possible arrival of one Demitri, I follow her eyes towards the crowd emerging from behind the sliding doors. At first, I can't see who she's waving at and then this vision appears in front of my eyes. At least six foot and with bulging muscles showing through his tight T-shirt, this couldn't possibly be Demitri. He flashes a mouthful of white teeth as his almost black eyes light up on seeing the object of his affection.

'*Eisai omorfi,*' he says, looking straight into her eyes.

Oh, my God! It's the sexiest thing I've ever heard. I'm mesmerised!

'He says I'm beautiful,' she says, turning to me to share this piece of news. 'Didn't I tell you he's wonderful?'

Yes, she did, and I didn't believe her for a minute. I'm speechless as I watch the two unlikely lovebirds head towards the exit, completely wrapped up in each other. Well they do say there's someone for everyone!

'This is much nicer than Gatwick,' I hear somebody say as they pass by, snapping me out of my daze. Here we go, the flight must be in. I smooth down my new jade-green skirt and reapply my lip gloss. Come on, Zahra – I'm ready for you!

CHAPTER 15

Ten minutes later, I'm still straining my eyes for the first glimpse of my virtual friend. I've checked the screens and her flight is definitely in, so I'm beginning to wonder if she's going to show up at all. Pulling my phone out of my bag I quickly tap into Twitter. Maybe she's left a message to say she's changed her mind.

> @*fionalee* Can't wait to see you later, Jenny. I'm leaving now so next time we speak will be face to face.

Nope, nothing from Zahra. At least it looks as though Fiona is definitely on her way. It occurs to me that I don't have phone numbers for any of the girls. It's strange; Twitter has always been our place of contact so we haven't needed anything else. But it's times like this that a phone number would be handy. But there are still crowds of people coming through so I'll give it another while.

Suddenly, there's a clash and shriek and I look over to see a young girl frantically trying to push her suitcases back onto a trolley. The poor thing looks mortified as people are whizzing past and not one person is bothering to stop to give her a hand. One of the cases has opened and the brightly coloured contents are spilling onto the floor.

What is it about people in this country? The Irish have a reputation throughout the world as being warm, inviting and friendly, but, to be honest, I'm not sure it's a true reflection of how we are. Only the other day I was trying to get out of my estate onto the main road and not one car would stop to let me go. Honestly, it was ridiculous. I edged Betsy's nose out bit by bit until I actually half-blocked the road but still people just swerved around me. It took me a good ten minutes to finally get out. Well, I'm not going to be one of those people.

'Here, let me give you a hand,' I say, rushing over to where the poor girl is trying to sweep her clothes back into the open case and balance the others on the trolly. 'Gosh, you've got a lot of stuff here.'

'T ... t ... t . . .t ... thanks,' she says. 'I always t ... t ... t ... t ... tend to over-pack. You'd just never know what you m ... m ... m ... m ... might need.'

Jesus! That's a mad stutter. I've never quite heard anyone that bad before. But stutter aside, this girl reminds me of my mother – not age wise, because she looks even younger than me, but by the clothes she's wearing. Her flamboyant orange leggings and matching heels are outdone only by her gaudy multicoloured bat-wing top. I have to stifle a giggle at the thought of Mam wearing this get-up – she'd probably love it.

'There you go,' I say, balancing the last of the cases on top of the pile. 'No harm done.'

'T ... t ... t ... t ... thanks again,' she says, not meeting my eye. 'I'd ... I'd better be off. I'm already l ... l ... l . . .l ... late to meet someone.'

'No problem,' I say, as I watch her push the trolley forwards with much effort. She must be roughly the same height as myself but together with her tubbiness and her orange fake tan, she puts me in mind of the Oompa Loompas from *Willie Wonka.*

But it's forty minutes since the Gatwick flight landed and there's still no sign of Zahra. Should I just go home and wait? She has my address so she can just get a taxi over to the house if she's on a later flight. It's almost four and if I wait much longer, I'll get caught in the evening traffic and won't get home in time to meet the others. Yes, that's what I'll do. I'll send her a message on Twitter in case she has a chance to read it and I'll head on home.

I notice the Oompa Loompa is still wandering around – seems she's been stood up too. I find an empty seat at arrivals and sit back down. My brain is exhausted. All of a sudden I just want to be back home, on my own, with no complications of visitors I don't really know.

All of a sudden a thought occurs to me. Jesus – the house! Zahra has my address. How do I know she's not part of an international crime ring targeting single, vulnerable women. She knows I live alone and that I'm here at the airport waiting for her. Maybe she's back at my house with her international cohorts ransacking the place! It's not beyond the realms of possibility – the internet really has a lot to answer for. I'll just quickly send a tweet and then hurry home.

@*JennyB* What's up @zahraglam? I've been waiting for ages for you? Where are you?
@*zahraglam* I don't see you – I'm here. I've been waiting too.

What? Sure I haven't even gone to the loo since I arrived in case I'd miss her and I'm bursting. I stand up and scan the arrivals area but the crowd has thinned out by now and I don't see anyone waiting around except for ... oh my *God*! She's got a phone in her hand. It must be her – it's Zahra! She's noticed me too and is now waving frantically. Well, that's just unbelievable. She looks nothing like her picture. In fairness, neither do I, but

I don't think the difference is so dramatic.

'Jenny?' she asks, tentatively, as I arrive over to where she's parked her luggage.

'Yes, yes, it's me. Jesus, Zahra, can you believe we actually chatted and didn't even recognise each other? That's mad, isn't it?' I'm not sure whether to shake her hand or go in for the hug but settle on a handshake for the moment.

'It's so g ... g ... g ... g ... good to meet you,' she gushes, squeezing my hand so tight I fear my fingers are going to break. 'I just can't b ... b ... b ... b ... believe I'm here.'

'I know, it's brilliant, isn't it?' I say, wondering how on earth I'm going to get through four days listening to that stutter. 'But how long are you planning to stay for? That's some amount of luggage.' I feel slightly uneasy about the fact that she appears to have brought enough to last a few months, never mind a few days! My suspicious mind is working overtime and now that I know she's not an international criminal, I'm thinking maybe she's sold her house and is looking to lodge at my place indefinitely. Oh, God!

'Oh, I'm s ... s ... s ... s ... sorry,' she says, blushing furiously. 'I can n ... n ... n ... n ... never make up my mind what I should bring when I'm going anywhere. It seems easier to t ... t ... t ... t ... take the lot!'

'Well let's hope Betsy can handle this lot then,' I say, taking control of the trolley and heading towards the exit.

'Betsy?' she says, looking around nervously. 'Who ... who's Betsy?'

'Oh, I should have said,' I laugh. 'Betsy's my car. I know ... it's sad, isn't it?'

'Oh not at all,' she says, a little too enthusiastically. 'That's just s ... s ... s ... s ... so cute. I can't wait to see it ... um ... her!'

Pushing the loaded trolley into the lift that'll bring us to the car park, we fall into an awkward silence. I'm struggling to keep

up with what's happening. This Zahra is way different to the
one I imagined – the one I've been talking to for the past year.
On Twitter, she always seems so self-assured, so confident. She
regularly talks to celebrities and seems to have a real easy and
relaxed way with them. I'd be shitting myself if I had to tweet
to a celebrity. I wouldn't have a clue what to say and I'd just
assume they wouldn't be interested anyway. But this girl beside
me is a different Zahra altogether. She seems pretty shy and I
can't imagine her commanding the attention of anyone, let
alone a celebrity. And that stutter – wow! I suppose it's under-
standable that she'd be more confident when she doesn't have to
speak but how on earth does she get by when she's dealing with
people face to face?

'Right, here we are,' I say. 'Betsy, this is Zahra, Zahra – Betsy!'

'Oh she's g. . . g … g … g … gorgeous. I'd love to have a c …
c … c … c … car like this. So cute.'

'But I'm sure you have something much slicker over in
London. What did you say you drive?'

'A BMW,' she says, starting to lug the cases off the trolley. 'But
it's a c … c … c … c … couple of years old, so no big deal.'

'No big deal?' I say, incredulously. 'What I wouldn't do for a
BMW. Maybe I'll get to have a ride in it some day if I go over
for a visit.' Good thinking – pave the way for a free trip to
London.

'Um … yes … of course. But I m … m … m … m … may have
changed it by the time you come over. I don't like to hang on
to the s … s … s … s … same one for too long.'

'Oh you're so lucky,' I say, squeezing the last case into the
boot. 'I'll probably have to hold on to this one until it just claps
out completely!'

'Well it's a really g … g … g … g … gorgeous car.

'Thanks. I think so. Right, that's everything in.' Thank God
for rear-view mirrors because there isn't a hope of seeing out

through the back window. 'We should be home in twenty minutes if the traffic isn't too bad.'

'Thanks, Jenny,' she says, sitting into the passenger seat. 'You're so g … g … g … g … good to come out and collect me. I'm really g … g … g … g … grateful – really, thanks.'

Jesus, I didn't even get a thanks like that when I shared my bingo winnings with Sally. She was grateful and all that, but not to the extent Zahra is grateful for a measly lift!

'All these new spaghetti junctions do my head in,' I say, as we emerge from the car park onto the main road. 'I find I have to have my wits about me or I'll end up in Belfast!'

'R … r … r … r … really?' she says, eyes nervously darting from side to side.

Ha! I have her worried now. At least it should keep her quiet for a few minutes while I try to digest everything. I feel as though I could have been to London and back myself for all the time I've spent in that airport. I take a little sneaky, sideways glance at Zahra and am happy to see she's concentrating hard on the road.

It's not that I don't like her – she seems like a really nice girl. It's just that I don't know her like I thought I did. I suppose the personality thing is my own fault. I'd made certain assumptions based on how she is on Twitter, but I should have known she may be completely different in real life. But the fact she's a celebrity make-up artist is puzzling because, quite frankly, her face suggests different. Honestly, the blusher is brushed on in two pink circles on her cheekbones and she has a horrible line along her chin where the foundation is a completely different shade to her tan. But maybe I'm doing her an injustice. Maybe she reapplied it quickly without a mirror before she got off the plane. That'll be it. Because looking at her now, I find it hard to believe anyone of any importance – actually anyone at all – would let her near them with a make-up brush. But at least her clothes are designer. Now I'm no expert, but anything that looks so off the wall as her outfit does screams designer to me. And her bright blue leather handbag is definitely Gucci and pretty gorgeous too.

The silence is a bit awkward, so I turn up the radio to fill the void. I know I'll have to get used to chatting to her – I'm just not sure how to handle her stutter. It must be a bit embarrassing for her and I don't want to make her feel uncomfortable. Adele's 'Make You Feel My Love' has just come on and I raise the volume even louder. It's one of my favourite songs ever.

'Oh I love this,' says Zahra, proceeding to sing along. I'm completely dumbfounded. Not only has she got the sweetest singing voice, but there isn't a sign of a stutter anywhere – not one!

I wait until the song is finished before talking to her. 'Zahra, did you know you didn't stutter once during that song? You're a beautiful singer too.'

'Thanks, Jenny. I never stutter when I'm singing and the music relaxes me so much, I don't tend to stutter after either. My speech is at its worst when I'm anxious or nervous. Sometimes, if I'm in a very relaxed situation, I may not stutter at all for days.'

'God, that's mad, isn't it? Well hopefully you'll feel nice and relaxed for the next few days with us girls.'

'I'm sure I will.'

'We're coming into Lucan now,' I say, indicating to come off the motorway. 'Just two more minutes and we'll be home.'

'Brilliant. I can't wait to see where you live and to meet the other girls when they arrive too.'

I can't help wondering if the other girls will be as much of a surprise as Zahra is. Well, I'll know before long. 'I was going to suggest I make us a cuppa while you sort out your stuff but, to hell with it, I think we'll crack open the wine. Start as we mean to go on and all that!'

'Perfect!'

Twenty minutes later, I'm in my kitchen organising drinks and nibbles while Zahra is sorting out her stuff upstairs. I almost knocked lumps out of the wall lugging her suitcases up the narrow staircase. What the hell is she doing bringing so much luggage? Does she need one for each day? It strikes me that maybe that's what celebrities do – not that she's a celebrity or anything but she certainly seems to spend a lot of her time with them. I set out a lovely spread of crackers, cheese and olives and open a bottle of both red and white. No sign of her coming down yet, so I'll take a look at Twitter and see if the others have been on.

@JennyB Just back from the airport with @zahraglam. Can't believe she's actually here. You must be due to arrive soon @kerrydhunt and @fionalee

@fionalee Yep. Almost there. Hopefull there'll be taxis waiting so I'll be out to you as soon as possible. How's Zahra?

@JennyB Ah, she's great. Just upstairs unpacking. Weird to meet in person, though. Can't wait till you get here.

@fionalee Me too. Kerry doesn't seem to have been on all day. Have you heard from her?

@JennyB No, nothing. I'm sure she'll be here soon though. She's driving so wouldn't be able to tweet.

@fionalee Right, train is pulling into the station. See you shortly.

@JennyB Great! The wine is out so hurry before it's all gone!

I log off just as Zahra comes into the room.

'Come and sit down,' I say, indicating one of my old chairs. 'I've just been tweeting with Fiona and she should probably be here in half an hour or so.'

'Fantastic,' she says, wriggling to make herself comfortable on the wooden chair. 'And what about Kerry?'

'No word from her yet, but she's probably on her way. Now I've poured a glass of red for you – that's what you said, right?'

'Yes, that's lovely, thanks. You have a beautiful house, Jenny. I really love what you've done with it.'

I give her a measured look, trying to decide if she's being sarcastic, but there isn't a trace of anything but admiration on her face. 'Thanks, my mother helped me to make it homely. She's a lover of colour, whereas I tend to play it safe with beiges and creams.'

'Well I think the colours are gorgeous,' she says. 'I love bright colours myself.'

You don't say! I try not to stare at her orange leggings.

'So tell me all about the celebrities you work with,' I say, leaning my elbows on the table. 'I'm dying to hear all about it. You're so lucky doing the job you're doing.' I'm starting to feel relaxed now that I have a glass of wine in hand.

'Well, as I said before, I can't really divulge who I work with.'

I never quite understood the logic in that. 'But why not? What's so secret about having make-up professionally applied?'

'Well I don't just d … d … d … d … do any old make-up,' she says, shifting uncomfortably in her seat. 'I'm sort of an emergency m … m … m … m … make-up artist, if you like. They call on me when things are bad – when their skin needs, let's just say, some extra l … l … l … l … loving care!'

'Oh, I see!' I don't really – is there really such a thing as an emergency make-up artist? I imagine her working in a special clinic that celebrities are rushed to when they've got a spot on their chin that they can't handle or if they're not getting the wide-eyed look quite right.

'You must work all sorts of odd hours then,' I say, determined to find out more, but the words blood and stone come to mind.

'Um ... yes, my hours c ... c ... c ... c ... can be a bit uncertain all right,' she says, looking more and more agitated by the questions. 'But I like it that way.'

Another uncomfortable silence. And why on earth has that stutter come back? She said it comes back when she gets nervous, but I can't for the life of me think why she's so jittery. God, I imagined having to get ear plugs to shut this girl up but, to be honest, it's a bit of a chore to speak to her. She's answering my questions, but not leading the conversation. I feel a bit like we're on the *This Morning* sofa and I'm interviewing her. Well at least it won't be just the two of us once the girls arrive. Fiona and Kerry are bound to have plenty to say to fill the silences.

'So how come you used a picture of yourself without the piercings and dyed hair on Twitter?' she asks. 'You look so different in real life.' Hooray – she's starting a conversation all on her own.

'Well, I don't think I'm that different,' I say, my hand automatically going to the piercings in my ear. 'Except for the piercings, my face is pretty much the same.' Anyway, she can talk. Her picture looks nothing like her!

'I like the piercings,' she says. 'They give you character.'

'Thanks, Zahra. I think so too. Although I could really do with lessons on make-up. I know you said you didn't want to get into doing makeovers while you're here, but maybe you could just give me a few pointers.'

She sighs heavily and I can't help feeling that I've said something wrong again. 'I think somebody's just pulled up outside,' she says. Is she purposefully changing the subject? Her chair is just under the little kitchen window that looks out onto my driveway. 'Maybe it's Kerry or Fiona.'

'Oh, brilliant,' I say, jumping up to take a peep. 'It's a taxi so it must be Fiona. I can't wait to see if she looks anything like her picture.'

'She's getting out now,' reports Zahra, excitedly. Honestly, we're like two little kids waiting for Santa.

'Ah sure I'd have recognised her straight away,' I say, catching a glimpse of her as she steps out of the taxi. 'She looks exactly like her picture on Twitter.' At least she's been honest about how she looks. That picture of her with pale, translucent skin and mousy brown curly hair looks as though it could have been taken today.

'Yes, yes, she does,' gushes Zahra. 'But ... hang on ... I didn't see that coming!'

Neither did I! And my heart sinks to my stomach. 'For feck's sake ... !'

CHAPTER 16

He must be her son. Jesus! I can't believe she's brought her four-year-old son along. I have nothing against kids – well not since I started to bond with Sally's two – but, firstly, this is meant to be an adult-only, girls' weekend, secondly, she has a bit of a cheek bringing him along without asking and, thirdly, what the bloody hell are we going to do with him? But hold on a minute, this is insane, she couldn't be that stupid. She's probably arranged for somebody to pick him up from here. Perhaps he's been minded by some friend or family member in Dublin. Yes, that must be it. She did say her husband was going to be away and she'd have to make other arrangements. Phew! Thank goodness for that. For a minute, there, I thought we were going to be stuck at home babysitting all weekend!

She's paid the taxi driver and is heading up the driveway so I plaster a smile on my face and go to open the door. 'Fiona,' I say, as cheerfully as I can muster. 'It's great to see you.'

'You too, Jenny,' she gushes, leaving her bags on the ground to envelope me in a bear hug. Gosh, there's hardly any of her. She couldn't be more than a size six.

'And this must be ... em ... ' I struggle to remember the child's name – it's something like Alex or Jack or—

'This is Ryan,' she says, pushing the boy forwards to greet me.

'I'm so sorry I had to bring him Jenny. It's just the way things worked out – it's always like that with kids.'

'Don't worry about it,' I say, generously, ushering them inside. 'Come and meet Zahra. We're not in too long ourselves.'

'Thanks,' she says, following me into the little kitchen.

Zahra is already standing up. She's pulling at her bleached hair nervously as though she's about to meet the Queen.

'God, is that you, Zahra?' asks Fiona, eyes looking Zahra up and down. 'I'd never have recognised you from your picture. You look completely different.'

'I k … k … k … k … keep meaning to change that picture. It's a c … c … c … c … couple of years old at this stage.'

'Mummmmmy,' wails the child. 'Why is that lady talking funny? She's scary and she's making me feel car sick.'

'Shhhh, Ryan,' says Fiona. 'It's not nice to speak about people like that – especially when it's true. Sorry about that, Zahra.'

'It's okay, Fiona,' says Zahra, flashing her pearly white teeth at Ryan. 'It doesn't b … b … b … b … bother me.'

'Mummy, I'm car sick and those colours are making my head hurt,' continues Ryan, dramatically placing his palm on his fore-head while giving Zahra the evils.

'Ryan! What did I just tell you,' shouts Fiona, glaring at her son.

'He's gas, isn't he?' I say, watching him skulk off out into the hall. I wonder what time he's leaving.

'So that stutter must be a right pain in the ass,' says Fiona, looking pityingly at Zahra. 'I don't think I've ever heard one quite so bad. I'd be mortified if that was me.'

Jesus, and I thought Paula was blunt. This girl could give her lessons in bluntness. I glance over at Zahra to see how she's taking it and pray to God Fiona's insult doesn't turn the poor girl into a stuttering mess.

'Oh, it's terrible,' she says, reddening. 'Especially when I'm in a bank or a shop and I'm trying to put my point across. People usually try to help me with my words, but that just makes me ten times worse.' Hmmm! Maybe Fiona has the right idea being direct with her. Zahra probably gets fed up with people dancing around the subject.

I realise we're all still standing and I'm suddenly feeling exhausted. At least we're not going out tonight, so I can stay as I am in my comfy clothes and melted make-up. 'Come on, girls, let's go into the sitting room and make ourselves comfortable,' I say, shoving the snacks and drinks onto a tray and leading the way.

'Oh what a lovely room,' gushes Zahra, sitting on the chair with my newly acquired lime green throw. 'You have such good taste.'

'Ah yes, lovely,' says Fiona, plonking down on the sofa. 'Ooh, I'd murder a glass of red – do you mind?' She indicates the bottle and picks up an empty glass.

'Not at all,' I say, glad she's making herself at home. 'So what time is Ryan being collected then?'

'Collected?' She's looking at me, puzzled. 'What do you mean collected?'

'Oh, do you have to bring him somewhere?' I ask. 'I won't be able to drive him because I've already had a glass of wine.'

'Bring him where, Jenny? I honestly don't have a clue what you're talking about.'

'To the babysitter, obviously,' I say, rolling my eyes at how slow she is on the uptake. 'Is there someone coming for him or are you dropping him off?'

'Jenny, I think we've got ... '

'Mummyyyy, I can't find any toys,' comes a voice from upstairs. 'Can you come and help me look?'

Oh, bloody hell. That's all I need. A four-year-old making a mess of the house I spent ages cleaning. Well, if Fiona doesn't call him back down, I will!

'There probably aren't any here, Ryan love,' shouts back Fiona. 'I'll get the colouring books and crayons out of the bag in a minute.' Shaking her head, she turns her attention back to our conversation. 'He never gives me a minute, that one. So what were we saying?'

I don't want him upstairs rooting around, but I don't have the heart to tell Fiona that. Well at least he'll be gone soon enough, so I'll keep quiet for the moment. 'I was just asking you about Ryan's babysitter,' I say, taking a slug out of my wine.

'Babysitter?'

'For this weekend,' I say.

'This weekend?'

Jesus, what is she on? Or maybe she's being deliberately vague. Maybe it's going to be a while before they're available and we'll have to hold on to him here for a few hours. Oh, God. I'm not sure I could handle that.

'Fiona, *who* is taking Ryan for the weekend?' I ask, exasperated. 'And do you need to bring him somewhere?'

'Ah I know what you're getting at now,' she says, smirking. 'I thought you were going a bit loopy there for a minute.' Erm ... hello! She thinks *I'm* going loopy?

'I think we've got our wires crossed,' she continues. There's no babysitter. I have nobody to mind Ryan this weekend – that's why I had to bring him with me. He won't be going anywhere.'

'He ... w ... won't?' I say, my voice falling to a whisper. 'I just thought ... I thought ... so you'll be keeping him here all w ... weekend?' God, now it's my turn to stutter! Surely this can't be happening.

'Well, yes, unless you can think of a better plan,' she says. Obviously in her world, it's okay to do things like this because she doesn't seem embarrassed in the slightest about the situation.

'Oh!' I can't think of another single thing to say. How is this weekend going to pan out now? We can't take him with us to nightclubs or pubs and what about the Keith Barry tickets that I've bought and paid for? Jesus, this is turning into a sham. It seems I wasn't wrong when I woke this morning and wondered if I was going to be living a nightmare today! I glance over at Zahra to see if she has anything further to add, but she's just sitting back watching the exchange.

'Well, I was thinking we could maybe do a bit of a rota with the babysitting,' says Fiona, making herself comfortable on the sofa beside me. 'It'll give us all a chance to get out and see the city. What do you both think?'

'That sounds fair to me,' says Zahra, finally opening her mouth. I wish she hadn't. *Fair*? She thinks it's *fair*? I invite these people that I don't really know to stay in my house for the weekend and one of them wants me to stay here and mind her kid for her while she's out on the town? I'm speechless. Thankfully, Ryan arrives back into the room, saving me from saying something I'll regret.

'This is a crap house – there's nothing to do,' he moans.

'Isn't it hilarious when they come out with words like that?' laughs Fiona. 'Here, Ryan. Hand me over that bag and I'll get you out your colouring stuff.'

Erm ... whatever happened to discipline? If my mother had heard me saying a word like that when I was his age, she'd have killed me. Although, there was this one time when I had a really bad earache, I remember it clearly because I thought it was weird that the pain seemed to be beating in a sort of rhythm – like it was playing the drums. Well I went to tell my mother about it and innocently said, 'Mammy, I've a pain in my hole' – and stuck my finger in my ear to demonstrate. It was only in later years that I understood why she suddenly choked on her tea and left the room in tears. But it's the one story that my mother still loves to tell.

'So what time is Kerry arriving then?' asks Fiona, spreading all sorts of colouring stuff over my lovely glass coffee table. 'I thought I'd be the last one here.'

'Actually, she should be here any time now,' I say, glancing at the clock and realising it's already gone seven.

'I think I hear someone coming now,' says Zahra. 'Sounds like a car has just pulled up outside.'

'Oooh, I'm going to have a peep out the front room window,' says Fiona, hotfooting it into the kitchen. Well, she's certainly not shy. It's funny, I was sure it would be Zahra who'd be the most forward and chatty out of everyone.

'Well this is a coincidence,' she shouts from her position at the window. 'Looks like I'm not the only one who's brought company!'

Oh, sweet Jesus. What now? Well Kerry doesn't have any kids so maybe she's brought a boyfriend, her mother, a patient from the hospital? Honestly, I don't think anything would surprise me at this stage. I head out to answer the door but Fiona has got there first.

'Ah, Kerry, it's brilliant to see you,' she gushes, flinging the door open and throwing her arms around the surprised visitor.

'And who's this handsome man with you?' she continues. 'Well you're certainly a dark horse, aren't you?'

I have to stifle a giggle at the scene as my mother and a stunned-looking Harry stand speechless on the doorstep. 'Fiona, this is my mother and her ... eh ... her partner, Harry.'

'What? Oh, I'm so sorry,' Fiona says, giggling. 'I just assumed ... but nice to meet you anyway.'

'And you too ... em ... ?'

'This is Fiona, Mam. I wasn't expecting you over tonight. There's nothing wrong, is there?' I'm feckin' raging at my mother. I know she was great last night with helping me out and all that but she knows I'm having a night with the girls tonight.

'Nothing wrong at all, love. We were just passing, so we

thought we'd drop in and say hello. So Fiona, you're the mammy from Galway, right?'

Wow! I'm impressed. I told Mam about each of the girls last week, but I thought she wasn't listening to me. I think I may have even got into a bit of a strop with her because I thought she was trying to watch *Corrie* over my shoulder as I was speaking!

'Well let's not stand here in the hall all night,' I say, remembering I have another guest in the sitting room. God, Zahra really is very quiet – if the roles were reversed, I'd say Fiona would be out here like a bullet to see what was going on.

'Zahra, this is my mother and her ... her ... Harry,' I say. Zahra jumps out of her seat as we all bundle into the sitting room.

'Oh, what a lovely surprise. It's good to meet you Mrs Breslin,' she says, without a trace of a stutter. Jesus, listen to me – in the past few hours I've become the stutter police! I've got to stop analysing everything she says, or I'll end up driving myself insane. But why did she stutter when meeting me and not when meeting Mam? Is my mother actually making her feel more at ease than I did?

'And it's lovely to meet you too, love,' says my mother, shaking her hand. 'And who's this little man then?' Ryan is still colouring, oblivious to all going on around him.

'This is Ryan, my son,' says Fiona

'Well isn't he gorgeous,' says Mam, not showing the slightest bit of surprise that a child has been added to the mix. 'And look at the gorgeous pictures he's drawing.' She tousles the hair on the top of his head. 'You're a right little artist, aren't you?'

'I drawed a damlation,' he says, holding up his page for all to see. It looks more like a car to me, but I suppose he is only four.

'So I see,' Mam says, crouching down on her hunkers to have a better look. It occurs to me that this is not a familiar sight. I don't ever remember my mother drawing pictures with me or playing anything at all, for that matter. It's like she's changing beyond recognition – but in a good way. I suppose that's down to Harry.

'I didn't realise you were bringing him along,' says Mam, turning to Fiona as she pulls herself back onto her feet.

'I didn't know myself until the last minute,' says Fiona. 'My husband had to go away on business for a few days and I couldn't get a babysitter.'

'Well he's a little dote,' says my mother, taking off her coat and flinging it on the arm of the sofa. 'It'll be nice to have a little one around the house for a bit, won't it, Jenny?'

I'm not listening. I'm rooted to the spot and can't decide whether to laugh out loud or run away screaming. Mam is wearing the very same multicoloured top as Zahra, with a pair of psychedelic pink leggings. Jesus, she even has matching pink dolly shoes. Standing beside Zahra, it looks as though they've been separated at birth – even their false tans have the same orangeness! I half expect them to burst into 'Oompa Loompa Doompadee doo'!

'Ahahaha, look at you two,' laughs Fiona, startling me out of my trance. 'Did you come as a seventies pop band?'

Jesus, she really doesn't think twice about speaking up, does she? But I couldn't have put it better myself.

'Well she's obviously got great taste,' says my mam, laughing along with Fiona. 'What's life without a bit of colour – isn't that right, Zahra?'

'That's true,' says Zahra, laughing too, but looking pretty uncomfortable.

'Well I think you both look lovely,' says Harry. Poor Harry. I don't know why my mother dragged him along here to a house full of women. He's shifting from foot to foot and I'd say he can't wait to get out of here.

'Do you want a glass of wine, Mam?' I ask, resigned to the fact that they're here and there's nothing I can do about it.

'Ah, no, love, not at all. We're not staying long. I just wanted to meet the girls. Where's the other one – the nurse?'

'Actually, I thought Kerry would be well here by now. I should really check Twitter and see if she's been on. I hope nothing's happened.'

'I'm just checking now,' says Zahra, tapping away at her BlackBerry. 'Nope, not a word from her since last night. I'll send a tweet and see if we get anything back.'

'So what are you going to do with Ryan while you're out and about these next few days?' asks my mother suddenly. 'What about Keith Barry's show tomorrow night?'

I can see this unfolding in front of my eyes. No sooner had my mother got the words out of her mouth than Fiona's eyes were out on stalks. I know exactly what her words will be before she says anything. Still, I'm quite interested to watch.

'Well,' says Fiona, slowly. 'There'll have to be one of us at home with him all the time unless we take him with us. But we can't take him tomorrow night so one of us will have to miss out – it seems such a shame!'

One of us! Bloody cheek!

'Well, why don't I come over tomorrow night to look after the little pet,' says my mother. 'Sure me and Harry will only be sitting at home watching *One Born Every Minute* anyway, so we may as well do it here!'

Jesus, *One Born Every Minute*? Will the real Eileen Breslin please stand up? The mother I know hates any soppy baby programmes like that, preferring anything that makes her howl with laughter.

'Oh, Mrs Breslin, Would you really? I hope you don't think I was hinting or anything – I never would have expected you to offer to do that.'

Liar!

'It's no problem, love. Sure I love kids. I can't wait to have some grandchildren to spoil rotten!'

She can't? That's the first I've heard of it. And she loves kids? I must be in the twilight zone!

'Mummy, mummy, I found a toy but I don't know what to do with it.' Jesus, he's back upstairs again. Nobody seemed to have noticed he'd disappeared from the room.

'Well bring it down and we'll take a look,' shouts Fiona.

But hold on, I don't have any toys in the house – not one. I don't even have friends who visit with kids, so there's nothing that could have been left behind. So what the hell has he got? With that, Ryan bursts in the door, clutching his precious toy.

'See, Mummy? I found it in a drawer with socks and things. Can you show me what to do with it?'

The faces in the room are a mixture of shock and amusement, and I just want to die as the four-year-old child holds my vibrator aloft. Shit!

CHAPTER 17

Thursday

I open a very begrudging eye and glance at the clock. Jesus, it's only six o' clock and there's already noise downstairs. Much as I want to bury myself back down into the comfort of my feather duvet, I don't feel right leaving one of my guests to fend for themselves. I'm guessing Fiona is the one clashing around, because I think Ryan has been awake for a while. I tried to close my ears to his whinging, but it's a bit like a clock ticking. The more I tried to blot it out, the louder it seemed to get.

And what about him appearing in the sitting room last night with my vibrator. Oh, God. I've never before really and truly wanted the ground to open up and swallow me. The look on Harry's face – how will I ever look him in the eye again? My mother and Fiona seemed to think it was quite funny, but poor Zahra just looked embarrassed. Although I'm not entirely sure her embarrassment was due to the nature of the toy or the fact she didn't know what it was!

But despite wanting to actually kill the little brat at that point, I felt quite sorry for him when he fell asleep with his head on the coffee table. He must have been exhausted from the journey.

I just made up a little bed on the floor beside Fiona's in the spare room and she carried him up.

Fair play to Zahra, though, she didn't flinch at all when she realised she'd have to share a room with them. But it's as though she doesn't really have an opinion about anything – she just goes with the flow and seems grateful for everything. God, it's hard to believe that I was actually nervous about meeting her. But people say that about those in the public eye, don't they? Sometimes they're nothing like what you expect. I know Zahra isn't exactly in the public eye but she certainly is *nothing* like what I expected.

And what about Mam coming up trumps again last night? I was tempted to challenge her when she said she loved kids, but, to be honest, if she's offering to babysit, I'm not going to say anything that will make her change her mind. All I can say is, thank God she's past the age where I have to worry about *her* getting pregnant! With her newfound love of little people, she could have been making an announcement if she was a few years younger. Oh the embarrassment – Harry as my stepdad and a baby sister or brother who's young enough to be my own child.

Judging by the amount of banging of cupboard doors, I assume Fiona is looking for the breakfast things. Shit. I'd really love another couple of hours sleep, but I'd better get down there. I manage to drag myself out of the bed and smooth out the wrinkles on my flannelette pyjamas. I keep meaning to buy some nice stuff to wear in bed to replace my grubby old stuff, but why bother? I go for comfort rather than fashion in the bedroom department and, anyway, grubby and old feels safe and familiar. Maybe I'll treat myself if I ever find a man to share my bedroom with.

Rubbing my eyes, I lift up the corner of my wooden blinds to check, as I have been doing for the past few weeks, for the promised snow. Nope! Not a single fluffy drop. Pity. It might have kept Ryan occupied for a while, giving us adults time to chat. One of my fondest memories of my childhood is me and Dad building snowmen on the green beside our house. We'd usually get fed up halfway through and it would end up in a snowball fight.

Maybe Ryan will go for a nap after his breakfast and we can all get back to sleep for a while. I search my brain to remember what Sally's kids do during the day. I know when they were babies they definitely slept a number of times each day but I'm not too sure if a four-year-old needs as much sleep. Maybe I can bribe him with a few sweets or something – it worked for Sally's kids. And there's only one of him, so I'm sure I can handle him.

Throwing on my warm robe and fluffy grey slippers, I pad quietly down the stairs. 'Morning,' says Fiona, yawning. 'Hope we weren't too noisy.' Jesus, what a mess! Just about every press is open and most of the contents are out on the worktops and the table. Ryan is sitting eating a very large bowl of what looks like Weetabix but there's definitely something chocolaty in there too as the brown milk is splashing all over the table.

'Eh ... morning,' I say, trying not to flinch at the mess. 'How are the two of you this morning then? Did you sleep well?' There's no point in me making her feel embarrassed by saying I've been awake listening to Ryan most of the night. Although I'm not sure anything would make this girl embarrassed.

'We're okay, thanks. But we didn't have the best night. Ryan was uncomfortable on the floor so he wanted to get in the bed beside me. But trouble was, the bed is so small that he kept falling out!'

'Oh, sorry about that. I had to get small beds so that two would fit in that room.' Why on earth am I apologising for the furniture in my own house? It's not as if she's paying for her stay or anything. And, on top of that, the child wasn't even invited so she should be grateful for any sort of bed.

'And I hope you don't mind that we've helped ourselves,' she continues. 'It's just that Ryan needs to eat as soon as he wakes up.'

It strikes me that what Ryan *needs* is a good kick up the arse! 'Not at all,' I say. 'You seem to have … em … found everything anyway.' I want to cry at the sight of my newly cleaned kitchen. It's back to a worse state than it was before, if that's possible.

'Mummy, I *need* some more chocolate sauce on my Weetabix.'

For fuck's sake! Chocolate sauce on Weetabix? Surely this woman can't be serious. Aren't mothers supposed to be concerned about feeding their children proper food? Sally would have a heart attack if she saw this. Although she did once admit to bribing Sinead with a sweet for every forkful of vegetables she ate. But having said that, she didn't actually mix the sweets in with the veggies!

'What's he like?' says Fiona, liberally squirting more chocolate sauce over his soggy Weetabix. 'It's a constant battle to get anything healthy into him. Sometimes the only way I can make him eat good stuff is to mask it with something sweet!'

Okay, well maybe I was a bit harsh in judging her. After all, it must be difficult to bring up a kid. The thought of it scares me to death. I want to have a family – I really do – but I just don't know if I have what it takes. Sure I haven't even found myself a man yet. Unless you count Tom but I can't see myself making babies with him. Oh God, I've just had a flash of me and Tom making love under the watchful eye of his mother! Eeek!

'So I'll just get him some toast and plonk him in front of the telly and we can have a good chat before Zahra wakes up.' Fiona is still talking and my head is pounding. I'd really prefer to go back up to bed, but I can't really say that. I'd better make a cuppa to wake myself up. I suppose it will be nice to have a proper chat with her. After all, that's what this tweet-up was supposed to be about – getting to know each other. Oh, yes, that and having some fun. But I'm struggling to figure out how fun is going to fit into this picture. Still, we've just got to make the best of it. At least Mam is babysitting tonight so we can have a good old girls' night out.

I make a pot of tea and head into the sitting room to switch on the telly for Ryan. His mother doesn't try to quieten his cries of 'this is a stinky house' and 'that lady is weird' and I try to resist the urge to slap him one.

Five minutes later, I'm sitting at the kitchen table with Fiona, Ryan safely tucked up on the sofa watching *Thomas the Tank Engine*. I had to bite my tongue when Fiona settled him with a plate of buttery toast and wrapped my new lime-green throw around him!

'I wonder what's happened to Kerry,' she says, taking a big gulp of her tea. 'She's been working so hard over the past few weeks and seemed so up for a good weekend.'

'I don't know,' I sigh. 'Maybe she'll turn up today. I can't believe we never bothered sharing phone numbers or anything. I wish she'd tweet us or something.'

'I'll check in a minute. But it must have been after one when we were getting to bed last night and I checked my phone just before. Whatever's happened, I hope she's okay.'

'Oh, God, now you have me worried,' I say, imagining all sorts of horrific scenarios. 'Do you think she might have had an accident or something?'

'It's possible,' says Fiona. 'Sure if she changed her mind or if something had come up, I'm sure she would have tweeted us.'

This weekend is really going down the toilet fast. First Zahra arrives and turns out to be quiet and nervous instead of the self-assured, successful diva I was expecting. Then Fiona comes with her kid and now it looks as though Kerry isn't coming at all. Furthermore, it looks as though she could be lying in a ditch somewhere or in hospital unconscious after an accident. Or worse still – maybe she's dead! Oh, God, the poor girl – and to think we were only tweeting with her yesterday.

'Jenny ... Jenny, are you okay?'

'Oh ... em ... yeah, sorry. I'm fine. Was just off in a daydream there.'

'So I was just saying,' she continues, 'your picture on Twitter doesn't do you justice at all. Was it taken long ago?'

'A few years – maybe two or three.' Or seven! I'm trying to take in what she's saying. I put up that picture because I looked so much nicer back then, but if I understand her right, she seems to think I look better now.

'Ah, so your piercings are only recent then. I love them, they're fab. You're so lucky, you know.'

'Lucky? Me? Why do you say that?' Zahra said much the same thing last night. I'm intrigued why these people would think *I'm* lucky when they both have lives that are so much more interesting and full.

'Sure look at you – you have it all sussed,' she says, sitting back into her chair and giving me an admiring look. 'You have a great job in the bank, your own house and car, you're beautiful and I bet you have your pick of men.'

'Em ... thanks, but my life is certainly far from ideal. To be honest, it's pretty lonely. I'd love to have what you have – a loving husband and an adorable child.' See, I'm back with the 'adorable kid' thing. But it seems appropriate in this scenario – even if it's not true!

'Well, to be honest, I don't have ... I'm not ... '

'Mummy, I want some more toast and I want chocolate spread,' shouts Ryan from the sitting room. 'This butter is disgusting!'

'Okay, love,' she says, immediately jumping up to pop some more bread in the toaster. 'Jenny, would you just go and take a peep in at him while I get this ready? Just to make sure he's not up to any devilment.'

I do as I'm told and stick my head around the door of the sitting room. The little brat is using my precious throw to wipe the butter off his toast and half of it is on the floor. I don't know how much more of this I can take. Sally's kids are angels in comparison to this one.

'You might want to get him to sit at the coffee table to have that toast,' I say, tartly, as Fiona heads in with a fresh batch. 'It's just he doesn't seem to be managing it too well, balancing it like that on his lap.'

I want to scream 'clean the fucking mess up' but I haven't sunk to the all-time low of swearing at a child – yet.

'Ah, he'll be grand,' she says, handing him the full plate. He doesn't say thanks or even move his eyes from the telly.

'So what was that you were saying earlier?' I ask, as we head back into the kitchen.

'About what?' she asks, filling the kettle again.

'We were talking about our lives and you started to say something about yours.'

'Oh ... eh ... it was nothing.' She looks agitated. 'I was just saying that it ... em ... that it's hard being married sometimes too.'

'I'm sure it is,' I say. 'But he seems to love you so much. I get so jealous when I see you tweet about him bringing home flowers and taking Ryan off so you can get some sleep. It must be brilliant to have somebody to take care of you.'

'Yes, you're right,' she says, eyes looking off into the distance. 'There's nothing better than knowing you're loved.'

Am I imagining it or are her eyes getting a little misty? Why on earth would she be tearful? Could it be she misses her husband already? Jesus! That would be some powerful love! Or maybe she's raging at him for choosing business before her this weekend.

'Good morning. How come you're all up so early?' Zahra's voice breaks into my thoughts and I turn to see her standing at the door, a vision in her satin, multicoloured, striped pyjamas.

'Good morning, Zahra,' I say, pulling another cup out of the press. 'Will you have some tea or would you prefer coffee?'

'Tea is fine, thanks, Jenny. But sit down, I'll make it myself.'

'Sure it's in the pot. Sit down and I'll just pour it. Bread's in the bin on the counter if you want to make yourself some toast.'

'Did you manage to get any sleep at all?' asks Fiona. 'Sorry my little monkey was so noisy.'

'He was fine,' said Zahra. 'I didn't hear a thing.' Her red-rimmed eyes say differently.

'We were just talking about how we envy each other's lives,' says Fiona, ready to quiz Zahra just like she did me. 'Yours must be so exciting. Do you just *love* your job?'

'Well … em … yes, I do,' she says, blushing. 'I feel very lucky to have it. It's a lot of fun all right.'

'And do you think you could introduce us to some of your celebrity friends if we go over for a visit some time?' asks Fiona. I'm curious to hear the answer. I wanted to ask that too, but I'm not quite as brave or blunt as Fiona.

'I don't know about that,' she says. 'We'll have to wait and see.' There she goes putting us off again. She did the same to me yesterday a couple of times. If I had a job and a life like hers, I'd be dying to show off. There's something just not right. I can't quite put my finger on it, but something just doesn't add up.

'So has anyone checked Twitter again to see if Kerry has tweeted?' asks Zahra, changing the subject. 'I hope she comes today.'

'Me too,' I agree. 'I haven't checked yet, so let's have a look.' I touch the Twitter icon on my phone and immediately see the message in my inbox.

@kerrydhunt Really sorry I can't make it, Jenny. Problem at hospital and have to work all week. Sorry.

'Well that's that then,' I say, throwing my phone down heavily on the table and relaying the message to the girls. 'I can't believe Kerry isn't coming after all.'

'Well at least she's okay,' says Fiona. 'Thank God nothing bad has happened.'

I think if something had happened to her, I couldn't be more disappointed than I feel now. I honestly thought that Kerry's arrival would help me make sense of this car crash of a tweet-up. I was imagining us drinking wine downstairs long after the others had gone to bed. We'd have laughed at how ridiculous Zahra looks in her seventies clothes and moan about how Fiona doesn't seem to have any control over her son. It's funny how even though we haven't met that I know she'd be on my wavelength. But now I'm stuck with these two and I just want the whole thing to be over.

'So it's just the three of us then,' says Zahra, smiling faintly.

'And Ryan,' adds Fiona. 'We can't forget about him.'

'Mummyyyyyyyyy.'

More's the pity!

CHAPTER 18

'Mummmmmmyyyyy!' I want to go to McDonald's *now*!'

I'm about to strangle the little brat. We're in Blanchardstown shopping centre and we've had nothing but moans and groans from him since we got here.

When we were having our breakfast, we decided that a sight-seeing day may not be the best idea with a four-year-old in tow. I had to resist the urge to shout 'yyyyyessssss!', because it was the one thing about the girls' visit that I was dreading. Well, when I say 'the one thing' of course that was back in the days when I was oblivious to all the other bad stuff that was about to befall me.

We decided that a bit of shopping would be the best way to go because we could bribe Ryan with the promise of McDonald's if he behaved. I'm coming to the conclusion now that Ryan just doesn't do bribes. Sure why would he need to when he can shout loud enough and his mother will give him anything he wants? Now, if he was mine…! Anyway, the other positive thing is that the girls agreed that the city centre mightn't be the best place to go with a child so we decided on the shopping centre.

'Shhhh now, Ryan,' says Fiona, half-heartedly. 'Remember I said the mummies want to do a bit of shopping and then we'll all go to McDonald's?' The 'mummies'? Is that meant to be a term of endearment or something? I've never been called a mummy before. Surely that sort of talk would just confuse a child.

'Sorry about the mummy thing,' whispers Fiona. 'It's just that in his little head, there are mummies, daddies and children – nobody else exists.'

Charming!

'Oooh, Fiona, look in here,' says Zahra, leading the way into a very colourful children's clothes shop. 'This stuff would be gorgeous on Ryan, with his black hair and everything.'

'I ... em ... I'm not sure I really like bright colours on a boy,' says Fiona, reluctantly following Zahra and myself into the shop. 'It's just that Ryan likes his tracksuits – they're so much more comfy.'

'Oh but look at this,' gushes Zahra, holding up a lime green tracksuit with dark blue detail. 'I could just imagine him in that.'

Now I've never been much of a fashion queen, and I've certainly never been shopping for children's clothes before, but I have to admit, the stuff in here is gorgeous. Of course the pictures of the perfect model children wearing the clothes help too. I can imagine myself with a little girl. I wouldn't put a frill anywhere near her. Instead, I'd dress her in the cutest jeans and leggings. Maybe for special occasions she'd wear a dress, but not one of those flouncy ones – she'd be comfortable in a nice wool one with soft tights to match. Jesus! Where did all that come from? The furthest thing from my mind at the moment is having kids. Especially when I can see first hand the trouble that comes with them.

'Honestly, Zahra,' says Fiona. 'He really doesn't need any of this stuff. It would be just a waste of money because he'd never wear it.'

'Okay,' sighs Zahra. 'It's up to you.'

'Are we finished now, Mummy?' asks Ryan, turning his pleading eyes to his mother. 'I'm staaaaaaaaarving.'

'I suppose we'd better go and get him something to eat,' says Fiona. I suspect she's glad to get Zahra away from the shops for a while.

'It's a little early for McDonald's, don't you think?' I say, wondering how anyone could stomach fast food at eleven o'clock.

'You promised, Mummy,' says a distraught Ryan, giving me the evil eye. 'She can go somewhere else.'

I'm tempted, but it would probably be a bit rude.

'Ryan,' says Fiona, in a half-soaked voice. God, I wish she'd be firmer with him. 'Don't be rude. Jenny has been very good to let us come and stay with her.'

'Don't want to stay in that boring house. I want to go home.'

'Look,' I say, in an attempt to save the situation. 'Why don't we just go to McDonald's and Ryan can get a burger or something and if we don't feel like eating, we can just have a cup of coffee. Maybe we'll stop for something else in a while.' At a more reasonable time, I wanted to add, but there's no point in making the situation any worse.

'Sounds like a great idea,' says Zahra, who'd been looking very uncomfortable during the exchange.

'Right, so,' says Fiona. 'You lead the way, Jenny. We're the blow-ins.'

Phew, disaster averted for now. I waste no time in getting us all through the crowds to the little cluster of fast food restaurants.

'It's manic in here, isn't it?' says Zahra, as we join the hundreds of shoppers stopping for a quick bite. 'We'll never get a seat.'

'Look – over here,' says Fiona, taking Ryan's hand and claiming seats that a few teenagers are just leaving. 'I'll grab these and tell you my order. I'll fix up with you when you come back.'

'Grand,' I say, happy to be rid of Ryan while I'm standing in the queue. 'So what are you both having?'

'Ryan will have a Happy Meal with nuggets and Coke and I'll have a large Big Mac meal with Coke too please.'

My stomach is churning at the very thought of it – and at this time of the morning too. 'I'll get yours too, Zahra,' I say. 'Just tell me what you want and go on over and sit with Fiona.'

'That's okay, thanks,' she says, glancing over at the table where Ryan seems to be playing some sort of game with the sachets of salt. 'I'm not sure what I want yet.'

I'm sure what she wants is not to have to spend a minute more than necessary in the company of the child from hell. And who can blame her? We're all bending over backwards to be nice to him but I'm beginning to wonder why I'm bothering. Fiona is clearly struggling with motherhood and her child is boss. I can't help wondering what her husband thinks, or if he plays a role in the discipline in the house.

Five minutes later, we're sitting at the salt-covered table – Zahra and I with coffee and apple pie and Fiona and Ryan with the full works. I noticed that Fiona wasn't putting her hand in her pocket to reimburse me when I got back with the food. Still, I'm sure she's just distracted with Ryan jumping all over the place. She'll probably give me the money later.

'I swear that guy over there is watching us,' whispers Fiona, nodding towards a guy sitting on his own reading the newspaper. 'When I caught his eye, he raised the paper up so I couldn't see his face.'

'Well why wouldn't he be looking?' I say, giggling. 'Three gorgeous girls like us sitting right across from him!'

'He's quite handsome too,' whispers Zahra, blushing. 'The bit I can see of him anyway!'

'I want ice-cream now, Mummy,' says Ryan, dipping his last nugget into the salt on the table and stuffing it into his mouth.

Gosh, for such a small little thing, he can certainly pack plenty away!

'Maybe we'll just have another look around and come back for ice-cream later,' suggests Fiona, picking bits of chewed nuggets off the floor and sweeping the mess of salt with her hand onto a serviette.

'Noooooo! I want it *now*!'

'Okay, okay! You wouldn't just get him a Smartie McFlurry, would you?' she says, turning to Zahra. 'I just want to clear this table up before they throw us out!'

'Sure,' says Zahra, jumping up. 'Anything for anyone else?'

'No, I'm done here,' I say. 'Maybe we'll just get out of here and Ryan can eat his ice-cream as we walk.' I notice that man is looking over here again. I can't see much more than the top of his head and his eyes but from what I can see, Zahra is right. He *is* handsome. His soft chestnut hair is swept back off his face in a sort of Hugh Grantish style. I can't help wondering if he has the Hugh Grant cheeky grin. Jesus, listen to me! What am I like – giving the eye to a fella in McDonald's?

It's only gone half eleven when we head back to the shops and I can't help thinking it's going to be a bloody long day. Now I understand why Sally doesn't go shopping any more. Given the choice, I think I'd poke my eyes out rather than put myself through shopping with a small child. Especially one like Ryan.

Thank God for Mam stepping in to babysit tonight. Maybe we'll get her to come over early, then we can nip out for a bite to eat before the show. Yes, that's what we'll do. We can give Ryan some pasta or a pizza and we'll get out of there at tea-time. The day is starting to look a lot more appealing.

'Right,' I say, cheerily. 'Where to next?'

'Let's go in there,' says Zahra, spotting a huge Penneys across from the fast food restaurants. 'I love all their stuff.'

'Oh, I thought you'd be designer all the way,' says Fiona. 'Sure with all your celebrity friends, surely you get freebies all the time. And didn't you tweet us once that you have a wardrobe full of designer gear?'

Is it my imagination or does she sound bitter? It wasn't said in a nice lucky-you sort of way but rather a damn-you-for-being-so-lucky sort of way!

'Well, I d … d … d … do have a l … l … l … l … lot of designer clothes,' Zahra says, blushing furiously. 'But, I l … l … l … l … like to team them up with ch … ch … ch … ch … cheap and cheerful jewellery.'

'Ah, Jesus, don't start that stuttering again. Sure I'm only having a joke with you,' says Fiona, nudging her playfully. 'Come on, let's go in. Sure I love the stuff in here myself.'

Poor Zahra looks mortified. I'm not sure whether it's because she realised she'd been bragging about her designer stuff or because her stutter has come back. Fiona really is a bit of a loose cannon. The insults just seem to trip off her lips and the funny thing about it is that she seems totally oblivious to it. She comes across as being so shy on Twitter – it's as though Zahra and her could have switched personalities!

'Can we go and look at the toys now, Mummy?' asks a bored-looking Ryan, after we've spent twenty minutes picking up bits and bobs from the accessories department. Zahra has a basket full of colourful bracelets and scarves and we haven't even hit the clothes yet.

'Ah, Ryan, stop your moaning, will you?' says Fiona, looking tired and a bit fed up. 'We'll go and look at the toys when the mummies are finished looking in here.'

'Why don't you bring him to the toy shop while we finish up here?' I say, seizing the opportunity to get him out of my hair for a while. 'That is unless you're looking to buy anything yourself?'

'No, I'm not buying today,' she says, glumly. 'I've had so many bills lately that clothes shopping has to be last on the list, I'm afraid. But I'm happy to tag along with you and just look at the stuff.'

So that explains the bitter reaction to Zahra and her designer gear. She must be feeling the pinch at the moment. Everybody is these days, but it must be so much harder with an extra person to feed and clothe. But maybe she should use her money more wisely. She didn't seem to have a problem splashing out on meals in McDonald's today and ... oh hang on ... she didn't splash out at all! I bought the meal and Zahra bought the ice-cream. Something tells me we won't see that money again. It's a bit of a cheek really, even if she is a bit broke at the moment.

'But Mummmmmmmyyyyy – I want to go now!' says Ryan, his voice rising to hysterical proportions. 'I *don't* want to stay in this smelly shop!'

Even though I'm not sure about Fiona's approach to parenting, I feel sorry for her. It can't be easy trying to handle a child like that twenty-four hours a day.

'Ryan,' I say, in the best Mammy voice I can muster. 'Your mummy just wants to have a little time to do her stuff and then we'll all go and look at toys with you. I think that's a good deal, don't you?'

There, he's quietened down now. He just needs a bit of proper parenting. I'm sure Fiona is a good mother, but she needs to stop giving in to his demands and try to teach him some manners. I'm quite surprised at how good I am at... 'Ouuuuuuuuuch!' The feckin' little monkey has kicked me hard, straight in my right shin. Oh the agony!

'Ah, Ryan, don't be doing that,' says Fiona, far too softly for my liking. When I manage to straighten myself up, I'll show her how it should be said. Little brat!

'She was making you not go with me to the toy shop,' he says, defiantly, as if that justifies half killing me. 'She's mean.'

'Are you all right,' says Zahra, worriedly. 'Do you want me to get someone ... get you some water or something?'

'No, no, I'm okay,' I say, although the pain is searing through my leg.

'Say sorry to Jenny, Ryan,' says Fiona.

'Will not. She's a bitch!'

I gasp at that. And I can see Zahra has visibly paled. Surely, Fiona won't let him away with saying something like that.

'No she's not, Ryan. Now come on. Let's get you to that toy shop before you cause any more trouble.'

Is she for real?

'Sorry girls,' she continues. 'I'll just bring him to have a look at the toys – it might quieten him down. I'll see you back here at the front door in twenty minutes.'

I'm completely speechless as I watch her walk away with Ryan, who has a look of smug satisfaction on his face. What a lovely lesson on parenting – kick the woman who's offered you shelter, bought you food and be rewarded with a trip to the toy shop! She must be very proud! Rubbing my aching leg, I decide to use the Ryan-free opportunity to have a browse around with Zahra and maybe pick up a few more bits. I think we'll be done with shopping when they come back, though I don't think I can put up with much more of this.

I wish Kerry was here. Things would be a lot more bearable if I had her to bitch to about the others. Damn that job of hers for keeping her away from us this week. I wonder if she is working today or tonight. Zahra seems happy, drowning in a sea of multicoloured scarves, so I'll just take a peep at Twitter while I have the chance. I think I'll go straight to DM though – because what I want to say should certainly not be read by the general tweeters.

@JennyB Hi, Kerry. Are you around? Could really do with a chat.

Feck! No response. I guess she's working – either that or sleeping off the night shift. I'll just leave her a message and hope maybe we might catch up later during a quiet moment – if I ever get one!

@JennyB I can't wait to have a bit of a goss with you. The goings on here are crazy. DM me back later.

Zahra's heading over my direction so I slip my phone back in my bag and try not to look guilty about having a moan to Kerry. Of course she'll have no idea that I did, but my face has a habit of telling tales on me.

'I think I'm done here, Jenny,' she says, balancing two full baskets of colourful bits and pieces. 'I just need to pay for this lot and I'm ready to go.'

'Great,' I say, marvelling at the amount of stuff she's managed to pick up in such a short time. 'Let's go and pay so. Hopefully, Fiona will be ready by then.'

Twenty minutes later, we're at the front door of Penneys. I'm feeling a little bit more relaxed after treating myself to some new leggings and two pairs of boots. But there's no sign of Fiona and the child from hell. I'd like to think she's on her way back to Galway, but since all her stuff is back at my house and she doesn't have a key, it's not very likely!

'Here she comes,' says Zahra, snapping me out of my reverie. 'And it looks like Ryan is a bit happier, thank God.'

'Well why wouldn't he be? Would you look at the number of bags he's got. Five minutes ago, she couldn't afford to look at anything in Penneys and all of a sudden she has the money to buy him half the toy shop!' It's none of my business really but it bugs me.

'Hi, girls,' says Fiona, looking much more relaxed than she was half an hour ago. 'God, that shop is great value altogether. Look at all the stuff I got for Ryan.'

She rummages through Ryan's goodie bags and produces cars and soldiers, board games and drawing stuff. Even if the shop is cheap, the sheer volume of stuff she bought must have added up to a tidy sum.

'Lovely,' I say, far more enthusiastically than I feel. 'I was thinking, unless you girls want to do anything else, maybe we'll just head home. We can relax for a bit before heading into town. What do you think?'

'Oh that suits me fine,' says Fiona. 'I think this fella has had enough and at least the toys will keep him quiet while we have a chat.'

'Yep, that's good for me too,' says Zahra. She looks just as relieved as I am. I'm guessing she has the same feelings as me when it comes to Fiona and her less-than-adorable son.

'Can I open my toys, Mummy?' asks Ryan, his head already in the bag.

'Wait till we're in the car, love,' says Fiona. 'You'll only lose bits if you open them here.'

'But I want to open one *now*,' he says, stopping dead and shaking off Fiona's hand.

'I said no, sweetheart,' says Fiona, wearily. 'Now, come on. The sooner we get out of here, the sooner we'll be home.'

I consider intervening and offering him a sweet from the bottom of my handbag but my shin is still sore. I think I'll let Fiona deal with this one herself. The little brat is now sitting on the floor, refusing to move.

'Ryan! I'm warning you!' Fiona is beginning to get really cross now and I feel like a spare tool just standing by.

'I'm opening them,' he says, smiling smugly. 'And you're not going to stop me.'

Zahra has obviously had enough and approaches Ryan, holding out her hand. 'Come on, Ryan,' she says. 'Don't be ... arghh-hhhh!'

He's ripped open a packet of marbles, sending them scattering all over the floor and causing poor Zahra to slip on one. I've never seen anything like it! Honestly, her feet just fly up in the air and she lands with a thud on her back! Everyone is stunned for a moment. You know when you're watching one of those comedy sketch shows where they're trying to emphasise something that's really hilarious and they play it in slow motion? Well, this is just like that. It feels as though the moment was taken from one of those shows and it would be hilarious except for the fact that Zahra is lying stunned on the floor.

'Jesus, Zahra! Are you all right?' I'm first to break the silence and get down on my knees beside her. 'Zahra, Zahra, can you hear me?'

'Mummy I want to go home now,' wails Ryan.

'Shhhh, Ryan. Can't you see Zahra is hurt,' says Fiona, at least having the grace to look embarrassed.

'Will I call an ambulance?' comes a shout from a passer-by, and I realise a crowd has started to form.

'No, no, there's no need,' mutters Zahra. 'I'm okay. I just got a fright.'

'Oh, thank God,' says Fiona, holding out her hand to help her up.

'No, don't get up, Zahra,' I say. 'Just in case you've broken your back or something. They say you shouldn't move after you've had an accident.'

'I'm fine,' she says, sitting up and rubbing her head. 'It's not my back – I just bumped my head. Come on, let's get out of here.'

This time, Ryan doesn't object! He's gone quiet and has his head down. Fiona is quiet too. I'd say she's mortified that he caused such a fuss and was almost the cause of a very bad accident.

After helping Zahra to her feet, we head out towards the exit. What a day it's been already, and it's still only lunch-time. I'll be glad to be back home with a nice cup of tea. Just as we get to the door, a man pulls it open, allowing us to go through first. As a blast of cold air hits us, I turn to thank him. It's the man from McDonald's. And, yes, he does have that Hugh Grant grin!

CHAPTER 19

Thank God for Zahra's fall! I know that sounds harsh but, honestly, it's the only thing that's shut Ryan up since he arrived. He's barely spoken a word since the incident and we're all enjoying the peace in the car.

'Where are we going?' asks Zahra, looking at me strangely.

'Em ... home – isn't that what we agreed?' Oh, God, please don't say she wants to go somewhere else. I don't think I could stand any more dramas. I just want to go home, have a nice cup of tea and put my feet up for a while.

'Oh,' says Zahra. 'Lovely.'

Phew! Yes, only ten more minutes and I'll have my feet tucked up underneath me on the sofa. Home never seemed so enticing.

'Ah would you look at my little man?' whispers Fiona. 'God love him, he's conked out.'

'He must have worn himself out with all his ... eh ... all his activities.' Jesus, I nearly said tantrums there, but I really don't want to start an argument with Fiona. I fear that if I started, I wouldn't stop. These girls are here until Saturday and I couldn't stand having an atmosphere in the house. I think an adult-only night out is exactly what we all need at the moment, to give us a chance to get to know each other properly without the distraction of Ryan.

'Well, hopefully, he'll be tired enough to go to bed early for your mam tonight,' says Fiona. 'It's very good of her to step in and mind him like that.'

'Where are we going?' asks Zahra, rooting frantically in her bright yellow handbag.

'We're going to see Keith Barry tonight,' I say, wondering what on earth she's looking for in such a panic.

'Not tonight,' she says, still rooting. 'Now – where are we going now?'

'Ah, you're half-asleep yourself, I think,' laughs Fiona, sticking her head in between the two front seats. 'Sure, you only asked that a few minutes ago.'

'And what are you looking for in that bag of yours, Zahra,' I say, intrigued. She's only short of sticking her whole head in.

'My keys,' she says, panicking. 'I can't find my house keys. And there won't be anyone home until after six.'

Jesus! What the hell is up with her? What's she talking about? 'Zahra, are you okay?'

'Yes, yes, I'm fine. But the cat will be going insane looking for her dinner and where am I supposed to go if I can't get into the house?'

'What are you on?' laughs Fiona. 'Are you having a laugh or what?'

'Fiona,' I say, just as I pull Betsy into the driveway. 'I think we might have a problem.' It's the bump on her head. I'm sure of it. I read about something like this before. Or was it in a movie? Yes, that's it. It was on telly only a few months ago. This priest slipped and whacked his head off the holy water font in the church. There were people waiting for him to start hearing confessions and they came to his assistance. He insisted he was fine but when he opened his little hatch to the first person, instead of hearing her confession, he began to sing to her. It was hilarious, but I'm guessing something similar is happening to

Zahra. God, I hope she doesn't start singing!

I jump out of my seat and rush around to the passenger door. Opening it quickly, I bend over and release Zahra's seatbelt. 'Come on, let's get you inside.'

'But my keys – I can't find them.'

'Well, you can ... em ... come into my house while you're looking for them, okay?' Jesus, I don't know if I'm doing the right thing by playing along with her. Maybe I should be trying to get her to snap out of it.

'Okay,' she sighs, reluctantly stepping out of the car.

'God, that's mad, isn't it?' says Fiona, following us into the house. 'I'm just going to make the couch comfy for Ryan and lay him there for a while. I might get a bit of peace for an hour or so to have a cuppa and see what's going on with her ladyship!'

'Fine,' I say, giving Zahra a gentle push towards a chair in the kitchen. 'Zahra, do you know who I am?'

'Of course I do,' she says, plonking down heavily on the chair. 'Why are you asking that?'

'Who am I then?' I ask, feeling stupid but I need to know how bad she is.

'Jenny, of course,' she says, looking at me quizzically. 'And that's Fiona carrying Ryan into the sitting room.'

Phew! Thank God. Maybe the bump just stunned her temporarily. At least we won't be making a trip to A&E. Oh, God, the thought of going into that place makes me want to run and hide.

'But when are we going shopping?' she continues. 'Didn't we say we'd go to that shopping centre you were telling us about?'

Shit! I shouldn't have spoken too soon! 'Zahra, don't you remember us going shopping already today? Do you remember falling and banging your head? I think you might be a bit confused from the bump you got.'

'What do you mean? We've only just had breakfast,' she says, looking at me as though I'm the mad one.

'So what's the story, then?' says Fiona, appearing at the kitchen door. 'Ryan's still fast asleep. How are things here?'

'I think Zahra is concussed from her fall,' I whisper, watching her resume rooting in her bag. 'She's seems to be confused and thinks we haven't gone shopping yet.'

'God, really?' says Fiona. 'I'll feckin' kill Ryan.'

'Well let's just deal with Zahra first,' I say, although I'm glad she realises who's fault all this is. I'll kill Ryan myself if we end up having to spend hours on end at the hospital!

'Zahra, are you still looking for your keys?' I ask, frantically trying to decide whether to pop her in the car and take her to hospital or just pretend it isn't happening.

'What keys?' she asks, suddenly stopping what she's doing.

'Your house keys,' I say. 'You were just looking for them in the car.'

'Was I?' she asks, looking even more confused, if that's possible.

'Yes, so is that what you're looking for now?'

'Jenny, are you okay?' she asks. 'You're acting very weird.'

'Ahahaha she's having you on, Jenny,' laughs Fiona. 'She's been just playing with us this whole time. Nice one, Zahra.'

I'm not convinced. Zahra is now staring at Fiona strangely. Her eyes look glazed and sort of scary.

'Zahra, are you okay? Have you just been having us on about forgetting things?'

'Of course she has,' says Fiona, clicking her fingers in front of Zahra's face. 'She's trying not to blink now, look.'

'Zahra ... Zahra ... come on,' I say. 'If you're messing with us, can you stop now please? I'm beginning to get a bit freaked out.'

Her eyelids haven't flicked at all and she hasn't taken her eyes off Fiona. Even Fiona has shut up and is beginning to look a bit spooked by the whole situation.

'Zahra ... '

Finally, she comes out of her trance-like state and bends over to whisper to me. 'That girl,' she says, pointing to Fiona. 'Who is she and why does she look familiar?'

Shit!

★

'Thanks for this, Mam,' I say, opening the door to my mother. 'I wouldn't have felt comfortable taking Zahra over to the hospital on my own.'

'It's fine,' she says, taking off her lipstick-pink coat and throwing it over the banisters. 'So how bad is she then?'

'See for yourself,' I say, indicating into the kitchen.

'Zahra, do you remember my mam? You met her last night when she dropped in.'

'Of course I do,' she says, smiling brightly at my mother. 'Nice to see you again Mrs Breslin.'

'And you too, Zahra,' says Mam, pulling out a chair to sit down beside her. 'And it's Eileen, remember? Mrs Breslin makes me feel so old. Jenny tells me you're not feeling too good at the moment.'

'Jenny means well,' she says, 'but I'm absolutely fine. I'm bursting for the loo though. Be back in a minute.'

'Well I don't see much evidence of concussion there,' says Mam, watching Zahra hurry out the door. 'She seems all right to me.'

'Jenny's right, Mrs Breslin ... em ... Eileen,' says Fiona. 'She was very confused up to a few minutes ago. One minute she knew who I was, and the next she didn't.

'Well what do you want to do about the hospital? I'm quite happy to stay here with Ryan if you two want to go and get her checked anyway.'

'Let's just decide when she comes back from the loo,' I say, exhausted by the whole situation. 'I don't want to go and waste hours in there if it's something that will just pass.'

At that very moment, Zahra arrives back into the kitchen but stops dead when she sees the three of us chatting.

'I'm terribly sorry,' she says. 'I must have come to the wrong house. Sorry about that.' She turns on her heel and heads for the front door. It takes us a moment to react to what just happened, but I'm first to jump up and run after her. She's already out the front door and halfway down the driveway before I catch her.

'Come on, Zahra,' I say, realising there's no decision to be made. 'Let's go for a little drive and we'll get the doctor to take a look at you.' She allows me to lead her by the arm and into the back seat of the car. I'm not having her sitting up front this time because I know I'll feel the urge to keep looking at her to see if she's okay. Fiona can sit beside her in the back. Fiona is already outside, so she gets in beside her while I run in to grab my handbag.

'There are a few bags of toys on the sitting room floor,' shouts Fiona out the window to my mother. 'You might need them when he wakes up.'

'He'll be fine, don't worry,' says my mother, waving us off before closing the front door.

I decide on Tallaght Hospital, but the Christmas shoppers heading to The Square Shopping Centre are out in force, so the traffic is heavy. Thankfully, Zahra is mainly quiet in the car but just to add to our panic, she's now beginning to get sleepy. I know from my diligent watching of *Grey's Anatomy* and *Casualty* that it's important not to let somebody go to sleep if they've had a head injury, so I instruct Fiona to make sure she stays awake.

Forty minutes and buckets of sweat later, we arrive at the hospital. At least Tallaght has plenty of parking and it's near to the A&E door too. I want to drop Fiona and Zahra off at the door while I go and look for a spot but Fiona won't hear of it.

'We won't leave you on your own,' she says, generously. 'Sure for the sake of a few more minutes, we may as well stick together.'

I suspect it's more the case that she doesn't want to be left with Zahra while she's in her scary mode, and I really can't say I blame her. Thank God Mam came to the rescue again or I would have had to spend the past forty minutes on my own in the car with Zahra. I'd surely have crashed the car, trying to keep her awake and drive at the same time!

We head into the hospital after nabbing a great spot just inside the entrance to the car park. Zahra isn't saying much and I'm a little afraid to question her for fear of what she'll say. She didn't object to us bringing her here, and in fact seems quite happy to go along with what's happening. I'd love to know what she's thinking – like does she even realise what's going on or is she just off in her own world?

My stomach lurches as soon as we set foot inside the busy A&E department. God, I hate that smell of disinfectant mixed with vomit and old people. I give Zahra's name to the nurse and give her a brief rundown of the problem. She tells us to take a seat and warns of a possible two- or three-hour wait. Wonderful!

'I hope the flight isn't delayed,' says Zahra, looking worried. 'I have to go straight to work when I arrive back in London.' Jesus, she thinks we're at the airport now. If it wasn't so worrying, it'd be funny.

'Ah I think it's on time all right,' says Fiona, winking at me. 'I'll go and double check for you in a few minutes.'

'Check what?' asks Zahra, looking at Fiona quizzically. Here we go again!

'Never mind,' sighs Fiona.

An eerie silence hangs over the waiting room except for the odd cough or sneeze. I look around and wonder what brings everyone here. There's nobody with an obvious injury, like a severed hand or a gushing head – although I suppose they wouldn't leave somebody like that just sitting in the waiting room.

The last time I was in an A&E was two years ago when I had an unfortunate episode while in a department store in the city centre. I was looking at nail polish and trying to decide between a blood red one and a dark wine one. I tend to wear black most of the time, but just fancied brightening things up a bit. Anyway, I had one in each hand, doing eenie meenie miney mo, when I heard a bang. It sounded as though it was right beside me, so I looked around to see what it was. It was only when I felt the sting in my hand that I realised the bottle of red polish had exploded in my hand and the shards of glass were cutting into my skin while the red polish rolled like blood down my arm. The manager of the shop almost fainted when she saw the mess and immediately called a taxi to bring me to A&E. On the sight of the blood and my obvious pain, they brought me in to be seen to straight away. I shudder at the memory of them picking each little shard of glass out of my palm with a tweezers.

So probably the ones that are left waiting are the ones that have no visible signs of injury. Though in fairness to the staff, they seem to be calling people quick enough into triage to be assessed, so I suppose they pick up on anything serious there. Well I certainly hope they call in the woman sitting facing me soon. She's looking seriously green in the face and I'm already recoiling in anticipation of her spewing up all over the place. She keeps making faces as though she's blowing up a balloon and it's making me really nervous.

'Zahra Burns, please,' comes a voice from the triage door and a tired-looking nurse is scanning the room with her eyes.

'Come on, Zahra,' I say, noticing she's getting sleepy again. 'Let's go and get you sorted. She stands up willingly and allows myself and Fiona to guide her into the little room.

'So which of you is Zahra then?' asks the nurse, smiling at the three of us.

'That's me,' says Zahra. Thank God, at least she knows that much!

'So you've bumped your head then, have you? Take a seat there and tell me what happened.'

'Um ... I don't think ... um ... I'm not really sure,' says Zahra, looking confused again. She plonks down on the chair and looks as though she's going to cry.

'Don't worry,' says the nurse, patiently. 'Maybe your friends can fill me in on what happened.'

Trying not to leave out any details (as learned from *ER* and *Casualty*), I tell the story from the moment Zahra slipped on those bloody marbles. Fiona adds in what she can remember too, although she seems more concerned with making the nurse understand it was an accident and that Ryan didn't mean to half kill Zahra.

'Right,' says the nurse. 'Do either of you know her medical history? We'll need to know that before we go any further.'

'Oh, God, I hadn't thought of that,' I say, feeling foolish. I bend over to the nurse to whisper so Zahra can't hear, though she seems to be in her own world at the moment anyway. 'We don't even know her that well. We've been friends on Twitter for a while and only just met her for the first time yesterday. She lives in London.'

'Don't worry,' says the nurse. 'Let's see how much she knows herself.' She bends down to talk to Zahra, who's starting to doze off again. 'Zahra, are you taking any medication at the moment or do you have any allergies?'

'Um ... I ... I don't think so,' she says. 'I sort of remember going to hospital one time with an allergic reaction but I can't remember what it was. Sorry.'

'It's okay,' the nurse says. 'Is there anyone we could ring and check, just to be sure? A husband? Mother? Who's your next of kin?'

'You could try my mum,' she says. 'Tell her I'll be a little late for dinner because my flight seems to be delayed.'

'Maybe you could take her phone and see if her mother's number's on it,' says the nurse, turning to us. 'She does seem to be very confused. I just need to do a couple of checks here and then we'll be getting the doctor to see her.'

'Okay,' I say, glad of the opportunity to get out of the room for a few minutes but not looking forward to telling her mother that Zahra had an accident. 'Zahra, can I have your mobile to get your mum's number please?'

'It's in there,' she says, handing me her handbag. 'You'll find it under "Mum".' I stifle a giggle. Like I was going to search under 'Dad'. I get her phone, leaving her bag back down beside her, and head outside with Fiona to make the call.

Bloody hell, what on earth is going to happen next? You couldn't write about this stuff. I thought by now I'd be on the sofa with a nice cuppa and a Twix and, instead, here I am in hospital with a girl I barely know, about to ring her mother in a different country to tell her she's had an accident!

'God, I hope she'll be okay,' says Fiona, worriedly. 'She doesn't look too good.'

'Don't worry,' I say, warmed by Fiona's concern. She's obviously not as tough as she looks. 'I'm sure it'll be just a concussion. She'll be fine.'

'And her poor mother,' she continues. 'Imagine getting a call to say your daughter's had an accident. Maybe you should be careful what you say.'

'Yes, yes, I will,' I say, scrolling down through the names on the phone.

'You know ... maybe you shouldn't tell her all the facts in case ... you know ... in case she worries too much and wants to come over.'

'Let's just take one step at a time, Fiona. And don't worry so much. Zahra will be fine, honestly.'

'Well, just ... just don't tell her how the accident happened, okay? After all, Ryan is only four and it wouldn't be fair if he was to take all the blame.'

Aha! Fiona is more worried about the consequences for her and Ryan than Zahra's well-being. Well I'm not the marble police, but I do think I should give the full picture to both Zahra's mother and to the medical staff here. Fiona can just like it or lump it! Right, found it. It's ringing. Eeeeek!

CHAPTER 20

'I don't believe it,' I say, sitting down heavily beside Fiona on the plastic grey chairs in the waiting area. 'There are more twists and turns to this tweet-up than a fairground roller-coaster!'

'Why? What's happened? Did you get her mam on the phone?'

'Yep, I got her all right. She's talking to the nurse now, but you'll never guess what she told me!'

'Oooh, come on then. What did she say?' Fiona's eyes light up at the prospect of a bit of gossip.

'Well, I introduced myself and she seemed to know who I was straight away. I told her about what had happened and where we are but tried not to panic her. I told her about some of the things Zahra was saying, including missing her flight and having to go to work as soon as she gets back to London.'

'So what did she say to all that then?' asks Fiona, on the edge of her seat. 'Was she upset about it all?'

'Well, yes, she sounded upset, but get this! She said Zahra must be thinking about Saturday when she has to go straight to the studios to work when she gets back.'

'Oh she must have another make-up job,' says Fiona. 'I wonder who she's due to do this time.'

'Well ... that's where you're wrong,' I say, enjoying drawing the whole thing out. 'It appears she won't be going to the studios to do somebody's make-up!'

'Well, what is it then?' asks Fiona, getting impatient. 'Are you going to tell me she's some hot shot movie star and we didn't know about it? Oooh, how exciting!'

'Well, apparently ... and you won't believe this ... apparently, she's a *cleaner* in the TV studios close to her house. She does a few hours every evening and she tried but couldn't get Saturday off. That's obviously what she was thinking about in the back of her head when she thought her flight had been delayed!'

I wait to let this sink in. I couldn't believe it when her mother told me. She said Zahra has an honest and decent job cleaning the studios. It pays reasonably well and since she only works in the evenings, she has her days to do whatever she wants. I asked her, in an attempt to cling on to the shreds of what Zahra had told us, if she uses her time during the day to do celebrity make-up. The woman laughed hysterically at this. She told me that Zahra is a dreamer and spends most of her time in a virtual world. She's celebrity obsessed and buys every magazine she can get her hands on to follow the lives of the rich and famous.

'Wow,' says Fiona, her mouth gaping open. 'God, I didn't see that one coming.'

'Me neither. And what's more, apparently, she doesn't live in her own swanky, state of the art apartment, she lives in a council estate with her mother and younger brother. She doesn't even have a car!'

'Oh, my God!,' says Fiona. 'I'm gob-smacked What do you think about it all?'

'I dunno,' I say, rubbing my temples in an effort to banish the headache that's been threatening all day. 'I don't really know whether to thump her or feel sorry for her.'

'I know what you mean,' says Fiona, 'but I think I feel sorry for her. The fact that she made herself out to be someone so important on Twitter must mean that she doesn't rate herself much. I mean, there's nothing wrong with the job she does or the life she has, but she must feel embarrassed by it and want people to see her as somebody more dynamic and exciting.'

I *never* expected such compassion and insight from Fiona, but she's right. Zahra is more to be pitied than ridiculed. I just can't help feeling cheated. I've been worried about meeting somebody so important, and wondering what she'd think of my mundane life when all the time my life is probably far more exciting than hers ever was. I feel I don't know her at all now. This past year of getting to know her on Twitter, all the conversations we've had online and even the chats we've had since she arrived yesterday – it's all been lies.

'Well she must have been very concussed if she told us to contact her mother,' I say, breaking the silence. 'Surely she would have realised her secret would come out if we got talking to her.'

'That's what has me worried,' says Fiona. 'If she's kept her secret for so long, she must be really sick to not care if it comes out. I hope they tell us something soon.'

'I'm sure they will,' I say, patting Fiona's hand. I know she's been worried that Ryan would get the blame for the accident, but I think she's genuinely concerned for Zahra. 'I'm sure it's just concussion. From what I've heard, it can make you really confused and forgetful but it'll pass.'

'I hope so,' says Fiona. 'Poor Zahra.'

'We probably shouldn't let on we know yet,' I say. 'She's confused enough as it is – we don't want anything adding to her distress. We can bring it up tomorrow or Saturday, if she's up to it.'

We sit lost in thought for the next half hour. It all makes sense when I think about it now. Zahra was so different to what I expected that I should have guessed she wasn't being truthful about everything. And Mam did whisper to me last night that her clothes were only fake designer. Apparently, my mother knew this because she'd bought the same top herself from a market in the Phoenix Park only last week and the label is slightly different from the real thing.

God, Twitter is a funny thing. Here's me worrying myself sick because of a couple of little lies about live-in lovers and being an all-singing, all-dancing aunty when, all this time, Zahra has portrayed herself as a completely different person. It's weird to think I know somebody who doesn't really exist. I really liked the Zahra from Twitter, even if she did scare me a little. Or maybe it was more the excitement of getting a glimpse into the celebrity world that I liked. Well either way, I've got to get my head around the new Zahra now. But if the new Zahra is the shy, over-appreciative, stuttering one, I like her too.

Thinking of Twitter has me wondering if Kerry has replied to my DM. I must get her phone number off her and maybe I'll ring her later. I'm dying to tell her what's been going on. She won't believe it. I sneak my phone out of my bag, conscious of being told off for using it in the hospital. Fiona has her eyes closed and has either dozed off or is deep in thought, so I'll see if Kerry is there. Sure enough, there's a DM she sent only five minutes ago.

@kerrydhunt Hi, Jenny. I have a couple of hours free before going in for a night shift. Are you there?

Hopefully she's still online. I'll stick with DM so we can have a private chat.

@JennyB Yes, I'm here. God, Kerry, you'd never guess what's been happening here. It's crazy.
@kerrydhunt There you are! I've been dying to know since your message. What's up?

@JennyB Well, basically, Fiona brought her son with her and it turns out Zahra is a cleaner – not a make-up artist!

@kerrydhunt Nooooo! What? I can't believe I've missed all that. Are you serious?

@JennyB Yep! And furthermore, we're in hospital with Zahra. Long story. What's your phone number – easier to fill you in that way?

@kerrydhunt Wow! That's a lot to take in. So it's been an eventful couple of days so far.

@JennyB You can say that again! Wish you were here so we could chat about it properly.

@kerrydhunt Me too. But gotta go now. I'll try to log on later for another catch up.

@JennyB Oh wait, you didn't tell me your phone number!

Shit! She must have logged off. There's only so much information you can get across on Twitter. I'd love a good old natter with her. Well, maybe she'll send her number when she's on later.

'Girls, you can come in and see Zahra now.' The nurse we'd dealt with earlier has just appeared in front of us, and I throw my phone hastily back in my bag. 'We're just waiting for a bed for your friend – we'll be keeping her in overnight.'

'Oh, no,' says Fiona, slapping her hand over her mouth. 'Is it serious then?'

'No, no, not at all,' says the nurse, sitting down beside her. 'We're pretty sure it's just a concussion. We'll be running a few tests to rule out anything else. She's just a bit confused and there are things she doesn't seem to be able to remember. But that's normal.'

'Oh poor, Zahra,' I say, feeling really sorry for her. 'She didn't bank on this when she was coming for an exciting few days in Dublin.'

'What are you trying to say?' says Fiona, defensively. 'Are you saying it's my fault?'

'Jesus, of course I'm not, Fiona. I'm just saying it's unfortunate. It was nobody's fault.' Except that out of control son of hers, but I'm not going to say that to her.

'Well, do you want to come in and have a chat with her,' says the nurse, getting up from the chair. I'm mortified. For a moment, I'd forgotten she was there. She must think we're right eejits, fighting about who's to blame when we should be in there with our friend. And Fiona must be feeling really guilty to have snapped at me like that. Oh, my poor head! I can't keep up with all of this.

'Hi, girls,' Zahra says, as we walk into the room where she's sitting on the edge of a makeshift bed. 'It seems I'm going to have to stay here all night. That's a bit of a pain, isn't it?'

'It's a shame all right,' I say, sitting down on the edge of the bed. At least she seems to know who we are and where she is. Thank God we don't have to start humouring her again about flights and lost keys.

'So do you remember everything now?' asks Fiona, sitting down on a stool beside the bed. 'Like you know who we are, right?'

'Yes, of course,' she says, her melting make-up giving the impression of deep circles around her eyes. 'I just can't remember how I got here. Last I remember, we were sitting chatting over breakfast and trying to decide where to go shopping.'

'God, that's scary, isn't it?' I say. 'So you don't remember shopping or slipping and banging your head?'

'No, not at all,' she says. 'But I don't feel bad otherwise. I had a throbbing headache but they gave me something for that so it's not too bad. Where's Ryan?'

'He's back in Jenny's house with her mam,' says Fiona. 'He

was asleep when we got back from shopping so Eileen offered to sit with him. She'd planned to come over tonight anyway to babysit while we went to Keith Barry.'

'Oh, yes, Keith Barry! What time is it? You two should go home and get ready. I'll be fine here.'

'What? No way, Zahra,' I say, shocked that she'd think we could go out enjoying ourselves while she spends the night here in hospital.

'Honestly, Jenny,' she says, generously. 'I want you two to go. Kerry is already missing so there's no point in everybody losing out. The tickets are bought and paid for, aren't they?'

'Well ... yes ... but ... '

'Well that's that then,' she says. 'I won't hear of you two missing out. Go and see him and you can tell me all about it tomorrow.'

'Zahra, you're brilliant,' says Fiona. 'Are you sure you don't mind? I mean, we can stay here for another while until you're settled in a ward.'

'Of course I don't mind, Fiona,' she says. 'I'd feel terrible if you missed out because of me. And why don't you get someone else to use the other two tickets, Jenny. I'm sure some of your friends would love to go.'

'Well ... I don't know ... I'm really not sure about this. It just doesn't seem right to me.' I should really learn to know when to shut up. It's a real Irish trait. We're the kings of looking a gift horse in the mouth. I couldn't tell you how many times somebody has offered me something that I really wanted but I feel I have to say, 'Ah, no, I couldn't.' Then the person says, 'Ah, go on, you may as well.' And then I say again, 'Ah, no, I shouldn't really.' And so it goes on and on until the person says, 'Okay then, if you're sure', and I kick myself for not just taking it and saying thanks. I won't let that happen today.

'But if you're really sure,' I continue, 'maybe I'll ask my friend,

Sally. She could really do with a night out and I think she'd enjoy the show.'

'Yes, that's settled then,' says Zahra, looking pleased with herself. 'Go on and ring this Sally and tell her to get herself ready. And what about the other ticket? You have two spares now. Don't let it go to waste.'

'Oh, maybe I'll ask Paula too then. You don't mind, do you Fiona?' I couldn't really care less if Fiona minds or not. I've paid for these tickets and I suspect I won't be seeing a penny of the money from anyone. The prospect of having both Sally and Paula out with us tonight is brilliant and has really cheered me up. I do feel sort of guilty leaving Zahra here, but, on the other hand, we've been with her most of the day and we've looked after her well. We can come back in tomorrow morning and probably take her home at that stage. Ooooh roll on tonight and let Keith Barry hypnotise me into believing my life is simple!

★

'Well look at you two,' says Fiona. 'You must be a miracle worker, Eileen.' We've just arrived back from the hospital to the sight of my mother sitting at the kitchen table making play dough with Ryan. They're both laughing and it occurs to me that I haven't seen Ryan smile since he arrived. My mother has obviously found a way to get the best from him – either that or she's bribed him.

'Hello you two,' she says, helping Ryan roll out a piece of blue dough. 'So how's poor Zahra then? God love her having to stay overnight in hospital.'

'She's okay actually, Mam. They just want to keep her for observation and they're going to run a few tests. She was fine when we left and insisted we go to the show. I've rung both Paula and Sally and they're coming to use up the spare two tickets. I assume you're still okay to stay?'

'Mummy, mummy, look what I've made,' shouts an excited

Ryan, proudly holding up something unrecognisable for his mother to see.

'I'm fine to stay,' says Mam, smiling fondly at her charge. 'Ryan and I have been getting along great. Sure he's no trouble.'

'That's lovely, darling,' says Fiona. 'How on earth did you get him to sit and do that, Eileen? I can't get him to sit still at all at home. You're really great with him.'

Am I imagining it, or does Fiona look as though she's going to cry. I think I've misjudged her. She gives the impression that she just lets Ryan get away with murder for an easy life and doesn't really try to control him. Maybe she just can't. Maybe she's given up or something. Yes, she's definitely wiping away a tear. I must try to have a chat with her later on when it's just the two of us. She hasn't said much about her husband since she arrived, except that he had to rush off on business. But maybe there's more to it. It must be a strain on a marriage having a, let's just say 'spirited', young child. Add to that money worries and surely it's a recipe for a very tough road. It strikes me that maybe Fiona hasn't been completely honest about her wonderful life either.

'So what's the plan then?' asks Mam, breaking into my thoughts. 'Are the girls meeting you in town or coming here first? Why don't you just get a taxi in so you can have a few drinks? There's no point in driving when there are four of you to share the cost of the taxi. And, besides, there's snow forecast, so you don't want to be driving in those conditions.'

'Good idea,' I say, already imagining the taste of a cool vodka and Coke on my tongue. 'I think that's exactly what we'll do.'

'Ryan, Eileen is going to mind you again tonight while Mummy goes out for a while,' says Fiona, stroking the child's head. 'Is that okay with you?'

'Yes, I like Eileen. She plays fun games. She isn't stinky.'

'Well, thank you ... I think,' laughs my mother, and I can't help smiling myself.

'Thanks so much for this, Eileen,' says Fiona, looking teary again. 'I don't often get a break from him back home. It's usually just him and ... ' She trails off, leaving me wondering if she was going to say 'him and me'.

'Doesn't your husband take him off your hands sometimes?' I say. 'He sounds like a right catch. Didn't he only take him off to the cinema last week to give you a chance to relax? I remember when you tweeted about it I thought how lucky you were to have such a supportive husband.'

'I ... em ... yes, he's good with Ryan all right but it's just ... it's just this damn job of his is taking up so much time lately.'

'Well you needn't worry about a thing tonight,' says my mam. 'Ryan and I are going to have a great time, aren't we, Ryan? Harry will be over later too and he's going to stop off at the DVD shop and get a couple of movies for us to watch. What do you think of that, Ryan?'

'Yay, yay!' squeals Ryan, jumping up and down. 'Can we have popcorn too? Can we close the curtains and make a cinema?'

'Now, Ryan, you have to be good. You can't keep asking Eileen for stuff.'

'Ah he's not a bother,' says my mam. Then bending to whisper to Ryan, 'We'll have a little party when they're gone – just don't tell them!'

'Well I don't think we'll have time to eat in town before the show, so how about I throw on a pot of pasta for us all so we can eat before the girls come over? They're coming at seven so we have a couple of hours yet.' I'll be damned if I'm making any fancy dinners at this stage – not that I'd know how to anyway. I'll add a pot of Dolmio stir-in sundried tomato sauce and sprinkle a bit of cheese on the top. Not a feast, but it will have to do.

Imagine this time yesterday I'd only just met Zahra, and Fiona hadn't even arrived with Ryan yet. I sort of know how Jack

Bauer feels now in *24*! It's like every hour of the past day could have been a stand-alone episode of a drama series. Seriously – it's unreal. But at least something good has come out of all this and I get to have a night with Sally and Paula too. Thank God the girls were available at such short notice. Maybe one of us will even be called onto the stage to be hypnotised. Imagine! Well, that would be something to talk about afterwards. And I hope Mam is right about the snow. I want oodles of white fluffy snow in my garden. I want to forget my worries, don my woolly hat and gloves and make a snowman. I want to have a snowball fight with anyone who's willing! I want to be a child again. *Let it snow, let it snow, let it snow*!

CHAPTER 21

Jesus, this is bloody hilarious. Just as we came back from the interval of the show, Keith Barry looked for volunteers to be hypnotised. I was full sure Fiona would be up for it or even Paula. But what I didn't expect was to see Sally hopping up on the stage! Seriously, I don't think I've ever laughed so much in my life.

There are about twelve people sitting on the stage and Keith has them doing all sorts of silly stuff. It's brilliant. Sally has been cuddling up to the man beside her because she thinks she's going to freeze to death and she claimed she was a Martian translator and was able to translate a message from a visiting Martian. Honestly, my sides are hurting from laughing so much. He's just put them back in a hypnotic sleep and Sally is sliding further and further onto the lap of the man beside her.

'Oh, God, look at Sal,' laughs Paula, tears streaming down her face. 'Another few inches and her face will be right in that guy's crotch!'

'You're friend's a howl, isn't she?' says Fiona. 'I'd be mortified up on that stage.'

'I know,' I say, still shocked that Sally volunteered. But fair play to her. She's been so stressed lately, it'll do her good to have a laugh. Keith Barry is shushing the crowd now.

'People on the stage, listen to my voice,' he says. 'In a few moments, I'm going to wake you up. Gentlemen, when I come and shake your hands, you're going to experience the best orgasm you've ever experienced in your lives.'

'Oh, God, my stomach muscles can't take any more of this,' says Paula, dabbing her eyes. 'Isn't it just hilarious?' She settles back into the well-worn red velvet seat in anticipation of the laughs to come.

'And ladies ... when I shake your hands, you'll experience the best multiple orgasm you've ever had!'

'Christ almighty,' screeches Fiona. 'I can't believe she's going to get a multiple from Keith Barry!'

'Lucky bitch,' I mumble under my breath, causing Fiona to splutter her drink all over the place. Thank goodness we're in the front row or she'd have showered everybody with red wine.

'Look, look, look,' says Paula. 'He's going over to Sally now. She hasn't a clue. Oh, God, what a howl!'

Keith is hovering over Sally's chair. 'So how are you enjoying the show so far?'

'It's great,' says a clueless Sally.

'And what did you say your name was?' He holds out his hand to shake hers.

'Oh, Sal, don't do it,' I wince, peeping through my fingers. 'I can't bear to watch!'

'It's Sallyyyyyyyyyyyy! Oh shit. I'm sorry. Oh ... ohhhh ... '

'Are you okay there? Still having a good time?' Keith is shaking her hand harder and harder.

'Yesss ... oh, God ... I'm ... ahhh ... ahhhhhh ... ahhhhhh-hoooooooh!'

'Go, Sally,' screams Paula, as the audience claps and roars its approval.

I can barely speak through the tears. I honestly can't remember the last time I laughed so much. Coming here was the best idea ever. It's been a while since I've been, but the old red and gold walls and ornate ceilings remind me of really happy times in my childhood when my mam and dad would bring me here to the pantomime at Christmas. It was the highlight of the year. Dad used to buy a box of Black Magic chocolates for Mam and a box of Maltesers for me and him. It was a magical time and I remember thinking I was the luckiest child in the world. Maltesers and a few laughs – how simple life was back then.

'Poor Sally. She'll be mortified when she realises what has happened,' says Paula, wiping her eyes.

'Poor Sally my arse!' I say. 'Does she look to you as though she's not enjoying herself? If I'd known he was going to do that, I'd have stood on heads to get onto that stage.' And I probably would have! The past few days have been a distraction from what's going on in my life, but I'm really missing having some male company. Maybe I'll give Tom a ring tomorrow and see if he wants to come over and meet the girls. I know things have been far from perfect between us, but I could definitely do worse. The words 'beggars' and 'choosers' spring to mind!

'And sleep.' Keith touches the heads of each of the volunteers and puts them to sleep again. He waits for the audience to settle down before he continues.

'People on the stage, in a few moments, I'm going to wake you up. You'll have no ill effects from your experiences. In fact, you'll feel energised and focused and feel on top of the world.'

'Of course they'll bloody well feel on top of the world,' whispers Fiona. 'Jesus, did you see Sally's face when she was ... em ... you know?'

Everyone is on their feet now as the volunteers are making their way back to their seats. Keith is rounding off the show. 'Let's hear it now for the real stars of tonight.'

'Sal, you were brilliant,' I say, hugging her as she comes back to the seat. 'What on earth made you go up there though – I couldn't believe it when you jumped up!'

'I don't know really,' she says, yawning. 'I suppose I just thought I may as well make the most of it. It's not often I get out.'

'And do you remember what you did?' asks Paula, standing up to let people pass by. 'Or were you completely out of it.'

'The funny thing is,' says Sally, 'I actually remember doing it all. It's like there was somebody else doing it and I was watching on. I can't really explain it. But, Jesus, I'm mortified now at the thought!'

'Come on, let's go get a drink in the bar,' I say. 'I'm parched.'

Ten minutes later, we're standing in a corner of the packed theatre bar, drinks in hand, talking about the show. God, Kerry would have loved this. I chatted to her on Twitter again this evening and I got the impression she was feeling a bit down about missing out on everything.

'Didn't you say you knew Keith Barry?' says Fiona, breaking into my thoughts. 'Weren't you going to introduce us to him?'

Shit! I was hoping she'd have forgotten that with everything else going on. 'I ... well ... I wouldn't say I *know* him exactly,' I say slowly, playing for time. 'I've chatted to him on Twitter so I suppose you could say I know him from there.'

'God, I didn't know that,' says Paula, looking at me admiringly. 'You never said.'

'Well, it's a different world on Twitter,' I say. 'Sure you can tweet to any celebrities who are on there. It's great that you can interact with people you wouldn't ever have the opportunity to talk to in real life.'

'Wow,' says Sally. 'I'm almost tempted to give it a try myself. It sounds interesting. Although I don't know when I'd find time, to be honest.'

'Hey look, Sal – looks like you've a bit of a fan base over

there.' I point over to a group of guys who couldn't be long out of their teens. They're giving Sally the thumbs up.

'Nice job up on that stage,' shouts one of them, making Sally blush furiously. 'Can you give me your address in case I ever need a Martian translator? You were brilliant at that.'

'Ah, no, you were better at the orgasm,' shouts another, causing a flurry of high fives amongst their group.

'Oh, God, I'm regretting it already,' whispers a mortified Sally. 'Maybe we should have gone somewhere else.'

'Ah, no, sure it's good crack,' I say, enjoying the banter. 'Let's have one more and then we'll head off somewhere else.'

'I should probably get back home after the next one,' says Sally, slipping back into her 'sensible Sal' mode. 'The kids will have me up at a ridiculous hour in the morning and I'm hopeless when I don't get sleep.'

'I suppose you'll be wanting to get back to Ryan too,' I say to Fiona, who's guzzling back her glass of wine. 'I'll give Mam a ring in a few minutes to see how they're getting on.'

'I ... em ... yes, I should really get back, shouldn't I? But maybe don't bother your mam with phone calls. It might just wake Ryan up if he's nodded off. We'll be home soon enough. Will we have that other drink then?'

Talk about opposite ends of the spectrum. Sally has already rung home two or three times to check on the girls. Fiona hasn't even bothered to ask for my phone number to check on Ryan. I'm not saying she's not as good a mother as Sally – in fact I think Sally is a bit over the top – but Fiona has just plonked her son into the lives of strangers and she seems quite happy to leave him there. Still, I'm not really in a position to judge. Someday when I have kids of my own, I might look back on all my criticisms of them and realise they were unfair. Jesus – thinking about *when* I have kids? Only a few weeks ago, even an *if* would be pushing it!

Back to the real world now, though, and it looks like it's going to be up to me to buy the drinks. Paula got the last round in and Sally is on the phone checking on the kids again. Fiona is sipping the last drops from her glass but I'm sensing we'd be waiting a long time before she'd rush to the bar!

'So same again, then?' I ask, throwing my denim bag over my shoulder to head to the bar.

'Oh yes, another red wine for me please,' says Fiona, draining her glass. 'Next round is mine.'

Oh sneaky – very sneaky. Next round, my arse! She knows full well we'll be leaving after this one and she won't have spent a penny all night. She even managed to dodge paying for the taxi since it came to just under thirty euro and myself, Paula and Sally threw in a tenner each. I manage to push my way up to the bar and go up on my tippy toes to try to get the attention of a barman. That's when I see him.

He's tall – but not so tall that I look small beside him. He's running his fingers through his long chestnut-brown hair while placing his order with the barman. I feel an instant rush of heat through my body and have to resist the urge to reach out and touch his silky smooth locks. God, he's *gorgeous*! He's not conventionally handsome, his teeth aren't completely straight and his eyes are small, but his dimples and naturally smiley face make up for that. He's just oozing sexiness.

'So what can I get you?' The voice of a barman bursts into my thoughts and I can't seem to remember the order.

'I ... em ... I'm not ... em ... sorry, it's just gone out of my head.' Oh fuck! The hunk is looking at me now and he must think I'm a total eejit. 'Oh, yes, it's a vodka and Coke, gin and tonic and a red and white wine please.' Phew! Bloody hell. I need to get a grip. But there's something strangely familiar about the man standing beside me. If I knew him from somewhere I'm sure I'd remember – he's not exactly forgettable – but something tells me we've met before.

'Your friend put on a good show tonight,' says the handsome stranger, looking right at me. 'Did she enjoy being up there?'

'Yes, yes, she loved it ... being up there I mean ... she loved being up there ... on the stage.' Oh, God, I'm babbling.

'That's good,' he says, taking his pint of Guinness from the barman. Go on, take a drink, I urge him. *Show me how you wear your Guinness tache!*

He must have read my mind because before walking away, he takes a huge mouthful of the creamy drink and I can't unglue my eyes from him. 'Lovely,' he says. 'You can't beat a pint of Guinness. Well it was lovely meeting you, Jenny.' He disappears into the crowd.

What? How on earth? I'm completely confused now. Did he really call me by name or did I just fantasise that whole scene? Jesus, it was like something from an erotic movie (not that I've seen any such movies but it's how I imagine them to be!). My drinks are ready and the barman is waiting for the money so I pay him and head back to the girls.

'That fella,' says Fiona. 'Isn't he the one from McDonald's this morning? He's a bit of a hunk, isn't he?'

'Ah that's why he looked familiar,' I say. 'How weird that he turns up here tonight as well.' I decide not to say anything about him saying my name because, quite honestly, I think I may have dreamed it. Maybe he didn't speak to me at all. It was probably just wishful thinking on my part. I can't help scanning the room as I take a big gulp of my drink but I can't see him anywhere.

★

'Shhhhhh!' whispers my mother, opening the front door where Fiona and I are struggling to get the key into the lock. 'Ryan is fast asleep and I don't want you waking him up.'

'Yes, Mammy,' giggles Fiona. 'We wouldn't want that now.'

'So I take it you've had a good time?' Mam asks, leading the way into the living room where Harry is sprawled on the couch watching the telly.

'Howarya,' he says, instantly sitting up and smoothing down the tousled throw. 'How was the night?'

'It was great,' I say, plonking down on the other end of the sofa. 'So how did you two get on with Ryan?'

'Ah not a bother at all,' says Mam, perching on the arm of the chair. 'Sure we had him well tired out before he went to bed. We did some drawing and then spent ages making Lego.'

'You're so good with him, Eileen,' says Fiona, sobering up suddenly. 'I only wish he'd behave like that for me. You seem to have a magic touch with him.'

'Nothing of the sort,' says my mother. 'It's just my age probably. I've had lots of experience lying down on the floor and making things with children. It only seems like yesterday when I was playing with my Jenny.'

Em ... excuse me? When did my mother ever get down on the floor to play with me? She's making herself out to be the all-singing, all-dancing mother but, in fact, she was quite the opposite. I don't ever remember a time when she played Lego or drew pictures with me. She wasn't a bad mother – just an unconventional one.

'Well I'm really impressed,' says Fiona. 'I only wish Ryan had a grandmother like you to spend time with him back in Galway.'

'Isn't your mother around then?' asks Mam, gently. 'Or your husband's mother?'

'We don't really see family much anymore,' sighs Fiona. 'It's a long story. It's just Ryan and me – twenty-four hours a day.'

'And your husband,' I add, just in case she forgot!

'Well, yes ... of course, my husband. I just mean it's Ryan and me most of the time because my husband is in work a lot.'

'Well that's a shame about your parents,' says Mam, shaking

her head. 'Well I'll be his adopted Dublin granny then. I love the idea of having a little grandson or daughter.'

Was that a dig at me? Surely not. My mother of all people can't preach about how I should live my life. She hasn't exactly been the best role model herself. And she knows the score with me. She's never tried to force me into any 'nice' relationships because she knows I just didn't want to go there. But I suppose it's only natural she's wondering if her only child will ever have children.

'You know, you're so lucky, Jenny,' says Fiona, tearfully. Here we go again – the 'you're lucky' speech! 'You've really got everything, you know.'

'What do you mean, I have everything?' I ask, intrigued. She's the one with the husband and child and a life of domestic bliss. It makes me feel like I have *nothing*!

'Well you've got such good friends who'll drop everything when you call. Sally and Paula are lovely. I wish I had friends like that. Then you've got your mother to support you too. Look at how fabulous she's been to me and she doesn't even know me.'

'Ah, go on out of that,' says my mother, blushing furiously. 'Sure anyone would have done the same.'

'No, seriously,' continues Fiona. 'It's great you have so many good people around you. There's nothing worse in the world than loneliness.'

'Well that's true,' I say, trying to size up where this is going. 'I know I live alone but it is good to know that there are people on the other end of the phone who'll be here in a flash if I need them.'

'We all need somebody to lean on,' chimes in Harry, chuckling at his own joke. At least he didn't burst into song!

'Well I think we'll leave you two girls to it then,' says my mother, standing up and brushing down her long, belted jumper. 'Give me a ring in the morning, Jenny, and let me know if there's any news on Zahra. Hopefully, she'll be out of hospital by then.'

'Will do,' I say, walking both of them out to the door. I can't help thinking of the last time they were here and the moment I realised I'd snogged Harry. It's only been days and yet it almost seems like in another lifetime. Harry is all right. He's not exactly the sharpest tool in the box, but he's kind and loving and, most important, my mother adores him. They're good together.

'Mummmmy,' comes a voice from upstairs. 'I'm scared.'

'Oh, God, Jenny. You wouldn't just go up to him, would you? I'm bursting for the loo and if he sees me, he'll only want to come down.'

'Em … okay then. But I'm not sure he'll be too happy to see me.'

'Ah he's probably half-asleep anyway. Just tell him I'll be up in a few minutes and he'll probably go back to sleep.'

I watch Fiona head off to the loo and wonder what on earth goes through her head. Her four-year-old son is in a strange house with strange people, she's left him with a strange woman all evening and now she won't even go up to him when he's upset! But I promised myself I wouldn't criticise anyone's parenting skills until I have children of my own, so I take a deep breath and head up the stairs.

'It's okay, Ryan,' I say, fixing the covers on his little bed on the floor.

'But I want my Mummmmmmyyyyyy,' he cries. 'Where's my mummy?'

'She'll be up in a few minutes. You just snuggle down and try to go asleep.'

'B … b … but is sh … sh … she going too?' he sobs. 'I don't want her to go.'

'She's not going anywhere, Ryan. Don't be silly.'

'But Daddy went,' he whispers. 'I'm not supposed to tell, but he went far, far away and he's never coming back – not even when I'm big and getting married. I don't want Mummy to go too!'

Jesus! I can't keep up!

CHAPTER 22

Friday

For one lovely, luxurious moment after I wake, I imagine it's a normal day. You know, one of those days that spreads out in front of me like a blanket of loneliness, the type that I used to moan about. How naive I was back then. In the past few days, my life has been transported from the world of mundane to this mad, multicoloured world where around every corner lays another surprise. Honestly, who would have thought that a simple tweet-up in Dublin could turn out to be so complex? What I wouldn't give now for one of those lonely, boring days!

I wonder if Kerry has had a chance to digest the information I gave her yesterday. I'll take a quick look before I head downstairs. Maybe she's remembered to send me her phone number so I can give her a buzz and have a proper natter. I grab my phone from the locker and tap into Twitter. Ah feck! Not a word from her since yesterday.

I miss talking to the girls on Twitter. I have other friends on there too, but I talk all the time to Fiona, Zahra and Kerry and it feels really strange not to have our four-way chats every evening. I know I can just talk to Zahra and Fiona face to face, but it's just not the same. Is that really weird? Twitter sort of sucks you right in and holds on to you for dear life. No matter what's going on around you, when you're in there, it seems like the most important thing in the world. It feels like a room where we all meet to have a chat and a laugh and escape the real world. I'm beginning to think I might be a teeny weeny bit addicted!

It's hard to believe that tomorrow is Saturday and if things had run smoothly, the girls would be going home in the morning and normal life would be restored. But in a moment of madness when talking to Zahra's mum last night, I offered to put Zahra up until Sunday. Poor Mrs Burns. She's beside herself with worry about her daughter, but the doctor said she wasn't fit to travel for a couple of days.

I know I should feel annoyed at Zahra for the lies she's told us, but I don't. She must be desperately unhappy with her life to live a completely different one through a social networking site. But I think the real Zahra is nicer than the pretend one, and I'm going to tell her that when I collect her from hospital today. When I think that I was worried about meeting her because I thought she'd be overpowering and maybe even look down on me. But she's actually the sweetest, most gentle girl with a heart of gold. She seems to only see good in people. Maybe I should have a think about my own view of the world and be a little more compassionate and understanding.

Well the new Jenny may have to wait for a while because I can feel my blood beginning to boil at the smell seeping up the stairs. Fiona must be cooking something – bloody cheek! I bet she has all the windows closed and that stench travels all around the house and can linger for days.

Gritting my teeth, I hop out of bed and grab my robe from the back of the door. Stepping into my slippers, I hurry downstairs to have words with Fiona about her carelessness and lack of respect. I'm not going to tip-toe around her any more so if there's a mess, I'm going to just tell her to bloody well clean it up. Honestly, she really has a cheek; and after I've been so good to her and Ryan too. I fling open the kitchen door, all fired up and ready to have a pop at her.

'Fiona, I really think you should ... ' I'm frozen to the spot. The table is set for three and Ryan is quietly drawing on the floor in the corner. The windows are open and the extractor fan on. There are plates in the oven keeping a variety of delicious-looking food hot. Despite the amount of stuff she's cooked, the place looks pretty clean. Jesus, she's messing with my head!

'Good morning, Jenny. I hope you don't mind, but I rustled around in your fridge and cupboards. I wanted to make a nice breakfast to say thanks for having us. What were you going to say?'

'I ... eh ... I was just going to say that I think you should relax when you're on holidays. I'm sure you do enough cooking and cleaning when you're at home.' Phew! That was quick thinking on my part. God, she's like a different girl this morning, all chirpy and appreciative. There's no sign of the lazy, sponging Fiona I've got to know over these past couple of days. Hmmm. Maybe I'm too cynical, but I can't help wondering what she's up to. Is she going to ask me for money? To babysit? For her and Ryan to stay for longer? Oh, God, she can have all my money but just don't ask to stay beyond tomorrow!

'Sit down there, Jenny,' she says, handing me a much needed cup of tea. 'Come on over and get some breakfast, Ryan.'

I do as I'm told and sit down. It feels strange to be waited on in my own house, but I think I quite like it. The domestic scene is sort of making me feel all warm and gooey inside – even if a little nervous!

'Wow! What a feast,' I say, marvelling at the plates of pancakes, omelettes and various other bits and pieces she's taking out of the oven. 'You must have been up at the crack of dawn making all this.' Now this is the Fiona I'd expected to see from day one.

'Well Ryan was awake since early and ... and ... I just wanted to do something nice for you.' Her face looks tired and pained as she pulls up her chair to the table. 'You've been really good to us, Jenny – to both of us. To be honest, it's been quite a difficult year for us ... '

She trails off just when I think she's going to spill the beans about her husband. God, when I think about the fact that so many times I was jealous of her. I thought she had it all – the wonderful marriage, the perfect child – how wrong could I have been? Jesus, all this deception is exhausting me!

'The past year hasn't really been great for me either,' I say, in an attempt to get her to open up. 'For starters, my love life is a bit of a shambles!'

'But what about that guy from work you were dating last week? He sounded nice.'

'You mean Tom? Yes, he is lovely but I'm not sure it's going to work out.' But maybe it will if I work on it. Don't they say relationships have to be worked on? I always wondered about that statement. I used to think if you find the right one, it just all happens naturally but apparently (well according to Sally) even the most perfect relationships need work. Sally and John are great together, but Sal just told me recently that in order to stay happy, they have to work on the relationship every single day. *Every single bloody day?* Well that was a revelation to me. I just need to figure out whether or not Tom is worth working on.

'Mummy, can I have another pancake?' asks Ryan politely, and for once he's not whining or demanding.

'You've already had three Ryan, so this is your last one, okay?' says Fiona, liberally spreading some Nutella on her son's fourth pancake. 'He's been so good this morning, Jenny. He even helped me make breakfast.'

'Good job, Ryan,' I say, smiling at the mess of chocolate on his face.'

'It's your mother's influence, you know,' says Fiona, stuffing her own mouth with a chocolaty pancake. 'Ryan said she told him that good things happen to good people, and so it's much better to be good. It's really worked too!'

I'm amazed. My mother – the child whisperer! Christ almighty!

'When is Granny Eileen coming over?' he asks. 'And Granddad Harry?'

Jesus, I've almost choked on my tea. Granny Eileen? I don't know whether to laugh or cry at that! 'When's she coming, Aunty Jenny?' he shouts, just in case I didn't hear it the first time.

All this 'Aunty' and 'Granny' talk is making me feel a little jittery. Sure I've only known these people for two days! Twitter made me think I knew them well, but nothing could be further from the truth. You can be anyone on Twitter – I only wish I'd realised that before I decided to open up my house to them all!

'Aunty Jenny, Aunty Jenny, when are they coming? I *want* them to come *now*!' He throws his empty plate viciously on the kitchen floor, smashing it into smithereens.

'Ah, Ryan, why did you do that? Now Aunty Jenny has a big mess to clean up.'

Ha! And normality is restored!

★

'Bloody rain,' I say, pulling off my sodden coat and throwing it on the banister. I'm beginning to give up any hope of seeing snow this side of Christmas. It's been forecast almost every day for the past couple of weeks and yet we haven't seen a single, solitary flake! 'I'd say you're dying for a decent cuppa, Zahra. I'll stick the kettle on.'

'Oh, yes, I'd love a nice cup of tea,' she says, following me into the kitchen, where Fiona is idly flicking through a magazine. 'That stuff in the hospital is horrible. And it's never hot enough.'

It looked pretty grim all right. A lady came around with a trolley of hot drinks while we were waiting for the doctor to discharge Zahra and she was kind enough to offer us both something. Zahra opted for the tea but upon seeing its brownish grey colour, I passed.

'Welcome back, Zahra,' says Fiona, hopping up to give her a hug. 'That was some fright you gave us all.'

'Sorry about that. And thanks for all you did yesterday – both of you – I don't know what I'd have done without you.'

'Anyone would have done the same,' says Fiona. 'I'm just glad you're okay.'

Fiona is acting sort of strange today. I can't put my finger on what it is about her, but she seems to have lost some of her fire. She was bright and breezy first thing this morning but, as the day has gone on, she's become a bit subdued. I think she wanted to tell me about her husband but then changed her mind. I didn't push her because I've enough dealing with one set of lies at the moment.

'Here we go,' I say, placing a pot of tea in the centre of the table and grabbing a few mugs from the cupboard. 'So where's Ryan then?' Having got used to the noise of a kid in the house, it seems eerily quiet.

'He's conked out on the sofa. I guess your mam did tire him out last night. He had a great time with her.'

'Speaking of mothers,' I say, seizing the opportunity to talk about what Fiona and I learned yesterday, '*your* mother seems lovely, Zahra.'

'How d ... d ... d ... d ... do you ... ? When d ... d ... d ... d ... did you? Oh, that's right. You spoke to her yesterday, didn't you?'

'Yes, we had a good chat,' I say, watching her carefully. 'And she told me, Zahra. She told me about your job.' I just let those words hang in the air for a moment. I can see Fiona is shifting uncomfortably in her chair. Zahra bows her head and looks completely defeated. Oh, God, don't let her cry. I seem to have spent the past few weeks willing everyone around me not to cry – Paula, Fiona, Zahra ... even Bootface and Tom! Jesus, maybe it's me!

She sighs heavily and continues looking down at the table. 'To be honest, I'm mortified, but at the same time, I'm glad it's all out in the open. I've wanted to admit the truth to you all so many times over the past year, but the lie just seemed to get bigger and bigger, until there seemed no going back.'

I look over at Fiona in the hope that she might wade in and help me, but she's giving me a look that says it's my mess and I should deal with it! She was never really sure that telling Zahra what we knew would benefit anyone.

'I'm glad we know, Zahra,' I say, doing my best to fix a comforting look on my face. I'm really not one of life's nurturers. 'But you're such a lovely person. Why did you feel the need to pretend to be someone else?'

'That's nice of you to say, Jenny. But it was just one of those things. When I joined Twitter, I never for a minute thought I'd make such good friends. I just thought it would be fun to create myself as a different person with a different life – the life I'd love to have. And then when this tweet-up came about, I thought it would be nice to meet the people who I've become close to and just to feel ... I don't know ... important, I suppose, for once in my life.' She takes a tissue out from her sleeve and dabs at her eyes before continuing. 'I suppose I was just trying to escape a pretty mundane existence.'

'I can understand that,' says Fiona, her face fixed in a grimace. 'Twitter allows you to escape from things you'd rather not deal with.'

I watch Fiona carefully as her eyes glaze over. I wonder if she will tell us about her husband leaving. I'm dying to hear the story, but I don't want to ask.

'I'm not very unhappy or anything,' says Zahra, dipping a biscuit into her tea. 'I just wish I'd done more with my life. It's not as though I don't have brains. I've always been interested in make-up and fashion and the celebrity world and look how I end up – a blooming cleaner!'

'A cleaner's not so bad,' I say, frantically searching my mind for something positive to say about a job that would be my worst nightmare. I mean, I can't even abide dealing with my own dirt, never mind that of others.

'And it certainly must pay pretty well if you can afford all those designer clothes,' adds Fiona.

Zahra sighs. 'They're not real,' she says. 'Wembley market on Sundays is a brilliant place for finding fake designer stuff. It's pretty good quality and looks like the real thing – and, best of all, it's cheap!'

'But the celebrities,' I say. 'I've definitely seen you chatting with celebrities on Twitter. You obviously have plenty of connections.' It's true – I've seen her chatting to loads of singers and actors. Once I even watched her having a conversation with Paula Abdul! I remember thinking how important she must be in the industry that Paula Abdul who has millions of followers would take the time to talk to her. I was in awe.

'It's easy on Twitter,' she explains. 'Sure you can follow any of those celebrities and tweet to them. You get to know which ones are friendly and they're the ones I tend to tweet with. Honestly, if you tweet to them enough, the chances are you'll get a reply at some stage.'

'Well you must have something special,' I say. 'I can't tell you how many times I've tweeted the boys from Westlife and haven't managed to get an answer from them. You'll have to let me in on your secret!' It's amazing to see how Zahra's face lights up at the mention of celebrities. She obviously loves that whole scene. I can sort of understand how she might have built up an image for herself when she's interacting with all those important people on Twitter. It must be a real let down to close her computer and head off to do her cleaning job – from celebrity make-up artist to celebrity loo cleaner!

A loud banging on the door makes us all jump out of our skin, but I'm thankful for a chance to get away from this far too depressing chat. 'Okay, okay, I'm coming,' I shout, as the banging stops for about five seconds and starts again. There's only one person I know who bangs on the door like that and completely ignores the doorbell!

'Hiya, Mam,' I say, opening the door wide for her to come in. 'One of these days you might actually gently press the bell like any normal human being!'

'Ah, Jenny, don't be like that,' she says, rushing straight into the loo. 'You know I'm a slave to my bladder. I'm only bursting!'

'Granny Eileen, Granny Eileen,' comes a little voice from the sitting room. 'I knew you'd come!'

'Thank God for that,' says my mother, coming out of the little downstairs toilet. 'Honestly, I don't know where it all comes from.'

'Your wee comes from your willy and your poo comes from your back bum,' says Ryan, knowledgably.

I have to fight back the ball of laughter that's threatening to escape my lips. Jesus, that's the funniest thing I've heard in ages. He's quite adorable when he's being good.

'Well aren't you a clever little thing,' says my mother, not at all phased by his declared knowledge of the workings of the human body. 'I bet you're the top of the class in your playschool.'

'So what brings you over again today, Mam?'

'Ah I just wanted to check if Zahra was okay and of course to see this little man!' She grabs Ryan and proceeds to tickle him, to his great delight.

'I'm fine thanks, Mrs Breslin,' says Zahra. 'I've a splitting head-ache but the tablets are helping with that.'

'Speaking of which,' I say, suddenly remembering the prescription in my bag. 'I'd better slip down to the chemist and pick up your tablets, Zahra. The doctor said you only have enough for one more dose.'

'You go on, love,' says my mother generously. 'I'll stay and have a chat with the girls.'

'And can we play again, Granny Eileen?' asks Ryan, pulling at my mother's hand to go with him. 'I need you to help me build a boat with Lego.'

'Sorry, Eileen,' says Fiona, not looking in the slightest bit sorry. 'He's been going on about you all morning. You have a real little fan there.'

'Well it's a mutual thing,' says my mother, ruffling Ryan's hair. 'Sure we have a great time together, don't we, Ryan?'

'Well it looks as though you're in demand,' I laugh. 'I shouldn't be more than an hour. Is that okay with you Zahra?'

'Oh that's perfect, Jenny, if you're sure you don't mind heading back out. It'll be nice to have a chat with your mum.'

I'm glad of the chance to escape, even if just for an hour. My head is in a spin with everything that's going on and I just can't keep up. Well at least Fiona will be heading off tomorrow morning. Hooray! I'll gladly drop her and Ryan to the station – just to make sure they actually get on that train!

CHAPTER 23

As I pull Betsy up into the driveway, I notice the sun trying to peep through the clouds. The rain has finally stopped and I'm suddenly feeling brighter. The hour away from the house seems to have done me good. I hadn't realised how suffocated I'd been feeling.

Life would be perfect if I was coming home to an empty house now, but, instead, I'll have to endure the guests for another while yet. In a funny and distinctly weird turn of events, I'm actually quite looking forward to going back to work on Monday. I'm not even put off by the thought of Bootface! I mustn't be well. But it's true.

On a positive note, the girls' visiting has made me realise that my life isn't as shit as I thought it was. Although I don't have loads of friends, the ones I have are great. Sally and Paula are true, loyal friends and I know I can rely on them. When these few days are over, I must do something nice for them to let them know I appreciate them. And it seems I actually have a real 'mammy' mother – yes, my mother has turned into a proper mammy and although it's weird to find her in this role after all these years, it's really quite lovely.

I don't think it's just coincidence that Harry appeared on the scene at the same time as this transformation took place. He's obviously been a great influence on her. He may be a bit of a gobshite at times, but he really seems to love her and there's no doubt he treats her well. Oh when I think back to a few weeks ago when I was met at the door by his hairy face, not to mention that horrific moment when I realised I'd snogged him! It's funny how all that seems irrelevant now.

But back to the real world and dealing with my guests. I'm going to suggest that we head down to the shops and get a few DVDs for later. We can get one for Ryan to watch before he goes to bed and we can order in pizza and crack open a bottle of wine when he's asleep. I'm still feeling sad that Kerry didn't come. It would have been nice to have a night with all four of us. I'll take a quick look at my Twitter before I go in. Maybe I'll catch her online.

@JennyB Are you there @kerrydhunt? I'm just peeping in for a minute. Dying for a chat.

@kerrydhunt Hi, Jenny. That's gas – I was just thinking about you. Guess what?

@JennyB What? What? I only want to know if it's good news – I couldn't face anything else bad!

@kerrydhunt Well, there's a chance I might be able to pop up to Dublin tomorrow for a few hours. How would you feel about me dropping in?

@JennyB Oh, that's brilliant, Kerry. Yes, yes, please come. I'd love to see you. I have loads of news!

@kerrydhunt Oh yes – is Zahra ok? You said she was in hospital.

@JennyB She's fine. Concussion. I'll fill you in tomorrow. She'll be here when you come. Fiona and Ryan heading off in the morning.

@kerrydhunt Great. I'll touch base with you later and let you know if I'm definitely going to make it.

@JennyB Okay. Talk to you then. x

I throw my phone back into my bag and head inside with a big grin on my face. I'm not going to say anything to the girls about Kerry's visit tomorrow because Fiona might decide to change her plans. Hopefully, she won't check her Twitter before tomorrow – maybe I'll ask Kerry to delete those tweets just in case. I know it seems a little selfish, but with Ryan around it will be hard to have a proper chat with Kerry. Zahra will be here but at least she won't command attention.

'Hello, I'm home,' I shout, delighted with the new turn of events.

'Shhhh, Jenny,' says Mam, coming out of the sitting room. 'Come on in here. I'm having a lovely chat with Zahra and Ryan is drawing in the kitchen. Fiona has gone up for a little sleep. She was exhausted, poor girl. Said she hadn't been sleeping well over the past while.'

Bloody cheek! She's unbelievable. Imagine heading off to bed and leaving my mother and a sick Zahra minding her son? Well I think I'll definitely have to give her a piece of my mind when she comes down. And to think I was softening towards her this morning. God she really takes advantage.

'Aunty Jenny, Aunty Jenny ... can you draw me a clown? Granny Eileen isn't really good at drawing.'

'Well ... em ... ' Popping my head into the kitchen, I feel myself getting agitated at the drawing stuff all over the table and I can see pen marks on the wood.

'Or Lego,' he says, jumping down from the kitchen chair and grabbing my hand. 'Granny Eileen is good at that. Are you?'

'Well I ... em ... I'm not really sure, Ryan,' I say, loathing the thought of sitting on the floor playing with a four-year-old. 'I think maybe I'll make some tea. I'm sure your mummy would love a cup when she comes down.'

'Okay,' he says, heading over to my mother, no doubt to engage her in some more Lego construction. It's weird but sort of nice to how well the two of them get on. He's really taken with her, and she is with him. I wonder if it'll be like that when she has her own real grandchildren? Jesus, listen to me – when she has grandchildren. There wasn't even a hesitation there – no 'ifs' or 'maybes' just a definite *when*! I must be growing up at last!

'How long has Fiona been up there?' I ask.

'She went up just after you left,' says my mother. 'She must have really needed the rest.'

Needed the rest, my arse! More like she saw an opportunity to take advantage. Well I think I'll go and call her. She's not going to stay there all day while we look after her child. It's just not on. I make a point of banging cupboard doors in the kitchen and even stick the washing machine on for good measure! It sounds like a plane taking off when it gets going so if that doesn't get her up, nothing will. I'll give it ten minutes and if she doesn't appear, I'll go and wake her up.

Twenty minutes later, I'm storming up the stairs, ready to haul Fiona's lazy ass out of bed. I don't know how she could have slept through that noise. Honestly, even my mother was giving out about me making such a din and she's deaf at the best of times. I knock on her closed door – well actually I bang on it pretty hard. I can always say I've been knocking quietly and she didn't hear. I'm fuming and she's still not answering.

'Fiona ... Fiona ... you need to get up now,' I shout, still banging on the door.

Nothing. Not a peep!

'Fiona, are you okay in there?' My bravado is beginning to diminish and I'm starting to worry something is up. Nobody could sleep through all that noise. Oh, God, I hope she isn't sick and has to end up staying here for another while. Maybe it was those pancakes she made this morning. She must have used the flour in the baking cupboard and since I don't bake, it must have been there for years. I wonder if you can get food poisoning from flour. I seem to remember someone saying that if flour is left open, it can develop these tiny little wormy things. Eeeew! Maybe that's what's made her sick. Thank God I only had the eggs and mushrooms!

'I'm coming in Fiona,' I say, pushing the door open. 'Are you not feeling well or something?'

What the fuck? The fresh lemon print covers are pulled neatly over both beds and the pillows sitting plumped up on top. She's not here. Confused and slightly alarmed, I go to check in my bedroom. Surely she wouldn't have the nerve to use my bed? Although maybe if she's sick she felt she needed to be close to the loo and my room has the en-suite. I swing open the door and for a minute I think somebody has ransacked the place. I'm about to panic until I remember looking for a decent pair of tights this morning and emptying most of my drawers in the process. But where the hell is Fiona?

I take the stairs two at a time. 'Mam, what exactly did Fiona say? Did she definitely say she was going to bed?'

'Of course she did,' says my mother, looking at me as though I'm mad. 'What's the matter love?'

'Gosh, Jenny,' says Zahra, jumping up from the sofa. 'You look dead pale. Come on and sit down. What's wrong?'

'My mummy is a sleepy head,' says Ryan, trying to stick two pieces of Lego together that clearly don't go. 'She went asleep ages and ages and ages ago!'

'Em ... well mummies need their sleep, Ryan,' I say, gesturing for my mother and Zahra to come out into the hall. 'I just need Granny Eileen and Zahra to help me with something in the kitchen. You keep playing there with your Lego.'

'What's wrong, Jenny?' my mother asks, following me out of

the living room and closing the door behind her.

'It's Fiona – she's *gone*,' I whisper. 'She's not in bed at all.'

'What? She ... she couldn't be gone,' says Zahra, paling. 'Gone where?'

'I haven't a clue,' I say, heading into the kitchen to have a look out the window. 'But she's definitely not in the house.'

'Maybe she woke up and went out for a bit of a walk,' my mother says. 'It's the first break we've had in the rain today, so she might have wanted a bit of fresh air.'

'Without telling anyone? Hmmm – doubtful! Although maybe she wanted a walk on her own and she knew Ryan would want to go if she said anything.' Yes, that'll be it. She's just slipped out for a walk to clear her head. She was very quiet earlier and said she'd a headache so she probably just wanted a bit of peace. She'll walk in that door any minute now.

'Granny Eileen,' says Ryan, peeping his head out from the living room. 'Are you coming back to play?'

'I'll be there in a minute, sweetie,' she says, flashing him a loving smile. 'Why don't you find me all the red pieces and we'll make a car now.'

'Okay,' he says, skipping off to do as he's told. 'Look, why don't we give her another ten or fifteen minutes and see if she's back then,' says Zahra, being uncharacteristically decisive. 'If she's just gone for a walk, surely she won't be longer than that.'

'Right,' I say, still not convinced she's just out for a walk. She really doesn't strike me as the walking-in-the-fresh-air type. And the way she was acting this morning has given me a real uneasy feeling. 'I'll make us some tea and we'll reassess things in a while.'

'Good girl,' says my mother, heading back into the living room. *Good girl?* Good grief!

Half an hour and copious amounts of tea later, there's still no sign. There's definitely something up. I bet she's gone off some-where for the evening. She'd been asking about the night life in the city centre and she said she'd have loved to go in and sample it if she didn't have Ryan with her. I swear, I'll kill her if she's taken the liberty of going out and leaving us to babysit. I know it must be hard for her if she's on her own with Ryan. She must never get a break. But honestly, this isn't the way to do it. If she'd been really keen to check out the city centre, she only had to ask. Mam would have willingly watched Ryan while we popped in for a bit.

An hour later, we're sitting in the living room watching *Alice in Wonderland* with Ryan. Well I'm not exactly watching it – just going through the motions. Ryan started to ask about his mother a while ago, so we just told him she had a message to do and would be back soon. He seemed okay with that, but what on earth are we supposed to tell him if she's not back before bedtime? And the general opinion is she won't be! At least the DVD is distracting him for the moment. Thank God for early Christmas shopping and the bargain of two-for-one DVDs that I'd snapped up last week in town for Sally's kids.

A ring on the doorbell makes us all jump. At bloody last! So maybe I did her an injustice. Fiona must have gone out for a long walk after all or down to the shop maybe. 'That's probably your mummy now,' I say, though I'm not sure Ryan is too bothered at the moment.

With my best cross face on, I swing open the door. 'At last,' I say. 'I thought you were ... oh!' I'm shocked and more than a little confused to see Tom standing there. 'Eh ... why ... how ... what brings you here?'

'Well you did invite me,' he says, holding out a bottle of wine. 'Didn't you tell me to come over around sixish?' Memories of a drunken conversation last night spring to mind. Jesus! How could I have forgotten that I rang him after the show and asked him to come and meet the girls before they go home? Shit! I don't need another complication at the moment. But I politely hold open the door for him to step inside.

'God, I'm sorry, Tom. There's been so much going on here that I completely forgot. Come in, come in.'

'So I take it things aren't exactly running smoothly,' he whispers, taking off his heavy overcoat. 'You said something last night about one of the girls being in hospital?'

'Yes, that was Zahra. She's fine though. I'll introduce you to her in a minute. She's in the sitting room with my mother, babysitting.'

'Babysitting?' he says, freezing on the spot. 'For ... for whom?'

'Oh, he's not mine,' I say, amused at his shock. 'One of the girls, Fiona, brought her four-year-old son with her and now she's done a vanishing act.'

'You're not serious?' he says, throwing his coat on top of the ever-growing pile on the banisters. I really must get some coat hooks or a coat stand for the hall. 'So when is she coming back? That's a bit rich, isn't it?'

'It's a cheek all right,' I say and proceed to give him a brief synopsis of the past forty-eight hours.

'It's certainly been an eventful few days for you,' he says, shaking his head. 'And are you sure this Fiona girl has actually just upped and left? Maybe you're forgetting she said she was going to visit someone or something?'

'Don't be ridiculous, Tom. How on earth could I forget something like that?'

'Em ... quite easily, I should think,' he says, smirking. 'Didn't you forget I was coming over tonight?'

'Well that's different,' I say, blushing slightly. 'But what are we doing still standing here in the hall? Come on in and I'll introduce you to the others and let's see if we can make sense of everything. I bet you didn't bank on coming to a mad house tonight!'

'Well if I can help at all, I'd be glad to,' he says, and I soften at his generosity. Plenty of men would run a mile from situations like this.

'Mam, Zahra, this is Tom. You know – my ... em ... my friend from work.' Shit! I almost said boyfriend. That would have been weird and totally embarrassing.

'And this little man is Ryan,' says my mother, tousling the top of the child's head.

'Well it's lovely to meet you all,' says Tom, sitting down on the arm of the sofa. 'Jenny has just filled me in on the ... em ... situation.'

'Ryan, why don't you go back into the kitchen and draw me another picture? All your stuff is still on the kitchen table.'

'Okay, Granny Eileen. I'll do you a picture of Granddad Harry.'

'Lovely!' she says, as he shoots out the sitting room door. She lowers her voice to a whisper. 'I just didn't want him to hear us talking about his mam.'

'Of course,' says Tom. 'Sorry about that. I presume you've looked in her room to see if she's left a note or anything?'

'You looked, Jenny, didn't you?' says Zahra. 'You checked for a note when you saw she wasn't in her room?'

Fuck! I'm a bloody eejit! 'I ... em ... I'll be back in a minute!' I take the stairs two at a time. Of course, she'll have left a note. I'm mortified that I didn't look earlier. Thank God Tom mentioned it. At least now we'll know one way or the other where she is and what she's up to!

CHAPTER 24

There's no note! I've watched enough Jason Bourne movies to know how to look for clues and I tore the room apart in the process. I'm back with the others in the sitting room now and we're all beginning to panic. Where on earth has she gone?

'Well let's just relax for a minute and think things through,' says Tom. 'It may not be what we're thinking. She may have just wanted to escape for a night and will be back later.'

'Jesus, why are you being so calm?' I say, pacing up and down the room. 'Can't you see what's happened? Fiona was in a really funny mood today and kept making references to how happy Ryan is here and how much he loves my mother. I'm telling you, she's abandoned that child! Bloody, bloody, bloody hell! What are we going to do?'

I'm close to tears. There's a lump of sick in my throat and I'm sweating like a pig. Thank God at least Ryan is distracted. He was beginning to get a bit upset with all the comings and goings, so I opened yet another of Sally's kids' Christmas presents, a giant pack of felt pens, and treated him to a bag of crisps.

'Come on and sit down, love,' says my mother. 'Tom is right, we need to think this through calmly. Do you have her phone number for starters?'

'No, I don't,' I say, realising how stupid that sounds. 'I've

MARIA DUFFY

always been in touch through Twitter or email, so I haven't ever needed to get her number. Do you have one, Zahra?'

'I'm the same as you, I'm afraid, and only talk to her on Twitter.' She's rubbing her head and I'm reminded that the poor girl is only just out of hospital. She's probably well overdue her painkillers and I told her mother I'd look after her. Jesus, my head is about to explode with all this responsibility!

'Where does she live?' asks Tom, breaking my train of thought. 'Do you have an address for her?'

Again, I feel foolish. 'I don't have that either – all I know is she lives in Galway city in a town house. I know she's close to Eyre Square, because she often talks about walking to the shops.'

'Well that's a start,' says Tom. 'Although I'm sure she'll be back before we have to worry about Galway.'

'Jesus, I hope you're right,' I say, not really believing it. I mean, I'm completely clueless here. What happens to a child whose mother deserts him like this? If she doesn't come back and can't be found, will he be taken into care? Will he be sent to an orphanage and spend the rest of his days there, hoping and praying a nice family will come along and adopt him? I can't imagine there'd be much demand for a four-year-old. I mean, if I was adopting a child, I'd want to pick a brand new cuddly one – one who'd just accept me as their mother from the start rather than one who'd answer back and kick me in the shins when they don't get their way! But maybe it doesn't work like that. And how would anyone ever know she's deserted her child if we don't tell them? But not telling them means we're stuck with him! Oh, God, I don't know what to think!

'We'll probably have to inform the police if she doesn't come back soon,' says Tom, breaking into my thoughts. 'It's not something we can cover up and would you really want to anyway?'

'We're absolutely *not* going to the police!' says my mother, banging her hand down on the table and startling us all. 'There's no way we should go to the police. They'd just take the child and he'd end up in a foster home – or worse still, a state institution. He doesn't deserve that.'

'But, Mam, what's the alternative?' I ask, worriedly. 'If she doesn't come back, are we going to just keep the child? Are you suggesting we hang on to him indefinitely? Jesus!'

I'm in full panic mode now. This is a nightmare beyond any I've ever had. Maybe all those weird dreams I was having before the girls arrived were a sign of foreboding – a sign that my worst nightmares would come true!

'I don't know, love,' sighs my mother, rubbing her temples. 'I don't have the answers but, look, she's only been gone a little while so let's not jump to any conclusions. Can you imagine if we called the police and she wandered back in here later saying she was sorry for worrying us?'

'I suppose,' I say, reluctantly. 'And from what I've seen, she really isn't a bad mother. I think she just lets things get on top of her.'

'What about her husband?' says Zahra, suddenly. 'We've forgotten she has a husband! I know he's away on business but even if the worst comes to the worst, he'll probably be back in a few days.'

'Oh, yes,' says my mother, clapping her hands together. 'I can't believe we almost forgot about him. And he's a great husband and dad, isn't he? Do you know his name, Jenny?'

Uh, oh! Why on earth didn't I question Fiona about what Ryan said last night? Maybe things wouldn't have come to this if I'd got to the bottom of what was going on with her. Now it seems we have absolutely no leads – there doesn't seem to be anybody else in that little boy's life except for his mother, and some use she's turning out to be!

'Em ... her husband may not be as lovely as we thought he

was. When Ryan was in bed last night, he told me his daddy had left and is never coming back!'

'Oh Jesus, Mary and Holy St Joseph,' says my mother, blessing herself like all good Catholics do when taking the holy names in vain. 'So she's been deserted by her husband as well! No wonder the poor thing is all over the place. I hope she's not planning to do anything stupid.'

'You mean anything *more* stupid than she's done already?' I say, annoyed that my mother is sympathising with her.

'I think your mother is thinking about something really serious, Jenny,' says Tom, shaking his head at the very thought of it. 'I think we should realise she's not right in the head to do something like this and we should consider her a danger to herself.'

'You don't mean ... you don't mean she could ... she might ... ' The words catch in Zahra's throat and she begins to cry quietly.

'Oh, Jesus, do you really think she'd do something like that?' I say, shuddering at the thought.

With things taking on a whole new sinister turn, I'm feeling sorry I sounded so harsh. God, maybe I should be a bit more sympathetic. Maybe the poor girl is having a breakdown or something. Oh bloody hell!

'I honestly think we should call the police,' says Tom, trying to take charge of a situation that's quickly falling apart.

'*No*,' my mother says again. 'If that little child gets into the system, he'll never live a normal life. We need to try and find her, that's what we need to do. We need to find her and see what the bloody hell she's playing at!'

'But we have no way of finding her, Mam,' I say, watching as my mother wipes her eyes. 'I told you, the only means of contact I have is Twitter.'

'So have you tweeted her?' asks Tom, looking at me expectantly. 'Maybe she's answered.'

Again I feel foolish! 'I haven't yet, but I'll do it now. I suppose I was hoping she'd arrive back and I didn't want to look as though I was panicking.' I quickly tap out a DM to her. I'm aware that it sounds pretty lame, but I honestly don't know what to say.

> @JennyB Please contact us, Fiona. We're really worried about you and haven't told Ryan you're gone. Come home before he knows.

Oh, God, I shouldn't have pressed send on that one. It just sounds so … so ordinary, as if I'm asking her to get some milk on her way home! But I don't want to sound too panicky. I don't want to scare her off. She needs to know we're not reporting her and we'll wait until she comes to her senses and come home.

> @JennyB We're not going to the police or anything – I know you love Ryan and won't stay away for long. Please come back.

There, that's better. Surely she'll read that and realise she can't do this. She knows Ryan will be fine here with us, but she also should know that we're not going to hold on to him forever. Maybe if she has some time away, she'll cop on to herself and come back, apologising for the whole mess. God, I hope so.

'Where's my mummy?' Ryan asks, appearing at the sitting room door. 'Why hasn't she come back yet?'

'Ah come on over here, lovey,' my mother says, gesturing her lap for him to hop up onto. 'Mummy had some messages to do, so she'll be late home tonight. Why don't we get you something to eat? You must be hungry after all that Lego building and drawing.'

'Okay,' he says, cuddling up to my mother. 'But can I have McDonald's? I love McDonald's.'

'I'll go,' says Tom, jumping up from the sofa.

'Well we were going to order in some pizzas for tonight, but why don't we just have McDonald's all round then,' I say, happy to go along with anything that'll keep Ryan occupied. If he starts his tantrums again, I honestly won't know how to handle him.

'Good idea,' says my mother. 'There's a drive-through in the village – you could go to that.'

'Hooray, McDonald's,' shouts Ryan, beaming from ear to ear and clapping at the decision. 'Can I have ice-cream too?'

'You can have whatever you want,' says my mother, stroking his curly hair.

'Oh, yes, ice-cream,' says Tom, tickling Ryan on the belly. 'We boys should always have ice-cream after our dinner to keep up our strength!'

I watch how Tom is interacting with Ryan and, I have to admit, I'm impressed. He's no problem talking to him on his level and Ryan seems to have warmed to him. If I tried to tickle him like that, he'd no doubt kick me, or at the very least cry!

'Right,' Tom says, grabbing his coat from the banisters in the hall and taking a pen out of the pocket. He tears off a piece of kitchen towel from the roll on the worktop. 'Shout out what you all want and I'll head down and get it. It's on me!'

I'm distracted from all the goings on for a moment by Tom's sudden manliness. I'm still not sure that I actually fancy him, but the way he's taking charge of the situation is certainly a bit of a turn on. I know I was annoyed at him for ditching me for his mother the other night, but maybe I was a bit harsh. He's a decent guy and I could do worse. And maybe I could persuade him to stay over tonight. I don't mean in my bed or anything – but if he wants to pay me a visit during the night, that might be okay too!

Half an hour later, we're all sitting around the kitchen table eating our burgers, chips and ice-cream. Ryan is in good spirits despite his mum not coming back and he seems to be oblivious to the fact we're all in bits about what's happening. Mam had a quiet word with me and suggested we keep everything normal for Ryan and we can all begin to panic again after he's gone to bed.

'Are you not finishing that, Ryan?' asks Tom, as the child pushes aside half his cup of ice-cream. 'The end part is the yummiest because all the sauce sinks right down.'

'That's what Mummy says,' answers Ryan. 'That's why I'm keeping it for her. Aunty Jenny, will you put this in the fridge for when she gets home?'

'Of course I will, Ryan,' I say, swallowing a lump in my throat. I suddenly feel terribly sorry for the poor child. God only knows what lies in store for him if his mother doesn't come back. For the first time since he arrived on Wednesday, I notice how cute he is. His bright-blue eyes are exactly the same colour as Fiona's and seem to be set right into his chubby face. He could really do with a haircut as the masses of unruly brown curls tumble all over his forehead. I suddenly want to pick him up and cuddle him. I want to tell him everything will be all right, but will it? I honestly don't know what's going to come of this mess.

'Come on then, Ryan,' says my mam, pushing her chair back from the table to get up. 'It's getting late, so why don't I bring you upstairs and get your pyjamas on.'

'But I want to wait up for my mummy,' he protests, big eyes almost popping out of his head.

'We'll tell her to come up to you when she comes home,' Tom says. 'Just think how happy she'll be if she knows you've been good and are all snuggled up in bed.'

Again, I'm amazed at Tom's easy way with Ryan. He's definitely made for this – unlike me who can't think of a single, comforting thing to say to the poor child. As Mam takes Ryan upstairs, I feel a little bubble of excitement at having Tom stay tonight. I know I shouldn't be thinking of anything but the situation with Fiona at the moment but it would be good to get to know Tom a little more and see if there's any hope for us. He's looking pretty comfortable and it's getting late, so I'm hopeful he won't want to bother driving home.

'Right, that's that done,' he says, sitting back down. 'So what now? Have you checked your Twitter to see if Fiona has answered any of your messages?'

'I've checked it every few minutes,' says Zahra, sighing heavily. 'It doesn't look as though she's going to get in touch.'

I think Zahra is right. I think we've been fooling ourselves thinking she might just be gone for the night. I think this girl has just walked away from her life. 'What the bloody hell are we going to do?'

'I know your mother is dead against it,' he says, watching me carefully. 'But I really think you should maybe give Fiona until the morning and if she hasn't turned up, you should ring the gardaí.'

'Well, that was my first thought,' I say. 'But looking at his little face at the table here before he went up, I'd hate to think of him going into care. I wonder is there anything we can do to find her. Surely there's a way – maybe we're just not thinking of everything.'

'The only thing I can think of,' he says, 'is to go down to Galway and see if you can find where she lives. Maybe Ryan knows his address or at least could give us an idea of the area.'

'Oh, that's a great idea,' I say, brightening up at the thought of me and Tom taking a trip down to Galway. I know it won't be all fun and games, but it would be good to have the time with him, just the two of us. He's a nice, kind and caring man, and I could certainly do worse than get together with him. Okay, the earth doesn't move when he's around or I don't feel like ripping his clothes off every time I look at him, but I do feel *sort of* attracted to him, so that's a start. Having him around this evening has just confirmed to me that I *do* want a man in my life. I want somebody to share things with. I want someone to lean on when things aren't going well or I've had a bad day. I want somebody to kiss under the mistletoe this year.

'Right, that's him down,' says Mam, cutting into my thoughts. 'The poor little thing was so tired he almost fell asleep while brushing his teeth.' Damn my mother and her rotten timing. Zahra has just gone to the loo and I was hoping for a bit of a private chat with Tom.

'Ah, poor fella,' says Tom. 'It's just as well he doesn't have a clue what's happening. Well I think I'll get off now and leave you girls to it. Don't forget to let me know what happens.'

What? He's *leaving*? Feck! Have I read the situation completely wrong? 'But, where ... why ... . I thought you were staying? What about Galway?'

'What *about* Galway?' my mother asks, looking from one to the other. 'What have I missed?'

'We were talking about going to Galway,' I say, looking at Tom accusingly. 'We thought if Fiona doesn't show up by morning, we might take a trip down there to see if we can find her.'

'Ah, Jenny, you misunderstood. I can't go to Galway with you. I have to bring Mammy shopping in the morning and I've promised I'd get stuck into the garden too. I was just suggesting you go down there yourself.'

'Oh,' I say, completely deflated. Never mind the fact he's not coming to Galway with me, but he's not even staying. I'm gutted. I know it's probably not appropriate to be thinking these things when my only thought should be getting Fiona back, but I can't help it. I'm obviously crap at reading signals!

'Well ... em ... why don't you stay over anyway?' I say, realising I sound pretty desperate. But I don't care. I suddenly feel the need to have someone put their arms around me and show me a bit of love. I don't even mean sex or anything – just a kiss and a cuddle. 'This sofa is pretty comfy and it would save you driving home. We could open a bottle of wine and have a chat about this whole situation.'

'I'm just ... eh ... going to check on Ryan again,' says my mother, hopping up from her chair and rushing out of the room. Either she's just giving us space to sort out whatever needs to be sorted or I've completely embarrassed her. And embarrassing my mother is no easy task!

'I'd love to, Jenny,' he says, continuing to fasten his coat. *Take it off, take it off!* 'But I've promised Mammy and I don't want to upset her. She hates it when I change plans.'

For fuck's sake! Mammy, Mammy, Mammy! I can't believe he's letting his bloody mammy ruin things for us again! Is he ten years old or what? No matter how much of a nice guy he is, this whole Mammy thing is a real turn off. It just takes all his manliness and pulps it into a withered, boyish blob!

'But I'll give you a ring in the morning,' he continues, heading out towards the front door. 'I honestly hope things work out. Do you think you'll go to Galway?'

'I'm not sure,' I sigh. 'Mam would have to stay here to mind Ryan since she's the only one who can handle him and Zahra wouldn't be well enough to come. This whole thing feels unreal. But if I honestly thought I'd find her in Galway, I'd head off there on my own anyway.' If I play it right, maybe he'll change his mind about coming down with me.

'Well if your mother is insisting on not calling the gardaí and Fiona doesn't make an appearance, it would probably be a good idea to go down yourself.' Huh! And his mother wins again!

'Well I'll just have to sleep on it. I'm going to check my

Twitter again just in case and I'll have a rethink in the morning.'

'All right,' he says, pulling his collar up around his neck as a blast of wind hits us when he opens the door. 'And, Jenny ... '

'Yes?' I look at him expectantly.

'Let's have a proper chat when all this stuff dies down.' He moves in towards me and kisses me gently on the lips. I close my eyes and enjoy the sweet, light touch that I've been waiting for. It's a lovely kiss. A soft, sexy kiss. But not a mind-numbing one. I enjoyed it, but it didn't make me want to pull him back inside and rip his clothes off. But still, it's more than we've had before so it's progress I suppose. I've got to remember what Sally told me – relationships need work. I'd expect to have my mind blown away if I was just in it for the sex. But I want more. I want a proper relationship so that might mean compromising on certain things. I watch as his car heads off into the darkness and close the door on the freezing cold.

'Are you okay, Jenny?' asks my mother, startling me. Jesus, was she standing behind me all that time? Has she no cop on at all?

'I'm fine, Mam, just worried about what's going to happen.'

'I know what you mean, love. But let's just wait until the morning and we can talk about it then.

'Will you come back, Mam ... in the morning, I mean ... will you come back over? I honestly don't know how Zahra and I will cope with Ryan. What if he wakes up during the night? I mean, I haven't a clue what I'll do if he starts one of his tantrums.'

'Jenny, love, I'm going to stay the night,' she says. 'I wouldn't leave you on your own with all this going on. Just get me a few blankets and I'll sleep on that couch in the living room. We can assess the situation bright and early in the morning. I've already rung Harry and told him the score.'

'What's this?' asks Zahra, appearing in the hall, a glass of water in hand.

'Mam's going to stay the night so that she can help us out if Ryan wakes up.'

'That's so good of you, Mrs Breslin. But if you both don't mind, I'm going to head on up. I just want to try to sleep off this headache.'

'Of course, lovey,' says my mother, giving Zahra a gentle hug. 'You get some sleep and we'll see you in the morning. We'll give you a shout if there's any news.'

'Thanks so much for this, Mam,' I say, as Zahra disappears up the stairs. 'I did think Tom might have stayed around but he couldn't tonight.'

'Hmmm! I noticed,' she says. 'So I take it you two haven't got it on yet then?'

'*Mam!*' I'm shocked she'd say something like that to her own daughter. 'You can't ask me that!'

'I'm your mother, Jenny,' she says. 'I don't *need* to ask – I could feel the sexual tension in the room!'

Jesus! I'm mortified.

'And if you want my advice,' she continues, 'he's not the man for you. He's a lovely fella – very kind and considerate – but just not for you.'

'Well we'll just have to see, Mam,' I say, wondering where that came from. 'We'll have a chat when all this calms down and we'll see where it's all going.'

'Fine, love. But just take my word, he's not the right one for you.'

I head up the stairs to grab a duvet and some pillows from the hotpress for my mother. What on earth possessed her to say that? How could she know if he's right for me or not? She's a bit of a cheek really. Just because she's my mother doesn't give her the right to decide who I see or who I don't. Doesn't she realise that good men don't grow on trees? And Tom *is* a good man. Well I'm going to forget what she said and see what happens. As soon as we get this whole sorry saga sorted out, I'll begin to concentrate on *my* life for a change. With a bit of luck, I'll be spending Christmas this year in the company of someone special. I'll have somebody to kiss under the mistletoe and somebody to swap special presents with. Yes, this Christmas is going to be the best one I've had in years. I just know it!

CHAPTER 25

Saturday

I'm running, faster and faster, stumbling and tripping in my effort to get away from my pursuer. I'm running in sand now and as it's getting deeper, I'm getting slower. Oh God, he's catching up – I can hear his insane laughter. He must be only a few feet away now and I can feel my legs give way. I'm finally thigh-deep in sand and can't move another inch. That's it. I close my eyes tight and pray.

'Aunty Jenny, Aunty Jenny – can you build me a car with my Lego? Can you bring me to McDonald's? Can you tie my shoelaces? Can you buy me some new toys? Can you … can you … can you … ?'

Arghhhhhhhh!

Bloody hell! They're back! The bloody nightmares are back! I haven't had a weird dream these past few days but this one tops them all. And that's probably because it's closer to the truth than I care to think about. Ryan woke up crying twice during the night. I'd naively thought that Zahra might have settled him back down since she's in the same room, but her drugs ensured she was in cloud-cuckoo land. I dragged my unwilling body in to check on him but thankfully a little soothing shhhh in his ear did the trick. I was quite proud of myself actually – I'm obviously not quite as bad with kids as I thought. But now it's seven o'clock and he's woken up again and this time he's well and truly awake. Jesus, I can't cope with this!

'Where's Mummy?' he asks, jumping on the end of my bed as though it were a trampoline. Honestly, he must never have been taught any manners.

'She's ... em ... she's had to go out to do a few more things,' I say, realising we'd have to come up with a better story soon if she doesn't turn up. 'Why don't you go and see if Zahra wants to play?' Well it's only right we take turns and, after all, I did the hardest part during the night!

'But Mummy didn't come and kiss me last night,' he says, still jumping up and down and scarcely missing a beat! 'You promised she'd come up to me when she got home. You told a lie and that's very, very naughty.'

He has me there! 'You must have been fast asleep when she came up, Ryan. She was very late and then had to go back out early this morning.'

Liar, liar, pants on fire!

'What's going on in here, then?' asks my mother, appearing like my fairy godmother at the bedroom door. 'Let's get you downstairs for a bit of breakfast, Ryan.'

'Hooray for Granny Eileen!' he squeals. 'Can we have sausages and put them in bread with brown sauce?'

'Of course we can, love,' she says, guiding him out the door. 'And maybe if you're really good, we'll even make some pancakes.'

God, I love my mother!

*

What a brilliant sleep that was. I must have dozed right off after Mam took Ryan. I was probably on tenterhooks all night, so I was more than ready to have a peaceful sleep. God, Ryan really is a handful. Imagine having to put up with that every single day

of your life. It's a scary thought. At least if there are two of you,
there might be some reprise, but it looks like Fiona is on her
own with nobody to take the reins off her for a while. I'm sort
of beginning to understand her need to escape.

But I think Mam is right. Fiona is, at heart, a good mother
and loves her son. I'm sure once she has time away to think
about this, she'll be back. I'm glad now we didn't call the police
last night. God, could you imagine if we had and she turned up
all apologetic this morning? Imagine we had to tell her that her
son had gone into care and she'd probably have to spend the
next number of years fighting to prove herself a worthy mother!

It's 10.30 already, so I suppose I'd better get up and face the
day. I'll just take a look and see if she's tweeted first. Grabbing
my phone from the locker I immediately click on the most used
button on the phone. Nothing. Not a sausage! She either isn't
checking her tweets or just isn't ready to communicate yet. Oh
but there *is* one here from Kerry.

> @*kerrydhunt* Hi, Jenny. I should be with you before twelve
> this morning. Looking forward to it.

Oh, shit! I'd forgotten Kerry was coming. I was so excited about
her visit when she tweeted yesterday and now it's just a bit of an
inconvenience. Sure I may not even be here if I decide to go to
Galway. What a bloody mess! I won't tweet her back because
she's probably already on the road. But I'll leave another DM for
Fiona. I'm sure she'll check at some stage and I want her to
know how worried we all are.

> @*JennyB* Fiona, please come home. I understand you're going
> through some stuff and we want to help.

Maybe I'll tell her about Kerry arriving – it might encourage her to come back. She was only saying yesterday how much she liked Kerry and how she was sorry we didn't get to meet her.

@JennyB You won't believe it but Kerry is coming today. We need you home so that the four of us can finally have our Twitmas party!

It sounds a bit lame and I really don't know if it'll make a difference, but I have to give it a try. I push the comfy duvet down off my warm body in an effort to entice myself to get up. All is quiet downstairs so I'm guessing Mam has it all under control, but we do need to make some decisions. Although I haven't even showered yet, a glance at my pale, tired face in the mirror scares me into sticking some make-up on. Honestly, I envy those girls who can go fresh-faced and make-up free. I'd scare small children if I ever ventured past the door without my mask!

'Morning, love,' says my mother, glancing up from her magazine as I arrive into the kitchen. 'There's tea in the pot – it's only made a few minutes so it should be hot enough.'

'Thanks, Mam,' I say, grabbing a cup from the press and sitting down beside her. 'Is Zahra not up yet?'

'She's just getting dressed now. I peeped in on her a few minutes ago to see if she was okay. We're forgetting that she has a head injury. We should really be keeping a better eye on her.'

'I know,' I sigh. 'It's just that there's so much going on at the minute, it's hard to keep up with it all.'

I do feel a little bit guilty. Since Fiona upstaged Zahra's drama, I really haven't been giving the poor girl the attention she deserves. The doctor suggested we should be keeping an eye on her while she's sleeping but other than a quick peep when Ryan woke up, I didn't bother. Still, she seems okay and at the moment all I can think of is getting Fiona back.

'Well it'll all settle down in a few days and we can all get back to normal,' says Mam, buttering a slice of toast.

'Let's hope so,' I sigh, wondering if life will ever get back to normal. 'What's Ryan up to?'

'Watching telly in the living room,' she says. 'He was asking about his mum again, so I thought it was best to distract him.'

'Good. So have you had any further thoughts about what we should do?' I cut myself a slice of the currant bread Mam has left on the table. I don't have much of an appetite but the cinna-monny smell is making my mouth water.

'Oh I've thought of nothing else, Jenny, love,' she says, sipping her tea. 'I take it she hasn't tweeted? Because if she hasn't, I think the best idea might be to see if Ryan knows any of his address and maybe go down to Galway for a snoop around.'

'You're probably right,' I say, although I'm not convinced. 'Do you want to have a little chat with him about it? You know how he is with you. If anyone can get information out of him, it's you.'

'I'll go and have a little word with him in a minute. The poor little mite. It doesn't really seem right to be questioning him, does it?'

'What doesn't seem *right*,' I say, raising my voice a little more than I should, 'is the fact that his mother has disappeared and left us to deal with this! We're only trying to do our best to get her back.'

'I know, love, I know. So I was thinking – I doubt Zahra is fit enough to travel down to Galway so she should definitely stay here. And I should really stay here to keep an eye on her. So either you head down on your own or take Ryan with you. He could be a help when you get down there and if you find Fiona, you could just pass him over to her.'

Oh, God, neither sounds like a very good option to me. I really don't fancy the thought of heading all the way down to

Galway on my own, but if the alternative is having a whiney child in the car, I think travelling solo wins! If Ryan is anything like Sally's two, the journey would be unbearable. I once went with her down to the Kildare Village shopping outlets which are around an hour from her house and, I swear, I was traumatised for days afterwards. From the time the engine started, Sinead said she felt sick. I was instructed to get into the back seat and sit between them both, holding a towel to catch any spew! I had the towel hovering under Sinead's face, disgusted at the thought of having to deal with vomit, especially since I'd worn my new Guess T-shirt. Anyway, ten minutes into the journey I was still holding the towel close to Sinead as she made all sorts of retching noises when out of the blue, Abbey squealed and proceeded to projectile vomit all over my back. It was the grossest thing I've ever experienced.

'Can I have something nice?' asks Ryan, appearing at the kitchen door. 'I ate up all my breakfast and you said I could have something nice after.'

'Okay, Ryan,' says my mother, ushering him back out of the room. 'You go on back in to watch the telly and I'll bring you in something yummy.'

He does as he's bid, with Mam following hot on his tail with a plate of chocolate-chip biscuits. I'm beginning to wonder if Mam is enjoying this Ryan experience a little too much! Just then, Zahra arrives downstairs, wearing the brightest canary yellow dress I've ever seen in my life. Her make-up is freshly applied and she looks the better for her long sleep. Lucky for her!

'Morning,' she says, flopping down on one of the chairs. 'That was a great sleep. Wasn't Ryan great not to wake up during the night? Has he been up long?'

'Eh ... he ... em ... yes, he was good and Mam took him down this morning so I could stay in bed for a while. I'm just up myself.' I was going to tell her he'd been awake during the night, but seeing how fresh and happy she looks today, I haven't the heart to.

'So I've checked Twitter,' she says, pouring herself a cup of tea. 'I suppose you have too. Nothing from Fiona. What are we going to do?'

'Well I think I'll head down to Galway and see what I can find out. It's a long shot, but what else can we do? Mam is checking to see if Ryan knows any of his address. Why don't you take your tea in to them while I head up for a shower?'

'I really enjoyed the chat with your mam last night, Jenny. She was giving me all sorts of ideas about how to go after the career I really want. I'm really beginning to feel I can make something of myself after all. I feel so much more confident now.' I watch as Zahra happily heads in to join Mam in the sitting room. Jesus! Child whisperer, guidance counsellor ... what next? I don't think anything could surprise me any more!

CHAPTER 26

Just as I'm heading up for a shower, the shrill noise of the door-bell makes me jump. Oh, thank God! It has to be Fiona. I take the stairs two at a time and just pause long enough to bless myself before swinging the door open.

'Hi, Jenny!'

What the fuck? 'Em ... who ... why are you ... em ... ' Words fail me. My head is spinning and I'm tempted to shut the door and when I open it again he'll be gone. It's the man from the bar at the Olympia – the one from McDonald's! What the hell is he doing here? Seeing him in the bar after seeing him in McDonald's could be put down to coincidence, but having him turn up at my front door is just plain stalkerish!

'Jenny, is that Fiona?' says my mother, appearing in the hall. 'I didn't want to rush out in case Ryan got his hopes ... oh sorry, I'll ... em ... leave you to it.' Shooting me a disapproving look, she disappears back into the sitting room. What must she be thinking? Another strange man arriving on my doorstep!

'You might need to sit down for this,' says the stalker, a mischievous twinkle in his eye. I'm completely confused now. Why would I need to sit down? Oh, God, I'm also aware that I must look a sight in my one-time-white-but-now-grey robe and hair sporting the 'just woken up' look! Thank God at least I've done my make-up.

'I'm sorry, but you must have the wrong house ... or person ... ' As I say the words, I'm fully aware that he's used my name – just like he did at the bar in the Olympia. I'd probably find it a bit scary but for the fact that he's pretty yummy with his long chestnut hair tumbling over his forehead. I feel a bit like Martine McCutcheon in *Love Actually* when Hugh Grant arrives on her doorstep. I'm no Martine, but he's a dead ringer for the scrumptious Hugh! Jesus, listen to me – drooling over my stalker!

'Jenny, it's me ... Kerry!' He doesn't say any more, but just waits to let the words sink in. What does he mean, Kerry? Kerry who? The only Kerry I know is Kerry from Twitter and she's meant to be com— what? Oh, fuck! What's he saying? I close my eyes for a split second and open them again but no, he's still there!

'Ker ... ry ... who?' I ask slowly, already fearing the answer.

He bites his lip and looks at me intently with those deep brown eyes. 'Jenny, I'm Kerry from Twitter. It's me – I'm a ... em ... I'm not a woman, I'm a man!'

Well, I can bloody well see that! Jesus! I can't get my head around what he's saying. Is he pretending to be the girl I've befriended on Twitter or ... or ... could he possibly be ... ?

'I'm really sorry, Jenny,' he continues, but he doesn't look really sorry. 'It's really me – Kerry Hunt – the person you've been tweeting. Ta da!'

Ta bloody da! Jesus, the cheeky pup. Is that meant to be a joke? 'Why don't you let me in and I'll explain everything to you.'

My world has ended. I may as well succumb to whatever evils this life throws at me. If he's telling the truth, I'm gutted! I've grown really fond of Kerry – well, the Kerry I thought I knew. She was the one I turned to mostly when I had a problem and the one who came across as so down to earth and likeable. So here I am, standing at my front door with the girl I've been friendly with for the past year who, apparently, is a man and, inside, there's a four-year-old child taking up residence in my house because his mother has abandoned him! Maybe I should move out and let them all take over my house and my life! Seriously, running away never seemed so enticing! But I need to snap out of it. I'm standing like an eejit in the doorway, not sure what to do. If what he's saying is true, I bloody well want an explanation.

'Well I suppose you'd better ... em ... maybe you should ... look, just come in for a minute, will you?' I still can't take it in, but I lead him into the kitchen and tersely point to a chair for him to sit down.

'Jenny, I know you must hate me right now,' he says, sitting down heavily on the chair, 'but honestly, you have to believe me when I say that this all just got out of hand. I really wasn't trying to fool anybody. And I certainly wouldn't want to hurt *you*.'

I try to ignore the cheeky grin, the smooth words. 'Are you *really* Kerry?' I ask, glancing out the window to see if the *real* Kerry is out there and this man will jump up and declare he's her brother/boyfriend/personal trainer!

'I swear, it's me,' he says, rooting in his pocket for something. 'Here's my driving licence so you can check out my handsome mug – just so you don't think I'm a stalker or something!'

Em ... never crossed my mind – well, okay then, it did! In my weirdly mixed-up head, I feel a little disappointed that he's not a stalker. I've never had one before and I have to admit, it would be fairly exciting. I was only reading last week about one of those supermodels – I can't remember which one – who had a stalker who turned up everywhere she went. She ended up having him arrested. I remember thinking how cool it must be to have somebody so interested in you that they would follow you everywhere. But back to the here and now and I take a long look at the picture on his licence. Yep! It's him all right and the name beneath – Kerry Hunt! He's waiting for me to respond but I honestly don't know what to say.

'Look, why don't we go out for a bit of breakfast or something and we can have a chat,' he says. 'I really want you to understand what happened.' He's looking more serious now. Thank God he's not continuing with that cheeky chappie routine, or I might well strangle him!

'Aunty Jenny, who's that man?' Ryan is peeping around the kitchen door and eying Kerry suspiciously.

'It's just a … a friend of mine, Ryan,' I say. 'Go on back into Granny Eileen.'

'She's gone to do her wee-wee. She said you have to go somewhere today. Is that man going with you?'

'No, Ryan, he is *not*. Now you go on back in and watch the telly and Granny Eileen will be in to you in a minute.'

'Is that Fiona's Ryan?' asks Kerry, puzzled. I thought he was going home with Fiona this morning. So they're still here, then? And where's Zahra?'

'Yes, that's Ryan,' I sigh. 'Zahra is inside with my mother but Fiona is gone. Honestly, Kerry, I'm telling you, you've no idea what's been going on here. It's been mental!'

'Gone? Gone where? Now I'm really confused.'

'Ha! You're confused! Try living with it for a few days! Basically, Fiona disappeared yesterday afternoon without Ryan. We thought at first maybe she was just gone for a walk or something but it looks as though she's abandoned him.' Why on earth am I talking to this man as though he's my best friend? I should be screaming and shouting at him, not getting him up to speed on the news. How dare he? How bloody dare he? He's just toyed around with my feelings for the past year and now he expects me to act as though there's nothing wrong. The amount of stuff I've told him on Twitter – things I didn't feel comfortable telling the other two. Jesus, I think I even told him about the trouble I was having with my periods! Imagine saying he was a nurse to suck me in and make me think she ... he ... he was a nice person!

'Bloody hell! You're not serious? I can't believe I wasn't here for all that. You poor thing; you must be out of your mind with worry.' Much as I'm annoyed with him, I can hear tones of the Kerry I've grown fond of in his voice. I know that sounds stupid because I've never actually heard her ... his voice, but he's actually just as I'd imagined Kerry to be – except for the fact he's a man! There's so much I want to know but, for the moment, I need somebody else to share this burden with, and Kerry knows Fiona just as much as I do. So I take a deep breath and begin from the moment they arrived on Wednesday through to now – taking in Zahra's fall, her revelation about who she really is, Fiona's departure yesterday and my plans to head to Galway shortly.

'Jesus!' says Kerry. 'This just keeps getting better and better. And now here's me turning up on your doorstep to complicate things even more. I wish I knew what to say or do to help. I know I haven't met her face to face but Fiona seems like a nice girl. I can't believe she'd want to abandon her child completely.'

'I know, we can't believe it either. Thank God for my mother, though. She's been great with Ryan. I don't know what I'd have done if she hadn't been around. There's no way Zahra and I would have been able to handle him ourselves. He can be ... let's just say ... spirited.'

'Um ... sorry, Jenny,' says Zahra, arriving into the kitchen. 'Your mam said you had company, but I just want to grab a juice for Ryan, if that's okay.'

'I think you'd better come in and sit down,' I say, pulling out another chair. 'I think you might know this man.'

'I ... em ... I don't think ... oh it's you from the theatre ... from McDonald's. But how?' She's babbling, but I know exactly how she feels.

'I'm Kerry,' he says, grinning. I swear, if he comes out with that 'ta-da' again, I'll kill him! 'And before you ask, it's Kerry Hunt from Twitter – the one you all thought was a girl!'

I watch Zahra's face as she sits down heavily on the chair. 'I don't know what to say,' she says, shaking her head. 'It's ... um ... nice to meet you, I suppose.'

'Lovely to meet you too, Zahra. Look, I know there must be a million questions you both want to ask me and I'm happy to answer anything, but for the moment we need to think about Fiona.'

He said 'we'! He didn't say 'you'! I feel slightly pleased that he seems willing to help with the situation. Oh for feck's sake! What the bloody hell am I thinking? This man is a pig of the highest order! He's lied in the worst possible way and made a complete fool of me. Bastard!

'Well? Any ideas?' he asks, slouching back even further on the chair and stretching out his long denim-clad legs. I'm tempted to be sarcastic and ask him if he'd like to lie down somewhere – but he'd probably only take it the wrong way. 'Do you really think it will do any good going to Galway?'

'I honestly don't know,' I say, rubbing at my temples in an effort to get rid of a blinding, pounding headache. I know I should just tell him to leave and block him on Twitter for what he's done but it's strangely comforting to have him here. 'But we have to do something. It's only two hours away and motorway all the way so I think it's worth a try. Mam is going to stay here with Zahra and Ryan. I'm really sorry you had a wasted journey.'

He's looking at me intently and I can't figure out what he's thinking. Maybe it's pity for the crap situation I'm in. Or could it be an admiring or lustful look? Huh, the latter is probably just my sexual antenna peeping out because of the close proximity to his maleness. I remember how I thought he was cute when I met him at the bar on Thursday night. And that's another thing – how come he's been hanging around all weekend? Maybe I wasn't too wrong about the stalker thing! But as his dark eyes catch mine, I feel a rush of something hot flooding through me.

'Maybe it's not wasted at all,' he says, a white-toothed smile appearing on his face. 'Why don't we go together? After all, two heads are better than one.'

'Oh that's a brilliant idea, Kerry,' pipes up Zahra, beaming. 'I was feeling guilty about you having to go on your own, Jenny. It's a perfect solution, don't you think?'

'Well ... I ... em ... I just need to check with my boyfriend first. He said he might come with me.' Oh fuck! Why on earth did I say that? It sounded like something a twelve-year-old would say: 'I can't go with you because I already have a boyfriend'! I know there's absolutely no way Tom is going to come with me – he made that plainly clear last night. And if Kerry comes, the journey in the car would give him time to explain himself properly.

'But I thought that ... ' Zahra trails off as I give her daggers. Thank God she has the cop on not to say any more.

'Ah well,' he says, shrugging his shoulders. 'It was just a thought. I wouldn't want to come between you and your fella, now.'

'Well, I'm not saying no altogether,' I say, in an attempt to redeem the situation. 'I just need to give Tom a call.'

Thankfully, my mother arrives into the kitchen and I avoid making any more of a fool of myself. 'Hi, there,' she says, holding a hand out to shake Kerry's. 'I'm Jenny's mam.' She raises an eyebrow at me that seems to be saying 'how many of these men have you on the go?'

'Mam, this is Kerry,' I say, wondering if she'll make the connection.

'Kerry? The Kerry from Twitter?' she says, shaking his hand but clearly not understanding what's going on. 'I thought Kerry was a girl.'

'So did we,' says Zahra.

'Well it's lovely to meet you, Mrs Breslin,' he says, flashing her a smile. 'I'm happy to do whatever I can to help.'

'Em ... right, thanks,' she says, looking at him doubtfully. 'I've managed to get a half-address from Ryan so at least that's something. We have a street name and he's said he can see the Eyre Square Christmas markets from his house, so that might help too.'

'Oh that's great,' I say, quite surprised that Ryan was able to give that much information.

'So I really think you should go as soon as possible,' she continues. 'If you can get down there before dark, you might be able to find something out. Even if she's not there herself, you might be able to get a phone number or something from a neighbour. I don't know – I'm stabbing in the dark really, but we have to do something.'

'I was just saying to Jenny that I could go down with her if her *boyfriend* isn't going,' chimes in Kerry. He emphasises the word 'boyfriend' as though it's a makey-up word and I scan my brain to remember what I've told him on Twitter about Tom. 'I'm off work for the next few days and I'd love to help.'

'Right, so,' says my mother, her eyes darting from one of us to the other. 'Well I'll head back into Ryan and you lot make up your minds what you're doing. I'll write down the details Ryan gave me. Fingers crossed they're right.'

'Right, I'll ... em ... just go and ring Tom and see what his intentions are,' I say, jumping up from the table. 'I'll be back in a minute.'

I leave him to catch up with Zahra while I run upstairs. Closing my bedroom door tightly behind me, I let out a long breath and try to control the palpitations that are threatening to explode out of my chest. Oh God, what on earth is going on? I feel I'm acting out a script that's been written for me. This can't really be happening. Just when I thought nothing else could surprise me, Kerry arrives. A male Kerry! I feel really cheated. I already miss the Kerry I know and love. This man isn't her – he's just someone who took on a persona for the fun of it. Both him and Zahra – God, how they had me fooled!

But right now, I need to think of finding Fiona so that I can reunite her with her son and finally put an end to this horrendous tweet-up. And if Kerry is offering his services to come and help me, I'm not going to turn him down. We'll concentrate on what needs to be done and then I can tell him what I think of his shenanigans.

Without any further thought, I run back downstairs. 'Right, Kerry. If you're up for it, you can come down to Galway with me. I could do with a second head, as you say, and Tom can't make it today.'

'Great,' he says, standing up and looking suspiciously like he's going to hug me. Well he'd better not think I've forgiven him or anything. That's completely out of the question. I'll just use him for a bit of support and I won't feel bad about it. He owes me after all!

'Will we go in my car?' he continues. 'It will give you a chance to relax after all you've been through.'

'Well ... em ... okay, then, that would be great.'

'And you know what women drivers are like,' he says, rolling his eyes.

The fecker! 'Well since you put it like that, there's no way I'm going in your car. We'll take mine and I'm an excellent driver, thank you very much!'

'Ah don't be like that,' he grins, turning on the little boy charm. 'I'm only joking with you. I just think it'll be a good idea for me to drive – as I said, you can take it easy and if you don't have to concentrate on the road, you can have a better think about where to go from here.'

'Well I suppose when you put it like that, it's probably a good idea.' It's a brilliant idea! I love the thought of him driving and me sitting back and enjoying the ride – so to speak! It's the least I deserve. As he said, I've had a shite few days and it's not over yet. 'I'll just go and tell my mother what's happening and I'll be ready to go in ten minutes.'

My head is spinning from wanting to be cross with him and kiss him for wading in and being so willing to help. My emotions are completely out of control and I don't know what I'm feeling any more. I'm exhausted from thinking. Well I'm going to shut my brain off on the journey down to Galway, close my eyes and imagine I'm heading off on a lovely spa weekend. Maybe when this whole sorry mess is over, I'll talk Paula or Sally into coming on a weekend away for real. Or maybe even Tom would be up for it. I wish it was Tom and not Kerry who was coming with me today but I'll just have to make the best of what I've got. And Kerry doesn't seem so bad really – for a lying, scheming pig!

CHAPTER 27

'So go on, then,' I spit, sitting back into the black-leather-covered seat. 'Tell me why you did it.' Thanks be to God Kerry's driving. I feel more in control this way. I can look at him and watch his reactions while he has to keep his eyes on the road. It also gives me the opportunity to check him out without him realising I'm doing it! Jesus, I need to stop seeing him as a fine thing and focus on the fact that he's a liar of the worst kind. I look out the window while I wait for him to explain. Good! Let him know I'm not going to be messed with!

'Jenny, I know you probably won't believe me but I didn't set out to lie to anyone. Honestly, I just joined Twitter as myself and people immediately made assumptions.'

Huh! Well, I'm certainly not letting him away with that. I've known him for a year – he could have put me straight! 'What do you mean "assumptions"? Surely you can't think we're to blame for all your lies!' Really, the cheek of him!

'Well I was completely honest with my profile information and it sort of annoyed me that people assumed certain things.'

There he goes again, talking about assumptions. Is he not going to take the blame for any of this?

'For starters,' he continues, 'people just *assumed* I was a woman because I'm a nurse. And with a name like Kerry, there was no reason for them to doubt it.'

'So ... so you actually *are* a nurse?' I say, staring at him now. I thought it was only in programmes like *Grey's Anatomy* that medical staff looked like that.

'Yes ... I told you ... everything I said about myself on Twitter is true. The only difference is I'm a man. And I didn't set out to pretend I was a woman – as I said, people just assumed! Sometimes I curse the romantic weekend my parents spent in Killarney all those years ago!'

Now I'm completely lost! What *is* he going on about? Bloody hell!

'Killarney ... in County Kerry,' he says, watching my blank face. 'I think they'd decided I was going to be a Kerry, regardless of whether I was a girl *or* a boy!'

'Oh!' This conversation is becoming more and more bizarre.

'And anyway,' he continued, 'if you girls could have just seen me, you'd have been in no doubt that I'm *all* man!'

'So let me get this straight,' I say, choosing to ignore his attempt at humour. 'The hospital, the shared house, the shift work – everything we've spoken about is true – except for the obvious of course.'

'Yes, Jenny. Yes, it's all true. I never lied to you over the past year. Honestly. I just didn't correct you.' He looks over at me for a little too long and has to pull the steering wheel hard as he almost swerves into the ditch.

'And does anyone else know? I know that Zahra and Fiona think you're a girl too, but are we the only ones?'

'Nobody knows,' he says, looking at me again.'

'Jesus, watch the road, will you?' I say, as the car swerves for the second time. 'I ... I just don't know what to say, Kerry. It even feels wrong calling you that. Kerry is ... was ... a woman – she was my friend.' I can feel the tears prick my eyes.

'I know it's a lot to take in, Jen, but I've wanted to tell you for ages. And really, if you liked Kerry, the woman, there's no reason we can't get along. I'm the very same person.'

Oh, God, the way he said 'Jen'! It just rolled off his tongue so easily and sounded so sexy and intimate. Only those very close to me call me Jen and I usually get annoyed with others just assuming they can shorten my name. But it seems right and natural for him to call me that. *Cop on, Jenny! You're annoyed with him, remember?*

'And to be honest, I think we've really connected – as friends I mean.' He's on a roll now! 'I've really enjoyed our chats and I suppose that's the reason I never really came clean. The longer it went on, the harder it was to speak up.'

'Come on, Kerry. I'm not buying that for a minute. You're trying to tell me it was easier to pretend to be a woman than tell the truth? It must have been really difficult to keep up the pretence. And I'm still not sure why you'd want to.' I can see how it would be funny to pretend for a day or even a week, but a whole year?

'I don't know if I'll ever be able to make you understand, Jenny,' he says, 'because it's just one of those things. I was always going to tell you tomorrow and then when tomorrow came it would be the next day and before I knew it, a year had passed.'

'But can't you see how cheated I feel? I thought I'd made a really good friend – somebody I could talk to easily and share my problems with. I thought you were somebody I could rely on and you were the one I always turned to when I had a problem.'

I really feel upset that there was never a girl called Kerry – it's as if someone has died. Was he just laughing at me for the past year? Was he thinking it was funny to hear a woman talk about personal stuff – women's bits and sexual encounters? Oh, Jesus, yes – I believe I did talk to her ... him ... about some ... em ...

stuff of that nature! I'm mortified. He must have been laughing at me all that time.

'Don't ever think I was laughing at you, Jenny. And I'd like to think that you have made a very good friend. Why should it be different just because I'm a man?'

'Why should it be *different*?' I almost wail! 'How can it *not* be different? The things I told you ... the personal stuff ... I would never share that information with a man. Never in a million years! You got me to say those things to you by default. I ... I ... I should really go to the gardaí!' Why did I say that? As if I don't already look stupid!

'And say what?' he asks, a smile forming on his lips. 'Report me for crimes against Twitter? Or tell the gardaí I should be arrested for having a name and a job that lends itself to misin-terpretation?'

He has a point, but I'm still far too annoyed with him to let him away with it. 'Don't be so smart, Kerry. You're lucky I'm bothering to speak to you at all. Just you wait until the others on Twitter find out about you. They'll probably come down harder on you than I have.'

He glances over at me and slips his left hand down to touch mine. I feel a tingle rush through me and I quickly pull it away. 'But I don't really care about the others,' he says, the serious look back on his face. 'Well, it's not that I don't care about them but you're my best Twitter friend and it's you I want to impress, not them.'

Did he say 'impress'? Why should he want to impress me? Yes, he should want my forgiveness and yes, he should want my understanding – but impress me? What's that all about? I'm really not sure coming on this trip was one of my best ideas. Now that we've had the whole why-did-you-do-what-you-did conversation, I really don't know what to say to him. And on top of it all, I'm finding him inconveniently attractive. I really don't want to notice, but between the light wisps of chestnut hair falling over his face to his tanned, manly hands gripping the steering wheel, I can't help but be distracted. If things were different, I'd probably flirt with him and even look forward to spending time with him, but because of what he did, I'd never allow myself to go there! And besides, I have Tom.

'Why don't we stop for a cup of coffee,' he says, breaking into my thoughts. 'I know we haven't been on the road long but maybe we can just sit down and finish this conversation and finally put it to bed, so to speak!'

Now why did he have to go and mention bed? It's been ages since I've had a man in mine and it doesn't help to be in such close proximity to one who smells muskily scrumptious. But maybe it's just the fact that I haven't been with a man in a while that's making me feel this way. Any port in a storm, as they say! To be honest, I wish it was Tom who was here with me. He's been so great about the whole Fiona saga. He was so level headed last night and really kept it together when I would have fallen apart. Yes, Tom is the only man I want in my bed at the moment. *Keep telling yourself that, Jenny, and you're bound to believe it!*

'Jenny, so what do you think? A pitstop for a cuppa?'

'Em ... yes, I suppose.' I'm trying to resist the urge to smooth his unruly hair back off his face. 'But not for long though – I don't want us coming home too late tonight. It's not fair on Mam and Zahra to leave them for too long with Ryan.'

'So what are you going to do with Ryan if we don't find Fiona?' he asks, pulling the car onto a slip road. 'I assume you're back in work on Monday?'

'Yes, I'm working on Monday all right but Mam has a couple of weeks off so she'll help out with Ryan until we get this sorted out.'

Jesus, that was quick thinking. I haven't thought beyond

tomorrow. I don't want Kerry to know I'm going about this completely cockeyed but the truth is, I'm just winging it. Mam has been great in all this, but I can't see her minding a child who isn't even her grandson indefinitely. And there's no way I can take more time off work. It was hard enough getting the three days off – I'm sure Bootface wouldn't be happy if I looked for more time off next week. Sure if Fiona isn't coming back, a day or two off work isn't going to solve the problem.

Up until now, I really believed Fiona would come back, even if it did take a little push from us, and everything would be sorted in time for me to go back to work. I don't know why I assumed that would be the case, but the alternative is just too unthinkable. It's looking less and less likely that things are going to get sorted easily.

I must give Paula and Sally a ring later and tell them what's going on. They won't believe it. They seemed to get on all right with Fiona on Thursday night, though I suspect Sally was a bit miffed by her parenting ideas. But they never would guess that she'd have upped and left like this.

'Here we are,' says Kerry, startling me back to reality. I was almost about to nod off there. 'I've been to this place a few times on my travels and it does the most delicious soup and sand-wiches.'

'Great,' I say, realising I'm actually starving. And he's right. It's a gorgeous place. The beautiful stone castle-type building, in the most unlikely setting just off the motorway, makes me feel as though we've stepped back in time. Inside, the cosy open fire throws out its heat into the room and casts a glow over the diners. The room is small and the tables close together but I like the intimate setting. It sort of makes me wish I was sharing it with someone special but, for the moment, I'll have to make do with Kerry. I must take note of where exactly we are and maybe see if Tom would like to come down here for a bite to eat some day. It's not much more than thirty minutes from my house so it wouldn't be too much of a drive.

We're informed by the waiter that the soup is leek and potato and I order without hesitation. It's one of my favourites and one I happened to have mastered myself. After all, you can't go wrong with a few potatoes, a bunch of leeks and an oxo cube. I've never been good in the kitchen but I've always felt I had an inner chef just waiting to burst forth. I have all these good ideas about making new and wonderful things, but never seem to get around to it. Kerry orders the soup too and we return the menus to the over-eager young waiter.

'So come on, then,' says Kerry, leaning forward on his elbows. 'I'm sure there's more you want to ask me, so hit me with it.'

'Well ... I ... em ... I suppose there are things I want to know,' I say, tripping over my words like a daft schoolgirl, 'like ... em ... how come you live with other women ... I mean nurses ... I mean, I assume they're women?'

Shite! Is that the best I can come up with? There are a million burning questions that need to be asked and I question him about his living arrangements? It's just when he bent across the table like that, I could almost feel his breath on my face and I'm sure he's trying to hypnotise me with those deep eyes and thick black eyelashes. I'd want to get a grip. I don't want him thinking I fancy him or anything. The problem is, I think I actually might fancy him – but I most certainly won't be letting *him* know that!

'See what I mean about assumptions,' he grins smugly. But, yes, I live with three other nurses and yes, they are women. I've known them for years and we get on great.'

'Oh,' I say, trying to appear as though it doesn't bother me, which, of course, it doesn't. Like why would I care about him living with three girls? I may think he's attractive, but when today is over, he'll just be a distant memory. Maybe I'll tweet him now and again, but it certainly won't go back to the way it was before when he was a girl.

'I suppose you want to know about me hanging around these last few days too, then?' he asks

'Yes, of course I do. I was just hoping you'd bring it up yourself. I don't want to have to drag the information out of you.'

'Well, I'd actually decided I was going to come to Dublin for the few days, just as we'd planned. I knew you probably wouldn't be too keen to have a man stay with the three of you so I organised to stay with a friend in Cabra.'

'Ah, so you didn't have to work at all – so you lied about that too!' Ha! Caught him out again – and this is the man who claims he hasn't lied about anything!

'True. You have me there,' he says, but not without a twinkle in his eye. 'But I only said that because I got panicky in the days leading up to the tweet-up and worried about the reaction I'd get when I appeared at your door. You've no idea how many times I cancelled and rescheduled in my head.'

'Well, I suppose I can understand how you'd be worried,' I conceded, 'but you do have to admit you brought it on yourself!'

'So, anyway,' he says, ignoring my jibe, 'I arrived up to Dublin on Wednesday night but chickened out of going to meet you all and just went straight to my friend's house.'

'Well it's probably just as well you didn't come. There was enough drama on Wednesday night what with Fiona bringing her son and everything.' Although I can't help wondering if he'd come then, would anything have turned out differently? Maybe with other things to focus on, Fiona might not have left. Although I'm not sure anything would have made her change her mind. I suppose we won't know if it was a planned decision or a spur of the moment thing until we find her – *if* we find her! God, the alternative doesn't bear thinking about.

'Anyway, I decided to come over on Thursday morning, which I did, only to see you all leaving to go out. I was parked across the road from your house so, when you headed off, I followed you all the way to the shopping centre.'

Aha! So I did have a stalker – of sorts!

'I kept trying to convince myself to go and talk to you,' he continues, 'but I just couldn't do it. I knew you were off to the Olympia too so I managed to get myself a ticket. The seat wasn't great but I didn't really care about the show – I just wanted to meet you all.'

'Ah, so that's why you were in the bar,' I say, starting to put all the pieces of the jigsaw together. 'Why didn't you say who you were at that point?'

'To be honest,' he says, looking into the delicious-looking soup the waiter has just put in front of us, 'I got a little rattled when I met you at the bar. I mean, I felt a real connection between us straight away. You were exactly as I imagined you'd be – even though your profile picture is a whole lot different!'

'I see.' I don't know how to react to this. Is he saying he was rattled because he fancied me? Or just rattled by nerves? The fact that he's blushing into his soup seems to suggest he felt or feels something more than friendship. I can't help it but the thought of that gives me a little thrill! Jesus! I'll have to stop letting my mind run away with me. I'm sure all he was feeling on Thursday night was butterflies in his cowardly stomach at the thought of coming clean!

'So was there any part of the few days that wasn't a drama?' he asks, dipping a piece of tomato bread into his soup. 'I mean, did you manage to enjoy any of it or has it been a hassle from start to finish?'

'Well it's still not finished!' I say, trying to avoid his eye. I'm sure he can read my mind. 'It was certainly all drama filled, but I have enjoyed getting to know Zahra. She's so different to how

I expected her to be and now that we know about her real life, I like her even better than I did. She's a really lovely girl.'

'Yes, she seems nice all right. I wish I had more time to get to know her. Still, maybe we can entice her over again sometime.'

'Not to my house, you won't,' I say, a little too quickly. But alarm bells are already ringing in my head. I think I've learned my lesson when it comes to having people stay in my house!

'Ha! Your face!' he says, chuckling loudly. 'Although I can't say I blame you. But I sort of wish I'd been part of the whole saga. I feel like I've missed out on so much.'

'Well you're part of it now,' I say, taking out my purse to pay for the food. 'But we'd better get going or it'll be dark by the time we get to Galway.'

'I'll get this,' he says, pulling out his own wallet. 'It's the least I can do.'

'You will not,' I say, haughtily. 'There's no need. We can each pay for our own.' I wouldn't want him thinking we're on some sort of date or the likes. Why would he pay unless he's expecting something in return? Well he'd better not be expecting anything, because I'm spoken for. How could I ever trust somebody who did something like that? Oh I know he explained it all away very nicely, but still. Nothing gets away from the fact that he's a man who's pretended to be a woman for the past year. And that's weird – even in my book!

I'm looking forward to seeing Tom again when this is all sorted. Hopefully we can start dating properly and I'll have my man for Christmas. But for now we need to focus on finding Fiona and reuniting her with her son. As we head out to the car, Kerry walks a little ahead of me and I notice how taut and plump his bum is. I imagine myself holding on to those cheeks while we're at it and I can almost feel the longing rise inside me. Oh, for fuck's sake!

CHAPTER 28

'So what now?' Kerry asks, turning off the engine and stretching his long limbs. 'Should we just knock on doors? It seems a bit lame really, doesn't it?'

'I think door to door is the only thing we *can* do,' I say, dreading the task ahead. As time passes, I'm beginning to wonder if we were completely mad to think that we'd get anywhere with this approach. The little bit of research we did before we left produced a few Fiona Lee's but not the right one.

With the help of Kerry's sat nav, we've found the street where Ryan says he and Fiona live. I've no reason to doubt him at the moment because we've just passed the Christmas markets that he spoke about. But the street stretches out in front of us and with no clue as to what number they live in, it seems like an impossible task.

'Should we split up or go together, do you think?' asks Kerry. 'We'd cover a lot more ground if we each take one side of the street.'

'Hmmm! It would be quicker all right but I'm not sure that a strange man knocking on doors alone is a good idea. I'd probably be okay since people aren't as easily intimidated by a woman but I'm not so sure about *you*. Someone might even call the gardaí and we certainly don't want that.'

'Good point,' he says, reaching around to take his coat and scarf from the back seat. 'Why don't we just stick together for the moment and see how it goes.' Phew! Thanks be to God. I'd hate to have to do this on my own. He's been a great help really and though I hate to admit it, I'm glad he came. I would have headed off completely cockeyed with no plan and just winged it when I got here. But Kerry suggested we print off a few copies of Fiona's Twitter picture, which is a surprisingly good likeness, so we can show it around.

Kerry also pointed out that we can't just knock on doors and expect people to tell us anything we want to know so he suggested we think up a story. The best we can come up with is that I'm Fiona's sister and haven't seen her in a couple of years. I'll say I remember the street but not the house number and I'm hoping to surprise her with a visit. Hopefully, it won't sound too creepy or suspicious but, to be honest, there really isn't anything else we can do.

'Right, here goes,' I say, ringing the doorbell on house number one. Thankfully the houses don't have gardens or drive-ways so we should be quick enough moving along the row.

'Yes?' says a little old lady, her face barely visible behind the door. She's kept the chain on, just allowing the door to open a fraction.

'Em ... hello there,' I say, fixing a smile on my face. I don't know why my voice has suddenly gone up an octave. Maybe it's just less threatening than my normal voice. 'I'm looking for my sister Fiona Lee. She lives on this road with her four-year-old son.' I hold the picture up to the open slit so she can see. She seems to stare at it for a while so I'm feeling positive. Could it be that we strike gold on our first house?

'You see, I haven't seen her in a while and want to surprise her with a visit,' I continue, trying to fill the silence. Still nothing. She looks from one of us to the other then closes over the door, rattling the chain. She must be undoing the chain so she can tell us about my 'sister'. Brilliant! Fancy hitting the jackpot at the first house! I stare at the door expectantly but as the seconds roll on and the chain stops rattling, my hopes of Fiona being delivered to us on a plate diminish fast.

'I guess that's it then,' says Kerry, already moving on to the next door. She's obviously not coming back so there's no point in hanging around.' Damn! This time he raps on the knocker and almost immediately, a young woman with a baby in her arms answers.

'I'm new to the area,' she says, before we even ask the question or give her our spiel. 'So I don't know anyone around here at all, so I'm sorry but I can't help you.' She gives us a half-smile and closes the door. Jesus! That was twilight-zone-ish! I'm guessing these houses don't lend themselves to privacy. She must have heard every word we said to her next-door neighbour. Or maybe it was my newfound high-pitched voice that carried!

In the next house, an old man with baggy trousers and old-fashioned braces answers the door. With his pot belly stretching the buttons on his shirt and his round face and little moustache, he puts me in mind of the fat guy from Laurel and Hardy (I never could figure out which was which). After we say our piece, he takes the picture in his hands. He runs his fingers over it while looking at it intently. He turns it over and stares at the back for a few moments. There's nothing on the back! He sucks in air and whistles it back out again while nodding his head. Fantastic! He seems to know her all right. He takes a deep breath and hands the picture back to me and I'm almost afraid to breathe.

'Nope!' he says, making to close the door. 'Never saw her before in my life.'

Oh for God's sake!

'Are you sure?' I say, pushing the picture back into his hands.

'Do you want to have another look?' There was definitely a flicker of recognition there – or am I just grasping at straws? Maybe he was just being polite.

'Positive,' he says, lodging the picture back into my hand firmly. 'The only one around here under the age of seventy is her next door.'

So it's on to the next house ... and the next ... and the next. My heart sinks lower and lower with every door we approach. Some people just close the door in our faces and some take a moment to look at the picture. Some are friendly, some not so much. But still, nobody knows Fiona. Each time we come across an empty house, I can't help wondering if it's Fiona's. If Ryan was with us, he'd be able to tell us straight away. But in reality, this is hard enough without having a four-year-old with us. Yes, we may have found the house but unless Fiona was in it, we would have ended up with a very teary-eyed child. I watch as Kerry remains determined, knocking confidently on every door and taking over the talking when I'm feeling just too deflated.

Two hours later, we have to admit we're beaten. Feckity, feckity, feck! 'So what now?' I ask, looking at Kerry and hoping he might have some bright ideas. 'This is useless, isn't it? What on earth were we thinking of, coming down here on a whim? We probably would have been far better staying at home and making some phone calls.'

'Phone calls to whom?' Kerry asks, pulling his collar up tighter around his neck to fend off the icy breeze. 'Don't you think if there was somebody to call, we would have done that?'

'True,' I say, shivering. 'But ... but I just feel so helpless. Are we just going to get in the car and drive all the way home again? It feels like such a wasted journey.'

'Listen, Jen,' he says. 'It hasn't been a wasted journey because if we hadn't come here, we would have just wondered if we should have. It may not have done any good but it didn't do any harm either.'

God, I love it when a man takes charge like that and sounds all manly. And he's really speaking sense. Maybe it's time I forgave him for his deception and stupidity.

'And look at it this way,' he continues. 'You've got to spend all day with me, so you win on that score!'

Huh! Or maybe he needs to do a bit more to earn my forgiveness! 'I do love a modest man,' I say, willing my face not to show how much he amuses me. But God, he's up himself. Does he think I'm going to fall at his feet just because he's cute ... and has nice hair ... and gorgeous eyes ... and he's sexy ... ? Jesus! Well, he can think again.

'Look, I don't know about you,' he says, as we head back towards the car, 'but I'm absolutely starving. There's no way I'd be able to drive the whole way home without having something to eat first. Will we go and grab a bite and we can use the time to brain storm?'

'Okay,' I sigh, resigning myself to the fact there's nothing much more we can do here. 'Will we just walk into Eyre Square and pick something up there?'

'Well I was here last year on a course and we stayed in the Radisson Hotel. The bar food was gorgeous and there's a big open fire and everything. How about there?'

I picture us sitting in front of an open fire, eating delicious food, drinking wine and whispering softly to each other. We'd order strawberries and cream for dessert and feed each other bites of the sweet fruit. The fire would heat us up so much that we'd be forced to go up to our room and slowly and romantically peel each other's clothes off.

'Jenny ... Jenny ... you're miles away. What do you think of heading to the Radisson for a bite to eat?'

Oh, Jesus. What on earth just happened there? 'Em ... yes,

yes, the Radisson sounds lovely.' I must definitely *not* order strawberries!

'Hello ... hello there,' comes a voice from down the street, just as we're about to get into the car. 'Glad I caught you. I've been thinking about that picture you showed me.' It's the Laurel and Hardy man. He arrives alongside us and has to lean on the car to catch his breath. But he mentioned the picture – maybe he does know something after all. My heart gives a little leap of anticipation.

'Are you okay?' I ask, noting his red face and short, sharp breaths.

'I'm fine,' he puffs. 'That girl in the picture – I think maybe I do recognise her. I couldn't be a hundred per cent sure, but I think I do.'

'Brilliant,' says Kerry. 'So what do you know about her? Do you know which house she lives in?'

'Well ... I'm ... a ... little ... puffed,' he says, patting his chest for extra effect. 'I was just heading down to the local for a swift one. Why don't you come down with me and we can have a chat.'

'Oh,' I say, not enjoying the thoughts of sitting with this man in a grotty pub. 'Well, you see, we're in a bit of a rush and we—'

'Yes, good idea,' interrupted Kerry. 'Let's all go down for a drink and you can tell us everything you know.' I shoot Kerry daggers, surprised he's agreed to drinks with this stranger, but he bends over to whisper to me, 'If there's a chance this man knows something, we shouldn't let the opportunity go.'

He's right, I know. But I was actually looking forward to the two of us sitting down and having a chat over a meal. The Radisson sounds gorgeous and just what we need after a few hours out in the icy cold. But I've got to remember why we're here in the first place. 'Right, where is this pub?' I ask. 'Do we drive or will we just walk to it?'

'Ah sure it's only a long spit away,' says the old man. 'Paddy's the name, by the way.'

Five minutes later, we arrive with our new friend Paddy into the most disgusting, spit-on-the-floor pub I've ever been in. The old dark-wood benches and tables remind me of something from the *Oliver!* movie and the old-sock stench hangs heavily in the air. Except for us, there's nobody here under the age of sixty and I can only see one woman in the whole bar. There must be a sale of soft caps on in Galway because every man seems to be wearing one.

'So what are you both having?' asks Kerry, leaning on the filthy old bar. I have a vision of the barman spitting on the glasses and drying them with a grubby tea towel. I've seen them do that in a few old movies and never really thought it happened. But somehow, in this place, it doesn't seem quite so unlikely.

'I'll just have a glass of water please,' I say, grimacing as a distinctly smelly man rubs up against me as he passes. I've no intention of drinking anything from a glass here so I'm not wasting mine or anyone else's money on a proper drink.

'Ah go on then,' says Paddy, smacking his shrivelled up lips. 'Sure I'll have a pint of Guinness with you.'

'Right so,' says Kerry, indicating one of the ancient benches for us to sit down. 'Won't be a mo.'

'And maybe just a little whiskey chaser,' adds Paddy, rubbing his wrinkled hands together. 'Just to get the heat in, you know?'

Feckin' cheek! He'd better come up with the goods now since we're funding his little excursion to the pub. 'So tell me about Fiona ... the girl in the picture,' I say, putting the picture down on the table. 'You said you recognise her.'

'Well, it's hard to say for sure,' he says, displaying a mouthful of broken brown teeth. 'But I'm almost certain I've seen her around those Christmas markets in the square. I go there most days, just walking about and having a look. There are some great cake stalls and they give out free samples. One of them even gives you whole mince pies for free.'

'Em ... yes, lovely,' I say, not in the slightest bit interested in how this man spends his day. 'But the girl ... my ... em ... sister. Do you know where she lives?'

'Here we go,' says Kerry, putting down the drinks on the manky table. 'So are we getting anywhere?'

'Well Paddy here says he's seen Fiona around the markets in Eyre Square.' I watch in shock as the old man knocks back the Guinness and takes a sip of the whiskey before he replies.

'To be honest, love, I'm thinking that maybe it's not even her I've seen.' He takes the picture up to look at it again. 'I really couldn't be sure. These young ones all look the same really and when the markets are open, sure there are loads of people about.'

'But you seemed so sure earlier,' says Kerry, looking almost as crestfallen as I'm feeling. 'Is there anything about her at all you recognise or remember?'

'Well, let me see, another whiskey wouldn't go astray if you're asking.'

The bloody cheek! He's downed the first two quicker than a professional darts player and now he's looking for *more*? I'm in no doubt now – this man is just playing us for fools.

'Paddy, do you or do you not know this woman?' I ask, slamming the picture on the table a little too heavily. Well, they do it in all the good westerns when they're bandying a 'wanted' picture about!

'Ah, there's Mick Malone,' he says, standing up. 'I need to go and have a word with him. Sorry I couldn't be of any help.' I watch, half in amusement and half in disgust, as he joins Mick, who promptly slaps a tenner on the bar to buy his buddy Paddy a drink!

'What a bloody waste of time,' I say, raging to have been taken in by that swindler. 'We could have been having our meal by now. The later it gets, the icier those roads will be.'

Grabbing our coats, we head outside to the bitter cold. There's definitely a smell of snow in the air tonight. Bloody typical! I've been dying for snow but, knowing my luck, it'll come in the next couple of hours and we'll be snowed in. God, what a disaster that would be. Hmmm! Or would it? Visions come to mind of a raging blizzard ... a warm fire ... Kerry feeding me strawberries! Jesus! Those bloody strawberries again. *Get a grip, Jenny*!

'So, the Radisson?' asks Kerry, breaking into my thoughts.

I try to avoid his eye so he won't see me blush. 'Oh, yes, I'm starving. But I'd kill for a shower first after that long drive down.'

'I'd offer to scrub your back but, unfortunately, I don't think they allow the restaurant-goers access to their rooms.'

'You'd be so lucky,' I say, still not looking at him. I now have the image of Kerry scrubbing my back to add to the ever-growing inappropriate thoughts in my head. 'Let's give ourselves an hour to have something to eat and then get on the road. We should be home by midnight all going well.'

'Fine by me,' Kerry sighs, disarming the alarm on the car. He looks tired. Is it wrong of me to expect him to drive all the way here and back in the one day? But what else can we do? He's been really great and I would have been lost without him, but I just feel tired and emotional now and I wish Tom or Paula was here. Or Sally – she's always good in a crisis. When we order our food maybe I'll make a few calls. I've texted Mam a few times during the day and I tweeted to Zahra. They seem to be all getting on just fine but I really need to ring them and fill them in.

As we pull up into the hotel car park, I feel strange. I'm away from home with a man I've known for less than a day. We're about to go for a meal in a lovely restaurant in front of an open fire. It's a perfect romantic setting. I feel a rush of resentment towards Kerry – I know it's unreasonable, but I just can't help it. I resent him for being one of the reasons I became hooked on Twitter. Only for Twitter, I wouldn't be in this situation now. I resent him for not being the Kerry I thought I knew. It's times like this I'd normally log on to Twitter and tweet 'her'. I still can't believe she doesn't exist. And I resent him for the fact that I fancy the pants off him! Bloody hell!

CHAPTER 29

I'm sitting alone in the reception area of the Radisson trying to make sense of everything that's happening. It's beautiful here, like something you'd see in a movie. The comfortable cream sofas are scattered around on beautiful, shiny marble tiles and the opulent, over-sized lamp shades add just the right amount of class to the place. If only I was staying here for a holiday instead of passing through on the mission from hell!

We managed to nab a lovely table in the bar right beside the open fire and as soon as we ordered the food, I excused myself to make a couple of calls. I feel a little bit guilty being down here while Mam and Zahra are managing things at home. Mam sounded tired when she answered the phone. She said everything was okay, but I could tell from her voice that it wasn't. I got her to put Zahra on the phone and she eventually told me that Ryan had been playing up and was asking questions about his mother. They'd only just got him to sleep, so they were about to settle down for a good old chat with a bottle of wine. I have to smile when I think of the two of them, with their matching orange tans and fluorescent clothes. They really seem to have hit it off.

Anyway, I'd better get back to Kerry before he thinks I've done a runner. Just as I'm heading back, my phone rings.

'Hello?'

'Hi, Jenny, it's Paula. I just thought I'd give a ring to see how you're getting on. Tom filled me in on what's happening. I can't believe it.'

'Tom? *My* Tom?' I'm aware that the use of 'my' may sound a bit possessive but why would Tom be talking to Paula when it's not even a work day?

'Yes, *that* Tom. He just dropped in this evening to see if I heard about what's been going on. He told me he was over with you last night.'

My brain is frantically trying to figure out, number one, why Tom would call in to Paula and, number two, how does he even know where she lives? But there are far too many things claiming prime space in my brain at the moment so I'll deal with that later. 'It's just been crazy, Paula. My brain is frazzled. And this trip to Galway has been a waste of time too. Honestly, I'm fed up.'

'Well let me know if there's anything I can do. What a nightmare. You poor thing.'

'Thanks, Paula. But, for now, I'd better get back. Kerry and I are grabbing a quick bite before we hit the road.'

'Oh yes, I heard about Kerry. Tom rang your house today because he couldn't get through to you on the mobile and your mam filled him in. How weird! What's he like?'

'He's okay, I suppose. Look, I'll give you a call tomorrow and we can chat more. I'm anxious to get back on the road as soon as we can.' So Tom knows about Kerry. I wonder how he feels about that. Maybe he's feeling guilty now that he didn't come with me. Maybe he's jealous. Well a bit of jealousy might be just the thing to add that missing spark to our relationship.

'Right, that's that done,' I say, rejoining Kerry and sitting back down into the big comfortable chair. 'No sign of the food then?'

'Not yet. I'm sure it will be along shortly. God, I'd murder a glass of wine though. How are things at home with Ryan?'

I feel the tears prick my eyes and I quickly try to blink them back in. Oh Jesus, please don't let me cry in front of him! 'He ... he's okay, I suppose, under the circumstances. Mam was making light of it all but Zahra said he's a bit unsettled. It's no wonder really, is it?'

'Poor thing,' he says, watching me carefully. 'God only knows what's ahead for the poor little man.' We both reach for our water at the same time as those words hang heavily in the air. The glow from the open fire is dancing on his face and I'm suddenly reminded of the strawberry-feeding scene. Bloody hell! I'm half afraid to look at him just in case he can read my mind! Thankfully, I'm saved from any such embarrassment by the loud ring of my phone.

'Hello,' I whisper, conscious of the looks I'm getting from other diners. You'd think they'd bloody well never heard a mobile going off before! Although to be fair, Homer Simpson's voice shouting 'Answer your God damn phone' was funny the first few times, but it's probably time I changed it to something more ... em ... grown up!

'Hi, Jenny, are you okay?' It's Tom. Oh God, why didn't I just ring him while I was out in the lobby? I really don't want to talk to him in front of Kerry.

'Yes, yes, I'm fine,' I say, lowering my head down towards the table. 'I'm just having a quick bite here with ... em ... with ... em ... before hitting the road.' Feck. Sure Paula said he knows I'm with Kerry so why the hell am I trying to hide it?

'I've been speaking to your mam and Zahra and they've been keeping me up to date on everything that's been happening since yesterday.' Hmmmm! Not sure I like him keeping tabs like that. Although I suppose he's trying to help. 'You must have been pretty shocked when Kerry turned out to be a man.'

'Mad, isn't it?' I whisper. 'I can't tell you what a shock it was.' I notice Kerry is sitting back looking very smug. What's that all about? It's as though he's smirking at my relationship with Tom. Well, I'll show *him*.

'But I'll have to fill you in on it all tomorrow, honey,' I purr, raising my voice slightly. 'I can't wait to have a *proper* catch-up.' Eeeeek! I don't know who's more surprised at my use of 'honey' and my sudden switch to seduction mode – Kerry, Tom or me! Why did I have to go and say that? I'm feckin' mortified. But at least it seems to have put Kerry in his place because he's now playing with his cutlery and looking uncomfortably around the room.

'Em ... yes ... okay,' Tom says, and I can tell he's more than a little shocked. 'I wanted to have a good chat with you anyway, Jenny. I think we need to get a few things sorted.'

'Oh, yes, of course, we'll definitely do that,' I say, more like an eager puppy now than a sex kitten! 'But gotta go now. I'll talk to you tomorrow.'

'Sorry about that,' I say, turning my phone onto silent and sticking it back into my soft, suede handbag. 'That was Tom.'

'I sort of guessed,' he says, the stupid grin returning to his face. 'So are you two serious then?' Am I imagining it or does he seem a little disappointed?

'Well, it's early days yet but I really think it's going somewhere. Tom is lovely. He was gutted he couldn't come with me today.'

'So is this the guy from the office you've only been out with a couple of times? The one you weren't too sure about?'

Oh shit! Damn Twitter. I'm beginning to regret ever sending out a single tweet. Twitter was great when it stayed in Twitterland but since it's taken a leap out of my computer and come to visit my real life, things have become more complicated than I could have ever imagined. Honestly, if you put this stuff in a movie, people would say it's just too far-fetched! I search my brain to remember what I might have said about Tom to Kerry. Bloody hell!

'Well, I may have been a bit wary at first but a lot has happened in the past few days, and let's just say we've grown a lot *closer*!' He can put that in his strawberries and suck them! I'll let him draw his own conclusions.

Thankfully, the food arrives and I'm saved any more awkward explanations. 'Oh, this looks delicious,' I say, eyeing the chunky chips that have come with my vegetarian lasagne.

'It's gorgeous all right but I'd murder a glass of red,' Kerry says, stuffing his mouth greedily. 'It's such a pity we're driving back tonight.'

'Oooh, yes. A nice cold glass of white would go down well.' There's no reason I can't have a glass or two but since Kerry can't drink, I've decided to keep him company and stick to the water. It wouldn't seem fair for me to get tipsy and fall asleep in the car while he's driving.

'Well,' he says, slowly, his chestnut hair doing that wispy thing over his face, 'why don't we see if there are any rooms free tonight? We could relax a bit more now and head off in the morning.'

Bloody cheek! I can't believe he has the nerve to suggest we stay. After everything he's done ... everything he's said ... all the lies ... and now he thinks we're going to spend the night down here together! But, oh God! I wish he wouldn't keep looking at me with those melting eyes.

'Come on,' he continues, still waiting for my answer. 'It'll be fun.'

'I can't, Kerry,' I say, not meeting his eyes. 'I really should get back home and have a chat to the others about what we're going to do and besides, it wouldn't really be fair on Tom for us to stay here together.'

'Well I wasn't suggesting we stay *together*, you know,' he says, grinning. 'Unless of course you wanted us to!'

Jesus, he's messing with my head! It's been a long day – a long *few* days actually – and I'm exhausted and vulnerable. '*Kerry*! Stop it! You can't keep saying things like that. I'm spoken for and the sooner you realise that the better.'

'Ooooh and fiery too,' he says. 'You really are a funny little thing, aren't you?'

I'll give him funny! 'And what do you mean by that?'

'Well it's just you seem to be going out of your way to let me know how much you and your *boyfriend* are in love. But you seem to forget the fact that we've had so many conversations on Twitter about things, including your love life!'

Oh, sweet Jesus! I wish to God I could remember what I've said. 'Well I've never once said we're in love, Kerry, only that we're getting on well. And anyway how do you know that I've been telling the truth on Twitter? Sure haven't you lot all lied through your teeth about almost everything?'

'It's funny,' he says, finishing his last bite of cod and mushy peas. 'You're exactly how you come across on Twitter. You're warm and funny and more than a little feisty. I really don't think you've lied about yourself – well not about anything important.'

'Oh, you mean like about being a woman?'

'Ouch!' he says. Kick me right in the nuts, why don't you? I thought we'd moved on from that.'

'I know I said we should move on, but you can't blame me for bringing it up now and again. I still feel sad and cheated about the whole thing.' It's weird but he's also exactly how he portrays himself on Twitter – except for the gender thing of course. I'm trying to make myself dislike him, to feel nothing for him, but I can't help feeling as though he's my best friend. Maybe I *should* consider staying tonight. I'm sure Mam would prefer if we stayed rather than put ourselves in danger by driving on icy roads.

'So what are you thinking about?' he says, breaking into my thoughts.

'I was just thinking that maybe we *should* see if there are any rooms available. It's getting really late and it's probably not fair to expect you to drive for two and a half hours in this weather.'

'Brilliant,' he says, his eyes twinkling. 'I'll just go and see if they've anything left. Two single rooms, I suppose?'

'Of course,' I say, trying to look cross but, to be honest, I quite like his cheekiness. I watch as he heads over to the reception desk, hands stuck in his denim pockets, his white T-shirt showing his modest, tanned muscles. God, I need to stop noticing these things and focus on why we're here in the first place.

It dawns on me that he'll probably try to play this to his advantage. He'll come back and say they only have one double room left. Oh yes, I've seen it in so many movies. He'll say gallantly that he'll sleep on the floor and let me have the bed. He'll keep me awake during the night tossing and turning and trying to get comfortable on the hard floor. I'll eventually give in and ask him into my bed, warning him to keep his distance. But then as we're about to drop off to sleep, we'll accidentally touch beneath the covers. And that will be that until we wake up in the morning completely naked with our legs knotted together and the covers all messed up.

'Two single rooms just down the corridor from each other booked!' he declares, throwing the two keys down on the table.

'Oh!'

'That *is* okay, isn't it?' he asks, looking puzzled at my reaction. 'You haven't changed your mind, have you?'

'No, no, that's fine,' I say. 'I just need to talk to Mam and make sure she's okay with it.' I try to shake off the strange feeling I have. Could it be disappointment? Surely not. If he really had come back and declared he'd booked a double room, I'd have been livid. Or would I? Of course I would. Hmmm!

'Well why don't we head out and have a look around the markets?' he says. 'I noticed a sign to say they're open until ten, so we could walk off some of this meal and then come back and have a few drinks. What do you think?'

'Good idea,' I say, wondering how I'm going to haul myself up out of this impossibly comfortable chair. 'I'm far too stuffed to have a drink now, so a walk sounds good.'

We settle the bill between us and I quickly dial home before heading out into the cold air. Mam sounds much more upbeat than earlier and, as I suspected, she'd rather we stay overnight than put ourselves in danger on the icy roads.

Within five minutes, we're right in the hub of Eyre Square where the very European-looking markets are set up. The stalls are beautifully constructed from a light-coloured wood, no tents or awnings like you'd find in Dublin markets. They display everything from cheeses and sweets to brightly coloured scarves and heavenly scented soaps. It's a hive of activity – even at this hour when it's almost time for them to close up.

'Nice here, isn't it?' says Kerry, stopping to take a look at belts on one of the stalls. 'I love markets.'

'Me too,' I say, checking out the handbags on the same stall. 'But I thought men were supposed to hate shopping. Isn't it part of the rules?'

'Haha! It probably comes from living with three women. They often drag me out to the Sunday markets and I've actually grown to like them. There's nothing like finding a good bargain.'

Be still my beating heart! A man who loves shopping? Is he *trying* to be the perfect man? Or maybe he just is! 'I'm exhausted,' I say, suddenly feeling my legs buckle. 'Can we just go back and have those drinks now before we turn in? I'm just ready for one now.'

'Sure,' he says, blowing on his hands. 'It's freezing out here anyway. Let's hope our seat beside the fire is still available.'

We walk back to the hotel in silence. What a fabulous city Galway is. I wonder how different things would be if Tom was here with me. We'd probably be holding hands now instead of swinging our arms by our sides as Kerry and I are doing. I half-expect him to take my hand as we walk. What would I do if he did? Would I pull away and act all indignant or would I just go with the flow and act as though nothing was different? Well, I'll never know because it's clear he's not going to do anything of the sort.

Back in the bar, we manage to reclaim our seats by the fire and order our long-awaited glasses of wine. Despite the fact it's a Saturday, it's fairly quiet. There's a man playing the piano just a little bit away from us and the beautiful soft sound makes for a lovely atmosphere.

'I really am sorry, you know,' Kerry says suddenly, as the waiter brings us our wine.

'Sorry for what?' I ask, taking a big gulp of mine. I'm quite thirsty so I should probably have had some water first.

'For the pretence,' he says, looking serious for once. 'You know, I honestly didn't lie to you about anything else. I know that sounds lame when the one lie was so big, but other than the fact I'm a man, you know a huge amount about me.'

'Well, I can see sparks of the Kerry I know,' I say, almost finishing my wine with the next mouthful. 'You really are exactly how I imagined you'd be, except for an extra few inches in the bedroom department.' I somehow find that hysterically funny and the tears pour down my eyes with the laughing.

'Well, I'm not admitting to any particular length, but I know what you mean.'

'Will we order another one?' I ask, already feeling the buzz. 'I think we deserve it after the day we've had.'

'Sure,' he says, beckoning the waiter. 'Same again?'

An hour later, we're sitting with a collection of empty glasses in front of us. I can't remember enjoying myself this much in ages. Kerry is lovely really. It's like having a girls' night out. He's very in touch with his feminine side, and yet he's all man.

'I'm just going to nip to the loo,' I say, trying with great effort to haul myself out of the chair. 'Maybe we'll finish up after this one. I'm knackered.'

The room spins when I stand up, so I wait for a moment for it to stop before I attempt to walk. Inside the Ladies, I take a look at my face in the mirror. Oh God, the state of me. Kerry must be thinking how lucky he is *not* to be in a relationship with me. My eyeliner has spread down as far as my cheekbones and my hair is sticking up all over the place from running my fingers through it. But why am I bothered about how I look if we're just friends? Why should I care? Because I wish we were more than just friends – that's why! Maybe I shouldn't be so caught up with Tom. Maybe I should be seizing the moment and seeing where it will take me. After all, I'm not really attached to Tom and, if I'm honest, there really isn't a sexual attraction there. Where would be the harm in just sampling what else is on offer?

Right, a quick wee and a touch up job on the hair and make-up and I'll be ready to see what the rest of the night has in store. I'd love to know what Kerry is thinking. Is he hoping something will happen between us tonight? He's certainly been giving off enough signals.

A few minutes later, I'm heading back to the lovely setting beside the fire. I can feel that rush of lust again when I see Kerry sitting back in the chair, looking relaxed and comfortable, with his left foot resting up on his right knee. He must sense me walking towards him because he looks around and gives me a lovely warm smile. Everything seems to fall into place now as we look at each other and I quicken my pace to be beside him.

But just before I reach our table, I catch my foot in the strap of somebody's handbag and manage to do a somersault any gymnast would be proud of. Honestly, I don't know how I manage to make such a drama out of the fall, but I do. I couldn't just fall gently on my face. Oh no, not me! I have to do the whole legs up in the air, skirt around my neck trick. I've literally fallen at the feet of two surprised women, and I'm momentarily stunned. It's only when Kerry rushes over to help me up that I realise that not only am I exposing myself, but I've also chosen that day to wear the most unflattering tights that pull up to my chest and my ugliest Bridget Jones knickers! Well those knickers may have worked for her but they've completely sobered me up!

'Jesus, Jenny. Are you okay?' Kerry is hovering over me and I'm aware of the two women looking at me from their chairs, unsure as to whether to help or not.

'I'm fine, I'm fine,' I say, mortified. 'Let's get out of here.'

'Don't you want to finish your wine?' asks Kerry, indicating the half-full glasses over at the table.

'No I do *not*,' I say, getting up and brushing myself down. 'You can stay if you like but I'm off to bed.' I can't get out of that bar quick enough and, as we leave, I can hear the giggles of the two women.

We're up on the third floor so we travel up in the lift. 'Here's where you are,' says Kerry, stopping outside a door and handing me a key. 'I'm just a few doors down in 312.'

'Thanks,' I say, wanting to just get inside on my own and go to bed. All the passion and longing I'd felt have been completely obliterated by my embarrassing fall. It was probably only the drink that had me thinking that way anyway. Kerry is just a friend. Tom is the one I want. He's gentle and loving and considerate – everything a man should be. Whereas Kerry is deceitful and cheeky and presumptuous – why would I settle for a man like that?

'Goodnight,' he says, pecking me on the cheek. 'I'll see you early in the morning. Give me a shout when you're up.' I can still smell his breath as he walks away, his hands dug deep into the pockets of his jeans. I notice for the first time how his long chestnut hair flicks up into little curls at the back of his neck. He stops at his door and turns to give me a little wave before heading in. Even from here I can see the twinkle in his eye as he gives me one of his cheeky grins. Yes, I'd be mad to settle for a man like that!

CHAPTER 30

Sunday

'I'll get you for that,' he laughs, shaking the icy snow from his hair. 'If a snowball fight is what you want, then that's what you're going to get!' I attempt to run away, but he's too fast and I squeal as a perfectly formed snowball catches me right on the back of the head, sending icy drops sliding down my neck. He's caught up with me now and I turn and put my arms around his neck. Despite the cold, I can feel the heat rising inside me. He places his warm lips upon mine and kisses me tenderly. What a perfect Christmas!

Hmmm! What a delicious dream. If only they were all as nice as that one. Strange that I didn't see the man's face though. I wonder who he was. Tom maybe? Well whoever he was, he was certainly making me happy.

I'm trying to remember what day it is, but a distinct fuzziness in my brain is scrambling my thoughts. I open my eyes to glance at my bedside clock but it's not there. Rubbing my eyes with the duvet, I force myself to focus. Think, Jenny! Oh God, it's all beginning to flood back. How on earth could I have forgotten? The Radisson ... Kerry ... me flashing my granny knickers! Oh the shame of it. I just hope Kerry was as sozzled as I was and doesn't remember the finer details!

Right, I really need to ignore my thumping head and the ball of vomit in the back of my throat and get myself organised. A glance at my phone tells me it's already eight o'clock and we really should be getting on the road soon. With great difficulty I swing my legs out to the side of the deliciously comfortable bed and note with disgust the mess on the top of the crisp white duvet. I really should learn to wash my make-up off at night.

I wonder how things are at home. I hope to God that Ryan gave them an easy time last night – otherwise I'll feel even guiltier than I do already. I'll give Mam a quick buzz after I hop in the shower. When I last checked in with her, she said Harry was coming over to lend a hand. I'm really glad she has Harry. He's really good for her. It's crazy really. Shouldn't it be the other way around? Shouldn't it be the mother who's happy to see the daughter settling down? But I really don't begrudge her a bit of happiness and, after all, it has to be a good thing if it's brought us two closer together.

I wish I could stop this horrendous drumming in my head. A nice hot shower might help. But first things first – maybe Fiona has tweeted. We're running out of time to help her because sooner rather than later, our own lives have to get back to normal. I think even Mam will agree to getting the police or social services involved if Fiona doesn't show up today. I take my bag from the floor at the end of the bed and root around for my phone. Shit! Two missed calls from Mam – one from last night and one from this morning. Uh oh! I forgot to take the damn thing off silent after Tom's phone call in the restaurant.

Oh God, I hope everything is all right. Although what else could possibly go wrong – I think we've exhausted all the bad luck in the world! I quickly dial the number, my heart beating out of my chest. But maybe it's actually good news for a change. Maybe Fiona has come back. Yes, that'll be it. Thank God for that. Oh, what a relief it will be to hand Ryan back over to her and not have this worry any more.

'Hello, Mam?' I say, expectantly, as soon as the phone is answered.

'Ah hiya, love,' she says, sounding even wearier than she did yesterday. 'I've been trying to get you. Why weren't you answering your phone?'

'Sorry, Mam, it was on silent and I'm just after waking up.'

'Silent? What for?'

'Forget about my phone, Mam. So what's up? Has she come back?'

'God I wish she had,' sighs my mother, and my heart sinks right back down again. 'I just didn't know what to do last night. Ryan was beside himself all night. Me and Zahra took it in turns to try and settle him. Even Harry had a go a couple of times. But he insisted on knowing about his mother – when she's coming back and if she's gone forever like his dad!'

'Oh, Mam, I'm sorry to have left you to cope with all that,' I say, mortified at the fact that I've been enjoying myself in a nice hotel while all that was going on in my house. 'We'll be leaving here shortly. How is he now?'

'He's actually sleeping now,' she says, whispering. 'The poor thing wore himself out. He knows there's something going on. He seemed happy enough that I was looking after him at first but then when there was no sign of Fiona coming home again, he got suspicious.'

'Right,' I say, balancing the phone between my chin and neck while grabbing my clothes from the floor. There's no time for a shower this morning. 'We're just going to have to get the authorities involved, Mam. I know you didn't want to, but we can't cope with this on our own. It's just not right – for anybody.'

'I know, love. I feel so sorry for the little lad but I'm definitely not cut out for this. I can play the granny very well, but I can't take on the whole responsibility and you've got work and everything.' I can hear the catch in her throat. Poor Mam. She'll really be gutted to see Ryan go into care – we all will – but there really isn't another option.

'Try not to worry, Mam. We should be there in a couple of hours and we can decide about things then. Just let Ryan sleep for the moment and you relax and make yourself a cuppa.'

I throw the phone on the bed while I quickly pull my tights on. Oh God, the very sight of them reminds me of the flashing incident. Not my finest hour. I take a sniff of my top and it's pretty whiffy under the arms so I run into the bathroom and rub some of the dry soap on it to try to disguise the smell. While I'm there, I wet a cloth and wipe off the remains of my make-up.

Right, I'd better give Kerry a shout and tell him he'll need to be up and ready in ten minutes. I hope for his sake that he's feeling better than me because, like it or not, he has a two-hour drive ahead of him. Grabbing the access card for the door, I head down to his room. I listen for a moment but there's no sign of life.

'Kerry,' I shout, banging loudly on the door. 'Are you awake?' Nothing. Not a peep.

I try again a little louder. 'Kerry ... Kerry, you need to get up. We've got to get going.' I wish I'd taken his mobile number and I could just ring him. A couple walking past are giving me funny looks and the woman has an understanding smile on her face. I don't know what she thinks she understands. I wish people wouldn't always make assumptions about a situation. I'm tempted to tell her to wind her neck in, but they disappear into the lift before I get a chance.

Damn! Kerry must be in a bad way if all this noise isn't waking him up. Just as I'm about to go back to my room, the lift opens and there he is, decked out in running gear, sweat dripping down his face.

'Morning,' he grins. 'I didn't expect to see *you* for a while.'

'Well I've been knocking on your door for ages,' I say, indignantly. How dare he go out without telling me! Or is that being a bit unreasonable? 'I've just been talking to Mam and they've had a terrible night with Ryan. We really should get home as soon as possible.' I can't help noticing his toned, muscular legs. I hadn't realised he was sporty – but, then again, there's a lot I don't know about him.

'Why, what's up?' he asks, dripping sweat onto the carpet. 'Did something happen?'

'Ryan is obviously missing his mother and has been awake crying for most of the night. I feel terrible for leaving Mam and Zahra to deal with the mess.'

'Well there's no point in you blaming yourself. You weren't to know all this was going to happen. Is your mam coming around to the idea of getting the authorities involved now?'

'Yes, I think she realises that it's the only thing we can do if Fiona doesn't turn up.'

'Well we've done all we can,' he says, looking at me with those gorgeous eyes. 'Just give me five minutes and I'll be showered and ready.'

'Okay. Just come and knock when you're done.'

'And Jenny … '

'Yes,' I say, swinging back around.

'You look much better without it.'

'Em … without what?' I don't know what he's talking about, but the way he's saying it sends tingles down my spine.

'The make-up, Jenny. You look gorgeous with your face bare.' He was still smiling as he went into his room.

Oh, feck! I'd forgotten I hadn't reapplied my make-up. Imagine me letting him see me bare-faced. Not even my mother has seen me like that since I was a child! But he said I was gorgeous. Me – Jenny Breslin – gorgeous! The last person to say that to me was my dad. I was always gorgeous in his eyes.

But God, Kerry looked good in that gear – even if he was sweating like a pig. Is it weird to be turned on by the beads of sweat trickling down his face? And those thighs, so toned and tanned. Oh for God's sake, I'm going to have to cop on to myself. It may have been okay having those thoughts last night when I was under the influence, but in the sober light of day, I've got to look at the reality. I'm going out with Tom and Kerry lives miles away. Hopefully things will get back to normal soon and my head will have a chance to untangle itself!

Back in the room, I throw myself on the messy bed and close my eyes. God, I feel terrible. That's the last time I'll drink so much wine. I can take five or six vodkas no problem but more than two glasses of wine and I'm plastered. A few sips of water and I manage to stall the nausea for the moment and pray it doesn't come back during the drive home.

I'm sure Zahra has been checking, but I must just take a look at Twitter. I touch the icon on my phone and wait while it loads. Nope! Nothing from Fiona. I didn't expect there would be really. Oh but there's Zahra tweeting to a few people. That's a good sign. Ryan must have settled, or otherwise she'd be up to her eyes. I'll have a few words with her before Kerry comes.

@JennyB Hi, Zahra. How are things there now? We'll be leaving here in a few minutes so should be with you in two hours.
@zahraglam Oh hi, Jenny. Much better now. Ryan is playing Lego with your mam and Harry and I are having a cuppa.
@JennyB Oh, thank God. I'm so sorry we ended up staying. But it just got so late and we were exhausted.

@zahraglam Oh don't worry at all, Jenny. I love spending time with your mam. She's great.

@JennyB You two really have hit it off. Pity you didn't get a chance to chat properly with everything else going on.

@zahraglam We had such a good chat this morning. I'll be going back to London with lots of ideas of new and exciting projects.

@JennyB Oh, that's fantastic. Can't wait to hear about them. We should have a few hours before I have to drive you to the airport.

@zahraglam Great. Better go and give your mam a break. See you shortly. x

I throw my phone back in my bag and I'm ready to go just as a knock comes to the door. 'Are you all set?' Kerry asks, sounding far more chirpy than he should be after a night of too much alcohol.

'Yep,' I say, opening the door. 'It's not as though I've got packing to do.'

Down at reception, we pay the bill and head straight out to the car park. Something seems to have changed between us. I can't figure out what it is and I can't really explain it, but there's an eerie silence between us now. The conversation that flowed before is strained. All day yesterday, we chatted comfortably and it felt as though we'd known each other – really known each other – for years. It's going to be a very long and awkward journey if we don't try to get over this ... this ... thing – whatever it is.

★

'So I didn't know you ran,' I say, turning down the volume on the radio. 'Are you very fit then?'

'I like to keep myself in shape,' he says, eyes fixed on the road.

I was hoping for more than that. I try again. 'And how come

you had your gear with you? I'd have killed for something clean to wear this morning.'

'I always keep a packed gym bag in the car. I often pop in on the way home from work.' Still he's staring at the road ahead.

Feck that for a game of soldiers! If he thinks I'm going to be bothered dragging the conversation out of him, he's got another think coming. Honestly, we're not even a couple and I feel as though we've had a lovers' tiff. Well if this is how it's going to be, I'll just have a little snooze. It's probably a bit rude to nod off while he's driving, but with the way the conversation is going, it'll be a relief for both of us.

★

'Jenny ... Jenny, I'm just popping into the garage for a packet of mints. Do you want anything?'

'What ... what's up? Where are we?' I open my eyes and am mortified to realise my whole body has shifted sideways to the right and I'm leaning against Kerry. God, that was some deep sleep! 'Sorry about that,' I say, straightening myself up and rubbing my eyes. 'I was out cold there.'

'So I noticed,' he laughs. 'Some company *you* are!'

'How long was I asleep?' I'm rooting in my bag for my phone to check the time.

'Well over an hour,' he grins. 'Just another half hour and we'll be back to dealing with the Ryan situation.

'Oh God,' I groan. 'I don't relish the thought of that. How did my life become so complicated? I wish I could just go home, get into my pyjamas and go to bed!'

'A bit forward, aren't you?' Kerry grins, his eyes twinkling. 'But I'd scrap the pyjamas – I'd only have them off in seconds anyway!'

I shake my head and give him a disapproving look. But I'm secretly delighted. He's back! The presumptuous cheeky chappie is back! Whatever was coming between us earlier seems to have resolved itself. I know I was annoyed at him for most of yesterday but now that we've made our peace, I'd hate to think of us falling out again.

'I'm sorry I was a bit short with you earlier, Jenny,' he says, his face turning serious. 'It's just ... it's just ... I'll just come out and say it. It's just that I've enjoyed spending time with you. I know the circumstances aren't great, but I feel a real connection between us. It's like we have something really special.'

Oh God, I knew it. He feels the same. 'I know what you mean, Kerry. It's been good to get to know you – *really* good.'

'Pity we live so far away – I'll miss you when I go back to Waterford. But hey, we can still tweet, can't we?'

Shit! No declaration of love! No plans to move his life to Dublin so that he can be near me! No happy ending! I feel a ripple of anger rising up inside me. How dare he mess with my feelings like this. How bloody dare he!

'You know what, Kerry. I don't think we'll bother. I mean, what would be the point? What you did was unforgivable and I don't think I can get past it.'

'Whoooooa! Where did all that come from? I thought we were having a moment there?'

'A moment – maybe,' I spit. 'But it was a moment of bloody madness. It must have been the drink last night that had me thinking we could carry on as normal but there's just no way we can be friends. You're a liar ... and ... and ... a horrible person.' Oh God, what am I saying? It's all just spilling out of me and I can't seem to stop. He's just looking at me, his big brown eyes almost popping out of his head. But I'm on a roll. 'And all the things I told you in confidence! All the moments we shared – the moments I shared with Kerry, the girl! You know how bad I was feeling about things, but you still had to come along and *trample* on me!'

'Jenny, Jenny, stop,' he says, reaching out for my hand. But I'm not having any of it. 'I'm so, so sorry about it all but it's because we were getting so close that I thought it was about time I told you the truth.'

'Well that's just not *good enough*,' I yell, not caring about the tears streaming down my face. 'You've used your power to break me. I'm such a fool – I'm such a bloody, stupid, gullible fool!'

'Jenny, you are *not* a fool. You're one of the most decent people I know.'

I'm sobbing my heart out now. Maybe I'm having a breakdown. Maybe it's all just been too much and Kerry just happens to be the one here to take the brunt of my outburst.

'And furthermore,' he continues, 'you're kind and funny and generous and loving. To be honest, I'm sick of hearing how you put yourself down all the time. Can't you see how fabulous you are? Do you really think you're such a bad person? Because from where I'm sitting you're pretty much bloody amazing!'

I stop sobbing for a moment and stare at him. Does he really think those things about me? Could it be that others see me in a different light to how I see myself? Or is he just trying to take the focus off himself?

'Well say something, will you?' he says, reaching over to take my hand in his. This time I don't stop him.

'Oh Kerry, I'm sorry I had a go at you. I think ... I think it's just everything's got on top of me and I couldn't hold it in any longer.' And I'm sure the copious amount of alcohol last night had something to do with it!

'It's forgotten, Jen. You're under a lot of pressure. Now just do me one favour – stop being so bloody hard on yourself! I'm not going to say it again but I meant what I just said. Right?'

'Right,' I say, sheepishly.

'Phew! Glad that's settled. Now let's get back on the road and see what the rest of the day has in store.'

We travel the remainder of the journey in silence – but it's not an uncomfortable one. Each of us is lost in thought. I'd love to know what he's thinking. God, those things he said about me. He said I was amazing. Nobody has ever said that to me before. I'll have to park my thoughts on this for the moment, though, because we're just up the road from home and there's other things that have to be dealt with first.

As he pulls the car up behind Betsy in the driveway, my thoughts turn to Fiona and I feel a sense of foreboding. I want to run away. I want to hide from all the responsibility that's waiting for me inside the house. When all this is resolved, I'll never complain about my mundane life again — in fact I'll embrace it. That's assuming it *will* all be resolved. Jesus, I hope so. Otherwise Fiona might not be the only one running away!

CHAPTER 31

'Don't cry, Mam,' I say, passing a box of tissues to my distraught mother. 'You've been brilliant, but there's nothing more we can do now.'

'I know, love,' she sniffs. 'It's just that I was full sure she'd come back or you'd find her down in Galway. I can't believe it's come to this.'

'Galway was a bit of a waste of time, to be honest,' Kerry says, briefly glancing over at me. 'But at least we gave it a shot.' God, he's so natural and relaxed here. It's as though he's known everyone for years. I love a man who's confident and can just fit in.

'And Social Services aren't going to just wade in and upset everyone,' adds Zahra, clattering around the kitchen, topping up the tea in the pot and making sure there's an unending supply of biscuits. 'I'm sure they'll treat the case sensitively and do all they can to help.'

'And what about Twitter?' asks Mam, for about the hundredth time. 'She's bound to tweet to one of you at some stage.

'Mam,' I say gently. 'We've been checking Twitter non-stop since she left. There hasn't been a word from her. We're just going to have to face the possibility she's not coming back any time soon.'

The words hang heavily in the air and the silence is broken
only by the squeals of laughter from the sitting room. Harry
tactfully took Ryan in there after we came back with a promise
of making the best Lego spaceship he'd ever seen.

'That poor little boy,' says Mam, dabbing at her eyes. 'He's
going to end up in care and if Fiona ever does turn up, she'll
have some fight on her hands to get him back.'

'Mam, we don't know that,' I say. I feel sorry for her but, I just
want to get things moving now. 'Let's start to make some calls
and we'll see what happens.'

'Don't worry, Mrs B,' Kerry says, putting his hand over hers. 'I
deal with Social Services regularly through my job and, honestly,
they'll have Ryan's best interests at heart. It'll all work out for the
best.'

I'm still watching Kerry closely and I wonder how I could
ever have been so cross with him. Oh God, I'm cringing at my
outburst earlier. He must have thought I was a mad woman.
He's a genuinely nice person. He really is the Kerry I befriended
on Twitter.

'You're right, Kerry,' says Mam. 'Let's not waste any more
time talking about it. We know what we have to do so let's just
do it.'

'Right, I'll just go and get the phonebook,' I say, glad we're all
being decisive about things. 'There has to be some number we
can ring on a Sunday.'

Ryan doesn't even look up when I come into the room. He's
guffawing at whatever Harry is saying and I can't help feeling
emotional myself. This may be the last time he'll laugh for a
while. Poor little thing.

I eventually find the phonebook amongst the junk in the
sideboard just as the doorbell rings. Bloody hell! This house is
becoming like Heuston Station. I must remind myself of this
moment whenever I'm complaining about being on my own!

Oh, but maybe it's Tom. Maybe he's decided to leave Mammy to fend for herself for a while and he's come to help out.

'I've got it,' I shout as I rush past the kitchen where the others are deep in conversation. I swing open the door and almost faint with a mixture of surprise and delight. I can barely believe it. 'Fiona,' I scream, unable to contain my excitement. 'Oh thank God you're back.'

I take a step outside and throw my arms around her. I can't believe she's just turned up like this. I could sing with joy. Whatever she's done, whatever her reasons, she's back! She's bloody well back! I let her go at last as Mam, Kerry, Zahra, Harry and Ryan all run out to see what the commotion is.

'Mummmmmmmmmmyyyyyy,' squeals Ryan, darting towards her. 'You came back, you came back.'

'Yes, sweetie,' she says, picking him up and planting a kiss on his curls. 'Of course I came back. Why wouldn't I?'

'But where have you *been*, Mummy? That message you went on took a very, very long time.'

'Well, I think we'd *all* like to know that,' I say, tersely. The need to hug her has completely passed and I'm tempted to slap her. 'You'd better come in and tell us what's been going on.'

'Did you buy me a present, Mummy, did you?'

'Of course I did,' she says, producing a Mars bar and a Twix from her bag. 'But why don't you take them into the sitting room and I'll come and play in a few minutes.'

'Come on, lad,' says Harry, tickling Ryan under the chin. 'Let's finish making that spaceship. I reckon it's going to be fantastic when it's done.'

'Yay! This is the best day *ever*,' he says, clutching his precious chocolate and following Harry into the sitting room. For just one moment, I'm brought back to my childhood. My nose is pressed up against the window waiting for my dad to come home. Dad always brought home a bag of chocolate on a Friday. I never knew what was going to be in the bag but, each week, I kept my fingers crossed for a Twix. There's nothing like a Twix dipped in a boiling hot cup of tea.

'Are you okay, Jenny?' my mother asks, watching me carefully. 'You look a bit pale.'

'I'm fine, Mam. I think I just need to sit down. Let's go into the kitchen.' As we pile into the kitchen, I realise Fiona is watching Kerry suspiciously and it dawns on me that they haven't met. 'Fiona, before we move on, I think you should meet Kerry.'

'Em ... it's nice to meet you, Kerry,' she says. 'Are you a family member?'

'It's me, Fiona,' he says, flashing one of his cheeky grins. 'It's Kerry Hunt from Twitter!'

'What? No *way*! But you're a ... you're a—'

'Yes,' he says, watching her carefully. 'I'm a man. But I can fill you in on all that later. For now we need to know what's been going on.'

'Yes, Fiona,' says Zahra, joining in. 'We've been really worried about you. Jenny and Kerry even went down to Galway to see if they could find you.'

'They did *what*?' she says, looking shocked. 'But why would you go down there? Didn't you read the note?'

'What note?' asks my mother. 'There was no note. Are you saying you left one?'

'There most definitely wasn't a note, Fiona,' I say, firmly. And I should know. Didn't I pull the room apart looking for one? No, if there'd been a note I most definitely would have found it. I'm beginning to lose patience with her. How dare she breeze in here with no apology and now claim she left a note! Even if she did, that doesn't explain her swanning off and leaving us with her kid for two days!

'Forget the note for a moment,' says Kerry, looking irritated. 'Just tell us where you've been.'

'Well, you won't know this,' she begins, 'because I haven't been exactly truthful on Twitter.' At least she has the good grace to look ashamed! 'I don't actually have a husband and an ideal life of domestic bliss. Ryan's dad and I were never together.'

'Oh, but Ryan told us his daddy had left,' I say, now doubly confused at this turn of events.

'Ross was ... is a good dad to Ryan but he just never wanted a relationship with me. He used to see Ryan every weekend and, I suppose, I always held on to the hope that he'd eventually want to come and live with us. But he's an out-of-work actor and was offered a job over in LA. He left six months ago and we haven't seen him since. Of course he rings and sends stuff, but it's not the same.' She pauses to blow her nose and I'm tempted to put my arm around her but I'm still waiting for the explanation about where she's been. Nobody utters a word, so I guess I'm not the only one.

'Anyway,' she continues, taking another tissue from the box. 'It's been doubly hard because I fell out with my family a while back so when Ross left, I literally had no one.' Jesus, it's like watching a movie unfold. We're hanging on her every word and I'm willing her to stop blowing her nose and get on with it.

'God love you,' says my mother, rubbing her gently on the back, as you'd do with a small child who isn't feeling well. 'It must have been hard without anybody at all to help you out. Sure you must have been going out of your mind.'

'Well, it's been hard all right,' she says, sniffing. 'But being on my own has made me think a lot more about my family. I have a sister who lives out beside the airport and I haven't seen her in two years. She has a little girl the same age as Ryan and I've been keeping an eye on her on Facebook and Twitter and I found out she's had another baby recently.'

'So is that where you went?' Kerry asks, impatiently. Men seem to just want to get to the point, whereas us women like to take the story right back to the beginning and get every nitty-gritty detail.

'Yes,' she says, finally giving us our answer. 'I was there, but I explained it all in the note.'

'But I pulled the bedroom apart looking for a note,' I say, realising that if what she said is true, we could have been saved a whole lot of heartache. 'Where did you leave it?'

'I left it right here on the kitchen table. There's no way you could have missed it. Ryan was in the sitting room playing with Zahra and Eileen when I slipped back downstairs and left the note right here!'

'I definitely would have seen it,' I say, trying to remember exactly what happened that day. 'I came back with the medicine and Mam and Zahra were in the sitting room. Ryan was drawing at the kitchen table and ... '

'That's it!' says my mother, jumping up from the chair. 'I bet that's what happened.' She gathers up Ryan's colouring stuff from the floor and throws it up on the kitchen table. Within seconds she's holding a note, neatly folded in two with my name on it.

'That's it,' says Fiona, triumphantly. 'I told you I left one. Well, if you just read it, maybe it will explain a few things.' My mother smoothes the letter out onto the table and reads aloud:

Jenny,
I'm not really good with words, so I'll do my best to explain myself. I've been very unhappy for a while now. Ryan's dad isn't around, as I've led you to believe. I've lost contact with my family and I'm desperately lonely. Being with you and your family and friends has made me feel happier than I've been in ages. I'd forgotten what it's

*like to have people around me and it's made me realise
how much I miss my family. I have a sister who I haven't
seen for a while. I've rung her and she's asked me to go
over and stay for a couple of days to see if we can work
through things. I'm leaving Ryan with you. I've just
been feeling so suffocated lately and really need a break.
I know it's a cheek and you must think I'm a terrible
person, but if it all works out, he'll have a real aunty and
cousins, and maybe we can finally begin to feel we're
part of a family. Please tell him I love him and I'll be
back before he knows it. I'm really, really sorry and I
hope you don't hate me.*
Fiona

'I'm so sorry,' sobs Fiona, as soon as my mother finishes reading
the letter. 'I'm really, really sorry. I know I should never have
left Ryan. Listening to that letter now, I feel pathetic. I'm a crap
mother. I can't explain why it felt okay for me to just up and
leave him. You must all really hate me.'

'Now, now,' says my mother, patting her back again. 'You're a
very good mother. Sure haven't I seen it with my own eyes?
That boy loves you. And we're all entitled to a little meltdown
now and again. I just can't believe we missed that note. It
certainly would have made things a lot easier if we'd known you
were coming back.'

'So what happens now?' asks Kerry. 'Fiona just heads back to
Galway after her little holiday and we all just pretend she hasn't
just turned our world upside down for a few days?'

'Kerry!' I say, shocked at how upfront he is. But really he's
only voicing what we're all thinking.

'It's okay, Jenny,' she says. 'Kerry is right. I've really messed up
and I'm sorry. I don't know what else to say except I'll do
anything to make it up to you all. I'm so ashamed.'

'But you didn't say,' says Zahra. 'How did things go with your sister? Did you manage to sort things out?'

'Yes we did. It was fabulous to catch up with her and once we'd got past the stuff that drove us apart in the first place, things were as natural and easy as ever. She even drove me back here today and just went up to have a browse in the shops to give me a bit of time. I'm to ring her when I'm ready and me and Ryan are going back to spend a few days with her and her family.'

'Well that's fantastic,' says my mother, getting up from her chair. 'I'm really happy things are working out for you, Fiona. But I think it's about time I grabbed my fella and headed off home. I could do with a quiet night watching those *Desperate Housewives* DVDs.'

I'm happy for Fiona too. To be honest, I want to hate her for the upset she's caused. I want to condemn her for abandoning her son. I want to slap her for the sheer cheek of thinking it would be okay to swan off like she did, but I can't help liking her. I can understand loneliness and how all-consuming it can be. And although I'm not a mother, I can also understand the need to get a bit of head space. Yes, she was wrong to do what she did, but she's back now and I'm daring to hope my life might return to normal very soon!

'So here we are,' says Kerry, cutting into my thoughts.

'The four tweeters together at last!'

'Oh yes,' says Zahra. 'But isn't it a pity we've only managed to get together at the end of our few days.'

'It's a pity all right,' says Fiona. 'And I really should apologise to you too, Zahra. I know you were only out of hospital when I left and had problems of your own. You really didn't need the worry and stress of me disappearing like that.'

'Honestly, don't worry about it, Fiona. It looks like we've both hit the jackpot from our visit to Dublin. You're all great, really you are, but I think I've made a friend for life in Eileen.

She's amazing. She's made me see that I have brains and drive and I've already made a list of goals to achieve within the next year. Being a celebrity make-up artist may not be as completely out of my reach as I've always thought!'

'Well good for you,' says Kerry, flicking back the strands of hair straying onto his face. 'I'm really happy for you. And I suppose I've been lucky too. My secret is out and you're all still speaking to me! You're fabulous, all of you.' He winked at me! I swear, he looked straight at me and winked when he said that. I may faint!

'I still can't believe you're a man, Kerry,' says Fiona, staring hard at him. 'I never in a million years would have guessed.'

'Well, you'd better believe it – I'm *all* man!' God, he's gorgeous. I have no doubt about my feelings for him now. I fancy him like crazy and I'd like to think he feels the same. But the bloody Waterford–Dublin thing is a bit tricky. Maybe if he stays around for a while today, we can have a chat about it. Fiona will be heading off with her sister and since she lives close to the airport, they might take Zahra with them. Yes, I think a good heart to heart is in order.

'We're off,' says Mam, peeping around the door. 'Ryan is still playing in there so I thought I'd leave him and let you lot have a chat in peace.'

'Cheerio,' says Harry. 'It was nice to meet you all. Maybe see you again sometime.'

I walk out to the door with them and give them both a hug. They've been fantastic and for the first time in years, I know I have a mother I can rely on. Just as I'm waving them off, another car pulls up outside. Oh for feck's sake! Jesus, why does my life have to be so complicated?

'Hi, Jenny,' says Tom, kissing me on the cheek. 'I just thought I'd pop over to see how things are going.'

'Well pretty good really. Come on in and see for yourself.'

'Gosh,' he says, after I make the introductions. 'So all's well that ends well, then. I won't pry into the details of what happened, Fiona, but I'm glad you're back.'

'Thanks,' she says. 'It's good to be back.'

'And thanks for looking after Jenny for me,' he says, looking at Kerry. 'I believe you've been very helpful since yesterday.'

'Ah it was no problem at all,' Kerry says, the cheeky grin replaced with an awkward smile. 'It was good to get to know Jenny a bit better.'

'Not too much better, I hope,' says Tom, pretending to give Kerry a warning look.

Everyone laughs at that, including myself, but I'm dying inside. Bloody, bloody, bloody hell! This is a nightmare!

'Well since you're all sorted here,' says Kerry, pushing back his chair and standing up, 'I might just head off now.'

'Do you have to go quite yet?' I ask, feeling inexplicably panicky at the thought of him leaving. 'Maybe we could all have a bite to eat before everyone goes their own way?'

'Thanks, Jen,' he says, his deep eyes meeting mine. 'But by the time I go and pick up the rest of my stuff from Cabra, it'll be late enough and I'd like to get home at a reasonable time.' Jesus, he said it again. What is it about the way he says 'Jen'?

'Well it's just as well to get the drive over before too late,' says Tom. 'You don't want to be driving if the roads are bad. There's snow forecast, you know.'

Kerry stands up and shakes Tom's hand. He gives both Fiona and Zahra a quick hug with the promise of seeing them again under better circumstances. I walk him to the door and feel my legs almost turn to jelly. Jesus, what's wrong with me?

'It was strange but lovely,' he says, treating me one more time to his hallmark cheeky grin. 'It'll be one to tell the grandchildren, that's for sure!'

I picture us both, old and grey, sitting in front of an open fire on a snowy, winter's day. We have two grandchildren – a girl and a boy – and they're sitting on our knees listening to us telling them tales of when we were young. We smile at each other, knowingly, remembering how it all started.

'Jen, are you okay?'

For feck's sake! There I go again. 'I'm fine. Just exhausted and so glad it's all worked out in the end. Thanks, Kerry. Thanks for all your help and for … well … you know – for everything.'

'No problem,' he says and his twinkling eyes turn serious for a moment. 'And I hope it all goes well for you and Tom. He seems like a really nice guy.'

'He's a good guy all right,' I say. *But it's you, Kerry, can't you see? It's you!* We stand in silence for a moment and I wonder, not for the first time, if he can read my thoughts. I wish I could read his. What is he thinking? Does he feel the same?

'Right so, I'll be off,' he says, breaking the magic. He bends over to kiss my cheek and I purposefully turn my face so he plants his lips straight on mine. He tastes delicious. He looks stunned for a moment, and then breaks into a smile.

'Bye, Kerry,' I say, storing that scrumptious feeling to remember later when I'm curled up in bed.

'Bye, Jen. Let's keep in touch.' He stares at me for a moment longer before heading out to his car. 'Tweet you later.' And he's gone.

CHAPTER 32

Friday – Twelve Days Later

'Oooh, look at you all busy and professional,' grins Paula, plonking herself down on the edge of my desk. 'So what time did you start?'

'Hey, watch where you're putting that bum of yours,' I say, indicating the neat pile of paperwork I've just sorted. 'It's taken me the last hour to get through all that. I've been here since before eight!'

'Oh God, I wasn't even awake at that time! What's got into you?'

'Well, I'm hoping to finish up at lunch-time, remember? That is if Brenda hasn't changed her mind!'

'Oh, yeah, I'd forgotten about that. Lucky you. The rest of us will have to suffer until the bitter end.'

'For feck's sake, Paula! Don't be so dramatic. And anyway, it's Friday, so you have the weekend to look forward to.'

I notice Paula's face seems to drop at that. I know she's still feeling hurt over Ian. Bloody bastard. She spoke to him the other day and it was clear that he'd only ever stayed with her because she was a soft touch, subbing him when he'd gamble all his dole away. She's so much better off without him but it might take her a while to realise it.

'Well roll on next weekend,' she says, suddenly brightening up. 'I can't wait. It's exactly what I need at the moment.'

'I think it's what we all need. Sally is already plucking and waxing in preparation.' It's been almost two weeks since the girls and Kerry left. When they went, I got to thinking about Sally and Paula and how they've been such good friends to me. After checking with John to see if he could babysit, I booked the three of us in for a spa weekend at the Osprey Hotel in Naas. Two full days of pure luxury – slobbing around in our bath robes, eating, drinking and just generally having some girlie time. It will set us up nicely for Christmas, which will be only days away.

'Poor Sal,' Paula says, breaking into my thoughts. 'I really like her, you know, but the kids are a handful, aren't they? She never seems to get a minute to herself.'

'That's true, but she's feeling so much better now that she's been getting out a bit more. She'd just let things get on top of her and she'd barely been out socially in the last twelve months. The weekend will be great for her – for all of us.'

'And of course I suppose her getting that orgasm from Keith Barry has nothing to do with her sudden joie de vivre?' Paula giggles. 'It would certainly have perked me up. And speaking of such things, any luck with sorting things out with Tom yesterday?'

'Paula! You know full well that my relationship with Tom doesn't involve anything of the sort! But to be honest, we've both been pussy-footing around things. I like him, I really do and I enjoy his company – but there's just no spark. We're going to meet up again over the weekend but I think we both know it will be to call it a day.'

'Look out, here he comes.' Paula begins pointing to imaginary things on my computer screen as though we're having an in-depth conversation about banking.

'Morning,' says a chirpy Tom. 'You girls are stuck into work early.'

I take Paula's lead and also pretend to be busy. 'Hiya Tom. Just trying to get a few things done before the weekend. You know how it is.'

'Well I'll leave you to it. Maybe we'll catch up at lunch-time?'

'That would be lovely, Tom.' No it bloody well wouldn't! I do like him – really I do – but I'm more than a little freaked out by having my every move monitored. I think I'd like to keep my business and personal life separate.

'Well, for what it's worth,' Paula says, looking down at the desk and fiddling with a paperclip as Tom walks away, 'I think he's really lovely. Any woman would be lucky to have him.'

'I'm inclined to agree with you there, Paula, but I don't think it will be me. We'll see how our chat goes at the weekend. Right, ten minutes to go before half past. I'm going to slip across the road and get a coffee to bring back to my desk – do you want one?'

'No thanks, Jen. I've already had two this morning to wake me up. I'm just off to the loo and then I'd better get started. Love the new look, by the way. It really suits you.'

Grabbing my bag from under my desk, I sling it over my shoulder and smile at Paula's last comment. I've finally realised that maybe I'm not so ugly after all. I plucked up the courage to go into Brown Thomas after work yesterday and got chatting to a lovely girl at the Mac counter. After she tut-tutted at my heavy covering of slap, she made me take it all off with copious amounts of wipes and then showed me how to achieve the less-is-more look. And I have to admit, I like it.

While I was there, I paid a visit to the underwear department and for the first time in my life, I got measured for a bra. The shop assistant was really lovely and I found myself telling her that I was considering implants. 'Oh you don't have to bother with surgery these days,' she said. 'Wait until I show you what we've got.' Sure enough, the woman performed a miracle. I'm not saying I'll never have a boob job, but for the moment I'm happy with what I've got.

Just as I'm about to go out the door for the coffee, I hesitate and come back in. I take a deep breath and head towards the office that used to terrify the life out of me only a few weeks ago. I tap gently on the door before letting myself in. 'I'm grabbing a quick coffee across the road to bring back. Would you like one?'

'Em ... thanks, Jenny, I'd love one actually,' Brenda says, rubbing her tired-looking eyes. 'I didn't get time for breakfast this morning.'

'No problem – milk with one sugar?'

'That's it, thanks – here, let me give you the money.'

'Don't be silly,' I say, heading back towards the door. 'It's on me.' I hesitate and wonder if I should ask, but I think it would be rude of me not to, considering our conversation earlier in the week. 'So ... eh ... how's your mum, then, Brenda? Any better?'

Her head snaps up and I wonder for a minute if she going to give me a bollocking for asking! 'She's not too bad at all actually. Now that we've had the family meeting and the others are pitching in more, she seems to be doing much better. I think she's just happier to see the family around more often, and that has to be a good thing.'

'Well that's great, Brenda. I'm glad it's all working out for you. Now I'd better get those coffees and get back to work or the boss will be on my back!'

She laughs at that – not just a smile or a grin, but a big bellowing guffaw. God, I've never seen her do that before and it takes me by surprise but it's good to see. Bootface is no more and Brenda Delaney is our lovely new boss!

After the tweet-up, I decided to make an effort with Brenda and find out more about the lady in the wheelchair. I carefully broached the subject with her last week in her office and I must have caught her at a vulnerable moment because she began to cry. Jesus! I almost died. My initial reaction was to apologise and leave her alone, but instead I offered her a tissue and asked her to tell me what was wrong.

She told me about her mother having had a stroke a few years ago that left her paralysed and how she's been steadily getting worse. She told me about being the only family member who wasn't married with kids and how she'd come under pressure from her siblings to care on a more permanent basis for their mother. She felt she'd no option but to rent her house out last year and move back in with her mother. By my reckoning, it was about the same time as I started working here. After we chatted for a good ten minutes, we fell into an uncomfortable silence, prompting her to shuffle a few papers and declare she'd better get back to work. But whether Brenda changed after our conversation or my perception of her was different, things in the office suddenly seemed a whole lot better. The atmosphere was different – less stuffy and more relaxed – and has been all week. I'd even go as far as to say I … em … quite like my job! Bloody hell. Will the real Jenny Breslin please stand up?

★

Sitting on the bus on the way home, I'm feeling great. It's only one o'clock and I have the whole weekend to look forward to. I've become so much more optimistic about everything since the tweet-up. Speaking of which, I wonder how Fiona and Zahra are getting on. Zahra rang on Wednesday night, full of excitement to tell me that she's enrolled in a college course during the day for beauty therapy. She's going to keep up the cleaning job at the studios for the moment as a means of income but hopefully one day she'll be able to get the job of her dreams. I'm so happy for her. She sounded so upbeat and positive. I tap the well-used button and send out a tweet.

@JennyB How are you girls today *@zahraglam* and *@fionalee*? Any news?

It's weird but I'm not including Kerry in most of my tweets since he went back to Waterford. We've had a few DM chats, but they've been stilted and awkward. He's sent me his phone number and asked me to ring, but I haven't yet. I need to get my head straight before I do because every time I think of him, my body feels like it's on fire and my heart speeds up to a gallop. And besides, I don't really have a clue what he's thinking. The last day we had together was such a mixed bag that it's impossible to know where we stand – if anywhere at all! Ah, there's Zahra online and she seems in great form.

@zahraglam Hiya, Jenny. Guess what. I plucked up courage to talk to one of the *real* celeb make-up artists while I was cleaning last night in studios.

@JennyB Oh, wow! That's great, Zahra. Tell me more!

@zahraglam I told her about the course and asked if she had any advice for me. She was lovely. Said I could come and watch her do someone up next week.

@JennyB Brilliant! That's just what you want. You go, girl!

@zahraglam Thanks, Jenny. And it's largely thanks to your mam that everything is working out so well for me.

@CoolEileen Ah don't mention it, Zahra, love. Sure I'm only too glad to have been able to help.

@JennyB Mam! For God's sake! Is nothing I do sacred any more? Are you even stalking me on Twitter now?

@CoolEileen Don't be like that love. Sure I had to check it out. Great, isn't it? I'm just about to see if Laurence Llewelyn Bowen is on here. See ya later.

@zahraglam Oh, your mam is hilarious, Jenny. How cool that she's on Twitter now.

@fionalee Hi, girls. Just noticed your tweets. And your mam's, Jenny. How funny!

@JennyB Hmmmm! Not sure about having her on here. We'll see. But how are you, Fiona? How's Ryan?

@fionalee We're both great, thanks. My sister has asked us to stay with them for Christmas so we're popping down to Galway to pick up some stuff this weekend.

@JennyB Ah that's great. I'm thrilled for you. And Ryan must be delighted to have his cousins around.

@fionalee He's thrilled and he's been so good. We'll stay for Christmas and the new year and then we'll see after that. One thing at a time.

@JennyB Looks like it's all working out. Great stuff.

@CoolEileen Will you be long, Jenny, love? You said you'd be here at half one and it's already twenty to two!

Bloody hell!

★

My beloved Beetle, Betsy, doesn't really have much room for boxes but I think Mam just wants me to be part of it all. Harry didn't have a lot of stuff in his little flat so between his car and mine, we've managed it all in one run. We're back in Mam's house now and I'm helping them to unpack boxes.

'Thanks for this, love,' says Mam, artistically scattering some of Harry's silver-grey cushions on her purple sofa. 'I know it couldn't be easy for you to ... you know ... to see another man moving in.'

'Actually, Mam, I think it's great. Honestly, you two were made for each other. I really like Harry and I can see he makes you happy.'

'That's very generous of you, Jen. But I know you must be thinking of your dad too.' She's not looking at me but continuing to busy herself with Harry's bits and pieces!

'I'll always think of Dad,' I say, watching her carefully. 'But Mam ... look at me!'

She stops what she's doing and turns to face me. She has tears in her eyes and I can see she's fighting back a lump in her throat. 'I love you, Mam. I should have said that to you before but I'm saying it now. I love you, okay? And I can see that Harry makes you happy so that's good enough for me.'

'Oh, love,' she says, flinging her arms around me. 'You're a brilliant daughter and I'm so lucky to have you.'

We hug each other for a few moments in silence and I feel an overwhelming sense of belonging. When we finally pull back from each other, I see Harry standing at the living room door. He's wiping the tears from his eyes and any doubts I may ever have had about him drift away in that moment.

★

It's been a long day and I can't wait to get home, have a nice long shower and get into my pyjamas. Mam and Harry wanted me to stay around for tea, but I made my excuses and left. I pull Betsy into the driveway and hop out into the cold air. God, it's freezing tonight. Although it's dark, the sky looks as though it's bursting with snow and I can see my hot breaths rising into the air.

'Well, I thought you were never going to get home!' comes a voice from the shadows and I almost jump out of my skin.

'Fuck! Jesus Christ! You scared the shit out of me.' My heart starts beating like mad and I'm suddenly not cold any more because there's heat rising up through my body.

'Hiya, Jen,' says Kerry, shooting me a cheeky grin. 'I just couldn't stay away.'

'I ... em ... I just ... what ... what are you doing here?' Oh, God, I look a wreck.

'I came to see you, of course. And you look lovely, so stop worrying.'

Oh, Jesus, there he goes again with the mind-reading thing.

'So can I come in, then?' he asks, raising an eyebrow. 'I had planned on us having a proper chat on the phone after the dust settled but ... but ... I just couldn't wait, Jen. I wanted to see you. Hope you don't mind.'

'Well ... no ... of course not ... come in, come in.' Hooray! He's come back for me!

'Oh wait,' he says, grabbing my hand as I'm about to put the key in the door. 'Look!'

At last! It's come at last! Big soft drops of snow begin to fall and cling to the cold, dry ground. It's beautiful, really beautiful. I just stand there, face turned to the sky and allow the flakes to gather on my face. Kerry slips his arm around my waist and I feel an overwhelming sense of happiness. I close my eyes tight and pray that this isn't just a dream!

SIX MONTHS LATER

I feel like a princess as I walk up the aisle in all my grandeur, stepping in time with the music. I'm trying not to look at the congregation, but I can't help noticing all the smiles and hearing the whispers of, 'Ah, isn't she gorgeous?' As I get nearer the altar, I feel a little lump in my throat as I catch my first glimpse of him in his chocolate-brown suit. Tom makes a truly handsome groom. Whoever would have thought he'd turn out to be so lovely. He's become my best friend and I love him dearly. We've come a long way from awkward exchanges in the staff canteen.

As I finally reach the top of the church, I begin to relax and I smile at the man who's been my rock. He gives me a wink and I nod my head in return. Then I step back gracefully for him to catch the first glimpse of his bride, Paula. For Tom, it was always Paula. Those sneaky looks in work, those shared conversations in the canteen – Tom never fancied me, it was always her. They make such a lovely couple and I'm proud that I was the link that brought them together.

I allow my eyes to finally scan the crowd. Before I take my seat, I meet the eye of a very special man. Kerry flashes me his cheeky grin and I know – I just know – things are going to be fine.

ACKNOWLEDGEMENTS

Where do I start? How do I put into words the debt of gratitude I owe to those who've helped, supported and encouraged me along the way? This last year has been a whirlwind and I've loved every minute of it.

I was going to save the best until last, but for once, I'm going to put the most important person in my life first. There just aren't enough words to express the love I have for my husband. Since we've met, Paddy has been my rock. He's always believed in me and ooh-ed and ahh-ed over my efforts through the years. When I decided I was going to be an artist, he insisted on hanging my 'masterpieces' on the wall and when I took piano lessons, he clapped loudly at the noise I produced. When I decided I wanted to pursue a career in writing, he was there, as usual, waving his pom poms in the air. Paddy is the voice of reason when I'm upset, a calming influence when I'm losing the head and an infinite source of love when I'm down. He's also the best tea-maker, kiddie juggler and ironer – living proof that a man can multi-task!

That brings me on to the little people who are my reason for being. I've been blessed with four wonderful children, Eoin, Roisin, Enya and Conor, and I'm thankful for it every single day of my life. I may scream and shout when their bedrooms resemble a war zone or when one of them informs me at ten o'clock at night that they need a homemade, fancy-dress costume for first thing the next morning; but they know I love them. I also want them to know that one day I will turn into Nigella, and offer them more than beans and toast or pasta with ready-made sauce for dinner.

Two people who deserve a huge thanks are my parents, who've always encouraged me to follow my dreams. They're an endless source of support and I love them very much. I'm very lucky to have one brother who I consider one of my closest friends. His wife, Denyse, is the sister I never had and I want to thank them from the bottom of my heart for always being there.

For as long as I can remember, I've dreamed of having a book published. I owe a huge thank you to the people who have been instrumental in making this happen. To all the team in Curtis Brown, especially Sheila Crowley, my agent and friend, thank you, thank you, thank you. Your support and unfaltering belief in me fills me with pride and I couldn't wish for a better agent. To Ciara Doorley, my editor, I can't thank you enough. I'm in awe of your ability to make words sparkle and I hope you'll be making my words shine for a long, long time. Thanks to Breda, Joanna, Ruth, Margaret and all the team at Hachette Ireland for their hard work and support. I also owe a debt of thanks to Vanessa O'Loughlin, my mentor and friend, for her tireless and selfless giving of her time and experience. Vanessa runs writing.ie and inkwellwriters.ie and I would advise any writers or aspiring writers to check them out.

To my long-time friends – Lorraine Hamm, Angie Pierce, Bernie Winston, Rachel Murphy and Sinead Webb – thank you for bearing with me during times when my writing was all-consuming and our phone calls and nights out became less and less. I owe you all copious amounts of wine! To Niamh Greene, Colette Caddle, Denise Deegan, Emma Hannigan, Cathy Kelly,

Sinead Moriarty, Melissa Hill, Monica McInerney and all the authors I've befriended and who have given so generously of their time to advise and support me along the way.

Twitter has become a big part of my life over the last two years. Yes, I'll admit it, I'm a Twitter addict! But not only has it opened up doors for me and is an endless source of information, it's a place where I've met some fantastic people. Two of my newest and closest friends, Niamh O'Connor and Mel Sherratt, are people I've met through Twitter. For the last year, Niamh and Mel have listened, reassured, encouraged and helped me and I'm eternally grateful for their unconditional friendship.

Through Twitter, I've got to meet and interview a number of celebrities, all of whom have been lovely and some of whom have given generously of their time to advise and encourage me. I'd like to say a special thanks to Eamonn Holmes and Ruth Langsford for their continuing support. Thanks also to Miriam O'Callaghan, Carol Vorderman, Angellica Bell, Ryan Tubridy, Sharon Marshall and Steve Huison. To Sarah Hitching, thank you for waving your magic wand! I've made so many other friends through Twitter that it would be impossible to mention them all but a huge thanks to the 'Breakfast in Avoca' brigade – you know who you are – and thanks to each and every one of you who brightens my day with your tweets.

I owe a huge thanks to Mary Kilbane, for tirelessly reading and sharing her views of my first book and for her constant belief that I would be published. I must also thank all the mammies (and daddies!) at the school who collect my children when I forget to because I've lost all sense of time while writing and for telling me I look great, despite wearing half my pyjamas and having last night's mascara running down my face.

I'm very lucky to live on a fantastic street and have wonderful neighbours I can call friends. Whether it's medical emergencies or computer meltdowns, there's always someone around to help.

I've lost track of the amount of tins of beans, teabags, dishwasher tablets and even (gasp!) toilet rolls I've borrowed in the last year alone! Thank you all for your support, encouragement and most of all for your parties! A special thanks has to go to one neighbour in particular, who allowed me to take his accident and twist it to fit for the purposes of the book. You know who you are!

A couple of years ago, I was hypnotised on stage by Keith Barry. If you've read the book by now, I needn't tell you why I won't discuss it! Suffice it to say, I had the time of my life! Keith has since become a friend and I'd like to thank him for allowing me to include him in the book as well as providing me with the best laughs I've ever had. If you haven't seen one of his shows, you're missing out.

Lastly, to you, my readers, I'm grateful beyond words that you've taken the time to buy and read this book. I hope you enjoy it and come away smiling. Please let me know what you think. You can contact me at mariaduffy2@gmail.com and on Twitter at @mduffywriter. I wish you all every good thing life can bring.

Maria

ABOUT THE AUTHOR

Born in Dublin, Maria Duffy knew from an early age that she loved writing, but she started out her working career in the bank after completing a business course. Maria went on to have four children with husband Paddy and became a stay-at-home mum, but she never stopped writing. When her youngest started school three years ago, she decided to dust off the book she'd once started, and as she began to write again, she knew it was what she wanted to do for the rest of her life.

A self-confessed Twitter addict, Maria also writes a blog for *Hello!* online magazine entitled 'Stars in the Twitterverse'.

Any Dream Will Do is her first novel.

Contact Maria at mariaduffy2@gmail.com or
on Twitter *@mduffywriter*

www.writenowmom.wordpress.com